Promising You

By Allie Everhart

Promising You
By Allie Everhart

Copyright ©2014 Allie Everhart
All rights reserved.
Published by Waltham Publishing, LLC
Cover Design by Sarah Hansen of Okay Creations
ISBN-13: 978-0-9887524-7-4

CHAPTER ONE

"Jade, you're awake." The man's voice is familiar. He comes up next to me and I see it's Dr. Cunningham, the doctor who took care of me after I fell and hit my head in the woods behind Garret's house. "How are you feeling?"

I open my eyes more and realize that I have no idea where I am or how I got here. The room I'm in looks like a small office with plain white walls and short beige carpeting. Across from me is a large wooden desk and a wall of bookcases. I notice a strong leather smell and see that I'm lying on a dark brown leather couch.

"Where am I?" I ask the doctor.

"You're just a few miles from Moorhurst. Your grandfather called me right after you passed out. Luckily I was still in town from seeing you earlier today." He smiles. "We really need to stop meeting like this."

"My grandfather?" I suddenly remember the scene outside the Student Services building on campus. An old man approached me, claiming to be the father of Royce Sinclair, my biological father who I learned about a few months ago. The man said his name was Arlin Sinclair and that he needed to talk to me. Two large men surrounded me and I knew that the old man wasn't just there to talk. He was there to kill me. To finish the job his son was supposed to do.

I bolt up from the couch and pain shoots from my knee, forcing me to sit down again.

"What are you doing?" My sudden movement startles the doctor and he quickly rests my leg back on the couch. "You know it's too soon to put weight on your knee like that."

I grab hold of his lab coat. "Tell me where I am! Tell me exactly where I am!"

"I told you," he says calmly. "We're at your grandfather's office."

"I don't have a grandfather! My grandparents are dead!" I'm panicking, searching the room for an exit. If the scene with Sinclair really happened, then why am I still here? I should be dead. He should've killed me by now.

"Your *maternal* grandparents are deceased." Cunningham remains calm as he tries to hold me still with one hand while using the other to take something from his lab coat. "Your grandparents on your father's side are very much alive. Now look right over here for me."

He shines a bright light at my eye, making me squint. I push the light away. "I have to find out what's going on." I attempt to get up again but he remains seated next to me and won't let me move.

"Jade, you have a serious concussion and you need to calm down. I believe your blackout was caused by stress. I want you to take some time to rest and relax this week."

Relax? Does this guy not get that my life is in danger?

"Take me back to campus. Please! I need to see Garret. I need to get out of this place."

"Your grandfather will be here any minute, and after he talks with you he'll take you back."

I grab Cunningham's lab coat again and yank him toward me. "That man is trying to kill me! Don't you get that? He wants me dead! He needs to bury the evidence of what his son did to my mom."

After I say it I realize that I was never supposed to tell anyone that. Then again, Cunningham was there the day Royce Sinclair was killed by Garret's dad. He was one of the doctors who took Garret away after he was shot. So maybe he already knows what happened. Still, I'm not sure if he knows the whole story or just part of it.

Dr. Cunningham removes my hands from his lab coat and sets them back at my side. "I can assure you that Arlin Sinclair is not trying to kill you."

"Why are you here?" I ask, still completely confused.

"I told you. You passed out and Arlin called me. Listen, Jade, I want you to take some days to rest. Stay home from class for a couple days. And make sure someone stays with you overnight. Garret, or your friend, Harper."

"How do you know about Harper? And why are you working for Sinclair? I thought you worked for the Kensingtons."

"I work for a private medical clinic that treats a very select group of individuals." He puts his hand on mine and looks me in the eye. "But you already know that, don't you?"

I nod.

"You also know that it's best not to ask questions, correct?"

"Yes." I decide to go along with whatever he's saying. Maybe doing so will buy me a little more time before they kill me. But if they're killing me, why is Dr. Cunningham worried about my concussion? And why did he just tell me to stay home from class? And have Garret stay with me overnight? Wait. What?

3

I'm slowly realizing that maybe I'm not going to be killed after all. But then why was Arlin Sinclair at Moorhurst today? And why did he kidnap me and take me here?

"Is she awake yet?" I tense up hearing his voice again.

"Yes, but she's a little confused," Cunningham says.

"Because of her head injury?" I glance back at the door and see the old man rushing over to me. "I thought you said she was okay!"

Cunningham stands up. "Yes. She is. What I meant is that she's confused by the situation. The confusion is not due to her concussion. Forgive me for not being clearer."

"I see. Well, I'll speak with her. If you're sure she's okay, you can go now."

"Jade, keep using the crutches," Cunningham says. "Don't try to walk on that knee. And call me right away if you have any of the head trauma symptoms on that sheet I gave Garret. Do you have any questions before I go?"

"Um, no. No questions." I don't want the doctor to leave me alone with the old man, but I don't know what else to ask him. He exits out the door, shutting it so fast I can't see what's on the other side.

The old man walks over in front of the couch. "So, Jade, let's try this again." He holds his hand out and smiles. It's a warm, friendly smile but I'm still leery of him so I don't smile back. "I'm Arlin Sinclair. Your grandfather. It's nice to finally meet you."

I cautiously shake his hand as he takes a seat on the leather ottoman that's in front of the couch. He doesn't seem nearly as scary as he did earlier when he was wearing his long black coat and was accompanied by his two ominous henchmen.

He's in his mid- to late-seventies, with a full head of thick white hair. His hair is a sharp contrast to his skin which has a deep, golden-brown tan like he just got back from vacation. His suit jacket is off, leaving him in a white dress shirt, blue striped tie, and black pants. He's average height and has a bit of a paunch in front.

"Are you going to kill me?" I blurt it out and it sounds crazy, but when I'm nervous I tend to spit out whatever's in my head. And if he truly is going to kill me, I want to know.

"No! Of course not." He puts his hand on my arm and I snatch it away. "I want to help you. I have no intentions of doing you any harm."

"But you kidnapped me."

"I didn't kidnap you. I'd hoped to talk to you at your school, but then you passed out. I called Dr. Cunningham and he told me to bring you here right away."

"Who were those guys you had surrounding me?"

"They're my security men. I was in Manhattan earlier and I always bring them with me when I go there. When we stopped at Moorhurst they didn't want to wait in the car, so I told them they could wait outside. But I can see how they might've scared you." He shakes his head. "I should've made them wait in the car."

"But your son tried to killed me. Aren't you here to finish the job?"

"No. That's not at all what's happening here." He lets out a long sigh. "Let me start by saying that I'm sorry, Jade. For everything Royce put you through. I didn't know what was going on until after my son's death."

"What do you mean? You didn't know he was trying to kill me?"

"I didn't even know you existed until Royce was gone."

I don't believe the old man. He has to be lying. "Your son raped my mother and left her on the side of the road to die.

You're saying you didn't know about that? Yeah, right. I'm sure you were the one who helped him cover it up."

"The story Royce told me was that he and your mother spent one night together and afterward she claimed it was a rape in order to get money from us. He said the rape story was completely false. And I believed him. As far as I knew he'd never forced himself on a woman. He had no criminal record. And you have to understand, we have people trying to extort money from us all the time. When it happened, Royce was married with a child on the way. He didn't want this to destroy his marriage. So yes, I did help Royce back then, but I was relying on what he told me. If I'd known the truth, things would've been different."

"Like how? You would've let the real story come out? Let your son go to prison?"

"I don't know what I would've done. It was a long time ago. The point is that I didn't know about you, Jade. Royce never told me your mother was pregnant."

I still don't believe the old man but I play along. "So when did you learn the truth?"

"After Royce died I was cleaning out his office and found the combination to his safe. When I opened the safe, I found a file that contained information about you and your mother as well as details from that night. I saw the original police reports. But until I saw that file I had no idea that's what really happened."

"What were you doing at Rockefeller Center that day you bumped into me? Were you following me?"

He nods. "Once I learned what really happened years ago, I was concerned for your safety. Even though Royce was gone, I didn't know if he had people who might come after you. So I've been keeping watch on you." He places his hand on mine. "When you were in New York, I purposely bumped into you because I wanted to see you. I assumed if I approached you and told you who I was you'd want nothing to do with me, given what Royce had done."

I yank my hand back. "If you knew I didn't want to see you, then why did you come to my school today?"

"Because I need to talk to you about some things. Do you have other questions before I begin?"

"Does anyone else know what he did? Did other people see what was in that file?"

"Luckily, no. If they did, you probably wouldn't be here."

"What's that supposed to mean?"

He sighs. "At first I feared the organization knew. They hold on to secrets like this to make sure people follow orders. It's blackmail basically, but they prefer to call it an incentive."

"What organization?"

He gets up and moves to a high-backed leather chair near the end of the couch. "I belong to a very elite organization that is composed of some extremely powerful men. My son, William, is also a member and so was Royce. I guess some people might call it a secret society although we don't care for that term. Anyway, because the group is so exclusive and its functions are so top secret we have to find ways to keep our members from speaking out. This file I found would've been an excellent tool to blackmail, or incentivize, Royce into keeping quiet. Not that they would've ever needed it. Royce wasn't the type to spill secrets, especially regarding this group."

"How do you know they don't have a copy of the file?"

"Royce's future was very important to the organization. If they knew about you, you would've been seen as an obstacle and they would've come after you. They would've done it years ago. I'm just thankful Royce never did it himself. Well, obviously he tried, but thank God he didn't succeed."

"I don't understand anything you just said, but before you go on, let me get this straight. So you're not going to kill me. You just wanted to talk. And then what?"

"You're my granddaughter, Jade. I want to take care of you. Help you with whatever you need. It's the least I can do given the way you grew up."

"I don't need to be taken care of." I glance back at the door, which is closed and probably has security guards on the other side. "I really need to go. Can you take me back to Moorhurst?"

"We're not done here. I have more to say. Do you have any questions about what I've said so far?"

I'm still trying to wrap my mind around what he said. I'm not prepared to start asking questions, but if he's letting me ask I better come up with something.

"Does this organization have a name?"

"Yes, but only the members are privy to that information."

"What does this secret group do?"

"I can't tell you that," he answers abruptly.

"You asked me if I had questions and now you won't answer them?"

"I can't answer those particular questions. But I can tell you that the organization I belong to had plans for Royce. Big plans. And now they're scrambling to correct the problem that interfered with those plans."

As cryptic as his words are, they're starting to make sense in my head. Big plans. Royce was trying to win the nomination for president. I would say running for president of the United States is a big plan.

"This group you belong to is involved in politics." As I say it I watch his face closely for any kind of response.

"I'm not going to deny that. But many powerful organizations have political involvement. Not just this one."

"I know, but your son was running for president. And he came out of nowhere and was suddenly the frontrunner. It's almost like he was hand-picked and this group was somehow going to make sure he won." I realize how ridiculous this sounds but I almost believe it.

Arlin clears his throat. "What other questions do you have? Would you like to know about your half-sisters? Or your cousins? Or my wife?" He gets up and goes over to the bookcase. "Let me show you some pictures."

It's obvious from his reaction that my statement about that group wasn't too far off. But it doesn't make sense. How did this group plan to make sure Royce won the presidency?

"This is my wife, Grace." Arlin hands me a framed photo. "Your grandmother."

It's weird to hear him say that. I've never had grandparents. The photo shows a nice-looking, older woman with short brown hair styled in a sleek and sophisticated bob. She's standing next to Arlin on what appears to be a yacht. I look closer and see that she has green eyes that are the exact same color as mine.

"That was taken a couple years ago. We were sailing off the coast of Greece. I'd love to take you there sometime. The Mediterranean coast is truly magnificent."

Is he out of his mind? He thinks we'll be travel buddies now? I just met the guy. And his son tried to kill me!

I give him back the photo. "I still don't understand what's going on here. Just tell me what you want from me so I can leave."

"As I said earlier, I want to do whatever I can to help you. Provide for your expenses. Pay for your college tuition."

"My tuition is already paid for. And I don't want your money. If you're trying to get me to keep quiet about your son, don't worry about it. I'll never tell anyone. I already made that promise to Mr. Ken—" Shit! I almost mentioned Garret's dad and I have no idea if this guy knows what really happened to his son. But he has to know. But who would have told him? I'm so confused.

"Were you going to say Mr. Kensington?" Arlin's eyebrows raise. "Is that who you're referring to?"

I keep quiet.

He slowly nods. "Yes, I know Pearce killed my son. That's another reason I wanted to speak with you."

"I don't know what you're talking about. Your son killed himself."

"Pearce, as well as his father, are members of the group I told you about. Everyone in the organization knows what happened to Royce. Pearce was forced to confess what he'd done when he came to us for help."

"What kind of help?"

"You think Pearce covered that whole thing up by himself? Of course not. That's not the work of one man. He needed all of us and all of our connections to get that done. But by killing my son, Pearce disrupted the plan. A plan that took nearly 20 years to develop and was almost brought to fruition. Pearce's actions didn't sit well with the organization and now he'll have to pay."

Have to pay? What does that mean? My pulse races as I begin to worry about Garret and his family. What if Arlin is keeping me here while this group he belongs to goes after Mr. Kensington? Garret said his dad was in trouble for killing Royce. He also said the punishment wouldn't be death but something that would make Mr. Kensington suffer. So would they try to hurt Lilly? Or Garret?

"Are they doing something right now?" I stand up and try to balance on my good leg, unable to find my crutches. "If they hurt Lilly or Garret, I swear I'll—"

"No, his children won't be harmed." Arlin comes over, helping me back down on the couch and sitting beside me.

"But you just said Mr. Kensington has to pay. And if you know he killed your son, then why aren't you punishing him yourself?"

"Pearce is an integral part of the organization and it's not up to me to decide his punishment. That's not how it works." Arlin grips my hand, his eyes suddenly desperate and pleading. "But Jade, for my own piece of mind, please tell me what happened that day. I need to know what Royce did. Did Pearce really shoot my son to save you and Garret? I've only heard Pearce's side of the story and I don't know if I believe him. You're the only one who knows the truth."

"Yes," I say with conviction. Arlin softens his grip on my hand. "Royce came there to kill me. He said he had to get rid of me because I looked too much like Sadie and people would start putting the pieces together and find out what he'd done. He didn't want me destroying his chance to be president."

"And he wasn't just threatening you? He really had a gun?"

"Yes. He pointed the gun at me and pulled the trigger. I'd be dead if Garret hadn't pushed me down. And Royce would've killed us both if Mr. Kensington hadn't shot him."

Arlin pulls me into a hug and I immediately stiffen up. "I'm so sorry that happened. But thank you for telling me. I needed to know the truth." He lets me go and I scoot farther back on the couch. "I wish Pearce had found a different way to stop Royce, but if someone pointed a gun at my child I'd do the same thing." I feel his eyes on me as I keep mine fixed on the wall behind him. He sighs. "Jade. Would you please look at me?"

My gaze returns to Arlin. He sits back a little, giving me some space.

"I'm not a violent man and I don't understand how my son ended up that way. His brother's not that way. I didn't raise either one of my boys to be like that. But Royce had issues. Once he got his mind set on something, he wouldn't let anything stand in his way. This offer to run for president was the worst thing that could've happened to him. It consumed him. I wish they never would've chosen him."

"So your son was chosen to be president? By this secret organization?"

Arlin looks down and fumbles with his tie. "When I said that Pearce and his family were safe I meant it, but Pearce will still pay for interfering like that."

Arlin has apparently decided to completely ignore my question.

He continues. "The loss of my son isn't a personal loss to the organization like it is for me, but it's a loss of a great deal of time and effort from a group of very important people."

"What's his punishment? Will they destroy his company?"

"They could, but the punishment being discussed is bigger than that. There are rumblings that it involves Garret."

My pulse shoots up again when I hear Garret's name. "You just said he was safe! Were you just lying to me so I'd sit here and listen to this?"

"Calm down. They're not going to harm him. In fact I shouldn't call it a punishment. It's more of a plan. A plan that involves Garret. His father doesn't know about it and if he did, he would never approve of it. He never wanted his son involved in anything this group does. So if this plan indeed happens, it will serve as a punishment for Pearce. That's all I can say."

"Are you kidding me? You can't say something like that and not tell me more. What are their plans for Garret?"

"I don't know the details yet. I've only been in on a few discussions. I don't even know if it's been finalized."

"It doesn't matter. He'll never go along with whatever it is. And I won't either. I'm dating him and we're getting more serious. We've talked about being together in the future. Maybe even getting married someday."

Arlin takes a deep breath and lets it out. "That brings me to the other reason we needed to talk. You need to end things with Garret."

CHAPTER TWO

"Are you serious? You don't even know me and now you're telling me to end things with Garret?" I shake my head, annoyed. "Yeah, well, I know you rich people have these rules about only dating other rich people but Garret and I aren't following your stupid rules. His dad has accepted that and so should you, or your group, or whoever else wants us to break up."

"This isn't an option, Jade. And it's not my rule. It's *their* rule."

"Whoever these people are, they can all go to hell because I'm not breaking up with Garret."

He grips my arm. "Listen to me. This is serious. You're getting caught in the middle of something very big and you need to get out before something happens."

"Caught in the middle of what?"

"This plan involving Garret. You're not a part of it and right now you're considered an obstacle. And yes, it's true that your background is the reason for that but you can't——"

"I'm half Sinclair. Shouldn't that buy me some points with these people?"

"They don't know you're half Sinclair. I told you, Royce somehow kept that a secret from everyone. The organization just thinks you're an underprivileged young woman from Iowa."

"But Royce is gone now, so they shouldn't care what he did. Just tell them I'm half Sinclair."

He shakes his head. "I can't. They'd be furious if they found out Royce lied. Members are supposed to disclose all information. Royce violated the rules and there are serious consequences for that. And since he's no longer here, the organization would punish my son, William, or me."

"So I can't date Garret because I'm poor?"

"It's more than that. Someone like Garret needs to be paired with someone who has had the proper upbringing. Gone to the right schools. Been immersed in this culture."

"Garret's dad got over the issues he had with my background so obviously it's possible."

"I know this is isn't what you want to hear, but I'm telling you this for your own good. I know how these people work. I'm one of them, and even when I don't approve of their techniques, I can't stop them."

"Why are you part of this group if you don't like what they do?"

"I wasn't given a choice. My father forced me to join just like he was forced to join. And once you're a member you can't get out." He shakes his head. "It doesn't matter. The point is that you need to know what's going to happen if you don't end things with Garret."

I sigh, rolling my eyes. "So what's going to happen?"

"If and when this plan regarding Garret is approved and finalized, you will get a visit from someone. This person will tell you to break up with Garret and will offer you a large sum of money. If you refuse to do as you're told, you will get another visit. These visits will continue, and as they do, they'll become less cordial and more threatening. Eventually you'll do as they say because you'll have no choice. And to punish you for your earlier disobedience, they'll destroy your future."

"How exactly would they do that?"

"They'll destroy your reputation. Get you kicked out of school. Make it so you'll never get a decent job. All it takes is a few fake photos. A fake story in the media. They can even fake evidence that links you to a crime. You could end up in jail for a crime you didn't commit. Even years later they can make sure an employer never hires you. Your life will be over, Jade. You'll end up like—"

He doesn't say it, but he doesn't have to. If this guy wanted to scare me he just did it. My biggest fear is turning out like my mother. It's not like I'd be an alcoholic or addicted to pills. Royce is the reason she turned out like that. But she had nothing in life. No job. No hope. No future. I can't live that way.

"If you stay away from Garret, you'll have a good life. You're a very smart girl and you can do whatever you want if you get away from all this. And I can help you. I'll send you to whatever college you'd like. I'll pay for everything. After college, I'll get you a place to live. Help you with whatever expenses you have."

For a moment he has me considering it. Then I come to my senses again. "No. I'm not leaving Moorhurst. And I'm definitely not leaving Garret. I don't even know why I'm listening to you. I don't even know you. Can I leave now? Garret's going to wonder where I am."

"I suppose you should be getting back. But please think about what I said. I'm not a crazy old man. Everything I told you is true. If you have questions or would like to meet to discuss this more, please call me." He gets up and pulls a business card from his pocket. "Here's my number. When you dial it, you'll be asked to input a security code. Everyone who calls me has a unique code." He smiles and again, it's a warm, kind smile which confuses me because I still don't trust this guy. "The code I've assigned to you is 1008. Your birthday. I'm sorry I missed it for so many years, but I hope we can celebrate it together in the future."

He seems really sincere and I'm starting to think that maybe he's not so bad after all. But that doesn't mean I want to see him again. I don't want a relationship with him or any other Sinclair. "Does anyone else in your family know about me?"

"My wife does. She's the only one. We should probably keep it that way for now. Grace wanted to come meet you today, but I told her I needed to talk to you first. But if you agree to it, she would love to meet you. You have her eyes, you know. You both have the same jade green eyes."

I give him a half smile as I scan the room. "Do you have my crutches somewhere?"

"Oh, yes." He gets my coat from a hook on the wall and hands it to me. As I put it on, he goes behind his desk and brings the crutches over. "Do you need some help?"

"No, I'm fine." I use the crutches to make my way to the door. I'm surprised to find it isn't locked. It opens to a long, empty hallway. I search for the security guys but they aren't there. Arlin leads me outside to where a car is waiting.

"Goodbye, Jade." Arlin pats my back. "I hope to see you again soon. Please call if you need anything."

I say I will, even though I have no plans to ever call him. Or see him. He seems like a nice old man and he *is* my grandfather, but none of that matters. His son destroyed my mom's life and mine. And telling me to break up with Garret certainly didn't win the old man any points.

As the driver takes off, I try to assess where we're at. It looks like the back of a strip mall. When the driver turns around the side of the building, we pass the drive-thru for The Burger Hut, a place that Garret and I sometimes go to eat. What is a rich guy like Sinclair doing with an office in a strip mall next to The Burger Hut?

I get my phone out to call Garret but there's no signal, which is odd because I always have a signal here. The driver sees me holding the phone in the air.

"The signal is disabled in the car," he says.

Arlin didn't want me using the phone? But why? It's another reason I shouldn't trust him. None of what he said made sense. He belongs to a secret society? The same one Garret's dad belongs to? I guess it's possible, but I still don't know what they do. Help rich people run for office? Keep people like me from marrying people like Garret?

The driver parks in front of my dorm, helps me out of the car, hands me my backpack, then drives away.

My phone immediately starts ringing. It's Garret. I've been gone for hours and he's probably been calling nonstop.

"Garret, I'm—"

"Jade, where the hell have you been? Are you okay?"

"Yes. I'm fine."

Actually I'm not fine. I'm feeling really dizzy all of a sudden. Stress must make the concussion worse, like the doctor said. And I've been under a lot of stress the past few hours.

"Where are you?" Garret asks.

"I'm just outside our dorm. Are you in your room? Because I could use some help down here."

"Yeah, I'll be right down." When he meets me there seconds later, I'm leaning against the building so I don't pass out. "What happened? Is it your head?"

"I feel kind of dizzy. I just need help with my bag."

"Something's wrong. I'm taking you to the doctor. Can you make it to the car?"

"I just saw the doctor. I'm fine. I just need to sit down."

"You saw Cunningham? That's where you were? How did you get there?"

"It's a long story. Let's go inside."

We go to my room and he helps me to the bed, sitting right beside me. He looks so worried. Nobody's ever looked that worried for me. Frank and Ryan worry about me, but not the same way Garret does.

He fastens his arm around me and kisses my forehead. "I knew I shouldn't have let you go to class."

"I'll be okay. I'm feeling a little better now."

"Dr. Cunningham called me earlier and said you're not supposed to go to class for the next few days. He knows you won't listen to him, so he called me to make sure you take some days off to rest. But he didn't mention you being at his office. Did you take a cab there? And why didn't you answer your phone?"

"There's something I need to tell you."

He gets an even more worried look on his face. "What is it?"

"After class today a man approached me outside of the Student Services building. It was the same man who bumped into me at Rockefeller Center. And I was right. He is connected to Sinclair."

"Are you joking here because this isn't funny."

"No. I'm serious. He had these men with him and I thought for sure he was there to kill me and then I passed out."

"Jade! What the hell? Why didn't you—"

"Just let me finish. I woke up at an office and Dr. Cunningham was there. He said I'm okay so you don't need to worry. Anyway the old man came into the room and said he wanted to talk to me."

"Who is this guy?"

"Arlin Sinclair. He said he's my grandfather."

Garret looks surprised and a little confused and then it suddenly hits me. "Do you know this man? Your family is friends with the Sinclair family and you dated Sadie, so I guess it's possible."

"Yeah, I know him. He's been to my house a few times. So that's who bumped into you in New York? I don't get it. How did he know about you? Does he know what Royce did to your mom?"

"He claims Royce told him it wasn't a rape and that my mom just made up that story to get money from him. Arlin said he didn't know anything about me until just recently. I don't know if I should believe him. Do you know anything about this guy?"

"He's retired. Does a lot of charity work. When I dated Sadie, she said he spends a lot of time with his grandkids. Takes them each on a trip every year."

"So do you think he was telling me the truth?"

"I really don't know him that well but my dad does." Garret gets his phone out. "I'll call him. We should tell him about this. I don't like Arlin just showing up like that." He starts to call his dad but I stop him.

"Wait. Let me tell you what else he said."

I start from the beginning and tell Garret what Arlin said about this secret organization and his dad's involvement in it.

"Do you know if any of this is true?" I ask him when I'm done.

"It's true that my dad is involved in some kind of secret organization, but I don't know much about it. I only know it exists because a few years ago I heard him talking about it with my grandfather. When I asked my dad about it, he admitted he's a member but he wouldn't tell me anything else."

"I think they do stuff to get people elected. Like maybe rig elections to get whoever they want in office. Like Royce."

"There's no way my dad or this group could pull that off, even if they wanted to."

"I'm not so sure about that. If you heard Arlin today and saw the way he looked when he talked about it, you'd know something strange is going on there."

"Did Arlin come out and say they were rigging elections?"

"No, but he acted like the organization had spent years getting Royce set up to be the next president. Something about him being chosen. And then your dad ruined their plans."

"So Arlin knows my dad killed Royce?"

"The whole organization does. They helped him cover it up."

"Then why haven't they done anything to him? Why hasn't *Arlin* done anything to him?"

"Arlin said it isn't up to him to punish your dad. It's up to the entire organization. He said they're definitely going to punish your dad for what he did to Royce but that they wouldn't harm you or Lilly."

"So what are they going to do? Does he know?"

"He said they have plans. For you."

"Me? Like what kind of plans?"

I scoot back on the bed and lean against the wall. "I don't know. Apparently they aren't final yet. He just said they have plans for you. And for *me* if I don't cooperate."

"What the hell does that mean?"

"You should really talk to your dad. I need to know if any of this is true."

"Jade. You're not telling me something. What is it?"

"He said if this plan they have for you gets finalized, I have to break up with you or they'll ruin my future. They'll get me kicked out of school and they'll destroy my reputation so I can never get a job."

"Okay, I've had enough of this asshole." Garret gets up and puts his coat on. "Where did Arlin take you? I need to go see if he's still there and have a little chat with him, man to man. Straighten this thing out."

"No, don't. Just talk to your dad."

"I want to hear it from Arlin. He seems to have all the answers." Garret picks his phone up from the table. "Will you be okay here? No, you can't be alone. I'll go down and get Harper to stay with you." He starts to leave.

"Garret, wait. I'll just go with you." I move to the edge of the bed and reach for my crutches. I feel dizzy again as I stand, but I don't tell Garret or he won't let me leave.

"You sure you're okay?" He gets my coat from the back of my chair.

"Yes. Besides, I can't let you go there alone. We don't need another Kensington killing another Sinclair." It's not at all funny, but it sounds funny when I say it.

Garret smiles as he shakes his head. "I'm not going to kill him, Jade." As I hobble to the door he stops and hugs me. "But I might have to punch the old man in the face for taking you like that. And then taking your phone. I was so damn worried about you when I didn't know where you were."

"Well, I'm okay now so you don't have to worry." He lets me go and we walk out to the parking lot.

"So where is this place?" he asks as we get in the car.

"It's in that strip mall next to The Burger Hut."

Garret laughs. "Funny, Jade. Where is it really?"

"I'm not kidding. It's in that strip mall."

"A billionaire doesn't put his office in a strip mall by The Burger Hut."

"I think it's in a pharmacy and the office is in the back. Arlin was probably just borrowing the office. Does he own pharmacies?"

"Yeah, he does. Their main business is the pharmaceutical company but a few years ago they started buying up local pharmacies. I forgot that he owns that one in the strip mall. Cunningham probably suggested meeting there in case he needed anything for whatever happened to you." He reaches over for my hand. "Are you sure you're all right?"

"I'm fine. You worry about me way too much."

"It's a side effect of being in love with you, so deal with it." He lifts my hand up and kisses it.

When we get to the strip mall, Garret comes around to open my door. I fumble with the crutches, which I'm still not good at using.

Garret's watching me. "Why don't I go in and check if he's there before you get out?"

"What are you saying? That I'm too slow?"

He's laughing. "You're kind of slow. Maybe I could carry you to the door."

"Just hold on." I yank on his sleeve as I get my balance on the crutches.

As we walk into the pharmacy a customer goes past us out the door, leaving only Garret and me. Garret goes up to the pharmacist, a tall, thin guy with wire-rimmed glasses wearing a lab coat. He's standing behind the counter, putting a new roll of paper into the cash register. He sees us there but doesn't even say hello.

"We're here to see Mr. Sinclair," Garret says. "Is he still here?"

The pharmacist gives us a strange look so Garret clarifies. "Arlin Sinclair? The man who owns this place?"

The guy starts laughing, which is surprising because he looks like someone who never laughs. "Arlin Sinclair? The billionaire?"

"Yes. Is he still here?"

"Why on earth would Arlin Sinclair come to this pharmacy?" He pulls on the register tape and notices he has it in the wrong way. He takes it out and tries again.

"Doesn't he own this place?" I ask the guy.

"He owns hundreds of pharmacies. He doesn't go visit them." He laughs again.

"Is there an office in the back?"

"There's a storage room, but not an office."

"Are you sure?"

The pharmacist is fighting with the register tape again. "I don't know what you kids are up to, but I don't have time for your college pranks. Go bother someone else."

Garret and I leave the pharmacy and go stand by the car.

"Are you sure this is where you were earlier?" Garret asks.

"Yeah. It was next to The Burger Hut and there's only one Burger Hut in town."

As we stand there I try to figure this out. I remember being here so what happened to the office I was in? Maybe the pharmacist was lying. But he didn't seem to be lying.

CHAPTER THREE

"I don't understand. I was just here an hour ago."

"It must've been someplace else," Garret says. "That's okay. Just forget it."

"No. I'm telling you this was the place."

"Let's not worry about it until we talk to my dad. His assistant said he's flying back from London tonight, so we can't talk to him until tomorrow."

"But what about—"

"Jade, stop. The doctor said you're supposed to avoid stress and this thing with Sinclair is totally stressing you out, so we're done talking about it for tonight." He points to The Burger Hut. "Are you hungry? As long as we're here we could get some food to take back."

"I'm not really in the mood to eat."

"You're eating something. I'm supposed to take care of you, remember? We don't have to go here. I'll take you wherever you want."

"Let's just go here. I love their cheeseburgers."

We get our food to go and take it back to my room. As we're eating, my mind is still on that office. How could it just be gone?

"So I have a surprise for you," Garret says, tossing his trash in The Burger Hut bag. "Should I go get it?"

"What is it?" I scrunch up my burger wrapper and add it to the bag.

"If I told you, it would ruin the surprise."

"Okay, go get it."

As he leaves, he turns on my blue ceiling lights. I stare up at them, remembering when he snuck in my room and put them up. It took him hours to do. Every time I look at them I think about how much I love him.

I can't imagine my life without Garret. There's no way I'm breaking up with him. I'm not following orders of some secret organization.

"You ready?" Garret pops his head in the door.

"Yes. I'm ready."

He kicks open the door and carries in a large, thin box.

"You got me a TV?" I practically yell it I'm so excited.

"I had to. You're sick, and when you're sick you have to lie around watching TV. And I knew you wanted one."

"I did, but Garret, that's too much money." I quickly cover my mouth with my hand. "Crap."

He just looks at me and smiles.

I'm laughing. "Okay, what do you want?"

Garret and I made a deal that if I ever mention money again, in regards to him spending too much on me, I owe him a striptease or I have to wear lingerie or a skirt. He acts like it's a punishment and I play along, but we both know I'd totally do those things for him anyway.

We made the deal a few weeks ago after Garret decided he couldn't take any more of my complaints about money. I was getting tired of it, too. We always ended up arguing and it wasn't worth it. Sometimes I still get annoyed when he buys me stuff but I try to let it go.

"I definitely want the skirt," he says, coming over to kiss me. "But not until after you get off the crutches."

"Okay, I can do that."

My friend, Harper, gave me a denim mini skirt for Christmas and as soon as Garret saw it on me, we had what he now refers to as "skirt sex." Now he keeps insisting I get more skirts. The boy really likes skirts. Then again, I think all boys do.

"Where do you want it?"

My head is still thinking about the skirt sex and I give him a funny look.

"The TV, Jade. Where do you want it?"

"Oh, yeah, the top of the dresser."

I watch as he removes the TV from the box and hooks up all the cables. He has such a hot ass. His jeans fit him perfectly. His arm muscles flex as he maneuvers the TV and it totally turns me on. I haven't been with him since I hit my head. Actually longer than that because before I hit my head we had a fight and didn't talk for days. So it's been almost a week, which for us is forever.

"It's ready to go." Garret hands me the remote. "It's your TV so you get to be the first person to turn it on."

I toss the remote aside. "The TV can wait. Come here." I pull him down on the bed with me and press my lips to his.

"Jade. Not yet," he says between kisses. "You know what the doctor said. No physical activity."

"I can't even kiss you?" I tug his t-shirt up to feel his ripped abs.

"You keep this up and there'll be more than kissing going on."

"I think I need that." I undo his belt. "I think it would help me recover faster."

"You do, huh?" He kisses my neck.

"Definitely. In fact, I think the doctor even mentioned that today." I flick open the button on Garret's jeans and yank the zipper down.

"Jade, stop." He says it softly by my ear, making me shiver. "It's too soon. You need to get better first."

"It's not too soon. I need this." I slide my hand over his black boxer briefs as his lips return to mine. "And so do you."

"Shit, Jade." His eyes close as I continue to touch him, and then he speaks against my lips in a hoarse whisper. "You know I can never say no to you."

So much for waiting. Guys are so damn easy.

I whip my shirt off while he does the same with his. Then he kicks off his jeans and boxers while I tug my jeans and panties down, letting him finish taking them off. Usually we take some time to kiss before moving on but not tonight. We've both missed being together and as soon as he gets on top of me he slips inside, rocking his hips in a fast rhythm that sparks small ripples of pleasure through my core. They continue to build until finally hitting a peak causing a release of all the tension in my body.

Yeah, it's definitely been too long. That was just what I needed.

Garret carefully moves off me so he doesn't hurt my knee. "Feel any better?"

"A lot better." I kiss him. "Thanks, Dr. Kensington."

He laughs as he kisses my cheek. "I recommend twice a day treatments."

"Twice a day? I could do that." I smile.

"I'm kidding, Jade. We probably shouldn't have even done that."

"Why? I feel better now than I have all day."

His face gets serious. "You're still not going to class tomorrow. Or the next day. And that's Dr. Cunningham's orders. Not mine."

"I know. I'll stay here."

"I only have one class tomorrow. The other one was cancelled so I'll be here with you all day."

"Really?" I pull his face to mine and kiss him again. "So I'll be able to get my twice a day treatments?"

He laughs. "What's gotten into you? I mean, not that you ever turn down sex, but you usually don't ask for it."

"I love you." My fingers trail over his chest and down his abs. "And you're hot. I can't help myself." I lean in and whisper in his ear. "I want you."

"Are you trying to get this twice a day thing going yet tonight? Because this new side of Jade you're showing me is really turning me on."

"If you're up for it." I glance down at the boxers he just put back on.

He flashes his cocky smile. "Give me a couple minutes."

We kiss until he's ready to go again, after just declaring this no-sex-until-Jade's-better rule.

I'll say it again. Guys are so damn easy.

After our second round, I try out the TV. The picture is crystal clear, almost 3-D. "Garret, this TV is awesome. Thank you."

"You're welcome. I would've got a bigger screen, but I knew you'd complain if I spent too much so I tried to limit my spending."

"Good. Because I don't need some $1000 TV set."

His eyes dart away.

"Garret, did you spend that much on this TV?"

"I got it on sale. And you like it, right?"

"Yes, but still."

He squints his eyes, waiting for me to say it.

"You spent too much money." I say it on purpose.

"Yes! Okay, this time it's a striptease. I'm keeping track of these by the way."

"I know you are." I scoot back into his arms and watch my new TV.

I should probably be spending the night thinking about Sinclair and worrying about what happened earlier. But I don't. Ever since I met Garret I don't worry about stuff as much. He has a way of taking my mind off all the bad stuff and making me focus only on the good.

The next morning when I wake up Garret's already at class but he left a cup of coffee and donuts next to my bed. I sip the coffee, which is still hot, and read the note he left. *A little something to help you feel better. I'll be back at 10 for your morning treatment. I love you.—G*

His note makes me laugh. But I think his sex treatments are actually working. I do feel better today.

It's 9 and normally I would be at class right now. It's weird not to be there. I never miss class.

I take the bag of donuts and turn on the TV. I can't believe I have my very own TV!

Morning talk shows are on and I stop at one that I used to watch last summer. It's hosted by a guy and girl duo who both have bright blond hair, deep blue eyes, overly tan skin, and super white teeth. They're practically identical and they're way too chipper for this early in the day.

I listen to their celebrity gossip as I eat my donuts and sip my coffee. This is so great. I don't even feel sick and I'm being forced to take a sick day.

After a commercial break, the blond girl introduces the first guest. "Fans from all over America have been anxiously waiting for it and now it's finally here. The Prep School Girls' Reunion debuts next week and we have one of the stars of the show with us today. Please welcome the beautiful Ava Hamilton."

"Are you kidding me?" As I say it I realize I'm talking out loud to myself.

Ava goes to school here at Moorhurst. She used to live on my floor but got an apartment off campus this semester. She dated Garret for a few weeks when they were 15 and acted as his fake girlfriend last semester, as ordered by Garret's parents. She was on Prep School Girls, a reality TV show, during her senior year of high school. While she was on the show, she pretended to be dating Garret and now she's pretending to date him again for the reunion show. Her made-up fantasy world has caused paparazzi to follow Garret around and celebrity tabloids to make up stories about him. And his dad won't get his lawyers involved because he doesn't want the bad publicity of a lawsuit. Plus the reunion show only consists of three episodes and Pearce thinks Garret's popularity will end once the show does.

"Ava, welcome to the show," the male host says.

"Thank you, Kurt," Ava says, smiling at him. She, too, has overly white teeth. She's wearing a tight red dress with a plunging neckline that shows off her fake breasts. Kurt seems to be having a hard time keeping his eyes off them.

"So tell us what we can expect on the reunion episodes," Cassie, the female host, says.

Ava pivots her body and talks directly to the camera. "Well, I'm not supposed to say too much but I *will* tell you that the fans who've been waiting for Garret to come back to me will be very pleased."

The audience oohs on cue.

Cassie clasps her hands together. "What else can you tell us about Garret? Because I have to say, I have a HUGE crush on him."

Seriously? Cassie's like 35. What is she doing crushing on a 19-year-old? I turn the volume up.

"I probably shouldn't say this on TV but..." Ava leans over like she's telling Cassie a secret. "If you think Garret's hot with clothes, you should see what he's got going on under those swim trunks."

The audience oohs again as Cassie pretends to fan herself.

"Ugh. Gag. I can't believe this!" For some reason, I'm talking out loud to myself again.

"So I take it you two are back together?" Kurt asks. He looks disappointed. He was probably hoping to get Ava to sleep with him after the show.

"You'll have to wait and see." Ava faces the audience as she says it. "The first episode airs next week, so don't forget to watch. And afterward, go to the show's website and you can rate Garret's hotness and download photos of him."

Rate Garret's hotness? What the hell does that mean? He's either hot or he's not. Where does the rating come in?

Cassie asks Ava about the other girls on the show and then Ava finally leaves the stage. The interview makes me so ill I shut the TV off and go take a shower.

Around 10:15, Garret comes back from class. "How's my patient?"

"Good. Thanks for breakfast." I kiss him as he sits down on the bed. He always wears this cologne that smells so incredible on him I just want to sit there and breathe him in. His face is smooth from his morning shave and his bright, aqua-blue eyes are wide awake. Today he's wearing jeans and a fitted gray t-shirt, a combo that would seem boring on most other guys but

Garret can make anything look sexy. And his t-shirts are the softest I've ever felt.

I smooth his shirt with my hand, feeling his tight abs underneath. "I think it's time for my treatment. You said 10 o'clock right?"

He laughs as I undo his belt. "Is this from your head injury? Because ever since you hit your head you've been—"

I put my finger to his lips. "Are you complaining?"

"Shit, no." He kisses my finger, then pulls my hand away and replaces it with his lips. His tongue tangles with mine and his warm breath tastes like mint.

Hearing Ava and Cassie talk about Garret that way makes me want him even more. He's hot and other girls want him, but he's all mine and there's something really sexy about that.

I unzip his jeans and slip my hand down them, taking him to the edge as we kiss.

"Jade, slow down. I'm supposed to be doing this for *you*."

"You want me to stop?" I start to pull my hand away.

He nudges it back and talks softly against my lips. "I didn't say stop. Just slow down."

He always tries to go slow for my sake but today I don't need to him to. I'm more than ready for him.

I break from his lips. "We can kiss later. Get naked. Hurry up."

He's laughing again. "You're supposed to *want* me to go slow. Give you time to warm up?"

"Yeah, well, I'm warmed up so let's go."

I yank back the covers on the bed as he strips his clothes off. I let him undress me, then pull him back over me to finish what I've been wanting to do since I got up this morning.

When we're done, he collapses on his back next to me. "You're wearing me out, Jade." He says it kiddingly.

"If you didn't want it you shouldn't have walked in here looking all hot."

He feels my forehead. "You're definitely sick. You want sex all the time and you just gave me a compliment. I'm taking you to the doctor."

I laugh and take his hand off my forehead. "I don't need a doctor. I feel a lot better today. No headaches. No dizziness."

"That's because you're not racing off to class or doing homework. You're going to rest here all day."

We get dressed and then I snuggle back into his arms.

I really like sick days.

CHAPTER FOUR

"Did you try out the TV today?"

"Yep. Still works."

Garret tickles my side. "Okay, smart ass. I meant did you watch anything."

"I watched Cassie and Kurt, that morning talk show. They had your girlfriend on as their first guest."

"You were on the Cassie and Kurt show?" he kids.

"Your other girlfriend. Ava."

"She's not my girlfriend so stop saying that."

"Well, this morning she basically told all of America that you're her boyfriend."

"Great. That's just what I need. Like I'm not getting enough emails and—" He stops.

"You're getting emails from fans of the show?"

He sighs. "Somehow my email got out and I've been getting like a thousand emails a day."

"When did you start getting them?"

"Last Saturday. At first it was just a few, but then more started coming in and now it's out of control." He reaches over me to get his phone from the table by my bed. "That reminds me, I need to get a new email address and shut the old one down."

"Did you read any of the emails?"

"A few. They're pretty much all the same." He swipes through his phone.

"What do they say?"

"Just stupid shit. I don't even remember."

"Can I read one?" I hold my hand out for the phone.

His eyebrows raise. "You're not going to like what they say."

I keep my hand extended. He gives me the phone and I open one of the emails and read it out loud.

"'Garret, I love you. Will you marry me? Kristy.'" I hold the phone up to him. "What do you think, Garret? Yes or no?"

He pushes the phone down and kisses me. "Email her back. Tell her I'm already engaged."

"That's a lie. You shouldn't lie to your adoring fans."

"It's not a lie. You and I are engaged."

I laugh. "Really. When did this happen?"

"Sunday. With your concussion you probably forgot."

He looks serious and for a moment I believe him. Memory loss is a side effect of a concussion. I glance down at my hand. No ring.

"Don't tease me like that. For a minute I thought you were telling the truth."

"And what if I was? Would it be so bad if we were engaged?"

"No." I smile as I say it, which is so unlike me. A year ago I didn't even want to date anyone and I definitely didn't want to get married. "But I'd like to be able to remember the proposal."

"When it happens, you'll remember it."

His comment has me imagining how he might propose. Not that I'm expecting a proposal anytime soon. Or ever.

He tucks my hair behind my ear. "You know, that's the first time you haven't totally freaked out when I brought up the marriage topic."

"That's not true."

"It's true. You hate it when I talk about it. In fact, I think Kristy or whatever her name is, would probably marry me before you would."

"Kristy is not getting you. And none of these other girls are either." I pick up his phone again and open another email. A photo pops up. "Garret, this girl sent you naked pictures!"

"Really? Let me see." He grabs the phone and checks out the photos.

"Hey! Don't look at those!" I reach for the phone.

He hands it back to me. "You're way hotter."

"You're just saying that," I mumble as I open another email. "This one says 'Garret, I want to lick your—' This is disgusting! She doesn't even know you and she's saying all these things she wants to do to you. *I* don't even do those things to you!"

"Maybe you should," he says, smiling as he gets up.

I scan the email again, seeing if I *would* want to try some of these things on Garret.

"I think you've read enough of those. I need the phone back. I've gotta see if my dad's lawyers are doing anything to get this stopped."

"You said your dad wouldn't get into a lawsuit over this."

"Yeah, but maybe they can work out a deal with the production company. Get them to stop pretending like I'm going to be on the show. I don't know, but they need to do something."

"I think it'll get worse before it gets better." I hand him the phone. "The show airs next week. And in the meantime Ava said girls can go on the website and rate your hotness." I laugh as I say it.

He's not amused. "This has to stop. They can't keep doing this shit without my consent."

"Well, they're doing it. They're also posting photos of you online. You should probably be monitoring that website to see what they're saying about you."

"I don't want to know." He swipes the phone and dials. "Hey, Dad. Are you back yet? I need to talk to you about some stuff." He listens. "No, it can't wait. We need to talk today. Can you come here to campus?"

"Let's just go to your house," I whisper to Garret.

He nods. "I guess we'll meet you at the house instead. Can you be there at 2?" He listens again. "We'll see you then." He hangs up and comes back over to the bed. "He would've met us here."

"I don't want to talk to him in my room. There's no place to sit."

"You're supposed to be resting." He kisses my forehead. "I was trying to keep you in bed, sick girl."

"I'm not sick." I kiss him back on the lips. "But I like that you want me in bed."

"Again?" He laughs and pulls away. "Sorry, but I'm cutting you off this time. Maybe tonight."

"You're turning me down?" I pout.

"Damn. Don't do that. You know how hard it is for me to say no to you."

"Then get over here." I reach for him and as I do there's a knock on the door.

"Jade? It's Carson." The knocking continues.

Garret rolls his eyes. "Are you gonna make me answer that?"

"He probably needs to talk about our chem paper. Go let him in."

Garret takes his time walking to the door. He doesn't like Carson. Actually he hates Carson. He's convinced the guy is trying to date me, which might be true, but I'm not interested in dating him so there's no reason for Garret to be jealous.

"Is Jade here?" I hear Carson ask Garret.

"Yes, but she's not feeling well so you can't stay long."

Carson walks past Garret into my room. He's a bigger guy than Garret, an inch or two taller with a stockier build. He has wavy, dark brown hair, dark eyes, and this incredibly cute dimple in his cheek when he smiles. He's very good looking, so he should have a girlfriend but he doesn't. He's very picky about who he dates.

"Hey, Jade." Carson comes over and sits on the bed and I notice Garret's jaw tighten. "Are you sick because of your concussion or are you sick like the flu sick?"

"It's my head. I'm supposed to rest for a few days."

"What do you need, Carson?" Garret stands there with his arms crossed.

Carson glares at him. "Don't you have to go to class?"

"Nope. I'm done for the day. And even if I *had* class I wouldn't go because I need to stay here and take care of my girlfriend." He emphasizes the word girlfriend.

I really wish these two could get along.

"So what did you come here to talk about?" I ask Carson. "The chem paper?"

"No. I already turned that in. I just wanted to check on you because you weren't in class this morning."

"Sorry, I should've called and let you know. You'll have to do the lab by yourself today. And I won't be in physics tomorrow either. Could I get your notes from class?"

"Sure. I'll email them to you. Anything else you need?"

Garret clears his throat. "What she needs is to get some rest. Visiting hours are over."

Carson keeps his eyes on me. "I think she can answer for herself. Jade, do you need anything else?"

"No. I'm good. I'll see you later."

"You have my number. Just call if you think of anything." Carson walks past Garret out to the hall.

Garret shuts the door. "The more I'm around that guy, the more I hate him."

"He didn't do anything. He just came by to check on me. As a friend. That's it."

"Why won't you just accept the fact that he wants you, Jade? Don't you see how he looks at you? And the way he's always trying to get rid of me?"

"It doesn't matter. I'm not interested in him, so you need to let this go and stop fighting with the guy."

"I'm not fighting with him. I'm just letting him know that I'm not going anywhere and that he needs to back off."

"He knows that. You've made that very clear. And so have I."

"And yet he's still trying to date you."

"Okay, let's just forget about Carson."

If Garret knew all the stuff I know about Carson, he'd never let me speak to the guy again. Carson is obsessed with Garret's family. He's one of those conspiracy nuts who believes everything he reads on the Internet, at least when it comes to the Kensington family. He claims he has a file full of stuff he downloaded that proves Garret's family is doing suspicious things. I don't have any idea what those things are, but Carson is convinced I'm in danger just being around Garret and his family.

I refused to see Carson's file and I told him that if he ever brought it up again, I'd stop talking to him. But he's piqued my curiosity and now I kind of want to see that file. Even if the stuff in there isn't true, I want to know what people are saying online about Garret's family and their company. When I did my own Internet research, I couldn't find anything other than boring company information, so I don't know where Carson is finding this stuff.

"Jade? Why aren't you answering me?" Garret is sitting in front of me, a worried look on his face.

"Sorry, I didn't hear you. What did you say?"

"I think that's a symptom." He races over to get the sheet of paper the doctor gave him for caretakers of people with head trauma.

"I'm fine. I just wasn't listening."

"Here. Slow response time." He scans the list. "And difficulty concentrating. You have two symptoms. I'm calling Dr. Cunningham." He gets his phone out but I grab it before he can call.

"Garret, really, I'm fine. I was thinking about something and I just didn't hear you." He reaches for the phone, but I hold it behind me and back up against the headboard. "I'll prove it to you. Ask me one of your stupid questions."

Ever since I got the concussion, Garret's been asking me questions to see if I'm confused or have memory loss, two symptoms on his caretaker sheet that warrant a trip back to the doctor. His questions are over-the-top ridiculous and always make me laugh.

"My questions aren't stupid." He sounds annoyed but he's smiling. "Are you ready?"

"Yes. Go ahead."

"Do you know what day it is?"

"That's a boring question. And it's already on that caregiver sheet. Come on. You can do better than that."

"Okay. When is my birthday?"

I take a moment to think. "Shit, I don't know. It's in August but I don't think you ever told me the exact date."

"Strike one. Next question. What's my favorite color?"

I try to remember but nothing comes to mind so I take a guess. "Blue?"

"Nope. Strike two."

"Wait. Did you ever tell me your favorite color? Why don't I know this?"

"Moving on. What sports did I play in high school?"

"Football and swimming. There, I at least got that right."

"Strike three."

"What? You told me you were on the swim team and were quarterback of the football team."

"Yes, but that's only two. What other sports did I play?"

"How should I know? You never talk about high school."

"Sorry, Jade. You failed the test." He reaches behind me and takes his phone, pretending to make a call. "You're obviously suffering from memory loss. I'm calling Dr. Cunningham."

I reach for the phone and he lets me have it. "What was that all about?"

"I was testing you. Making sure your head's okay."

"No, you weren't. You were testing me on how well I know you. And I failed. How could I fail?"

"Forget it, Jade. I was just kidding around."

"Yeah, but still, you're my boyfriend. I should know this stuff about you. Why don't I know this stuff?"

"Maybe you don't want to know." He smiles and kisses my cheek. "Maybe you're just using me for sex and have no interest in getting to know me."

"That's not funny, Garret. I feel like the worst girlfriend on the planet. Later today, I'm going to make a whole list of questions to ask you and I'm going to keep asking them until I know everything about you."

"You're making too big a deal out of this. I was kidding."

"Doesn't matter. I need to know everything about you."

"Not everything." He kisses me. "You need to leave a little mystery."

"So what day is your birthday?"

"August 22."

"And your favorite color is . . . black?" He shakes his head. "Purple?" He laughs, still shaking his head. "Red?"

"Nope. You're running out of colors, Jade."

"I don't know. What is it?"

"Green. That's why I love looking at your eyes. Plus I like the outdoors, green grass, green trees. I've always liked green."

"And what other sports did you play in high school?"

"Besides football and swimming, I played basketball, baseball, lacrosse, and soccer."

"How did you have time for school?"

"I didn't do all of them in one year. Football and swimming were every year and then I added one or two other sports. Freshman year was baseball. Sophomore year was soccer. I just tried different sports to see what I liked best."

"You were a total jock. No wonder your body looks like that." I lift his shirt up to see his abs.

He slowly puts it back down, taking my hand away. "Okay, we're not going to start that. We need to leave soon. Do you want me to get you some lunch before we go?"

"Let's eat out. I need to get out of this room. Let's go someplace next to your house. Or maybe Charles has some leftovers we could eat. Yeah, let's do that. I love Charles' cooking."

"You should tell him that when we see him. I don't think Katherine or my dad ever compliment his cooking. They're used to it now, so they don't even think to compliment him."

We get our coats and head to the car. It's almost March and the weather is starting to warm to the point that we only need a light jacket. I'm looking forward to better weather. I miss running, although now I have to wait for my knee to heal before I can start up again.

When we get to Garret's house, his dad isn't there yet. Katherine's there, unhappy to see us as usual. But she puts on her fake smile and tells us that her husband will be home shortly.

We go straight to the kitchen where Charles, the family cook, is already prepping dinner.

"What are you two doing here?" he asks when he sees us.

"We came to talk to my dad but he's not home yet."

"Hi, Charles," I say.

He nods and smiles as he cuts carrots into thin coins. I like Charles a lot. He's in his fifties and although he doesn't have kids, he seems like he'd be a good dad or a good uncle. He's super friendly and easy to talk to.

"Jade's missed your cooking, Charles. You got any leftovers for us?" Garret opens the door of one of the massive refrigerators.

"You don't have to eat leftovers. I'll make whatever you want. What would you like?" He puts his knife down and wipes his hands on the kitchen towel hanging from his shoulder.

"Ask Jade. She's the sick one."

"I'm not sick," I insist. "Would you stop saying that?"

"Are you feeling any better?" Charles asks.

"Yes. I'm fine."

"She's not fine," Garret says to Charles. He takes two sodas from the fridge. "She couldn't even remember what day my birthday is. She's suffering from major memory loss."

Garret hands me a soda, smiling before taking a sip of his own.

"It's August 22," Charles says.

"See? Charles remembers what day it is."

I give Garret a look to cut it out. I already feel bad enough for not knowing. We talk about maybe getting married someday and I didn't even know his birthday or his favorite color.

CHAPTER FIVE

"My mother used to make grilled cheese sandwiches when I was sick," Charles says.

"I'm not sick," I mumble.

"My mom did, too," Garret says. "Jade, you like grilled cheese?"

"I love grilled cheese."

"We'll have two grilled cheese if it's not too much trouble," Garret says to Charles.

I'm expecting a couple thin slices of white bread with a slice of bright orange processed cheese, but that's not how Charles makes it. He uses thick slices of homemade bread that he slathers with real butter and tops with white cheddar cheese that he cuts from a large block. The resulting sandwich is much better than the ones I grew up eating.

As we finish up lunch, Pearce walks in the kitchen. Charles nods hello at him as he walks by.

"Hey, Dad," Garret says. "We're almost done."

"No rush," he says. "I'll be in my office. Just come in when you're ready. How are you doing, Jade?"

"Fine." I cover my mouth, which is stuffed with the homemade cookies Charles gave us for dessert.

Pearce takes a bottle of water from the fridge and leaves.

Charles points to the tray of cookies. "I'll wrap some of those up for you to take back. In fact, I'll make up a whole box of things. I have some brownies and some caramel nut bars. Would you like some as well, Garret?"

"No, thanks."

"He's always been a healthy eater," Charles says quietly to me. "Always limits the sweets. That's how he stays in good shape like that."

I look at Garret. "That's true. You really don't eat sweets that much."

"I do sometimes, but not every day like you do."

"I really need to start paying more attention to you. I feel like I don't even know you."

He laughs as he gets up from the table. "You *know* me. Let's go talk to my dad."

Pearce is yelling at someone on the phone when we walk into his office. "I need those reports by this afternoon. No excuses." He sets the phone down, not even saying goodbye to whoever he was talking to.

"You want us to come back later?" Garret asks.

"No, I'm just having some problems with the plant manager in Detroit. It's under control now."

Garret and I sit in the leather chairs across from Pearce's desk.

"So is this about that reality show?" Pearce sits back in his chair. "Because I've talked to our attorneys and aside from getting those photographers banned from Moorhurst, there isn't much we can do."

"But how can it be legal for them to make up stories about me like that?" Garret asks. "Can't we sue them for libel?"

"We could, but that would take a lot of time and effort and the lawyers think it's best if we just wait this out. Once those three episodes air, all this press you're getting will likely just go away. By April, nobody will care what your favorite food is or what cologne you wear." He chuckles.

"Dad, it's not funny."

"I know. I just find it surprising how people have taken such an interest in you. You're not even on the show and yet you've got millions of fans."

"Millions? Really?" I look over at Garret who seems just as surprised.

"Anyway, we've been advised by the lawyers to keep quiet and lay low until all this blows over. They want you to stay on campus, Garret, as much as possible so the photographers can't get to you. And they want you to avoid travel of any kind. I know you mentioned going with Jade to Des Moines over spring break but I don't think you should. You'll have photographers following you around and given what happened last time, you could end up getting hurt. Or getting Jade hurt."

Garret glances at me, then turns back to his dad. "Jade and I will talk about it later. We actually came here to talk to you about something else."

Pearce leans forward, resting his arms on the desk. "Okay, what it is?"

"Jade, you want to tell him?"

"Um, yeah." I feel nervous all of a sudden. Garret's dad can be very intimidating and sometimes I find him hard to talk to, especially when all the attention is on me. "Arlin Sinclair came to see me at school yesterday."

Pearce sits up straighter, rubbing his chin with his hand. "I see. So what was the purpose of Arlin's visit?'

"He wanted to meet me and tell me some things."

"What kind of things?" Pearce is a busy man so he likes people to get to the point, but I'm having trouble doing that and I can tell it's frustrating him.

"You want me to tell him?" Garret asks, sensing my nervousness.

"No. I'll do it. Sorry, Mr. Kensington. I'm still trying to make sense of what he said so—"

"It's okay, Jade. Just take your time."

I retell the entire story including the supposed plans for Garret.

Pearce listens intently, but his face never changes. No look of surprise or worry or anger. Nothing.

When I'm done, the room gets quiet for a moment. Then Pearce does this thing he's done before where he looks me right in the eye so intensely that I feel like I'm being hypnotized or brainwashed.

"Jade, you understand that knowledge of this organization Arlin and I are part of is strictly confidential. I trust you'll keep the secrecy of this organization intact. Is that correct?"

With the look Pearce is giving me and his somewhat threatening tone, I find myself unable to respond.

Garret squeezes my hand and I'm finally able to speak. "Yes, I understand. I won't tell anyone."

"Arlin never should've told you about it. It's against the rules and he knows that. It just proves that he's not as sharp as he once was."

"But what about the other stuff he said? Was any of that true?"

"No. Absolutely not."

"So there's no secret plan for me?" Garret laughs a little as he asks it.

"Of course not. That's ridiculous." Pearce smiles, but I notice his body stiffen up and his eyes shift to his desk and I wonder if he's really telling us the truth. Or maybe I'm just being paranoid. Being in this house and around Garret's family seems to make me that way.

"What about that stuff he said about Royce?" I ask. "Was the group you're part of really going to make Royce president?"

Pearce smiles again as he sits back in his chair. "We aren't in the game of picking presidents, Jade. It's true we're involved in helping people get elected, but strictly through donations. Helping with fundraising events."

"But why would Arlin make up lies like that? Why would he say that stuff about Garret?"

"Because he doesn't want his granddaughter dating a Kensington." It's so odd to hear myself referred to as someone's granddaughter. "Given the circumstances, it's understandable why he wouldn't want you to be with my son." Pearce stands up. "I really need to get back to work. I'm sorry, Jade, if Arlin frightened you with those stories he told you. I'll have a talk with him at our next meeting."

"No, you don't need to. I'm just glad none of that stuff was true."

I pretend to believe Garret's dad, but I really don't trust what he said. It doesn't make sense. Arlin wouldn't go to all that trouble to tell me those things if they were just made-up stories. And he seemed really sincere when he told me. Like he really believed everything he was saying.

Garret and I get up and leave and Pearce shuts the door behind us.

"Feel better now?" Garret asks, putting his arm around my shoulder. "Arlin is just a crazy old man trying to get you to break up with me because I'm a Kensington. Just forget what he said. My dad will talk to him. He won't bother you again."

"Yeah, okay." I decide not to share my suspicions with Garret. He and his dad have been getting along better lately and I don't want to mess that up. Besides, maybe Pearce *was* telling the truth.

"Ready to head back?" Garret grabs our coats which we left sitting on a chair in the living room, mainly just to piss off Katherine who likes everything to be neatly put away.

"Not really. It's a nice day and we don't have class so maybe we could do something."

"Like what?"

I look up at him and smile. "Take a drive in my new car? Since I can't drive yet, you'll be the first one to drive it."

"I already drove it. I've driven it several times."

"Garret!" I punch his arm. "Why didn't you tell me?"

He rubs his arm, laughing. "Because I knew you'd be pissed."

"I'm not pissed at you for driving it. I'm pissed because you didn't take me with you."

"Well, I'm taking you now." He kisses my cheek, then walks off. "Wait outside. I'll go to the garage and bring it around front."

Mr. Kensington bought me a brand new, white BMW convertible and gave it to me last week. It was a gift for finding his daughter, Lilly, when she ran off and got lost in the woods behind their house. Finding her is what landed me with stitches in my knee and a concussion.

Garret and I are taking my new car to California this summer. We're living on the beach for three whole months. We still haven't decided on a place, but we've narrowed down our options. We don't want to be in a big city so we're trying to find a place in one of the small coastal towns north of LA. Harper

51

and her boyfriend, Sean, will be there, too. They're hoping to get a place right next to ours so the four of us can hang out together all summer. I'm so excited about this summer. I just want it to hurry up and get here.

The car pulls up into the circular driveway and I get in the passenger side while Garret tucks my crutches in the back seat.

"Nice, huh?" He gets back in and speeds off.

"Really nice, but slow down a little."

"I'm showing you what it can do." He speeds up again once we're past the gate.

"It goes fast. I get it. Now slow down or you're going to get a ticket."

"I get tickets all the time around here. The cops probably keep a stash of them already made out with my information. The speed limits in this town are way too slow."

"Well, there's another thing I didn't know about you. You get too many speeding tickets."

He swerves fast around a corner. "I like to think of it as supporting the city services."

"Where are you taking us?"

"I'm going to that park where we went sledding. I'm guessing nobody's there right now so we'll have the entire parking lot to ourselves. You can test out the car without killing someone."

"I'm not going to pass out while driving."

"That's not what the head trauma caregiver sheet said."

The parking lot at Bryant Park is empty, just as he predicted. He gets out of the car and I climb over to the other side, not bothering to walk around the outside.

"Someone's anxious to drive," Garret says as he gets into the passenger side. "You shouldn't climb over the middle like that. You could've hurt your knee."

"My knee is fine." Actually it does kind of hurt after bumping it on the steering wheel just now, but I'm not telling Garret that. It's my left leg so at least I can still drive. I pull the seatbelt over me and adjust the seat. "I feel like I'm 16 again learning to drive in a parking lot."

"Who taught you to drive?"

"Ryan did, in that old car of his. It's so huge I felt like I was driving a bus." I look over at Garret. "Hurry up. Put your seatbelt on."

"I don't need one to drive around a parking lot."

"Yes you do. I might pass out."

"Oh, now you believe me?" He reaches back for his seatbelt and clicks it in place.

I press on the gas and the car takes off so fast I have to hit the brakes before we run into the curb.

"And you thought *I* was a fast driver?" Garret's hands are against the dashboard like he was bracing for a crash.

"I didn't mean to do that. This gas pedal is really sensitive. You barely have to press down on it. Same with the brakes. With Ryan's car, you had to press really hard." I drive down the parking lot and turn around. "This steering wheel is so easy to move."

"Yeah. Power steering." Garret's laughing at me. "It's been a common feature in cars for the past 20 or 30 years."

"Well, Ryan's car doesn't have it. And that's the only car I've driven other than yours that one time." I continue to go up and down the parking lot. "When Ryan taught me to drive, he was so worried I'd crash his car. He's sick of that car now, but back then he loved it. It was his baby."

"Then I'm surprised he let you drive it."

"It was right after my mom died. He took me out every night and let me drive. Even after I was already pretty good at driving

53

he still made me practice. I think he just wanted to find something to get my mind off what happened. He didn't want me sitting in my room thinking about . . . you know, finding her that way."

Garret puts his hand over mine on the steering wheel. "Why don't we take a break and go sit on the picnic tables over there?"

I laugh. "Are you getting tired of going around the parking lot? I guess it is kind of boring, especially when you're not the one driving." I pull into a space next to the tennis courts.

We go sit on a picnic table by the swings. It's sunny out, but the wind is chilly.

"So you know how you said earlier that you don't know me as well as you should?" Garret asks.

"Yeah." I pick up his hand, which is toasty warm, and place it around my cold fingers.

"Well, I feel the same way about you sometimes. I think we need to work on that."

"Okay, so tell me about yourself." I gaze into his eyes, smiling. "Do you like long walks on the beach? Sunsets? Rainy days?"

"I'm serious, Jade. You never talk about your past."

"Neither do you."

"So I think we should start talking about it."

"What do you want to know?"

"Whatever you're willing to tell me."

"Um, okay, but I still need you to be more specific."

He hesitates and holds my hand a little tighter. "Do you want to tell me about the day your mom died?"

I shrug. "There's not much to tell. It was a Tuesday. I came home from school, went to use the bathroom and there she was. Lying on the bathroom floor. I yelled at her to get up but she didn't move. I don't know why I yelled at her like that. I knew she was dead. Her eyes were rolled back in her head and she had some weird liquid coming out of her mouth."

Garret watches me as I tell the story, probably thinking I'll burst out crying. But I never cry over that day. When I think about it, I don't feel anything really. Maybe I'm a bad person for reacting that way, but it is what it is.

"And then what happened? Did Frank come over? Or who helped you after you found her?"

"Nobody. I just called the police. I wasn't sure who you're supposed to call when something like that happens. Frank was at a doctor's appointment with Ryan. Anyway, the police came over and asked me some questions and the coroner came and took the body away. Then they left and I waited for Frank to get home."

"You just waited there all alone? And the police allowed that? But you were a minor."

"I lied and told them my aunt was coming over. I don't even have an aunt, but I must be a good liar because they believed me."

"So you went to Frank's house when he got home?"

"Yeah, and I stayed there that night."

"And what happened the next day?"

"I just got up and went to school."

"But your mom had just died."

"I didn't want to sit at home all day and think about it. Frank took care of the funeral and whatever else needed to be done. And that's the story. Now you know."

"When did it happen?"

"In the fall. Okay, now you have to tell me something about *your* past."

"When in the fall?"

Dammit. He's going to make me say it and then he's going to overreact. This is why I never tell this story.

CHAPTER SIX

"It happened in October. October 6th."

And there's the look. Shock and sadness cross Garret's face, mixed with a good helping of pity.

"October 6th? That's just a couple days before your birthday."

"Yeah, I know when my birthday is." I pick a rock off the ground and run it along the grooves in the wooden picnic table. "Sometimes I think she planned it that way. The morning it happened she came in my room and told me she was going to order pizza on Thursday for my birthday, which was weird because she never did anything for my birthday. But whatever. She broke her promise, just like she always did."

Even though I know now that my mom was drugged and didn't mean to be that way, I still haven't fully accepted it. And because of that, I still hate her. I feel guilty about that, but it hasn't changed how I feel about her. I think it'll just take time.

Garret's quiet and I can't stand the look he's giving me. Like I'm broken because of this one day in my past. Like he has to try and fix me now. Make me whole again.

"Well, this is depressing." I laugh a little to lighten the mood. "Do you want to just leave?"

"No." He's still staring at me with that same look.

I focus back on the table, digging the rock into a knot in the wood. "I shouldn't have told you that story. It was 4 years ago, and I hated her so it really wasn't as traumatic as it sounds. Your story is way more sad. You actually loved your mom and then she died in a plane crash."

"But I had people around me, helping me get through it. You were all alone."

"I wasn't alone. I moved in with Frank and Ryan the next day."

He takes the rock from my hand and waits for me to look at him. "Is that why you don't celebrate your birthday?"

"No. I don't celebrate it because I didn't grow up celebrating it. It was just another day." My tone is harsh and I don't care, because I really don't like where this conversation is going. I wasn't prepared to tell him that story and I'm kind of mad at him for even asking. "Are we done? Because I really don't want to talk about this anymore. What else do you want to know about me?"

"Okay. Here's an easy question." His face brightens as he thankfully moves on. "If you could go anywhere in the world, where would you go?"

"I never thought about it. I never thought I'd leave Iowa. But I guess if I had to pick, I'd probably pick some country in Europe. I've always wanted to go to England and see a real castle. Have you ever been to a castle?"

"Yeah. Several. I lived in England for a few months."

"That's right. Boarding school. I did know *that* about you."

Some clouds cover the sun making it feel chillier. Garret takes his coat off and drapes it over me.

"I'm not that cold." I hand it back to him. "You can wear it."

"You're sick." He wraps it around me again and kisses my cheek. "I'm taking care of my patient."

"For the last time, I'm not sick. I'm injured."

"Yeah, so let me take care of you. I like taking care of you."

"That's sweet, but I don't need to be taken care of. When I got sick as a kid I used to—never mind."

"Tell me, Jade."

"No. You'll give me that look again."

"When you were sick you used to what?"

"I just took care of myself. That's it. My point is that I don't need someone getting me grilled cheese sandwiches or sitting by my bed all day."

"You may not need it, but I want to do those things. So go ahead and yell at me, but I'm still taking care of you."

"So tell me where *you'd* want to go if you could pick any place in the world."

"I've actually already been to all the places I wanted to go. I've been to almost every country in Europe. I've been to so many tropical islands I can't remember them all. I went to Australia a couple years ago. You already know all this. You'll have to ask me a different question."

"Do you think you'll go back to any of those places?"

"I'm going back to all of them," he says, confidently. "But next time I'm taking you with me."

The idea of that causes a smile to instantly form on my face. I've always wanted to travel to far off places and there's no other person in the world I'd rather go with than Garret. Thinking of traveling reminds me about spring break.

"Garret what are we going to do for spring break? Your dad said you shouldn't leave Connecticut."

"I know. And he's probably right. I should hide out at home so the photographers can't get to me. It pisses me off that we

59

can't fight this, but like my dad said, fighting it will just bring more attention to it. More photos. More articles. More online gossip."

"Well, I can't stay here. I need to go home and see Frank and Ryan since I won't be there this summer."

"I didn't expect you to stay here. You should go. You already have your plane ticket."

"I know, but I really wanted you to come home with me."

"I'll go home with you some other time. I can't have photographers following me around at the airport or showing up at Frank's house. They're too aggressive and I don't want you around that. It's just a week, which I know will seem like a month, but you fly back on Friday, so we can spend the entire weekend doing whatever you want." His smile implies he already knows what I'll want. "Cards. Board games. Movies."

"After a week apart, I guarantee we won't be playing board games." I kiss him. "We should get back. I think it's time for you to give me another one of your treatments."

We drop the car off at his house and drive his black BMW back to campus. We eat dinner in the dining hall with Harper, then watch my new TV before going to bed.

Garret stays with me again and I realize that I'm starting to get used to having him beside me every night.

"I like this," I say softly to him as he tugs my back closer to his chest.

"I like it, too." He moves my hair aside and kisses the back of my neck.

"I mean, I like it so much that I want to do this every night."

"What are you saying, Jade?"

He sits up and I turn over on my back to look at him.

"I'm saying I want to live with you next year. I want to get an apartment together in the fall."

"Really?" I can barely see his face in the dark room but I can hear the happiness in his voice. "But you said you wanted to test out living together this summer first."

"I don't need to test it out. I love you and I love being with you and sleeping next to you like this." I flip on my side to face him. "When we were at Frank's house and you asked me to move in with you, I really wanted to say yes. I was just afraid to because I wasn't sure where this was going. But I've decided to stop listening to that part of me that keeps telling me this will never work and that I can't count on anyone, even you."

"You can count on me, Jade. I promise. I know I screwed up in the past and you didn't trust me, and I didn't deserve your trust back then. But I hope I've earned it back now. I promise you. I'm a hundred percent committed to this and I'm not going anywhere."

"I think I'm finally starting to believe that."

"So we're really doing this? After this semester we'll be done living in these shitty dorms?"

"Yes. And in the meantime, maybe we could do these sleepovers more than once or twice a week?"

"We could definitely do that." He gives me a kiss, then lays his head back down on the pillow.

"And Garret?"

"Yeah."

"Thank you for taking care of me. I know I said I didn't need it but—I do."

"I know you do. Goodnight, Jade."

It's true. He knows exactly what I need even when I don't. I'm not sure how he knows me so well, but he does. He knows that when I try to push him away, it means I need him even more. And when I say I don't want to talk, it means I really need to. I'm crazy that way and other guys would've given up

61

on me months ago. But Garret's still here and he isn't going anywhere. Just thinking about that makes me feel like the luckiest girl alive.

Thursday morning I go back to class. I haven't had any dizzy spells or headaches, so taking a few days to rest was probably a good idea. My knee is feeling better and the doctor said I'll get the stitches out next Tuesday. Spring break starts a few days later on Friday and I fly out that afternoon for Des Moines.

"You're finally back," Carson says when he sees me in chemistry class. He takes my crutches and helps me into my seat even though I don't want or need his help.

"Yeah, I'm better now. And I'm a lot better with the crutches." It's my hint for him to stop helping me, but I'm sure it won't stop him. I haven't talked to Carson since he came by my room the other day, but he's been texting and emailing me.

"Did you get the notes I sent you? You should have some from physics yesterday and the chem notes from Tuesday."

"Yeah. I got them. Thanks for doing that."

"What are your plans for spring break? Are you staying here with Garret?"

"No. I'm flying home on Friday. Garret's staying here."

"Why isn't he going home with you?" Whenever he mentions Garret, Carson's tone always makes it sound like he's making an accusation or a judgment.

"He's having some problems with that reality show and all the publicity around it, so he needs to hide out at his house."

"I've seen the promos for that show. The way they promote it, you'd think Garret's the star of it. And his face is all over the Internet. Well, not just his face. Where do they get all those photos anyway?"

I assume he's talking about the photos that show Garret shirtless or only wearing swim trunks. They have a ton of them on the website for the reality show. "I don't know where they get the photos, but they shouldn't be on the Internet without his consent."

"Why isn't Garret's dad suing the producers? I'm sure he has a whole team of lawyers."

"He does, but they advised him to ignore it and keep quiet until the show is over." My laptop's low battery signal is flashing and I search my bag for the power cord. "So what are your plans for spring break?"

"I'm going home. But I decided to drive instead of fly because I wasn't sure when I was coming back. None of my friends will be home and I'm not sure I want to sit around with my parents for a week."

"That's a long drive." I reach down and plug in the power cord.

"I don't mind. It's not like when you're a kid stuck in the back seat. I actually had a good time driving out here."

Class begins, and I spend the next hour trying to catch up from what I missed. I feel so behind from missing just a couple days.

The same thing happens at my classes on Friday. The professors have moved on to new material that builds on what I missed when I was out. It's like I missed two weeks of class.

By Friday afternoon I don't feel so good walking back to my dorm. My dizziness is back and my head hurts. When I get to my room, Garret's there, swiping through his phone.

"Hey, how was class?" He kisses me as he takes my backpack and sets it on the desk.

I collapse on the bed. "I'm exhausted. I think I'll skip dinner and just go to sleep."

"You're not skipping dinner." He comes over and sits beside me. "What's wrong? Did you overdo it the past couple days?"

"Yeah. I think I did." I rub my head, trying to make the aching go away.

"Then we'll have a quiet weekend. What do you want to do?"

I groan. "Study. Write a paper."

"When's the paper due? Can it wait?"

"It's not really a paper. It's a lab summary for chem. It's due on Tuesday, but I have to do it this weekend or I won't get it done on time."

"Make Carson do it."

"He did the last one. I can't make him do this one, too."

"I'm sure he'd do it, Jade. Just let him write this one and you can write the next two. You need to rest up so you'll feel better when you go home over break."

"Yeah, that's true. I'll call him quick. Could you grab my phone?"

He brings it over to me and I call Carson. He agrees to do the paper and even seems happy about it.

I set the phone down. "Well, that's one thing I don't have to worry about."

"Come on." Garret tugs on my arms until I sit up. "Let's go upstairs and watch a movie. And later I'll order something for dinner."

I yawn. "I'll probably fall asleep."

"That's okay." He kisses my forehead. "You sleep and I'll watch a movie."

"That's a really boring Friday night. You should go out and do something. Call Decker and see what he's doing." My head slumps down on Garret's shoulder.

"You're not getting rid of me, sleepy girl. Do I need to carry you upstairs?"

"No, I can make it. But could you grab my pajamas so I don't have to come down here later?"

He goes to my drawer and pulls out some pajamas, then we head upstairs to his room. I fall asleep right away and stay asleep the rest of the night.

We stay in the dorm all weekend so I can rest and Garret can avoid any photographers. The reality show airs Thursday night so he's a wanted man. I've tried to avoid the Internet, but I have to use it for class and when I do I keep seeing ads for the show. Everyone else on campus has as well, and now the girls at Moorhurst are showing interest in Garret. They did even before all this happened because he's extremely hot, but now they're more aggressive. It's another reason why we need to hide out in his room.

On Tuesday afternoon, Garret takes me to a medical clinic in town to get my stitches out. Dr. Cunningham doesn't work there, but for some reason he's allowed to temporarily use their facilities. I don't ask questions about it because I know I won't get answers.

"Your knee is healing nicely," Cunningham says as he removes the stitches.

Garret's standing there holding my hand like I'm five, but it's sweet so I let him.

"When do you think I can ditch the crutches?" I ask the doctor.

"Let's go another few days and then you can try walking without them."

"I'm dying to run again."

"No running, Jade. You'll just do more damage. Wait another month."

"I'll have to hide her running shoes," Garret says. "Otherwise there's no way she'll wait a month."

"It's true." I look down at my now stitch-free knee. "I can't wait that long."

"Hide her running shoes," Cunningham whispers to Garret, knowing I can hear.

Garret laughs as he helps me off the table.

Cunningham goes to the sink to wash his hands. "Any spring break plans for you two?"

"I'm staying here and Jade's going home," Garret says.

"Back to Des Moines?" Cunningham asks me. I nod as I put my coat on. "I'll be there as well. I'm checking in on Frank next week. That's good. I can check in on you, too, and make sure you're not running on that knee."

"Great," I mumble, annoyed but smiling.

He swipes through his tablet, stopping briefly to type in some notes. "Who's driving you to Iowa? You don't plan to drive yourself do you? Because I don't want you driving until you go a full week without any dizziness."

"I'm not driving. I'm flying."

He looks up from his tablet. "You can't fly with your concussion. If you weren't still having the headaches I'd say yes, but since you are, air travel is out."

"But I have to fly. I have no other way to get there. And I have to get home. I won't be there this summer." I'm talking really fast as if doing so will somehow change his mind.

Garret puts his arm around me. "Jade. Relax. I'll just drive you."

"Are you sure that's a good idea?" Cunningham asks him. "I don't want Jade to be knocked around by a photographer or one of your fans. You know what happened last time."

"Yeah, I know. We'll figure something out. Is she done here?"

"Yes. You're all set, Jade. I guess I may or may not see you in Des Moines next week. Either way, have a nice break. You, too, Garret."

We leave and I find myself getting really angry on the drive back to campus. "Who does he think he is telling me I can't fly?"

"He's your doctor, Jade. And you need to listen to him."

"Why? What's so dangerous about flying? I just have to sit there for a few hours."

"It probably has something to do with the air pressure. Look it up if you don't believe him."

"Maybe I should get a second opinion."

"That guy is one of the best doctors in the country. I guarantee he's better than any doctor you'll find around here."

"Then what am I gonna do? Frank and Ryan are all excited about having me home and I really want to see them. And Ryan already rearranged his work schedule so he could get some time off while I'm there."

It makes me hate Ava even more. If it weren't for her, Garret could just drive me home and this airplane ban wouldn't even be a problem.

CHAPTER SEVEN

Back at the dorm, my phone rings just as we walk in my room. I answer without looking to see who it is.

"Hey, Jade. Did you get your stitches out?"

I recognize the voice. "Hey, Carson." I glance at Garret who gives me his why-is-he-calling-you look as he closes my door. "Yeah, the stitches are out, but I still have to use the crutches for a few more days."

"At least when you're back from spring break you'll be able to walk to class without them. So when are you leaving?"

"I can't go now. The doctor won't let me fly."

He's quiet for a moment, then says, "Just come with me. I'll give you a ride home."

"No, that's okay. Besides you're going to Illinois."

"Des Moines is only four hours away from my hometown. That's nothing. I told you I like driving."

"But then you'd have to pick me up again a week later, unless I got Ryan to drive me to your house."

Hearing "your house" Garret's eyes narrow and he starts shaking his head no.

Carson's talking again. "Either way. Doesn't matter to me. I can easily go pick you up. It's no problem."

"Let me think about it and I'll get back to you."

"Okay. And hey, I'm totally flexible on when we leave and when we come back."

"Sounds good. I'll see you tomorrow." I hang up, set the phone on my desk, and turn to Garret. "Now before you get all—"

"Tell me you did not just agree to drive halfway across the country with that asshole." Garret stands in front of me, his arms crossed over his chest.

"He's not an asshole. And he offered, but as you heard, I didn't say yes." I pause. "But it's not that bad of an idea. He seemed like a safe driver when he drove me to the coffee shop that day. His car is new so it shouldn't break down. He's very mature and responsible."

Garret throws his hands in the air. "And he's trying to sleep with you! Did you forget that part?"

"He's not trying to sleep with me."

"Are you seriously thinking of going with him?"

"Well, yeah. It's just a car ride." I go over to the bed and sit down.

"It's a two day drive! That means you two will be spending the night in a hotel. No fucking way that's happening."

I hadn't thought about the hotel issue. "I'll tell him we have to drive all night. No stopping at any hotels."

"You can't drive, Jade. So he'll have to drive the whole 22 hours or however long it is. He'll fall asleep at the wheel and then you'll roll into oncoming traffic and die."

"That won't happen. I'll be there to keep him awake. I'll make sure he drinks lots of caffeine. Last fall Ryan drove the whole way back without stopping to sleep."

"Yeah, and that was stupid. He even admitted that himself when we saw him after Christmas. He only did it because he had to pick up Frank at the hospital."

"I want to see them, Garret. I want to see Frank and Ryan. That's all this is about. If Carson wanted to try something, he could've done it by now. I've been alone with him plenty of times."

"Not alone in his car for 22 hours! This is exactly what he wants, Jade. To get you alone so he can convince you to stop seeing me. He'll be saying shit about me the entire time while he tries to move in and take my place."

"Nobody is taking your place. Would you just come over here so I don't have to yell this across the room?" I wait for him to sit next to me. "You know how you always say I'm stuck with you?"

He doesn't answer. His mind is still on Carson.

"Hey, you. Over here." I laugh as I push on his shoulder to get his attention.

He finally looks at me. "Yes, I heard you. I always say you're stuck with me."

"Yeah, well, you're stuck with me, too. Carson can say whatever he wants about you, but it won't change anything. I'll still want to be with you. I don't want to be with anyone else. And I don't mean just now. I mean not ever."

His expression softens as I continue to say the things I should've said months ago.

"I know sometimes I say or do things that make you think I won't stick around, but it's not how I feel. I *want* to stick around. I want this—us—to be my future. I don't want this to ever end."

It takes a few seconds for my words to register with him and when they do, the corners of his mouth tick up a little. "You've never said that before. How long have you felt this way?"

"For a while. I was just afraid to say it."

We're both quiet for a moment and then he says, "So I'm stuck with you, huh?" He says it like he's not sure that's a good thing.

I punch his arm. "Hey, you're supposed to be happy about this."

He lays me down on my back and props himself up beside me. "I am." He gives me a kiss, then runs his hand up and down my arm. "But I'm still not sure about this trip. It's your decision, but can you just think about what I said before you decide?"

"Yes, but I want you to think about what I said, too. You have nothing to worry about."

"I'll always worry about you. You know that. And I'm not just worried about Carson hitting on you. I'm worried because I hardly know anything about this guy, and it really does concern me that he'll be driving the whole time without a break. It's dangerous and it's still winter so you might hit bad weather."

"Okay, I got it. So can we make up now?" I ask with an anxious tone.

He looks confused. "Why? Did we have a fight?"

"Well, yeah. Where were you?"

"That was more of a disagreement, not a fight. Hang out with my dad and Katherine for an hour or two and you'll hear a real fight."

"I don't want us to fight like that. To me, what we just had was a fight."

His sexy smile appears. "Then let's make up." He takes his t-shirt off, then kisses me softly and trails more kisses down my neck to the opening of my shirt. He undoes each button until he's at the end, leaving kisses all the way down to my stomach. The area just below it is scorching hot and begging for attention. He undoes my jeans and slides his hand down them. Then he kisses his way back up to my mouth as his hand does whatever the hell he does down there that is pure magic.

"Garret," I say breathlessly.

"What?" he says against my lips.

"You're so damn good at this."

I feel his brief smile on my lips before he kisses me again. My body is on fire with sensations, the tension building under the direction of his hand until it finally releases.

Garret strips the rest of my clothes off, then quickly takes off his. My body is still reeling with sensation as he enters me. His slow, deep thrusts cause another wave of tension to build. His hand slips under me, pulling us closer as his hips move faster until the tension releases yet again with him following shortly after.

He stays there for a moment, his body covering mine, laying soft kisses along my shoulder. "I love you, Jade."

"I love you, too."

He shifts onto his back and holds me close against his chest. I feel him kiss my forehead before I drift off to sleep.

We wake up a few hours later. Garret stretches his arms out, then relaxes them around me again. "I'm starving. How about you?"

"I'm pretty hungry, but the dining halls are closed."

"I wasn't going to eat there anyway." He gets up and starts dressing. "You want pizza?"

"I always want pizza."

He picks my clothes off the floor and tosses them on the bed. "When we get our own place we'll be able to cook something instead of always getting takeout."

"I like takeout. I never got it growing up, so to me it's like a special treat."

"Did your mom cook much?"

I laugh at the thought of my mom cooking. "If you call making a vodka tonic cooking."

"So I take it you did all the cooking?"

"If we had stuff, then yeah." I laugh again as I wiggle into my jeans while lying on the bed. "It'll be nice when I can stand up to put my pants on again."

"You didn't have stuff? You mean like food?"

"What?" I almost forgot what we were talking about. "Oh. Yeah. We didn't have money. You need money to buy food."

After our earlier conversation, I'm finding it easier to talk about my past. Telling him the story about the day my mom died was a big deal. Now that it's out there, I'm not so worried about telling him other stuff.

"What about food stamps?"

I sit up and put my shirt on. "Sometimes they run out before the end of the month." I smile. "And they don't call them food stamps anymore. They give you a card to use at the store."

"Couldn't you go to a food pantry when you ran out of food?"

"We didn't have a car so there were no trips to the food pantry."

"So you just didn't eat?" Garret stands next to the bed as I button up my shirt.

"I ate the free lunch at school."

"Are you saying that was the only food you ate all day?"

"If we didn't have anything at home, then yeah."

"What about weekends?"

He looks so sad and concerned. I reach for his hand.

"Garret, just forget it."

"You went all weekend without eating?"

"Sometimes. But it's not just me. A lot of people live that way." I pull him back down on the bed and kiss him. "So what are we getting? Pepperoni?"

"What?" He's in a daze.

"The pizza. Are we getting pepperoni?" I laugh. "Are you still asleep or something?"

"No. I was just thinking."

"About what?"

"I didn't realize how bad things were for you growing up. I mean, I know living with your mom was bad, but I didn't think about things like not having food."

"It doesn't matter. It was a long time ago."

As I start to make the bed, he stops me. "Jade, you'll never go without anything ever again. I promise."

I kiss him again, then push on him to get up. "Well, you already broke your promise because I'm going without pizza and I'm starving."

"I'm calling right now." He gets his phone out to call in the order. "Shit! How did this get out so fast?" He's swiping through messages on his phone.

"What are you talking about?"

"My phone number. My email. I just changed all that and now I have over 800 new text messages and almost 300 emails."

"More naked pictures?"

He swipes the screen. "Yep." He stops and looks.

I grab the phone. "Garret! You're supposed to delete those, not look at them."

"I'm a guy. Of course I'm going to look. *Then* I'll delete them." He gets his wallet from the desk as I flip through some of the emails.

"You got another marriage proposal. Actually you've got one, two—at least five marriage proposals. And lots of girls asking you to take them to prom. You probably have 100 of those."

"Come on, let's just order the food. I'll delete those later."

When the pizza guy arrives, Garret meets him outside, then comes back shaking his head. "The delivery guy asked for my autograph. Can you believe that?"

"So now you have male fans, too?"

"The autograph was for his little sister. Apparently, she has pictures of me all over her bedroom wall." He sets the pizza on his desk and gets some sodas from the fridge.

"Did you give him the autograph?"

"No. If I did, his sister would tell her friends and then they'd start following me around town asking for one."

I don't mention it to Garret, but I'm starting to get a little worried about his fans. A few preteen girls is one thing, but some of the girls who emailed him sounded more like stalkers than fans.

This reality show can't get over fast enough. Only three more weeks and everything will go back to normal.

Later that night I consider Carson's offer to drive me home and decide to accept it. I know Garret won't like it but I don't always like his decisions either.

Wednesday morning I call Frank and tell him about my change in plans. He insists that Ryan drive to Carson's house in Illinois to pick me up instead of making Carson drive another four hours, and I agree.

I call Carson and tell him the plan. He's really excited. Almost too excited, which makes me think Garret's right and Carson wants to be more than just friends, which could make this an awkward trip. But Carson knows I'm committed to Garret and I'll remind him of that if necessary.

At dinner I tell Garret the news. "So I've decided to let Carson give me a ride home."

Garret stops eating and looks up from his plate. "Um, okay. And you're not worried about him driving for 22 hours straight?"

"He'll only have to drive for 18 hours, which is still a lot, but it's better than 22. We'll drive straight to Carson's house and Ryan will pick me up there."

"Maybe Ryan has to work."

"I already checked and Frank said Ryan's off those days so he'll be able to pick me up and drop me off."

"You already told Frank this? So you told him before me?" Garret drops his fork on his plate, making a loud ding sound. "Did you purposely tell him first so you couldn't change your mind?"

"What? No. I just wanted to let him know what was going on."

"What about Carson? Did you tell him yet?"

I focus on my plate and use my spoon to pile up the corn I never ate. "Um, yeah. I told him."

I feel Garret's anger without even seeing his face. "What the hell? You didn't even consider anything I said, did you?"

"I considered all of it but you're making a big deal out of nothing. I'm not interested in Carson. And if he starts saying things about you, I'll tell him to stop. We won't even talk about you."

Garret takes his tray and gets up to leave.

"Where are you going? I need help with my tray." He comes back and takes my tray and drops both of them off at the conveyor belt.

I follow him as he walks out of the dining hall. He doesn't wait for me as I take forever on the crutches. I meet up with him in his room.

"Why are you getting all mad about this? You said it was my decision."

"Jade. I just need a few minutes, okay?" He's standing by his desk not looking at me.

"A few minutes to what?"

"To calm down so I don't say something I'll regret later."

"Just go ahead and say it. You think I'm stupid or naïve for thinking Carson won't try something on this trip. Is that it?"

He walks to the door and holds it open. "Why don't you come back in an hour? I really need to calm down before we talk."

"I'm sorry, Garret. I just want to see Frank and Ryan. That's the only reason I'm doing this. I wasn't trying to piss you off."

He doesn't say anything so I leave. I don't go back up there later and he doesn't come downstairs. At 10 I call him.

"Aren't you sleeping down here tonight?"

"Do you need me to?" He still sounds mad. "You haven't been having any dizziness or headaches today, right?"

"No."

"Then I'll probably just stay up here."

"But we only have two nights left before I leave and then we'll be apart for a week."

"Do you need me to sleep down there or not? Just tell me what you want."

"Forget it. I'll sleep alone."

He hangs up without saying goodbye or goodnight or that he loves me. I know he said he needs some time to calm down, but I wish he'd find another way to manage his anger. When he pushes me away like this and refuses to talk to me I start to lose faith in our future. All my fears about committing to him come flooding back into my mind. I revert back to the old Jade. The Jade who doesn't want or need anyone in her life because people just let you down.

Whenever I feel like this, I have to keep reminding myself that I'm not the old Jade. I can't think like her anymore. I can't let her doubts and anger and fears taint my judgment. Doing so will just turn me back into the person I don't want to be.

It's almost midnight and I can't sleep. I'm so used to having Garret beside me that the tiny twin bed feels big and empty without him. As I reposition my pillow for the hundredth time trying to get comfortable, I hear a soft knock on the door. I grab my crutches and get up to answer it.

"Hey." It's Garret, dressed in the navy shorts and white t-shirt he often wears to bed. The anger in his eyes is gone and he seems more relaxed. "Am I still invited?"

"Yeah. Of course."

He comes in and shuts the door. "I'm sorry about how I reacted earlier. I shouldn't have shut you out like that. It's just that the thought of you with him for all that time—" He stops and takes a deep breath. "Never mind. I'm sorry. That's what I came down here to say. I love you and I don't want to fight about this."

"I don't want to fight either."

Garret sets my crutches down on the floor and picks me up and carries me back to the bed. He lies beside me, wrapping me in his arms. "Sorry if I woke you up. I should've come down earlier."

"You didn't wake me up. I couldn't sleep."

"Me either. I'm so used to sleeping next to you that now I can't sleep unless you're beside me. I'm really going to miss you next week. I wish I was going with you. If it weren't for this fucking reality show. I'm so sick of this."

I feel him tensing up.

"It'll be over soon." I tug his arm closer around me and feel him relax again.

I shut my eyes, but part of me still feels anxious about our fight. In the past I would've said nothing and just gone to sleep, but that just makes things worse. If I want this relationship to work, I need to just say what I need to say.

"Garret?"

"Yeah."

"I know you were mad at me tonight, but I can't have you telling me to go away like that. It makes me feel like you don't want this anymore. And then I get mad at myself for getting involved with you in the first place. I know I can't react like that every time we fight, but until I get over it could you maybe not throw me out of your room when I piss you off?"

"I'm sorry, but I just didn't want to yell at you and say something I didn't mean. And you didn't piss me off. I was pissed off at Carson and I needed some time to calm down."

"Well, maybe next time we could just sit together and not talk."

"We could do that." He sits up on his side and I turn to face him. "But Jade, you need to understand that we're going to fight. It's normal and it's okay. We won't always agree on stuff. Sometimes I'll be mad at you and sometimes you'll be mad at me. But that doesn't mean we'll break up."

"I know we'll fight, but I still don't like it."

"I don't either, but it's part of being in a relationship." He runs his hand down the side of my face. "Even if we fight, don't you ever think I don't want this. I want this more than I've wanted anything. I want *you* more than anything."

I nod.

He kisses me. "So are we okay now?"

"Yes." I yawn as my eyelids get heavy and close.

"Hey." I feel him nudge my side.

"Yeah." I open my eyes again.

"Don't be afraid to tell me when I'm being an ass. I do stupid shit all the time, especially when I'm pissed, so feel free to call me on it. I won't get mad at you for it."

"I know. I just don't like yelling at you."

"You don't have to yell. Just tell me. I can handle it. I know this may come as a shock, Jade, but I'm not perfect." He can't even say it without laughing. "And neither are you."

I sit up, trying not to laugh. "Hey, I'm totally perfect!"

"You're not." He lays me back down and drops a kiss on my lips. "Neither one of us is. But together we're kind of perfect. So it works."

"Yeah, it does."

He lies behind me again. I flip on my side and scoot my back into his chest.

It's exactly where I belong. Not just tonight, but forever.

CHAPTER EIGHT

When I go to class on Thursday, I hear people talking about The Prep School Girls' Reunion. The first episode starts tonight and it sounds like everyone on campus plans to watch.

During chem lab even Carson says he plans to watch the show. "Are you and Garret watching tonight?"

"I don't know. Maybe we will just to see what they say about him."

"Has he talked to Ava since all this started?"

"No. I don't think she wants to talk to him. I think she prefers to live in her fantasy Garret-land where he does and says whatever she wants." I set up the bunsen burner while Carson lines up the chemicals we need.

"On the promo for tonight, Garret shows up at Ava's apartment and—"

"Garret's not on the show, okay? So unless Garret has a twin, that's not possible. Let's just focus on the experiment. What chemical do we start with?"

As Carson checks the lab book I hear Amber and Mackenzie, the two girls behind me, talking about Garret.

"Did you go to the website and download those photos of him?" Mackenzie asks Amber.

"Yes. Oh my God. So hot. Next year I'm totally going to the swim meets."

"Why wait? He's always over at the pool. We should just go over there and get our own photos. Up close and personal."

They both laugh. I want to turn around and punch them but of course I don't. But what the hell? I'm sitting right in front of them. They have to know I can hear them.

That night, I go up to Garret's room after dinner. It's officially spring break and our last night together before I leave to go home. Since I won't see him for a week, I planned something special for him but I'm going to wait and surprise him with it later.

"Are we watching the show?" I ask him.

"No. Why would we do that?"

"To see what they're saying about you. Carson said the promos made it look like you were actually going to be in one of the scenes. He said they showed you at Ava's apartment."

"How is that possible?"

"Maybe they got some actor who looks like you." I turn the TV on and flip to the channel. "We should at least watch a few minutes."

The show is starting and some cheesy music plays in the background as photos of the "stars" fade in and out.

I lean back against Garret as we sit on the bed. "It already looks bad. I can't believe so many people like this."

"I can't believe you're making us watch this. It's our last night together. I don't want to spend it watching this shit."

"It's only an hour and we don't have to watch the whole thing. And we have plenty of time to do other things later." I rub my hand over the front of his jeans.

"Hey, don't be starting that unless you plan to finish it."

I take my hand away. "Fine."

He puts my hand back. "Well, go ahead and start so we can finish."

"We're watching the show. We'll do that later."

He turns my face toward his and kisses me. "We need to start early. We're not doing it just once."

"Then I guess I won't be sleeping tonight."

Ava's voice booms from the TV and I look over and see her face, covered in way too much makeup, smiling back at me. She's sitting in a chair talking right to the camera. "Garret and I were high school sweethearts. We started dating when we were 15. He was my first. Most girls say their first time isn't great, but mine was. Let's just say that Garret's talents go way beyond swimming."

"Okay, we're not watching this." Garret takes the remote from me and turns the TV off.

"You need to know what she's saying about you." I take the remote back and turn the show back on. Slow, soap-opera type music plays in the background as Ava and some guy make out on her bed. You can only see the back of the guy. He's on top of Ava, shirtless but wearing jeans.

"Garret, look! They did just what I said they'd do. They hired some actor so people would think it's you. I was kidding when I said that, but they actually did it!"

"This can't be legal." Garret gets his phone out. "There's no fucking way." He calls his dad as the show goes to commercial. His dad answers and Garret mutes the TV and puts the phone on speaker.

"Yes, Garret," his dad says before Garret even says anything. "I'm watching the show and I saw the scene with Ava."

"Yeah? So? What can we do about it?"

"Nothing. In that scene, she didn't actually say your name, so technically it could've been anyone."

"But everyone assumes it's me."

"Yes, that's implied, but that's not enough for a case."

"So she just gets away with it?"

"There are only two more episodes after tonight. We're not going to start a legal battle over this. We just need to get through the next couple weeks. I've hired some additional security here at the house until all this is over."

"Why do you need extra security?"

"Earlier today we had photographers waiting outside the front gate along with some teen girls camped out across the street. I assume they'll be there tomorrow as well so I'm sending the driver to pick you up. You can't drive your car. You need to be in a vehicle with dark windows. I don't want anyone seeing you come home."

"What time is the driver coming?"

"In the morning, around 9."

"Tell him to come later. Jade doesn't leave until noon and I want to be with her until she leaves."

"You just call him and tell him when to be there. I'll see you tomorrow."

He hangs up and I turn the volume back on the TV. Ava is talking to the camera again, recapping last year's episodes for people who didn't watch the original show. It all sounds scripted and not at all how she normally speaks. She mentions Garret again and as she talks, they cut away to some photos of her in high school, including ones of her and Garret together.

"I wasn't dating her when those photos were taken," Garret says, annoyed that I'm making him watch this. "She's lying. This whole thing is a lie."

"And this is just the first episode. I wonder what she has planned for the other two episodes."

"I don't know and I don't care." He slips his hand under my shirt. "It's time to get you naked."

"But the show's not over yet."

He shuts the TV off and tosses the remote on the floor, then works his hand down my jeans, hitting the spot that makes my whole body go crazy. "You really want to watch it?"

"Watch what?" I ask.

His cocky smile appears. "That's what I thought."

Right after we do it, I get up and start getting dressed.

"Where are you going?" Garret asks.

"We're going down to my room. Get dressed."

"Why would we go down there? Let's just stay here." He holds his arm out for me. "Come back to bed."

"Nope. Get up. We need to go downstairs." I toss his clothes at him.

He laughs. "What's going on with you?"

"Just hurry up." I'm dressed now and I sit down next to him and put my shoes on.

"You're acting very strange, but okay." He leaves a kiss on my cheek as he gets out of bed.

As he's getting dressed I try walking around the room without the crutches.

"You sure you don't need them anymore?" he asks, watching me.

"Yeah, it's still a little sore but I can walk on it." I stand in front of him. "You ready, yet?"

"Yes, I'm ready." He smiles and takes my hand as we leave.

We go down to my room and I open the door and pull him inside.

"What's this?" he asks as he shuts the door and sees the movies and snack foods piled up on my desk.

"It's Garret night. I picked out your favorite movies and made you a concession stand."

A huge grin crosses his face. "Why? It's not my birthday."

"It doesn't have to be your birthday. I just wanted to do something special for you and I wanted to do it before I left for spring break. I've wanted to do something for you for a really long time but I didn't know what to do. I never have money so I can't really buy you anything."

Garret goes over and looks through the movies. I took them from the box in his room. They're all action films and I don't really like them but this night is about him, not me. I bought his favorite snacks, too. Buying them used up my laundry money for the week but I'm going home tomorrow so I'll just wash my clothes at Frank's house.

Garret's not saying anything.

I go up to him. "You don't like it, do you? I guess it *is* kind of lame. We watch movies all the time, so it's not that special but I didn't know what else—"

He takes my face in his hands and kisses me before I can finish.

"I love it," he says, still holding my face. "And it *is* special because you did all this just for me."

"I got you something, too. Well, I kind of made it and I'm not very crafty so if you don't like it you can—"

"Wait." His smile gets even bigger. "You seriously made me something?"

I nod, now a little nervous that he won't like it.

"Can I see it?"

"Yeah. It's in my dresser." I walk over and open the top drawer. "Promise me you won't laugh or say it's stupid."

"I'd never do either of those things. I guarantee if you made me something that I'll love whatever it is."

I take the navy blue photo album from my drawer and hand it to him. It's one of those photo albums where you peel back the clear cover on each page and put photos on the sticky surface. I made it into a scrapbook of Garret's years on the swim team during high school. It's divided by each year with photos and a list of all his swim meets along with his times and where he placed in each event. I hand wrote the stats on small pieces of paper using different colored pens for each year. Then I mixed the photos with the swim meet stats so that each page is like a collage. That's where the craft skills come in, and as I said, I'm not at all good at crafts.

Garret takes the photo album over to my bed and sits down. As he opens it up and I see the pages again, it looks like something a kid made. I should've asked Harper for help. She's way better at crafty things.

"Where did you get all this?" Garret asks. He's still smiling so maybe he likes it.

"I asked your dad for help."

"But my dad hardly went to any of my swim meets. Where did you get all these photos and the stats?"

"Your dad gave me your high school coach's number and I called him and he emailed me the stats. And your dad had some of the photos and Decker helped me get the other ones."

Garret's quiet as he flips through each page. When he's done he sets it on the table next to my bed and says, "Come over here." I go up to him and he pulls me onto his lap. "That's the nicest thing anyone's ever done for me."

"So you like it? You're not just saying that?"

"I love it. Really." He slips his hand around mine, his other hand wrapped around my waist holding me in place on his lap.

"How long did it take you to get all that stuff and put it together like that?"

"I don't know. It doesn't matter. I just wanted you to have a record of all your swim meets. Your dad said you didn't have anything like that. And I'm making you one for college, too. I've already got some photos and all your stats for the meets up until you got hurt. But I'll do a better job on the next one." I glance back at the album. "Sorry that one looks so bad, but I warned you about my craft skills."

"Jade." He turns my face back to his. "Stop apologizing for it. The book is perfect. I love it. Thank you for doing that for me."

The look on his face causes a warmth to spread through me that goes deep within my soul. He's happy. Really happy. And I know it's not just because of the scrapbook, but because of what it means. Garret knows I can't always express my feelings the way he can. Telling him how much he means to me is still hard for me. But this book I made for him, even if it's kind of a mess, is my way of telling him how much I care about him, and appreciate him and everything he's done for me.

Now I wish I'd done something special for Garret a long time ago. I'm not sure why I didn't. If I'm truly honest with myself, I think it's because I was still afraid to give Garret too much of myself. I was afraid to give him all of my heart because I've already had so much pain and loss in my life that I didn't think I could handle the emotions I would feel if I opened my heart completely to him and this didn't work out. But I'm tired of being afraid. Garret's given his whole heart to me and I'm ready to give him mine. In fact, I feel like I already have and I'm not even sure when it happened. Now I just need to make sure that he knows that. Not just with words, but with actions, and tonight was the first step in doing that.

When I look at Garret again, I see him smiling at me. "You're really sweet, you know that?"

The tough-girl side of me does not like being called that, so I roll my eyes and say, "I am *not* sweet."

"You're sweet. Deal with it." He kisses me, then backs away just enough to look at me. "That took a lot of time and effort and it was really nice of you to do that for me."

"It's just a photo album. It's not that great." I glance away but he turns me back to him.

"Don't do that."

"Don't do what?"

"Don't put yourself down like that."

"I didn't." I try to look away again but he cups my cheek with his hand, forcing me to face him.

"Yeah, you did. And I don't want you to do it anymore."

"I didn't say anything about myself. I was talking about the album."

"Yeah, but you did something really nice and then I tell you that and you get all uncomfortable, like you don't believe me."

"Because doing this one little thing doesn't make me nice. Or sweet. If I *were* those things, I would've been doing stuff like this the whole time we've been dating instead of waiting until now."

He sighs.

"What?" I ask, not sure where this is going.

"Why do think all these bad things about yourself when none of them are true?"

I don't respond because I'm not sure I know the answer.

His hand is still cradling the side of my face and I feel his thumb brush my cheek as our eyes meet.

"You're so many good things, Jade. You're thoughtful and caring and whether you like it or not, you're sweet. And when I think about the hell you went through as a kid and how you got through that—" He stops. He seems frustrated. "You're a fucking amazing person, Jade, and it pisses me off when you can't see that."

His words make me smile but also make me tear up a little because nobody's ever described me that way. Nobody's ever said I'm thoughtful or nice or caring or anything like that. Most people would probably describe me as being the opposite of those things because I shut people out and keep them at a distance. But I don't want to be that way and I've been trying to figure out how I even got like that. I think it's because I tried for so many years to do nice things for my mom so that she'd like me, maybe even love me, or at the very least stop yelling at me. But no matter what I did, no matter how hard I tried, she never changed. And so I gave up trying to make her love me. I gave up trying to make *anyone* love me, but then Garret came along and loved me without my having to do anything other than just be me.

And now that he knows me, the real me, he knows that deep down I don't think I'm a very good person. I know that's why Garret said that to me just now. He wants me to believe I'm the person he described as much as he believes it. And maybe someday I will.

I give him a hug, squeezing him really tight. "I love you so much."

He rubs my back and kisses the top of my head. "I love you, too."

I hold on to him a little longer, then finally let him go and stand up. "Now can we start Garret night?"

He laughs. "Okay, but I still don't know why we're having Garret night."

"We just are, okay?" I go over to the movies. "Which one do you want to watch first?"

"Where did you get the DVD player?" he asks, seeing it next to the TV.

"I borrowed it from Harper."

"And you made me cookies?" He points to the container of cookies, which is sitting next to the snacks I bought.

"No. I asked Charles to make them. He said those are your favorite. He made them this morning."

"And he drove here and delivered them?"

"Actually Decker picked them up for me since I can't drive yet."

"You really put a lot of effort into Garret night," he says, wrapping his arms around my waist.

"Yeah, well, given that it's the first one I figured it better be good."

"So this isn't a one-time thing?"

"Nope. Garret night will continue but you won't know when. I'll just surprise you."

"You're so damn sweet," he says, tickling me as he kisses me.

"For the last time, I'm *not* sweet," I say, laughing as I try to squirm away. "Now go pick out a movie."

We watch two movies, then have sex again before finally going to sleep. Garret wakes me up early and we do it again. I think he's trying to make sure I remember how good he is at that when I'm spending all those hours alone with Carson. As if I'd even consider doing anything with Carson. Not gonna happen.

We go to Al's Pancake House for breakfast since we'll miss our traditional Sunday breakfast. Luckily, there aren't any photographers there. They must all be hanging out at Garret's house.

When we get back to my room I finish packing. At 11:30 we say our goodbyes before Carson arrives.

"So you'll call me every hour from the road," Garret confirms.

"Yes. But Carson's going to think I'm crazy calling you that much."

"I don't give a fuck what he thinks. I need to know you're okay and not dead in a ditch somewhere."

"He's a very safe driver. And don't start getting upset. He'll be here in a few minutes and I don't want you two fighting before we leave."

"I won't fight with him." Garret doesn't sound at all convincing.

"Garret, I mean it. If he says something that pisses you off, just ignore him."

He drops his head down, shaking it side to side. "I can't believe I'm going along with this. Why the hell am I letting some guy I can't stand drive the person I love most in the world halfway across the country? Your life is in his hands. He could veer off the road into a ditch and kill you. Or hit another car." Garret runs both his hands through his hair. "Shit! I can't let you do this, Jade. I can't trust this guy."

I take Garret's hands in mine. "Relax. Everything will be fine. Nothing bad will happen. Isn't that what you always tell me when I worry about stuff?"

"Yes, but this is different. You sure you don't want to stay here? We could watch movies at my house all week. Charles will make you whatever you want. You could hang out with Lilly."

"Those are all good things but I need to spend time with Frank and Ryan."

"Just make sure you call me, okay? And leave your phone on."

"I will."

He gets his wallet out and takes out four twenty dollar bills. "Here. Take this."

"I'm not taking your money, Garret."

"You'll need it for the trip."

"Carson said I didn't owe him gas money. His dad's paying for it."

"You still need money for food and drinks and whatever you else want. Just take it." He holds the bills out in front of me.

I take one of the bills. "I don't need $80. Twenty is fine."

"That's not enough for two trips, there and back. You'll be stopping at gas stations and they jack the price up on stuff. Trust me. You'll want the $80."

"Okay, but I'm giving you whatever's left when I get back."

He rolls his eyes. "You're keeping it. I swear, Jade, you drive me crazy with this money thing."

I take the remaining bills and put them in my empty wallet, then go back over to him. "Thank you."

"You're welcome."

We kiss just as Carson starts knocking on my door. "Jade, it's me."

Garret sighs as I pull away. "It's me? Seriously? Tell him you're not on the 'it's me' level."

"Don't start." I kiss him quick, then go to answer the door.

"Hey, Carson. I'm ready to go. Are you parked out front?"

"Actually I parked by the side door so you wouldn't have to walk so far on the crutches."

"I'm trying not to use them anymore. My knee feels a lot better."

Garret picks up my crutches. "You're still bringing them, just in case."

"Let me take your suitcase." Carson steps inside my room to get it but Garret blocks his way.

"I'll take it," he says, glaring at Carson.

"Whatever, man." He turns back to me. "Jade, after you."

Carson waits for me to go, then follows me out as Garret walks behind us with my stuff. We load up the Jeep, then Carson holds the passenger door open for me.

Garret goes up to him. "I'd like to say goodbye to my girlfriend."

Carson doesn't even look at Garret as he shuts the door. "I'll wait in the car, Jade."

Garret and I move off to the side, away from the Jeep.

"It's just a week," I remind him. "A week is nothing."

"A week seemed like a month last time." He rubs my arm.

I sigh. "I know. This is really gonna suck, isn't it?"

"It won't suck for you. You'll be out doing stuff with Ryan and Frank. It'll suck for me being trapped at the house for a week."

"Just do stuff with Lilly. She loves playing with her big brother."

"I can't play with a six-year-old for more than a couple hours. I'll probably spend the week swimming. Lift some weights. Start getting in shape for next season."

"You're going to be the hottest guy on the beach this summer." I smile at him as I get a final feel of his abs. "I won't be able to let you out of my sight. Those California girls will be all over you."

"Jade, we should get going," Carson yells from the car.

"She'll be there when we're done," Garret yells back. "God, I hate that guy."

"Maybe when I get back we can finalize our place for the summer," I say, trying to get his focus off Carson.

"Yeah, we need to do that soon. Go online when you're home and check out those condos Harper suggested. I'll do the same and we'll compare notes."

Carson starts the Jeep. Garret rolls his eyes.

"I better go before he bugs us again." I hate goodbyes and I just want this one over with so we can skip ahead to the reunion. "See ya next Saturday." I give Garret a quick kiss, then turn to walk away.

"Hey. Get back here. That's not a goodbye kiss." He pulls me into his arms and kisses me in a way that makes it nearly impossible to say goodbye. "I love you. Be safe. And make sure to call me."

"I will. I love you." I hug him once more.

I get into the Jeep just as Garret's driver shows up.

"What's with the fancy car and chauffeur?" Carson asks as he pulls out of the parking lot. "Garret can't drive himself places anymore? He has to hire someone?"

I take a deep breath and let it out. "Okay, Carson. We're going to be together in this car for a very long time and we need to set some ground rules. We are not going to talk about Garret. At all. Not one word about him. Got it?"

"I was just asking a question." Carson drives down the small road that leads away from campus.

"For the last time, Garret and I are a couple. We are not breaking up no matter what you say." I take my cell phone out of my purse and set it in the cup holder between us. "So it's no use trying to convince me to stop dating him and start dating you."

"Jade, I'm not trying to date you. Why do you keep saying that?" He stops at the end of the road, looking both ways several times before turning onto the main road. He definitely seems like a safe driver.

"Because you act like you are. You call me and text me all the time. You put down my boyfriend. You always invite me to go out with you."

"Yeah, as a friend."

"Guys aren't friends with girls. They always want more."

"Who told you that? He-who-must-not-be-talked-about? Because he's wrong. I have several female friends and I'm not trying to have sex with any of them. Besides, I might be getting back with my ex-girlfriend. She's on break from school at the same time as us and wants to get together while I'm home."

"That girl you showed me a photo of?"

"Yeah. Madison. She wants to see if we can work out the long distance thing. So who knows? Maybe we'll get back together."

"Oh. Well, that's good. I hope it works out." I feel like a total idiot. Here I am accusing him of trying to date me and his mind is on his ex-girlfriend. His ex is really pretty. She has a face like a model and long, blond hair. He showed me her picture when we first met. She's a senior at a small college in Chicago. She broke up with Carson when he moved to Connecticut because she didn't want to do the long distance thing. But apparently she's changed her mind.

He reaches over and puts his hand on my shoulder. "So will you relax now? We're just two friends taking a road trip. That's it."

"Okay, but I still don't want you to talk about Garret."

"Fine by me."

Maybe this trip won't be so bad after all. I'm glad we got this out in the open and settled right away.

As Carson gets on the interstate, I position the pillow I brought with me up against the seat and rest my head on it. I'm so tired from my lack of sleep last night that I can't stay awake.

"Jade." I feel Carson tapping my arm. "I need to stop for gas. Do you have to use the restroom or anything?"

Stop for gas? What's he talking about? We just got on the road.

"Why didn't you fill up before we left?"

"I did, but the tank's getting low and there's a station just up ahead so I'm going to stop."

"How long was I asleep?"

"About four hours."

I sit up. "What? How is that possible?"

"I guess you were tired. Why? What's wrong?"

"I told Garret I'd call him every hour. Shit! He probably thinks I'm dead in a ditch somewhere." I reach down for my purse to get my phone.

"Why would he think that?"

"Where the hell is my phone?" I don't have a very big purse and my searching has turned up nothing.

"It's right here." Carson points to the cup holder in the center console. "I didn't want it to wake you up so I put it on vibrate."

"You what? No! You can't do that." I grab the phone and see the long list of missed calls from Garret and a string of texts. I call him back.

He answers right away. "Jade, what the hell? It's been four hours."

"I know. I'm so sorry. The phone was on vibrate and I fell asleep."

"Why was it on vibrate?"

"I don't know. I must've hit it by accident." I feel guilty lying to Garret but I don't want him hating Carson even more.

"I was freaking out here, Jade. I thought something happened. I was about ready to have the state patrol start looking for you."

"It won't happen again. I promise. So how's everything at home?"

"Boring. I miss you already. This totally sucks."

"I know. I miss you, too." I turn away so Carson can't hear. "Did you have people waiting around your house when you got there?"

"Yes. It's crazy. Girls are lined up on the street taking photos of the house and trying to climb the gate. Photographers are waiting by the entrance. My dad doesn't want me leaving the house until school starts again, but I don't know if I can make it that long."

"Well, it's only a week." Carson pulls into the gas station and parks at the pump. "We just stopped for gas and I really have to go to the bathroom so I'll call you later, okay?"

"Yeah, but it better not be another four hours. And turn your ringer on."

"I will. Bye."

We hang up and I go in to use the restroom. Then I grab some energy drinks in the gas station so I won't fall asleep again.

"Let me get those." Carson walks up to me holding his own collection of caffeinated beverages. "You want anything else?"

"I have money. You don't need to pay."

"My dad gave me trip money. Might as well spend it." He turns to the rack behind him and grabs three bags of potato chips.

"You must really like potato chips," I say.

"These are for you. I know they're your favorite."

He does? How does he know that? Did I tell him that? I can't remember, but the fact that he wants to buy me my favorite food seems a little more like something a boyfriend would do than a friend, doesn't it? But he wants to get back with his ex-girlfriend. I'm so confused by this guy.

CHAPTER NINE

When we get to the register, Carson takes my energy drinks and sets them on the counter. As I'm getting my wallet out, he pays for all it before I can stop him. I just let it go and don't say anything because I don't want to argue about it here in the gas station.

We stop for dinner a few hours later and he tries to pay again but this time I pay for myself. Now I'm really glad Garret gave me that money. I don't like Carson buying me stuff. And I definitely don't want him buying me dinner, which would make it seem like we're on a date.

I call Garret and check in once we're back on the road. "Hey, it's me again."

"Hey, you. What's up?"

"We just stopped for a late dinner and now we're in the car again. I probably shouldn't call you every hour for the rest of the night. You need to sleep."

"I won't sleep unless I know you're okay. You have to call."

"How about every couple hours? Then at least you'll get a little sleep. Or I'll text you instead of calling and you can check your phone whenever you wake up."

"Fine. But I'll be up until midnight so keep calling until then."

We talk a few minutes more before hanging up.

"Does he really make you call him every hour?" Carson asks.

"We aren't talking about him, remember?"

"I'm just saying it seems a little controlling, doesn't it? You can't go more than an hour without checking in?"

"We're only doing the hour thing during the road trip. When I get home we'll only talk once or twice a day."

"He doesn't trust my driving, or what?"

"You're driving all night without a break, so yeah, he's worried about it."

"I'm a safe driver, Jade. I've never had an accident. I rarely speed. Never had a ticket."

"He still worries. Let's just leave it at that."

I find a radio station and turn it way up so we can avoid talking for a while. Around midnight I turn it off and talk to Carson to keep him awake. I ask him about his hometown, his family, his friends, what sports he played in school, and other random questions. By the end of this trip I'll probably know more about Carson than I know about Garret.

By five in the morning I'm really tired, so I know Carson's even more tired than me since he's had to pay attention to the road the whole time.

"You want another energy drink?" I ask him.

"No, I'm okay. You know, this lack of sleep is good practice for our residencies after med school. My dad had to do 35-hour shifts when he was a resident, but he said they changed the rules and now they only make you do 16-hour shifts."

"I haven't decided for sure if I want to be a doctor."

"Really? Why? You're getting A's in chem and physics. It's not like you can't handle the classwork."

"Yeah, but that doesn't mean I should be a doctor."

"You'd be good at it. You'd have a good bedside manner. You have a lot of empathy for people. You're a good listener. You're easy to talk to."

This conversation is getting way too personal so I try to change the subject. "The weather seems a lot colder here than in Connecticut, don't you think?"

He ignores the question. "So why are you changing your mind about med school?"

"I'm not changing my mind. I was never set on going in the first place. It was just an idea. I'm good at math and science so it seemed like I should at least consider it. But it would mean a lot more school and I don't have the money."

"You can get scholarships and financial aid."

"Yeah, I still need to think about it."

He arches his back to stretch. "I could use a break. Do you mind if we stop and get some coffee?"

"No, not at all. Honestly I don't know how you're holding up so well. I'm exhausted."

He smiles and puts his hand on my arm, gently squeezing it. "It helps to have a good travel companion."

I'm not great at figuring out when someone is flirting but Carson's gesture just now seemed very flirtatious. I can't even describe exactly how or why. It was more of a feeling. Maybe I'm reading too much into it.

After our short break, we're back on the road with two giants cups of coffee wedged in the cup holders. It's 6 but the sun still isn't up.

My phone rings just as I'm sipping my coffee. It's Garret.

"You're up early," I say when I answer.

"I barely slept. I told you I can't sleep unless you're next to me."

"Well, that's a problem since we have to live in separate rooms until we get our own place."

"We don't have to *sleep* in separate rooms."

"I don't think Jasmine will allow that. She doesn't mind if you stay over a few times a week, but every night might get us in trouble."

"She doesn't care. So you must be almost there, huh?"

"Just a couple more hours. Ryan called me last night and said he'd pick me up around 11." I notice another call coming in. "That's him now. He's probably getting ready to leave. I should talk to him quick and make sure his plans haven't changed. I'll call you later."

I switch over to Ryan's call. "Hey, Jade. I just got up but I'll head out at 7 and should be there by 11 like we planned. You guys still doing okay? No car problems?"

"Nope, everything's good. See ya soon."

I put the phone down and sip my coffee again.

"I didn't mean to listen in, but it sounded like you might be moving out of the dorms," Carson says.

"Yeah, Garret and I are getting a place together next fall. Oops, I didn't mean to say his name. Let's change the subject."

"You sure you want to commit to something like that so soon?"

"Soon? By next fall, it'll be a year since we started dating. That's not soon."

"I mean soon as in young. You're only 19. Do you really want to move in with a guy at 19?"

"I'll be 20 in the fall and yes, I do want to move in with him. Age doesn't matter."

"It *does* matter. You're still figuring out your life at 19. Or 20. Like you said, you're not even sure what you want to do after college."

"Yes, but I'm sure about Garret and me. When you know it's right, why wait? Waiting's not going to change how I feel about him."

"It might. A lot happens in college. You change. You make big decisions that affect the rest of your life. And you don't want to make a decision based on what someone else wants instead of what you want. When you do that, you end up making sacrifices and then you resent the person."

"It's normal to make sacrifices in a relationship."

"Yeah, when you're older and have the big stuff figured out."

"And what makes you an expert on this?"

"Madison broke up with me because she didn't want me sacrificing my future to be with her. She didn't want me staying in Illinois, going to a college I didn't want to go to, just so we could still date. And she was right. I'm way happier going to Moorhurst, living in Connecticut."

"But you said she wants to get back together with you."

"Yeah, because she's not as worried about the long distance thing anymore. Now that we're both doing what we want to do, she feels better about the relationship."

"Won't it be hard to only see her a few times a year?"

"We're both busy, so even if we were in the same town we wouldn't see each other much. Besides, it's not healthy to spend all your time with one person."

There he goes again. Trying to send me a message about Garret. Putting down our relationship. I turn to look out the side window, hoping Carson will get the hint that I'm not happy with his comment.

The car gets quiet and I watch the sun rise over the open fields that line the interstate. I'm more awake now thanks to large amounts of coffee and the emerging daylight.

Carson messes with the radio and finds a station that sort of comes in but not really. It's almost impossible to get a station in these rural areas. He gives up and turns the radio off just as his phone starts ringing.

"Hey, Mom," he says when he answers it. "We have about an hour left." He's quiet as he listens. "I don't know. Do you want to ask her?" I feel Carson nudging me. "My mom wants to talk to you."

I turn to see him holding the phone out in front me. I stare at it, confused why Carson's mom wants to talk to a total stranger. I mouth "why" at him but he just smiles and pushes the phone at me.

I take it from him. "Hello."

"Hi, Jade. This is Carson's mom, Judy. I can't wait to meet you. Carson's told us a lot about you."

"It'll be nice to meet you, too." I have no idea what to say to her.

"We can talk at the house, but I just wanted to ask what you'd like for breakfast. I'm making pancakes, eggs, bacon, and some other things but if you want something else, my husband can run to the store quick."

"No, don't worry about it. Whatever you have is fine. That all sounds good."

"Are you sure? Because it's really no trouble. We want you to feel welcome, so don't be shy. If you want something, just ask."

"Really, I don't need anything, but thank you for offering."

"If you think of something, just call. We'll see you soon."

I hand the phone back to Carson who listens as his mom continues to talk. "Yeah, she is nice." He smiles at me as he says it. "Okay. Love you, too."

That's odd. Carson tells his mom he loves her? After a phone call? Does he always do that? I'm not at all used to that type of family interaction. I don't even understand it. I never had anything close to a loving relationship with my mom. And I've never heard anyone in Garret's family say that they loved each other.

"My mom already likes you." Carson picks up his coffee and takes a drink.

"She doesn't even know me. We talked for like two seconds."

He puts his coffee down. "Well you won her over in those two seconds."

"You seem to really get along with your mom."

He shrugs. "I get along with both my parents."

"That's unusual."

"Not really. A lot of people get along with their parents. Doesn't Gar—" He stops. "Never mind."

"Good catch," I say, laughing. "Anyway, your mom is way too concerned about breakfast."

"She loves having company. She'll have a big buffet set up when we get there. She always makes too much."

An hour later we arrive in a neighborhood in Carson's hometown. The street is lined with short, stick-like trees that look like they were just planted last fall. The houses look nearly identical—large, two-story homes with three and four car garages. The exteriors are either gray or beige stucco combined with stacked stone. Each house is set far back from the road with large lawns which are currently covered in snow. The driveways are neatly plowed with sharp edges that could only come from a snowblower. I would know. I used to shovel the sidewalk growing up and it never looked that neat and clean.

It's definitely an expensive neighborhood. Carson's mom is a trauma nurse and his dad is a doctor so I know they're rich. Not Kensington rich but richer than most people.

"These houses all look new," I say. "When did you move here?"

"In January. My parents couldn't take being in the old house after my sister died. Too many memories." Carson turns into the driveway of a two-story house with a dark gray exterior and pulls into the three-car garage.

As soon as we're parked, a woman comes into the garage from the house. She has straight, dark-brown hair that hits just above her shoulders. She's taller than me, maybe 5'8, and thin. She has a pretty face and doesn't wear much makeup; just a little blush and some mascara.

"You must be Jade." She smiles and comes over to hug me. I just got used to people I know hugging me, so having a stranger hug me is a little much. But she doesn't linger. She moves on to Carson and gives him a hug.

"Hi, honey. I'm glad you're home. We've missed you."

"Where's dad?"

"He went down to the bakery to grab some donuts." She comes over to me again. "This bakery down the street has the best pastries. Let's go inside. I've got some coffee brewing."

"Um, I was going to help Carson get his stuff from the car."

She holds the door open. "He's a big boy. He can handle it. Let me show you around."

We go inside and Judy gives me a quick tour of the house. It's big, but feels homey. The walls are all painted in warm, rich colors. The kitchen walls are red, the dining room is dark beige, and the living room is a light chocolate brown. The furniture all looks soft and comfy. An oversized couch covered in a navy blue fabric sits in the living room across from a flat-screen TV and a stone fireplace.

As she leads me back to the kitchen I glance around, noticing all the family photos everywhere. In the hallway there are photos of Carson at different ages, along with a girl who I assume is his now deceased sister.

This house is such a stark contrast to Garret's house, which is all white. Cold, white tile floors. Stiff, white furniture. Empty white walls. There is only one family photo at the Kensington house and it's a professionally taken photo where the four of them are all dressed in—you guessed it—white. I'd never want to live in Garret's house but I'd love to live in this house. I've only been here a few minutes and I already feel comfortable.

CHAPTER TEN

"Have a seat." Judy points to the tall chairs that line the kitchen island. "Cream and sugar or just black?" She hands me a big ceramic mug filled with coffee.

"Cream, please."

She reaches in the stainless steel fridge and pulls out the pint of half and half. "We'll eat in a few minutes, as soon as my husband gets back. Everything's ready. I'm just keeping it warm in the oven."

Carson walks in loaded up with luggage. "Did she give you the tour?"

"Not all of it," Judy answers. "I didn't show her the basement."

"Come on, Jade. Let's go downstairs. You've gotta see this."

I'm not sure what's so great about a basement, but I follow him anyway, taking my coffee with me.

I see why he likes it. The basement looks like a sports bar. On one end there's a small kitchen with a tall counter and six barstools. Red glass pendant lights hang above the counter and there are two TVs hung on the wall, I'm guessing so you can watch multiple sporting events at once.

In the middle of the room is a pool table and next to that is a big, wraparound couch in a bright red fabric that faces a massive flat-screen TV. Carson turns it on and sound booms from speakers mounted in the ceiling.

"Pretty cool, right?" he says. "And of course they get this after I go to college."

I follow him down a hallway that leads to his bedroom. I wait outside the door as he walks past me into the room.

"You can come in," he says, putting his suitcase on the bed. "I only spent a couple nights in this room and then I left for college so it doesn't have that lived-in look yet."

I remain at the door and check out his room. It's painted a grayish-blue color and he has a king-size bed covered in a dark gray comforter and neon green throw pillows. It's masculine, but you can tell his mom decorated it. The colors all coordinate and everything's neatly organized. Across from the bed is a desk and bookcase which has some trophies and medals on it.

"Anyway, that's the tour." He meets me back at the door. "Let's go upstairs and eat."

We go back to the kitchen to find the entire length of the island covered in food. Pancakes, scrambled eggs, hash browns, bacon, fresh fruit, and baskets filled with baked goods.

"Ready to eat?" Judy asks.

A man walks in and stands behind her, wrapping his hand around her shoulder.

"Hi, Jade. I'm Howard. Carson's dad."

"Hi," I say. "Do you guys always eat like this for breakfast?"

They all laugh.

"Judy tends to go overboard when we have guests," Howard says. "But she always makes a big spread on the weekends." He kisses her cheek. "She likes to feed her boys, don't you, honey?"

Judy smiles. "Go ahead, Jade. Grab a plate and get started. We're pretty casual here, so sit anywhere you want at the table."

Again, this is so different than Garret's family. Casual is not a word I would ever use to describe them. Everything at their house is formal. You sit where they tell you to sit and your food is always plated and served, except at breakfast.

"So Jade, Carson tells me you're thinking about med school," Howard says once we're all seated around the table.

"Yeah, I'm considering it."

"Well, I'll be honest with you, it's a challenging field. Treating people is just one part of it. You also have to deal with insurance companies and manage a staff. You're really running a business."

"Great, Dad, now she'll never want to be a doctor," Carson says.

"It's important you both know what you're getting into. That's all." He takes a muffin from a basket on the table. "Personally I find the hardest thing about being a physician is that sometimes you try everything and you still can't make the person better. You'd think with all the technology available they would've found some cures by now, or at least some more effective treatments, but it doesn't seem like they ever do."

There's a sadness to his tone and I'm sure it's because he wished he could've done something to save his daughter. If he only knew that there actually *are* better treatments available. Ones that regular people aren't allowed to have. Maybe not a cure for cancer, but Garret did say his grandfather had lung cancer and it just went away. How is that possible?

As grateful as I am to Garret's dad for hiring Dr. Cunningham to take care of Frank, it makes me sick to know that the private medical group Cunningham's part of is keeping their cutting-edge treatments reserved only for rich, important people.

"Enough about work, honey," Judy says to Howard. "Jade, did Carson tell you his grandmother lives in Des Moines?"

"Yes, he mentioned that." I hear my cell phone ringing from the kitchen where I left my purse. "Sorry, but I have to get that. It might be Ryan."

"Sure, sweetheart. Go ahead."

Sweetheart? I don't even know Judy and she's calling me sweetheart? Maybe it's a thing moms do. Obviously not all moms because *my* mom never called me that. And Katherine's never called me that. Just imagining Katherine calling me 'sweetheart' makes me laugh as I answer the phone.

"Hey, did you get there yet?" It's Garret. "And what's so funny?"

"Nothing. And yes, we're finally here. I was going to call you, but then we sat down to breakfast."

"Carson made breakfast?"

"No, his mom made this huge breakfast for us. We just sat down to eat. Can I call you back?"

"Don't you want to talk now that you don't have Carson listening in?"

"Yeah, but I don't really have much to say. I'm so tired from staying up all night I can't even think straight."

"How are Carson's parents? Hopefully better than their son."

"They're nice. And they have a great house. It's in one of those new neighborhoods where every house on the street looks the same. But I really like the inside. It feels comfortable. Lived in."

"You mean unlike my house?"

"Well, yeah, kind of."

He laughs. "It's okay, Jade. I know you don't like my house. But technically it's my dad's and Katherine's house. I'd never live in a place like that."

"So our apartment won't be all white with furniture nobody wants to sit in?"

"Of course not. You know that. In fact, you can pick out whatever you want for our place. It doesn't matter to me as long as it's nothing Katherine would ever buy."

I'm so relieved to hear him say that. I knew Garret didn't want a place like his parents' house, but I wasn't sure what that meant.

"I should probably get back to breakfast. I'll call you when I'm on the road with Ryan."

I hang up and turn to see Carson behind me, refilling his plate. "Was that Garret checking in again?"

"Yeah. I told him I'd call him back later." I put the phone in my purse. "Hey, you said his name. That's against the rules."

"The rules only applied in the car, not here." He smiles as he walks back to the dining room.

The four of us finish breakfast, then linger at the table, drinking coffee and talking. Around 10:30 Carson asks his dad to check something on the Jeep because it was making a noise whenever we turned the heater on high. They go to the garage and Judy gets up to clear the table.

"I can help," I say.

"That's okay. You're tired from the trip. Just relax."

"I'm happy to help. Just tell me what you need."

I follow her to the kitchen and watch as she pulls out a stack of plastic containers. "Could you put the leftovers away?"

"Sure." I scoop the food into the containers while Judy loads the dishwasher.

"I'm so glad you and Carson became friends," Judy says. "Growing up in the Midwest, I wasn't sure how he'd fit in on the East Coast, so I was relieved when he found you."

"I was happy to find him, too." Crap! I hope that didn't sound like I considered Carson anything more than a friend. I was just agreeing about the Midwest thing, not Carson specifically.

"It sounds like he's made some friends. Even had a girlfriend for a while."

"Yeah, he has a lot of friends at Moorhurst." I'm not really sure if that's true but I know it's what she wants to hear.

Judy dries her hands on a dishtowel and puts lids on the plastic containers I just filled.

"Carson's ex-girlfriend is coming over later today." Judy lowers her voice even though there's no way Carson could hear her from the garage. "Madison's a lovely girl. Very pretty. Very smart. But I just hate to see her break his heart again. I'm worried she wants to get back together with him, but I don't think it's a good idea."

I don't know why Judy thinks this is any of my business. I keep quiet and focus on filling the remaining containers.

She raises her voice back to normal. "So do you have a boyfriend?"

"Yes. He goes to Moorhurst. He's a Connecticut boy, born and raised."

I'm surprised Carson hasn't mentioned Garret. It sounds like he told his parents everything else about me.

"Well, maybe you could find a nice girl for my son." She stacks the leftovers in the fridge as I hand them to her.

I try not to laugh. Carson would die if he knew his mom asked me to find him a date. "Okay, I'll keep my eye out for someone."

The doorbell rings and Judy goes to answer it. I hear her calling me. "Jade, your brother's here."

I race to the front of the house to find Ryan standing there. I give him a huge hug. "Finally."

"What are you talking about? I'm right on time."

I step back and look at him. He cut his hair. It's much shorter now, cut close to his head. But it looks good. More of a cute college guy look and less of the slacker artist look he used to have, which never really fit him.

"You changed your hair," I say to him.

"Yeah, I didn't think they'd let me into med school the way I looked before."

"You're going to med school, too?" Judy asks.

I cringe. Ryan was not supposed to know about my possible plans for med school. I hadn't told him or Frank. I knew if I did they'd start scrimping on food and other things trying to save money to pay for it and they already scrimp enough trying to pay for Ryan's school.

"Um, yeah," Ryan says. "I took a short break from college so it'll be another year." He looks at Judy. "Did you say someone else is going to med school?"

"Yes. My son, Carson, is also going. And of course, Jade. So all three of you."

Ryan stares at me. "Yeah, I guess we all want to be doctors."

"Well, the world can always use more doctors," Judy says, clueless that she's just spilled my secret.

Carson and his dad walk into the room and I introduce them to Ryan. They make small talk about Des Moines for a few minutes.

"Ryan, could I get you something to eat before you get back on the road?" Judy asks. "We have plenty of food."

"Thanks for offering but Jade and I should get going. I don't like to leave my dad alone for too long."

That comment causes another 10-minute conversation about MS and Carson's dad telling Ryan about different treatments Frank could try.

It's 11:30 and I'm starting to think we'll never get out of here. Carson's parents have a way of making you want to stick around.

Finally, Ryan heads to the door.

"Jade's stuff is in my car so I'll meet you out by the garage," Carson tells Ryan.

"I can get it," I say, following Carson to the garage.

I hear Judy talking to Ryan as I leave. "Let me pack you up some food in case you two get hungry."

She's so funny. She's one of those moms who's always worried that people aren't getting enough to eat. Totally unlike my mom who never even noticed or cared if I ate.

"Do you have any plans for the week?" Carson hits the button to open the garage door and a rush of cold air blows in as the door lifts. "Or are you just hanging out?"

"Just hanging out. We'll probably watch some movies. Play cards. How about you?"

"Not sure yet."

"Hey, I hope things work out with Madison." I'm sure Judy wouldn't like me saying that but whatever. Carson seems to want his ex back.

"Can I call you when you're home or did Garret ban that?" Carson opens the back of the Jeep and pulls my suitcase out.

"You probably shouldn't. I don't think Garret, or your ex, would like that." I spot Ryan by the car with Judy at his side, holding bags full of food.

"You gotta get over this no-guy-friends rule of yours, Jade. I can be a great friend if you just let me."

"We're already friends. You just can't be calling me all the time. It's not a good idea."

"Well, have a good trip." He gives me an unexpected hug. I sort of hug him back, then pull away.

"Thanks again for the ride. I'll see you next Friday."

Ryan loads my stuff into his car and we take off. I turn up the radio, trying to put off the talk I know is coming.

As expected, Ryan turns the radio back down so that we can barely hear it. "Carson seems like a good guy. His parents were friendly."

"Yeah, they're nice. It looks like Carson's mom gave us a ton of food. Do you want something?"

"Maybe later." He turns onto the entrance ramp to the interstate. "So anything you want to tell me?"

"Like what?"

He checks his mirror as he merges into traffic, which seems heavy for a Saturday. "I don't know. Like maybe the fact that you've decided to be a doctor?"

"That was just an idea. I haven't decided for sure."

"Jade, why didn't you say anything? That's big news. Plus, I'm a little offended that you didn't ask me for any advice."

"What advice would you give me?"

"I've had three years of pre-med classes and I'm studying for the MCAT. I must have something to offer. And Chloe's already in med school, so she could've answered your questions."

"I don't have any questions. I told you. I'm just considering it."

"What else are you considering? Something in a science field?"

"That's the thing. Every time I think of other careers I keep coming back to the doctor thing."

He jabs my arm. "You're totally going to be a doctor." I look over and see him wearing his proud, big-brother smile. "Dad's going to be so happy." He pauses for a moment, then says in an annoyed tone, "Thanks a lot, Jade."

"What did I do now?"

"You'll be Dad's favorite kid again. I thought going to med school would score me some major points with him, but now you have to go and copy me."

"Fine. Then we won't tell him. He doesn't need to know until it's for sure."

"I was kidding. You're telling him."

"I'm not his favorite kid by the way. I'm not even his kid."

"You're his daughter. You always will be. So don't ever say you're not. You'll hurt his feelings."

I wish Frank really was my dad. My life would've been so much different if I'd grown up with him instead of my mom.

"Why didn't you tell us?" Ryan asks. "Why were you keeping this a secret?"

"Because if I do this, I have no idea how I'll pay for it and I didn't want Frank thinking he had to come up with the money."

"You'll get financial aid, just like I'll be doing." Ryan turns the heater up. "I'm glad you didn't consider asking your billionaire boyfriend to pay for it because that would not be a good idea."

It's true. Garret's family has already given me way too much, and I would never ask them to pay for med school.

"I just got this heater fixed and it's still not very warm, is it?" Ryan's fiddling with the dials and adjusting the vents.

Now that he knows about the med school thing I figure I might as well tell him the other things I've been keeping from him and Frank.

CHAPTER ELEVEN

"I have some other news to tell you," I say to Ryan.

He stops messing with the vents. His eyes get big and he grabs my arm. "You're not pregnant, are you?"

"No!" I yank my arm back. "Geez, Ryan, what the hell?"

"What? It's not like it couldn't happen." He hesitates, then cautiously asks, "You're still on the pill, right?"

"Ryan! I am NOT talking to you about that."

"Just make sure you take it at the same time every day. Otherwise it's less effective. And you should really be using other protection as well."

"Oh my God, Ryan. Please stop." I turn away. I'm so embarrassed I can't even look at him.

He laughs. "Fine. I won't say anything more about it. Now tell me your news."

I turn back to him. "Garret and I are getting an apartment together next fall."

I'm expecting a lecture followed by a fight, but instead he says, "Yeah, I figured you would."

"You did?"

"Sure. I know you don't like living in the dorm and you two are living together this summer, so Dad and I assumed you guys would be getting a place together next year."

"And you're not mad? Frank's okay with it?"

"He'd rather have you stay in the dorm and do stuff with other girls instead of always hanging out with your boyfriend, but there's not much he can do about it. But how does that work with your scholarship?"

"We're going to ask Garret's dad to put my room and board money toward the apartment rent."

"How will you get to campus?"

"Mr. Kensington got me a car." I wasn't going to tell Ryan that yet, but he took the moving-in-with-Garret news well so maybe he'll be okay with this, too.

"He got you a car?" From his tone I can tell Ryan's not okay with it. Crap! I should've waited.

"Yeah. A few weeks ago. I'm not supposed to drive yet, so it's still parked at their house."

"So this isn't a car he's just letting you borrow. He actually bought you your own car?"

"Yes." I really wish I'd waited until later to tell Ryan this.

"Why did he give you a car?"

"I've been babysitting Lilly a lot so he wanted to thank me." That's the lie I'd planned to tell Frank and Ryan when I shared my news about the car, but now that I've said it out loud it sounds ridiculous.

"He gave you a car for babysitting his kid? That doesn't make sense, Jade."

"To you and me it doesn't, but to a billionaire it makes perfect sense. He knew I needed a car and he felt he owed me for all that babysitting so he got me one."

"What kind of car is it?"

I hesitate as I consider lying again, but he'll find out eventually so I tell him. "A BMW convertible. Garret and I are taking it to California this summer."

Ryan coughs like he's choking. "A BMW? He got you a BMW? What kind?"

"I told you. A convertible."

"I mean what series? Like a three series?"

"Oh, um, I think Garret said something about it being a six series. What does that mean?"

Ryan practically chokes again and I offer him the bottle of water sitting next to him on the seat.

"A six series? Are you kidding me? That's like an $90,000 car."

"It is? Damn, that's a lot of money."

Ryan swigs his water and hands it back to me to put the cap on. "Yeah, that's a shitload of money. That's more than our house cost. You can't tell me he bought you a car like that just for babysitting."

I should've made up a better lie. This one sucks. But what was I going to say? I can't tell Ryan the car was a gift for finding Lilly in the woods after her family thought she'd been kidnapped by bad guys wanting revenge for Garret's dad killing a presidential candidate. Yeah, that would go over well.

I try to find another way to explain this. "The guy is super rich. To him, $90,000 is like $90 to you and me."

Ninety thousand dollars? Is that really what the car costs? Ryan knows a lot about cars, so I'm sure he's right. I knew the car cost a lot, but not that much. I purposely avoided looking up the price online because I didn't want to know.

"Jade, you can't accept that."

"He registered the car to me. It's mine. I already accepted it."

"We can't afford the insurance on a car like that. Or the registration. Or the maintenance. It'll cost over $100 just to get the oil changed."

"Mr. Kensington is taking care of all that."

"That makes even *less* sense."

"No, it doesn't. He gave me the car and he knows I can't afford to keep it if he doesn't pay for that stuff."

"And what happens when you're no longer dating his son?"

"Oh, thanks a lot, Ryan. That's real nice. You just assume this isn't going to last?"

It's already a fear that lingers in the back of my mind, so hearing Ryan say it really pisses me off.

"I'm being realistic. You two are 19. You're probably not going to stay together forever."

"Really? So then I guess you and Chloe won't either."

"That's different. I'm 22 and she's 23. You're only 19. People mature a lot between 19 and 22."

He should NOT have said that. You know how there are certain topics that set you off? Push your buttons? Make you so pissed off you can't think straight? For me, this maturity thing is one of those topics.

"So now you're saying I'm not mature? Fuck you, Ryan."

"Jade, stop it. Don't talk like that."

"Don't swear? Like you never swear? Or can only 22-year-olds swear? And by the way, your birthday was a couple weeks ago. You're barely 22."

"I didn't mean you're not mature. I'm just saying that—"

I'm now beyond angry and I start yelling at him. "For as long as I can remember I had to take care of myself! I was doing my own laundry when I was five, Ryan. Five! Maybe even before then. I can't remember. I was also making my own meals at that age. Peanut butter sandwiches every day until I learned how to use the microwave. And I took care of my mom for all those years. Did the cooking. Paid the bills. Did the grocery shopping. I was a child taking care of a grown woman! So don't you ever fucking tell me I'm not mature!"

I face the side window, taking a deep breath to calm down. My phone rings and I pick it up and see that it's Garret.

"Hi, Garret."

"Hey, are you on the road again?" He's in a good mood, which isn't unusual. He almost always is, which is good, but I can't be around it right now. I'm too pissed off, and as crazy as it sounds his happy mood is making me more pissed off.

"It's not a good time. Can I call you back later?"

"Why? What's wrong?"

"Nothing's wrong. I'm just tired and I can't talk right now."

"Okay. Call me later then. I love you."

"I love you, too." I keep the phone in my hand as I gaze out the side window at the snowy farm fields. As I start to calm down I feel guilty for yelling at Ryan like that. He doesn't have any idea how close Garret and I have become. He doesn't know what we've been through together, so it's not surprising he thinks we'll break up.

Ryan doesn't talk for the next three and a half hours and I don't either. He plays some of the cassette tapes I got him for Christmas until we're just outside Des Moines and can get a radio station to come in again.

"Are we going to end this before we get to the house?" Ryan asks, shutting the radio off.

"We don't need to. It's over. We're good." I face forward again. "Sorry I yelled at you. It's the lack of sleep. I'm not in the best mood right now."

"Jade, what's going on with you? You used to talk to me all the time about stuff and now you never tell me anything."

"There's nothing to tell."

"A few hours ago you told me three major news events in your life that you've been keeping a secret from me. Why are you keeping secrets? We've never been like that with each other. Even if you don't tell my dad stuff, you at least tell me."

"That was back in high school when I lived with you. Things have changed. Now I'm on my own and you're busy with work and Chloe. We don't talk that much anymore."

"Yeah, and it shouldn't be that way. I want us to talk, Jade. I want things to be like they were before. Us telling each other stuff. Yeah, I'm busy, but I'm never too busy to talk to you. I haven't called you as much lately because when I do you don't return my calls, so I thought you needed some space."

"It's not that. It's just that we're both moving on with our lives. We're not going to be as close as we were before."

"Why not?"

"Because you have Chloe now."

"I still want to talk to you. Chloe has nothing to do with it. And she's not the type of person who would tell me I can't talk to you or spend time with you."

"Are you going to marry her?"

He laughs. "So I guess you decided we're confiding in each other again?"

I shrug. "You're the one who suggested it."

"Okay, then yes. I'm planning to marry her, but not anytime soon. We've talked about it and she wants to wait until she's done with med school."

"That's a long time."

"She's almost done with the first year, so three more years."

"When are you going to propose?"

"Probably next fall sometime. Or maybe at Christmas."

"That's big news, Ryan. See? You've been hiding stuff, too."

"It's not exactly a surprise. You know I've never dated a girl for this long."

"Yeah, I figured you'd marry her. I just didn't know when."

"So how about you and Garret? Does the marriage topic ever come up?"

He looks at me and I look back at him like he's crazy. "Marriage? A few hours ago you said I was immature and had no future with the guy."

He sighs. "I didn't mean that. I only said it because it's what *I* want."

"I don't get it."

"You're my little sister and I don't want you to grow up. I still picture you coming over to my house when you were 12 with your hair up in a ponytail, wearing one of your mom's dresses that was way too big on you, trying to look older so I'd notice you."

"Yeah, well, I was a stupid kid. I didn't know what I was doing. My mom didn't talk to me about boys."

"It was cute. You were trying so hard. And as a 15-year-old boy, I had no idea what to do with this annoying girl who kept following me around. But then I kind of liked having you around. I liked pretending to be your big brother and now I'm not ready to lose my little sister."

I look down as he reaches over for my hand. "I know you're growing up and moving on, but I don't want us to grow apart. I'm sorry for what I said. You're not immature, Jade. In fact you're more mature than most people twice your age. And I really hope it works out with you and Garret." He laughs as he takes his hand away and picks up his bottle of water. "But if you two get married, his family's not going to make you live with them in their mansion, are they?"

"No. I'm never living in that place. You should see it. It's all white like an insane asylum."

The mood in the car has changed. I can already feel the two of us getting closer again. The tension is gone and I feel like my friend is back. Ryan was my first best friend and I've missed the talks we used to have. I hope he's serious when he says we'll still be friends when he gets married.

"Ryan, I should've told you and Frank about the car, but I was afraid you guys would tell me I couldn't have it. I know I probably shouldn't have accepted it, but when I saw it in the driveway and Mr. Kensington said it was mine, I really wanted it. I've never had anything that nice."

"I know. I would've taken it, too." He kiddingly punches me. "I'm just jealous that you get to drive around in a Beemer while I'm stuck in this old thing. If that's how rich people pay their babysitters I might have to spend a few months babysitting for some wealthy family. Does Lilly need a sitter over the summer? Because I'm available."

"I don't think so, Ryan. You'll be taking classes all summer trying to catch up from your year off from school."

We're at the house now and Ryan gets out to open the garage. He has to open it by hand because Frank doesn't have a garage door opener. It's only a one-car garage and it's really small but from the outside it looks almost the same size as the house.

Frank's house and this neighborhood are such a huge contrast from the mansions and wealth that surround me back in Connecticut. That's why it's good to come home. I need to get back to reality.

Ryan gets back in the car. "Do you want to go inside? I'll bring your stuff in."

The front door opens and Frank appears, wearing his high-waisted, old-man jeans and a plaid flannel shirt. I get out of the car and meet him on the porch.

"Hi, Frank. You look really good." I hug him which I'm sure still shocks him since hugging was never my thing until Garret came along.

126

"You do, too, honey. Come inside. You must be tired."

"I was earlier, but I feel more awake now."

We go in the living room which is right when you walk in. There's no big, fancy foyer in Frank's tiny house. He sits in his recliner and I take the couch.

"You're not using your wheelchair?" I look around and see it folded up, leaned against the back wall.

"I've been feeling stronger and haven't had any dizzy spells so the doctor said I could try going without it. He said it's good for me to get around on my own. How about you? How's your knee?"

"It's better. I stopped using the crutches and so far I've been able to walk on it without any pain."

Ryan comes into the kitchen with the grocery sacks Judy gave him. "Jade, you want to put this food away while I grab your stuff?"

"Sure." I go into the kitchen which is just off the living room. "Carson's mom gave us some leftovers. Do you want anything, Frank?"

He comes into the kitchen and sits at the table.

"No, I thought I'd take you out for an early dinner unless you want to sleep instead."

"I can sleep later. Dinner sounds good."

Ryan brings my suitcase to my room, then comes back to help me in the kitchen.

"I bet you and Jade talked the whole four hours and now she'll have nothing to say at dinner," Frank says to Ryan.

"No, she slept the whole time." Ryan smiles at me. He won't tell his dad about our fight. Frank doesn't need to know.

"Well, if you two are ready, let's head to the restaurant."

My phone rings and I see it's Garret calling. "Just a minute. I'll be right back." I go down to my bedroom and shut the door.

"Are you in Des Moines yet?" he asks.

"Yes. I'm finally home. That's a really long drive. I wish I could fly back."

"Maybe you can. Ask Cunningham when you see him out there."

"I will."

"Do Frank and Ryan have anything planned for you tonight?"

"We're going out for dinner in a few minutes, so I can't talk long."

But I really want to. Now that I finally have some privacy I just want to talk to Garret for the rest of the night. I'm so used to having him around that it feels weird when he's not. It's like something's missing. I know I'll see him in a week but that doesn't make this any easier. I still miss him. A lot. And I hate how much I miss him. I should be able to go a day without feeling like this.

Stupid love. It really messes with your head. And your heart. Basically your whole body.

"Jade, every time we talk you rush me off the phone."

"I know. I'm sorry. I really want to talk to you. I'll call you when I get back from dinner."

"Let's just talk tomorrow. You sound really tired. You need to sleep after being up all night."

"Okay." I hesitate, because for some reason I'm embarrassed to say it, but it's how I feel and I need to start saying this stuff to him. "I miss you, Garret. I miss you so much that I think something might be wrong with me. I shouldn't miss you this much."

I swear I feel him smiling through the phone. "Nothing's wrong with you, Jade. I feel the same way. I missed you as soon as you left."

"I don't know, Garret. I've never missed someone this much. You sure there's nothing wrong with me?"

He laughs. "I'm positive. Have a good time tonight. I love you."

"I love you, too."

When I come back out to the living room, Ryan and Frank are waiting by the door with their coats on. For dinner, we go to the casino. Frank doesn't gamble, but he likes the restaurant there. It's not the greatest atmosphere, but Frank thinks it's one of the nicest places in town. They do have really good food.

During dinner I tell them all about my classes. Our phone conversations are very brief, so they haven't heard any of this stuff.

When there's a lull in the conversation, Ryan says, "So why are you taking all those sciences classes, Jade?" He can't help but smile.

I roll my eyes. "Because I'm thinking of going to med school."

"Really?" Frank puts his fork down. "That's wonderful. When did you decide this?"

"I've been thinking about it ever since you got diagnosed."

Frank's quiet and then I see his eyes get all red and watery.

I reach over for his hand. "Frank, I didn't mean to make you cry. But it's the truth. When you got sick, I wanted to do something to help you get better, but I couldn't. And that's when I started thinking about being a doctor."

"Oh, honey." He dabs his eyes with his napkin.

"See? I told you he likes you better," Ryan says, as he scoops some mashed potatoes into his mouth.

We finish dinner, and when we get home we sit and talk some more.

"Garret's dad bought Jade a car," Ryan says. I glare at him. Even though I told him he could tell Frank, I meant later in the week, not tonight.

"A car? Really?" Frank puts his glass of water on the table next to his recliner and gets that concerned look I know so well. "What kind of car?"

"BMW convertible." I say it like it's not a big deal.

"Six series," Ryan adds.

I glare at him again.

"That's a very expensive car," Frank says to me.

"Yes, but Mr. Kensington is paying for the insurance and maintenance, so you don't need to worry about it." I wish Ryan hadn't brought this up tonight. I'm too tired to argue about it.

"She got the car for babysitting his kid," Ryan says. "I told her I might have to start babysitting if they're paying in BMWs now."

Frank doesn't find the comment funny. "Did you accept the car, Jade?"

"It's in my name, so yeah. I can't drive it yet because of my concussion so it's sitting at Garret's house."

"I see. Well, that was a very generous gift." He takes a drink of his water.

It's obvious he wants me to give the car back, but why should I? Mr. Kensington wants me to have it and I'm sick of being the only person on campus without a car.

Frank's looking at me like I'm a different person. He knows the old Jade would've refused the car, but the old Jade also wouldn't give him a hug or show emotion. I've changed. I'm growing up. So he needs to accept the new me and take the good with the bad, or whatever he considers to be bad.

CHAPTER TWELVE

"I'm really tired. I'm going to bed." I get up and leave the room before they can say anything more about the car.

My lack of sleep hits me as soon as my head hits the pillow. I'm out until noon the next day. When I get up, I see that Garret called and left some text messages. I call him back.

"Did you just get up?" he asks.

I hear his voice and feel myself smiling. Damn, I think I miss him even more today. I'm so pathetic.

"Yeah. I was wiped out. Did you get some sleep?"

"Not really. My bed's too empty."

"And it better stay empty."

"Jade, don't joke about stuff like that."

"Well, you've got female fans lined up outside. You might give in and let one of them inside."

"If they actually watch that show, they're not my type."

"So what's going on at the Kensington estate?"

"Not much. I swam this morning. Lifted some weights. Showered."

"Okay, stop. You're totally turning me on."

He laughs. "It's that easy, huh? All right. My turn. What are you wearing?"

"That's so lame. But for the record, I'm wearing a sweatshirt and pajama pants. Nothing special." I'm actually wearing several layers of clothing because Frank can't afford to turn the heat up and the house is freezing. I was used to it when I lived here, but now I'm used to the dorm which is kept really warm, so Frank's house feels like a freezer.

"Jade, wake up." Ryan's knocking on the door.

"I'm up," I call back. "I'm on the phone."

"We're leaving soon so get yourself ready." I hear Ryan walking away.

"Do you need to go?" Garret asks.

"Yeah. Sorry. We'll talk later."

As I head to the bathroom Ryan purposely bumps my shoulder on his way to his room. "We're going to a movie at 1, so hurry up."

I stand there, rubbing my eyes. "I'm not awake yet. Did you make any coffee?"

He continues down the hall. "You're not at Garret's house. I'm not your butler. You have to make your own coffee."

"Geez, you could be nicer to me since you never see me," I yell at him.

I hear him laughing from his room. He yells back, "I'm making you feel at home. Treating you like any big brother would."

All three of us go to the movie, which is weird because we never used to do that. We always rented movies. This is the first time we've gone to a theater. After the movie we go home and order pizza, then play cards the rest of the night.

Monday morning, we take Frank to see Dr. Cunningham who's in town for the day. He has an office at a clinic that's inside the hospital.

While Frank and Ryan are filling out paperwork in the waiting room, I pretend to go to the restroom but I really sneak back to see Dr. Cunningham to ask him if I can fly home. As I expected, he says no because I'm still having headaches. But at least he's okay with me not using the crutches anymore.

The rest of the week goes by slowly. A March blizzard traps us inside on Tuesday and Wednesday. Frank doesn't have cable so there's nothing to watch on TV and we quickly get tired of playing cards. Thursday Ryan and I go to another movie while Frank rests at home and then we all go out for a farewell dinner since I have to leave the next morning.

After dinner, Ryan drops Frank and me off at home, then leaves again to pick up Chloe from her part-time job because her car's in the shop.

Frank and I sit in the living room. As I reach for the TV remote he stops me.

"Let's talk, Jade."

That's never a good way to start a conversation. I put the remote down. "What do you want to talk about?"

"Tell me about your involvement with Garret's family."

"They're paying for my school. That's it."

He rubs his jawline which has two days worth of stubble on it. "I feel like there's something going on. Are they making you keep secrets? Bribing you to keep quiet about something?"

"What?" I let out a nervous laugh. "Of course not."

Where is this coming from? Do I look like I'm hiding something? Then again, Frank was a reporter for 25 years. He tends to pick up on stuff.

"You can tell me, Jade. This is just between you and me. How did you really get that concussion and hurt your knee?"

"I told you. I tripped when I was running on the trail."

"I've interviewed a lot of people over the years and I can tell when someone's lying. Now what's the real story?"

I know Frank will keep prying until I tell him the truth. Or at least part of it.

"Okay, here's what happened. Garret's sister, Lilly, ran away and everyone thought she'd been kidnapped because bad people have kidnapped her in the past to get ransom money. So Garret and I searched the property to see if maybe she just ran into the woods behind the house. And that's where she was. We were searching at night and I tripped over her and fell. My head hit this huge log and my knee scraped over some rocks."

Frank continues to rub his scruffy jaw. "Why did you lie about it? And why did Garret's father lie to me about it?"

"He didn't want to scare you with the whole kidnapping thing."

"Why would it scare me? You weren't the one in danger of being kidnapped."

"Just the fact that dangerous people come after his family sometimes. That's the scary part."

"Do they ever come after Garret? Threaten him?"

"No. I don't think so."

Frank doesn't look like he believes me. He sighs. "Jade, I realize that you're becoming more serious with Garret, but being with him won't be easy. I hope you know that."

"I can handle it." I keep my eyes on the couch, tracing the lines in the plaid fabric with my finger.

"He'll have to deal with the same problems his father has to deal with. Problems with the company. Lawsuits. People making threats against him and his family."

"That won't happen. Garret's getting away from all that. He doesn't want to run Kensington Chemical. He's getting his

134

business degree, then an MBA, and then he'll start his own company."

"It may not be that easy. He may have obligations he's not able to get out of. He's his father's only son. And in wealthy families like his, sons are often expected to follow in their fathers' footsteps. They're not given a choice."

"Garret already told his dad he's not taking over the company and his dad's okay with it. Well, I'm sure his dad isn't happy about it, but he's accepted it."

Frank's quiet and I look up and see him watching me.

"What is it, Frank?" It comes out sounding angry because I already feel like he's lecturing me and I'm sure he's not done yet.

"Garret has grown up with wealth and privilege. People taking care of his every need. Is he planning on continuing to live that way when he's on his own? Because that doesn't seem like the type of lifestyle you'd want to be around. That's not how you grew up."

"Garret's not going to live that way. He doesn't want maids and cooks and he doesn't want to live in a mansion." I'm really getting pissed off now. It doesn't matter how Garret grew up or how I grew up. I've finally accepted that and I don't want to start worrying about it again. "Do you want me to break up with Garret? Is that what this is about?"

Frank leans over and rubs my arm. "No, of course not, honey. I just want you to think about these things. Although I like Garret, I do have concerns about his family. Maybe I'm reading too much into it, but I find it a little strange that his father would give you such an expensive car. I suppose to him it's not that expensive, but that's just another thing for you to consider when you think about being with Garret. Being around that type of wealth will take some adjustment."

"What are you saying, Frank? That I have to be poor the rest of my life because I grew up that way or because my mom was?" I yank my arm from him and move over on the couch. "I'm half Sinclair. That means half of me is rich. And I really wish I could tell people that because I'm sick of people at school acting like I'm not one of them. Acting like I'm just some poor kid from Iowa. I deserve to live in a nice house and drive a fancy car just as much as anyone else at Moorhurst."

He nods slowly. "If that's what you want, then okay."

The way he says it infuriates me. Like it's wrong for me to want material things. "It's not what I want! I mean, I guess it is, but who wouldn't want that stuff?"

I'm such an idiot. I shouldn't have said that to him. Frank doesn't have much when it comes to material things. His house is sparsely decorated and he wears worn-out clothes, yet he's still happy. He's always told me that he'd rather have his health and his family than material possessions, and I used to agree with him. I still do, but can't I also have a few nice things?

"I'm sorry, Frank. I don't know what I'm saying."

"You're right. You're part Sinclair, but look what that lifestyle did to Royce. It turned him into a monster."

"I know, but the whole family isn't like that. His dad came to visit me a couple weeks ago and he—"

Shit! Why did I just say that?

Frank shoves the footrest of his recliner down and grips the edge of the couch. "What did he want? Did he threaten you? Try to hurt you?"

"No. He just wanted to talk."

"This happened weeks ago? Why didn't you tell me this sooner?" Frank's really mad.

"I thought I'd wait until I got here." Actually I wasn't planning to tell Frank at all because I knew he'd overreact like this.

"Does he know what happened to your mother?" Frank huffs. "Of course he does. He helped Royce cover it up."

"No. It's not like that. Just let me explain."

I tell Frank the story about Arlin, leaving out the part about the secret organization. Instead, I say how Arlin never knew the truth about my mom and didn't know I existed until he found the file Royce had locked away.

When I'm done, Frank is quiet for a moment and then asks, "Did you believe him when he said he didn't know about you or what happened to your mother? Did he seem sincere?"

"Yes. So he's either a really good liar or he was telling the truth. He apologized repeatedly for his son and admitted that Royce had problems. Do you think he was lying? I don't know enough about the guy to know if I should believe him."

Frank leans back in his chair. "I did some research on Arlin and the whole Sinclair family back when your mother told me about Royce. I've continued to follow the family over the years and I haven't come across anything that would cause me to think Arlin is dangerous. But that's not saying much given that he could've just covered up whatever he's done."

"I don't think Arlin's like his son. After we talked, I got this gut feeling that he's not."

"And after he told you this, he asked if he could see you again?"

"Yes. He said he wants to get to know me and he asked if I'd meet his wife." I shrug. "The whole thing's really weird. I've never had grandparents before and then this guy just shows up saying he wants a relationship."

"Jade, do you want to see Arlin again? Because you don't need my approval to do so. He *is* your grandfather and it's okay if you want to talk to him or have him introduce you to your grandmother."

"I don't know yet. I have to think about it." I focus on the lines in the couch, not looking at Frank. "But what if I let him pay for some stuff? He offered to pay for the rest of my college and I was thinking that might be a good thing. It's kind of weird to have Garret's dad paying for my school. Arlin also said he wanted to help me with other expenses, not that I would ask him to, but . . . I don't know. What do you think?"

"If you need money for something important, like school, and he's offering, then I think it's okay to consider that. I understand how you might feel a little awkward having Garret's father pay for school, so maybe letting Arlin pay for it is a better option. As for other expenses, that's up to you. Just make sure that Arlin's doing this for the right reasons. If his offer includes any kind of conditions, then I think you should refuse his money. But it sounds like you didn't get that feeling from him."

"No, I didn't." I look at Frank again. "He seemed like a nice old man. That's why I'm so confused. About all of this. Letting him pay for college. Meeting his wife. I feel like I shouldn't even want to see him again, but he's my grandfather and part of me kind of wants to get to know him."

"Then maybe you should. Maybe just have lunch with him and his wife and see how it goes." Frank sighs and shakes his head side to side.

"What's wrong?"

"I just never thought I'd be encouraging you to get involved with the Sinclairs."

The back door opens and we hear Ryan in the kitchen, his keys jingling as he hangs them on the hook.

He comes in the living room and sits down. "Jade, is your boyfriend on some reality show on cable?"

Frank laughs like his son is kidding but Ryan looks serious.

"The Prep School Girls' Reunion," I say.

"You know about it?" Ryan asks.

"Of course I know about it. How did you find out?"

"When I dropped Chloe off I went in her apartment for a few minutes and was flipping through the channels and I heard Garret's name. And then I saw him with some girl. At least I think it was him. I could only see the back of him."

"That's not Garret. He's not on the show."

I explain everything and when I'm done Frank and Ryan don't seem to believe me. But they never watch those reality shows. They don't get how much of those shows are fake.

"That's why Garret couldn't come home with me," I explain. "He's hiding out from the photographers. They've been following him around and some of his fans are following him around, too. That's why I didn't tell you about the show. I didn't want you getting all worried about me being around all that. But tonight was the second episode and next Thursday it ends. After that, people will forget about it and everything will go back to normal."

"Garret's father should sue the production company and everyone else involved," Frank says.

"The lawyers told him it would be better to ignore it. Fighting it would just end up getting Garret even more unwanted press. I should talk to him quick and see if he watched tonight's episode."

I go in my room and call Garret. "Hey, did you watch tonight?"

"How about a greeting before you jump right in with the questions?"

"I'm sorry. Hi, Garret. How was your day?"

"Same as every other day this week. I'm so sick of hanging out here I'm actually looking forward to going to class again."

"So did you watch the show?"

He laughs. "You don't even care what I did today, do you? And no, I didn't watch the show."

"Garret, you have to know what they're saying about you. I don't have cable here so I didn't see it, but Ryan saw part of it when he was at Chloe's so then I had to explain the whole story to them."

"They would've found out eventually. I don't know why you were hiding it from them."

"Did you hear from anyone who saw it?"

"Decker called right before you did. He watched it. He said I took Ava skiing up in Vermont. Apparently we had a great time."

"It works out well for the show. They could cover up their Garret look-alike with ski clothes and nobody would guess it wasn't you."

"Jade, just forget about it. There's one show left and then we can move on and pretend it never happened. What time are you leaving tomorrow?"

"Ryan and I are leaving around 8, so we should be at Carson's around noon."

"Will you call me this time?"

"Yes. Will you be around?"

"I'm a prisoner here. I'll be around all day. I'm spending tomorrow night in the dorm so that I'll be there when you get back on Saturday. We have a lot of catching up to do."

"I may need a few hours sleep before we start catching up."

"I don't care what we do. I just need to see you. A week apart is way too long. Don't make me do this again."

"Me? This is your fault! Or Ava's!"

"I'm just kidding. Oh, I almost forgot. I got that place reserved for the summer. It's all ours. And Harper and Sean got the one right next to it."

A couple days ago, Garret and I picked out a beachfront condo to rent in a town a couple hours north of LA. It's a condo that Harper found and once we checked it out online, Garret and I liked it, too. It's a furnished condo and we even liked how it was decorated, clean and simple with comfy-looking furniture.

"Are you serious?" I'm so excited I want to jump up and down but I can't or I'll hurt my knee again. "So this is really going to happen?"

"Well, yeah. Did you think it wouldn't?"

"Kind of. You know me. I never trust that things will work out."

"Stop thinking that way. I've told you that a hundred times. I'm good luck. Stick with me and things will always work out." I can feel his famous cocky smile through the phone. "The guy who owns the place even gave us a deal because we're staying all summer."

"This is so great! I have to call Harper."

"I talked to Sean earlier and he said they'd be out all night with her sisters, so you might want to wait."

"I'll just text her. So tell me again. Are we really living on the beach in California all summer? With Harper and Sean right next door?"

"Yes, Jade. And you're freaking adorable when you get this excited. Even over the phone. Damn, I love you."

"I love you, too. I need to go spend some more time with Frank before I go to bed but I'll call you tomorrow. And hey, don't get used to sleeping alone because when I get back we're having sleepovers every night for at least a week."

"A week? Try the rest of the semester." I smile because that's really what I want, too. "Have a safe trip and make sure to call me from the road."

"I will. Bye, Garret." I hang up and go back to the living room where Frank and Ryan are watching the news. "Guess what? Garret reserved that place on the beach so we're definitely going there this summer. Isn't that great?"

"Yeah, great." Ryan pretends to be annoyed but I know he's happy for me. "And I'll be stuck here in summer classes. Can I at least come visit?"

"Of course you can visit. That's a great idea. Bring Chloe if you want. You should come, too, Frank."

"I think my traveling days are over. But you should go, Ryan."

Ryan yawns as he gets up. "I'm really tired. I'm going to bed. I want to leave on time tomorrow, Jade, so set your alarm clock."

"I should probably go to sleep, too," Frank says. "I'll see you in the morning, Jade."

I wasn't expecting them to go to bed at 11. I thought since this was my last night here we'd all stay up late.

I go to my room but I'm not ready to sleep. I'm too excited about my summer. A whole three months living with Garret on the beach with my best friend right next door. It's like a movie, but it's actually my life. How did this happen? A year ago I was here in this house thinking I'd go to college, get a boring job, and live alone in an apartment the rest of my life. Now everything's changed in ways I never could've imagined.

Since I can't sleep, I make a pros and cons lists to fill the time. I've never been much of a list person, but now that I have decisions to make I find it a useful exercise. First I make one for being a doctor. The result? Almost all pros. Then I make one for meeting Arlin and his wife for lunch. There are quite a few cons, but the pros still win out. Lastly, I make a list for marrying Garret, just in case he asks me someday. The list is all pros except for one con. His family. But that only applies to Katherine so I scratch out family and put Katherine's name down. There's no way I'd let Katherine be a reason for not marrying Garret.

So as of tonight, it looks like I'll be going to med school, having lunch with my grandparents, and marrying Garret. Yeah, things have definitely changed the past year.

CHAPTER THIRTEEN

Friday morning I get up at 7 and find Ryan in the kitchen making breakfast. He's already showered, dressed, and ready to go. He's a morning person, which I don't understand. I barely function before 8 and that's even after having a large dose of caffeine.

"You got donuts?" I grab one from the box and take a seat at the kitchen table with my mug of coffee.

"I went to the gas station to fill up and they'd just delivered these so I thought I'd get some as a going-away gift."

"Thanks. I love donuts."

"I know you do, but drink some orange juice so you at least get some nutrients." He sets a glass of it in front of me. "I made scrambled eggs. You want any?"

"Yeah, I'll have some."

"Morning, everyone." Frank comes into the kitchen. His hair is still wet from his shower and he has on jeans and an old green sweater. "You ready to go back to school?"

"I guess." I pass him the donuts.

Ryan sets a plate of eggs in front of each of us, then joins us at the table. "Come on, Jade. We know you can't wait to get back. You miss Garret. You've been moping around all week, counting the hours until you could see him again."

"That's not true! I've hardly thought about him all week."

Frank and Ryan both give me an eye roll.

"Fine. Maybe I miss him a little, but it's not like I have to spend every minute with him. I can date him and still be independent. And for the record, I was not moping around all week."

"You were totally moping," Ryan says as he eats his eggs. "Even Dad noticed."

I look at Frank to deny it but he doesn't.

"It's okay to miss him," Frank says. "You love him. It's normal to want to be with him."

"I don't love—" I stop because I can't even say it. I love Garret so much that I can't even pretend not to.

Ryan laughs. "Jade's in love." He sings it like an annoying little kid.

"Shut up." I punch his arm and he keeps laughing. "You're in love, too."

"Yeah, but at least I admit it. You're over there trying to hide it, like it's some big secret."

Frank sighs. "You two will both be married off by the age of 25. I guess I'll be a young grandpa."

Ryan chokes on his eggs. "Grandpa? I may be married when I'm 25, but there aren't going to be any kids for a long time. Chloe and I have to get through med school, then a residency before we even think about having kids."

I take another donut. "And I'm not having kids, so don't look at me to help you out with the grandpa thing."

"Oh, please. You'll have kids," Ryan says. "Maybe not by the age of 25, but you'll have them."

"Why does everyone keep saying that? Do I seem like a kid person? I don't even like kids. They're loud. They think they know everything. They don't listen."

145

"Yeah. Just like you." Ryan laughs. "You'll get along great with kids."

I punch him again. "You better stop this right now or I'll kill you before we make it to Illinois."

"All right, you two. No fighting at the table." Frank's face breaks into a smile as he says it. "Someday you'll both have kids and you'll both come back to visit and your kids will be here fighting at the table instead of you two."

I sling my arm over Ryan's shoulder. "We'll still be fighting. We'll just fight in a different room."

Frank looks at Ryan and me. "Even with your fighting, I'm so proud of you two, and I love you both." His eyes get watery.

I get up and give him a hug. "Frank, don't make me sad before I leave. Saying goodbye is hard enough."

He wipes his eyes. "I just wanted to say it."

"We love you, too, Dad," Ryan says, biting into a donut. "But you're still not getting grandkids anytime soon."

His comment makes us all laugh and lightens the mood.

"So, Jade, are we going to see you at all this summer?" Frank asks.

"I hope so. Garret and I haven't figured out our itinerary yet. I was thinking maybe we could stop here on the drive out and again on the way back."

"You're driving to California?" Ryan asks. "I figured Garret would hire someone to drive the car out there and you two would fly. Isn't that what rich people do?"

"I don't know. I'll talk to Garret about it. But I'll come home at least once this summer."

Frank pushes away from the table. "Well, I suppose you two need to hit the road."

"Yeah, hurry up, Jade," Ryan says. "We have to leave soon."

I quickly shower, dress, and finish packing and a half hour later I'm ready to go.

"I'll see you later, Frank." This is my new way of saying goodbye. I find it easier to tell him I'll see him later than to tell him goodbye, which seems so final.

"Bye, honey. Have a safe trip." He hugs me, then stays close and lowers his voice. "I know you don't always tell me everything, but if you need to, I'm here. It can be hard to keep secrets to yourself."

What does he mean? Does he know something? If not, what secrets is he referring to? Maybe it's just the reporter in him. He's always thinking there's more to the story. And he's right, but I can't let him know that.

Frank lets me go just as Ryan comes into the living room. Ryan doesn't know about the incident with Sinclair or the story about my mother or any of that, and Frank and I have decided it's better if he doesn't know.

"You ready?" Ryan has his coat on, his car keys in his hand.

"Yeah, let's go."

Frank follows us out and watches as we drive away.

As we're leaving Des Moines, I get a text from Garret saying he had to go somewhere with his dad and won't be back until late afternoon. I text him back asking where he's going, but he doesn't respond.

The drive to Carson's house goes by fast this time because Ryan and I are talking instead of giving each other the silent treatment. Every hour, I call Garret to check in but his phone goes straight to voicemail. I'm guessing he has it turned off, which doesn't make sense given how insistent he was that I call him during the trip. But maybe he's someplace where they make you turn your phone off.

When we get to Carson's house, Howard's at work but Judy is there, preparing more food. She packs a lunch for Ryan to eat on his way back to Iowa and fills a foam cooler with food and drinks for Carson and me.

After Ryan leaves, Carson and I head out. As we're pulling out of the garage his mom yells, "No speeding, Carson. And don't text and drive. Love you!"

He waves at her as we drive off. "She sees all these kids come into the ER because they were texting while driving so she always says that."

"Your mom is funny. She really likes to feed people."

"I know. I'm surprised I don't weigh 400 pounds." He turns the heat up when he sees me put my gloves back on. "So did you have fun at home?"

"We got snowed in for a couple days, but we found stuff to do. How about you? Did you get back together with Madison?"

"No. After we talked about it, I decided I didn't want to. I used to be okay with the long distance thing, but now I think I'd rather date someone I can see every day."

"But you made this big deal about how people should have their space and how it's not healthy to spend your time with one person."

"I know, but then I thought about it some more and I changed my mind. I don't want to date someone I can only see during the summer and once or twice during the year."

"I guess I better start looking then."

"What do you mean?"

"Your mom told me to find you a nice girl to date in Connecticut."

"Did she really?" He shakes his head. "God, that's embarrassing."

"I thought it was sweet. She just wants you to be happy."

"She shouldn't have asked you that. I can find my own girls." He picks up his soda from the center console and takes a drink. "So what's Garret been up to all week?"

"The rule still applies for the trip home. No talking about Garret. But to answer your question, he's been playing with his little sister, watching movies, and swimming. He has a movie theater in his house. And an indoor pool."

"I saw his show last night. Did you watch?"

"It's not his show, but no, I didn't see it."

"He—or the fake Garret—took Ava skiing in Vermont. They rented a suite at a lodge. They mostly showed Ava talking to the camera, so Garret wasn't on that long."

"He wasn't on the show at all! It wasn't him!"

"Yeah, but you know what I mean."

"I'll be so glad when this is over." I check my phone and still have no messages from Garret. I send him another text.

"Do you have to check in with him every hour again?" Carson asks.

"I don't have to, but I was going to. He went somewhere with his dad and his phone is off. I'll have to try later."

We drive for six hours and I don't hear anything from Garret. No phone calls, no texts. Nothing. I'm getting really worried. I've been calling him and texting him and I can't get any response. I even called his dad, but the phone went straight to voicemail.

At 8 Carson and I stop to eat dinner. There's plenty of food in the cooler but we need to get out of the car.

We're back on the road at 8:30 to begin the overnight drive that I've been dreading. Another night of no sleep as I try to keep Carson awake with loads of caffeine and nonstop conversation. My mind is a mess worrying about Garret and why I haven't heard from him. Every time we stop for gas or bathroom breaks, I tell Carson I'm calling Garret so he won't pick up on the fact that something's wrong. The last thing I need is Carson coming up with reasons for why Garret isn't returning my calls.

By 6 the next morning, I can't take another minute in the car. I just want to get home. I call Garret again but his phone goes straight to voicemail. I try calling his dad again but he doesn't answer. I leave messages for both of them to call me back even though I've already left the same messages several times now and gotten no response.

I'm now beyond worried and I have no outlet for my nervous energy. I need to get out of the car and run for an hour to burn off the stress, but instead I have to sit here for at least two more hours.

"Jade, I want to say some things before we get there." Carson says it in the tone he uses when he lectures me about Garret. "I've been waiting to say this until now because I know you'll be mad when I tell you."

"If I'll be mad, then don't tell me."

"It's about Garret and his family."

I tip my head back toward the roof of the car. "Carson, please do not start with this. I'm so tired and I'm not at all in the mood to hear your conspiracy theories or whatever bad things you're going to say about Garret's family."

"Just listen. You need to hear this." He pauses. "I think Garret's dad belongs to some type of secret society."

Shit! How the hell would Carson know that?

I react as I always do when he tells me stuff like this and act like he's crazy.

"Garret's dad does not belong to a secret society. Those things don't even exist."

"Of course they exist. You never heard of Skull and Bones? The one at Yale? They even made movies about it."

"Well then it's not that secret, is it?"

"There are other ones that very few people know about. Like the one I think Garret's dad belongs to. My uncle told me about it. He said it's been around for over 100 years. It's made up of very rich, very powerful men. Women aren't allowed in. You're born into it so if I'm right and Pearce Kensington is part of it, then Garret will be a member soon, if he's not already."

"That's a funny story. I'm going to sleep. Wake me when we get there." I lean my pillow against the seat and pretend to sleep.

"This group finds out stuff about its members—things they don't want to get out. That's how they keep people in line. You can't ever leave this group. You're in for life. Members have to do things, Jade. Bad things. That's why some people try to get out."

"I'm not listening," I tell him, my eyes still closed.

"They rig elections. It used to be harder to prove, but with these new electronic voting machines a reporter was able to prove they rigged the voting machines in Ohio and Florida during the last presidential election. You know what happened to that reporter? Shot in the head the day before he was going to announce this on a talk radio show. They said it was a suicide, but the guy never showed signs of being suicidal."

"Are you done yet, Carson?"

Although part of me wants to hear what he has to say, the other part of me doesn't. If this group does bad things, I'd rather not know. Garret will never be part of that organization. He already knows about it and he's never been told he has to be part of it.

Carson keeps talking. "We've had presidents who never should've been in office. This group is controlling the system. And the party affiliation doesn't matter. Democrat or Republican. They switch it up so people don't get suspicious. They just find a person to act as a figurehead, someone who's likable and looks good on camera. They get him elected, but the guy has no control. This group controls what he says and does."

"Do you realize how crazy you sound? You really need to stop this, Carson. If you tell this to anyone else, you'll end up in a mental hospital."

"They pick key senators as well. Men who will head important committees to help this group with their agenda."

"And what is their agenda?"

"I don't know. Get more power? Control the masses? Make more money? Being a member of this group has benefits. You're guaranteed to be rich. Not average rich but super rich, like Garret's family."

"Where do you get this stuff?"

"News articles, websites, videos. A lot of times something gets published online that shouldn't and then it disappears. Like that reporter who died? An article went online right after his death saying he was shot. It had statements from witnesses who said they saw someone enter his apartment before it happened. Then an hour later, the article was taken down and replaced with the suicide story. This time the so-called witnesses said they hadn't seen anyone go in his apartment all day."

"And you're saying this secret group killed the guy?"

"Yes. They had to get rid of him. That's what they do. They get rid of people who know too much and then they just make up some story to cover their tracks. What they don't get is that there will always be people who search for the truth. Some guy took a screen grab of the original article that came out about that reporter, the real story, and put it on his website. I printed it out if you want to see it."

"I get it, Carson. You don't like Garret's family."

"It's not that I don't like them. I've never met them, so how would I know? What I'm saying is that if this is true, you should be aware of it because you may not want to be involved in this. These people are dangerous, Jade."

"Well, now I know, so are we done with this topic?"

"I still have that file in my room. I have proof for at least some of the things I told you about."

Carson's really starting to freak me out. And if any of what he said is true, he could end up getting killed if he pursues this any further.

"Carson, what exactly do you plan to do with this information? You're not a reporter. You're not a journalist. You want to be a doctor, so why are you so obsessed with this? What's your goal here?"

He considers it. "I don't know. It's not like I can stop them. I guess my goal is just to find out the truth."

"But it's *not* the truth. You're just believing stuff you find on the Internet. People can make up whatever they want and put it out there and make it sound real."

He sighs. "Fine. I'm done trying to convince you. I thought I was being a friend by telling you this. I was trying to protect you. But it's obvious you'll never believe me. Just be careful."

"I seriously need you to stop bringing this up."

"I just told you I would."

"Yeah, and you've said that before and then you bring it up again. I just want this to end. You don't need to protect me. And you really need to stop obsessing about Garret's family. Just let it go."

"I told you I'd stop talking about it and I will. Let's just leave it at that."

I'm guessing that means he'll keep investigating this, but I can't seem to change his mind so I don't bother trying. Instead I close my eyes and end up falling asleep for the rest of the drive. I wake up when I feel Carson's hand on my arm.

"Jade, we're here." Carson is talking beside me. He sounds normal again, his conspiracy tone gone, hopefully for good this time.

I slowly sit up and see that we're in the parking lot in front of our dorms.

"It's a lot warmer here than in the Midwest," he says. "And there's no snow. Guess we should've just stayed here for spring break."

He gets out of the Jeep and goes around to the back to get the luggage.

While he's back there, I check my phone. Still no messages from Garret. What the hell? I haven't heard from him since yesterday morning and it was just that one text saying he had to do something with his dad. So is he still with his dad? But his dad isn't answering his phone. What if something bad happened to both of them?

I've gotta figure this out. Something is definitely wrong.

CHAPTER FOURTEEN

When I step out of the Jeep, Carson is standing there with my suitcase and the crutches I never used. I offer to take something, but he insists on carrying it all to my room.

"Thanks for bringing my stuff in," I say as Carson sets my suitcase by the closet. "And thanks again for the ride. I really appreciate it."

"No problem. Need anything else?"

"Nope. I'm good. I'll see you in class on Monday." I just want Carson to leave so I can figure out what's going on with Garret.

"Okay, see ya."

When he's gone, I phone Garret again. No answer. I send another text and wait for a response but I get nothing back. Then I call his dad who also doesn't answer. I don't know who else to call so I call their home number. The maid answers and says nobody's home.

I run up to the second floor. I'm sure Garret's not in his room. If he was, he would've answered his phone or sent me a text. But I figure I might as well rule out all the options.

His floor is quiet because people are still on spring break. I knock on his door several times but as expected, he doesn't answer.

So he's not at home. He's not at school. Where the hell is he?

I check my phone again and still have no messages. As I'm walking back down the hall I hear a door open. I look back and see that it's Garret's door, so I run back.

"Garret, where have you—" I stop because I can't believe what I'm seeing. He's standing there in jeans and a wrinkled black t-shirt, holding a half-empty bottle of vodka.

"Hey," he says, tipping the bottle up at me.

His hair is a mess and his normally bright blues eyes are glassy and distant. He reeks of alcohol and I notice three other bottles of liquor on his desk.

My chest gets heavy and tight and I'm only able to take short, shallow breaths. Time seems to slow as I try to process what I'm seeing. Try to make sense of it somehow.

"What is this?" I ask him. "What's happening here? What are you doing?"

He walks slowly to the bed and slumps down on it, still holding his bottle.

I snatch it from him. He looks up briefly, but otherwise doesn't seem to care.

"Tell me what's going on here." I set the bottle on the floor, then shake his shoulders to get his attention. "Garret, talk to me."

"I'm sorry," he says quietly.

"Sorry about what?" Tears are now streaming down my face. I don't know what's going on, but I know it's bad. It's really bad. "What happened? Why are you drinking?"

"I couldn't deal with—" His eyes close.

"Couldn't deal with what?" I shake him again, then stop because it might make him throw up. I sit next to him. "Garret, look at me." His eyes slowly open. "Why are you drunk? Would you please say something? Anything?"

He puts his hand on my face, wiping the tears off my cheek. "Don't cry, Jade. It's my fault."

"What do you mean? What's your fault?"

He's quiet again.

I'm exhausted from being awake all night, but I use every last bit of energy I have to stop crying and focus on figuring this out.

"Garret, you need to tell me what's going on. You're scaring the shit out of me. Please just talk to me."

"I didn't know about any of this. I swear."

"Any of what? You're not making any sense."

His head drops down to his chest. "If I knew, I would've kept you away. I would've kept you out of this."

"Kept me out of what?"

He lifts his head again and I can tell that he's struggling with something he can't express. Something painful. And it's killing me to see him like this. All I want to do is help him, but I don't know how. I don't know what he needs. I don't know how to make this better.

I reach over and hug him tightly against me because whenever he does it to me, it always makes me feel better. And although I don't think it will help, I don't know what else to do.

He doesn't really hug me back but just wraps his arms loosely around my waist.

"I love you, Jade. More than anything. I love you."

"I know you do. I love you, too."

"I'm sorry. I'm so sorry."

I slowly pull away from him. "What are you sorry for? What did you do?"

"They did it. I didn't."

"Who's they? Your dad? Katherine?"

His head collapses on my shoulder. I push him up but his eyes are closed like he's passed out. I lay him on the bed and call his dad again. No answer. Where the hell is his dad?

Maybe his dad is screening his calls and doesn't want to talk to me. That would explain why he didn't return any of my earlier calls. I spot Garret's cell phone on the dresser and use it to call his dad.

Pearce answers on the first ring. "Garret, where are you? I've been looking all over town for you. Let's just talk about this. We'll figure something out."

Figure what out? What is he talking about?

I hear Pearce's voice again. "Garret, are you there?"

"It's me, Mr. Kensington. Jade. I'm with Garret."

There's silence and I'm sure he's going to hang up, but then he speaks. "Where is he?"

"He's in his dorm room. He's been drinking. A lot."

More silence and then, "Put him on the phone."

"He's passed out." I see Garret lying there and my stupid tears start flowing again. "Can you please tell me what's going on? I just got back and found him like this. Yesterday morning he sent me a text when I was leaving Iowa. And that was it. No more texts. No phone calls. Nothing. And then I get here and he's drunk. He never drinks, at least not since he met me. Something's really wrong and I don't know what to do. I don't—"

"Jade, just calm down."

"Calm down? Garret was fine when I talked to him Thursday night and now he's passed out drunk! At 8:30 in the morning! What the hell happened? Before he passed out he kept saying he was sorry. Why is he sorry?"

"Just wait there with him. I'm in the car now. I'll be there in 20 minutes to take him home."

"You're not even going to explain what's going on here?"

"I'll explain later." He hangs up.

I set the phone down on Garret's desk and pick up all the liquor bottles and take them down to the bathroom. It's the guy's bathroom but nobody's in there. Even if a guy walks in I'm not leaving until this alcohol is gone.

I dump the vodka and the whiskey down the sink, turning my head to avoid the smell. But I can't avoid it. It's all around me and images of my childhood come flashing back.

This scene is all too familiar. Jade's desperate attempt to get rid of the alcohol. I feel like I'm 6 years old again, dumping my mom's vodka down the sink when she wasn't looking, hoping it would make her stop drinking. It never did. She'd just hit me to punish me, then walk to the liquor store and buy more.

I toss the empty bottles in the trash and start dumping out a bottle of rum and another bottle of vodka. The rum smell is so strong it almost makes me vomit.

I go back to Garret's room, grab a clean towel, and race down to the bathroom to soak it with cold water. When I return to his room, he's still lying there passed out. I wipe the cold, wet towel over his face. It's what I used to do for my mom when I was a little girl and wasn't sure if she'd wake up after she passed out drunk. Sometimes it woke her up, sometimes it didn't. And when it didn't, it scared the crap out of me. I was sure she was dead. I know Garret's not, but I still get that same panicked feeling seeing him lying there, not moving.

I fucking hate that Garret is making me do this! Making me relive the worst part of my life. Bringing back memories I try so hard to forget.

He wakes up a little and pushes the towel away. "Jade?" He squints like the light from the window is making his head hurt.

"Yes. It's me. Let's get you in a different shirt. This one smells really bad." He slowly sits up and lifts his arms. I pull his shirt over his head and toss it on the floor, then grab a clean one from his drawer. He starts to fall over, but I hold him up and manage to get the clean shirt on him.

"Whatever's going on here, we'll get through it, Garret. This is nothing we can't handle." I'm saying it to him but it's really more for myself. "We've been through worse things than this."

"I'll miss you, Jade." His head falls forward onto my chest and his arms hug my waist. "I already do."

"Why would you miss me? I'm right here."

"Because it's over," he says softly.

"What's over?"

"You have to go away."

"What are you talking about? I'm not going anywhere." I lean him up against the wall so I can get a bottle of water from the fridge. Keeping an eye on him, I quickly get the water, then sit next to him again.

"You need to drink some of this." I hold the bottle to his lips and he tips his head back just slightly, hardly getting a drop in.

"Garret, sit up. Just take a few sips. It'll make you feel better."

He bolts upright and shoves the plastic bottle from my hand. It hits the floor, bouncing a few times and splattering water all over the place.

"What are you doing?" I reach to pick it up and he grabs my wrist so tight it hurts. "Garret, stop it!"

I pry my wrist from his hand and pick up the water bottle.

"Just go!" He yells it at me.

"Go where?" I yell it back, slamming the bottle down on his dresser. "I don't understand you! What is going on here? Why are you acting this way?"

"They said if you don't go they'll—" He falls back against the wall, his head hitting it so hard it makes a thumping noise.

"You're hurting yourself!" I race over and place myself next to him so his body doesn't fall over. "Just hold still. Your dad will be here any minute."

"I hate him," he mumbles. "That bastard should've told me." His head falls to the side, resting on my shoulder.

"Told you what? Did you have a fight? Is that what this is about?"

"He said he didn't know, but he always fucking lies."

"So he lied to you? About what?" I don't know why I keep trying to have a conversation with him. He just keeps stringing together disconnected words and phrases that make no sense.

"I'm sorry." He says it softly against my shoulder.

"Yeah, you said that already," I say softly back.

We're sitting on the bed, leaned up against the wall. I slip my hand in his and feel my heartbeat slowly return to normal. I stare straight ahead at the shelf above his desk, focusing on the spines of each book and saying the titles in my head to keep my mind off what's happening. *Fundamentals of Accounting. Microeconomics. Introductory Financial Analysis.*

I read them again but my mind doesn't even recognize the words. It's like they're in a foreign language. I give up and let my mind return to Garret.

He's quiet and I feel like I should say something but I don't know what to say. So instead I keep trying to figure out what might've happened. It sounds like he had a fight with his dad. But Garret wouldn't get drunk over that. He fights with his dad all the time. Something else happened and it must've happened yesterday.

Garret adjusts himself on my shoulder. His breathing is slow and I assume he's asleep, but then I feel him lightly rubbing the top of my hand with his thumb.

"I was going to marry you, Jade."

Great. He says this when he's completely wasted. Real romantic. And what's with the past tense?

"If you get yourself cleaned up, maybe you still *can* marry me." I gaze down at our hands, noticing how big his is and how small mine looks by comparison.

"No!" He sits up straight, ripping his hand from mine. "It's over!" He yells it at me, then drops his voice to almost a whisper. "This is over." The way he looks at me, it's like he's trying to tell me something. Trying to make me understand.

"Nothing's over." I reach for his hand again. "You're just drunk and saying stuff you don't mean."

Suddenly the door whips open, slamming against the wall. Pearce storms in. "Garret, get up!" He goes over and yanks hard on Garret's arm, pulling him up to standing.

"Stop it!" I hurry off the bed. "You're hurting him!"

Pearce slings Garret's arm over his shoulder and storms back out of the room, Garret's feet half walking, half being dragged by his dad.

"Where are you taking him?" I follow them down the hall.

When we get to the stairs, his dad hoists Garret's body over his shoulder like it weighs nothing at all and walks down the stairs.

"Are you going to answer me?" I yell at him.

"I'm taking him home," Pearce says, his voice calm but stern.

"Then I'm going with you."

We get to the bottom of the stairs and he stops and sets Garret down.

"My son got some bad news yesterday. We both did. And we need to figure this out as a family."

Garret's eyes close and he sinks into his dad, who then hoists him up again to a partially standing position.

"Please tell me what's going on. Garret keeps telling me he's sorry. Why is he saying that? What is he sorry about?" Here come my tears again.

Pearce sighs, a look of pity on his face. "I need you to listen to me. Don't call him. Don't text him. Don't try to come to the house. I'm sorry, Jade, but this is how it has to be. I truly am sorry. You're a nice girl and I wish you the best."

I hear his words, but they're not registering with me. My attention remains on Garret, who's now standing on his own a little more but still out of it.

"Will he be coming back here?" I ask Pearce.

"Yes. But I'm afraid you won't. You need to leave Moorhurst. I won't be funding your education anymore. You have today and tomorrow to pack up your things. I'll have them shipped back to Iowa for you. You'll be flying home Monday morning. I'll get you a plane ticket and have it delivered here. My driver will take you to the airport. I talked with Dr. Cunningham and he'll be stopping by later to check on you to make sure you're okay to fly."

My brain is finally getting what he's saying but I don't believe it. This can't be happening. My legs give out and I sink down on the stairs.

"Jade?" I hear Garret's voice and feel his hand touch my shoulder. I grab hold of it and find the strength to stand up again and face his father.

"No! You can't take him away from me! Not again! I won't let you. I love him. You can send me home, but we'll still find a way to be together."

"That's not going to happen. I'm sorry, Jade." He yanks Garret up again, tearing his hand from mine. He walks out the door to the parking lot with me right behind.

"Garret's not going to just let me go. He loves me."

"Yes. He does. And that's why you need to leave." Pearce stops and opens the passenger side door of his shiny black Mercedes.

"What? I don't understand."

He puts Garret in the car, shuts the door, and walks to the driver's side.

"Why are you doing this?" I scream it at him, but he pays no attention as he gets in the car.

There's a clicking sound as the doors lock, followed by the sound of the engine starting up. As Pearce backs up, I see Garret leaned against the window, his eyes now closed.

The car speeds off down the road.

And Garret is gone.

I think I might be hyperventilating. I can't seem to get enough air in my lungs. My legs don't want to move, but I manage to make it back to my room.

My phone rings and I practically rip the pocket of my jeans getting it out. I don't know why I'm racing to answer it. It's not like Garret's calling me. "Hello?"

"Hey, Jade. It's Harper." Her voice sounds so happy I almost can't stand to listen to it. I'm sure she's having a great time with Sean, a normal guy who probably has a normal family who will never force him to break up with Harper. "Sorry I couldn't call sooner, but Sean and I had to go to this party last night with my parents. Anyway, are you back at school yet?"

"Yeah, I'm back."

She keeps talking but it all sounds mumbled. I can't concentrate on anything she's saying.

"Jade? Are you there?"

"I'm here."

"Well, aren't you excited?"

"About what?"

"About the condo on the beach. Garret said he reserved yours and Sean and I got ours so we're all set. This is going to be the greatest summer." She pauses as she waits for me to agree. "Why aren't you saying anything?"

"Harper, I have to go. I feel kind of sick from the car ride. Can we talk later?"

"Sure. Sean and I are on our way to the airport, but I'll call you quick before I get on the plane. And when I get back tonight I'm staying over at Sean's so I probably won't see you until Sunday night."

"Yeah, sounds good," I say, trying to hurry her off the phone.

"Okay, well, I hope you feel better. Oh, and I got you something for our summer on the beach. I'll show it to you tomorrow. Bye!"

"Bye." I shove my phone back in my pocket. There's not going to be a summer on the beach. And I don't know why because nobody will tell me.

I need to talk to someone about this, but there's nobody I can talk to. I can't call Frank or Ryan. They have no idea what I've been through with Garret's family. I get my phone out again and text Ryan to tell him I made it to Moorhurst so he won't call me.

I collapse on my bed and replay in my mind all the scenes from last semester when Mr. Kensington kept trying to break Garret and me apart. Is that what he was doing today? But why? He acted like he liked me, like he'd finally accepted me. He let me stay at his house. He got me a car. He was nice to me. So did Katherine make him do it?

My shock, sadness, and confusion quickly turn to pure rage. Mr. Kensington can't do this to me. He can't take Garret from me again. And neither can Katherine. I won't let either one of them take away what Garret and I have together.

I search my desk drawer for my laundry money and stuff the bills in my wallet. Then I look up the number of a taxi company and call them to come pick me up. If Mr. Kensington won't take me to his house, I'll go there myself. I have to see Garret.

The taxi arrives and when I tell the driver my destination, he says it will be $70 for the half hour ride. I dig in my wallet and count the bills. I only have $75 and that money was supposed to last me for months.

When I arrive at Garret's house, there's a line of photographers and teen girls all along the street. The taxi driver drops me off and I give him the entire $75 to include the tip.

Now I'm stranded here. If Mr. Kensington doesn't let me in, I'll be camping out for the rest of the day with Garret's fans. At night they'll all go home and I'll freeze to death. Okay, so maybe this wasn't the greatest idea.

I walk up to the gate and press the button. Brad, one of the security guys, answers. He's a good guy. I've talked to him many times. His wife runs a day care center and they have twin girls who are Lilly's age. He's shown me photos of them.

"We don't allow people on the premises," he says. "Please stay—"

"Brad, it's Jade. I need to speak to Mr. Kensington. Can you let me in?"

I hear him mumble something to another guard. "I'm sorry. We can't let you in."

"What? Why not? Brad, it's me. You know me."

"I know, but . . ." He sounds like he really wants to let me in and yet the gate remains closed.

"But what? Just open the gate."

"I can't. We've been ordered to not let you through."

"By who? Katherine? Mr. Kensington?"

He clears his throat. "No. By Garret."

CHAPTER FIFTEEN

"But that doesn't make sense. Why would Garret—"

"I'm sorry, Jade."

That seems to be the word of the day. Everyone's sorry but nobody will tell me why. I sink to the ground, but a security guy I've never met before reaches under my arms and pulls me up. "You can't be on the property. You need to be across the street or at least a foot from the gate."

I don't move, so he pushes me until I start walking. I join the young girls lined up across the street. Some have lawn chairs. Others are sitting on sleeping bags. The girls next to me have signs that say *I love Garret* and *Marry me, Garret.*

"Are you waiting for Garret to come out?" a girl asks. She's looking up from her spot on a pink and green sleeping bag. She's probably around 12. Her blond hair has blue streaks in it that match the puffy blue jacket she's wearing.

"Yeah, I am." I stand there with my arms crossed, staring at the iron gate.

"Are you one of the moms?"

Moms? Is she blind? Do I seriously look like a mom? I'm only 19! Then again I probably look really old given that I stayed up all night and have dark circles and bags under my eyes. But still.

"No, I'm not a mom." I'd love to tell her I'm Garret's girlfriend, but that would cause all kinds of problems, so I pretend to be just another one of Garret's fans. Apparently the oldest fan he has by the looks of this crowd.

This is so ridiculous. I'm not standing here all day. I'm getting past that damn gate and then I'm going to force Garret or his dad to tell me what the hell's going on.

I walk down the street past the crowd of young girls until I'm by myself. I'm standing in front of another large mansion that's surrounded by an iron gate that looks just like the one at Garret's house.

Now what? I need a plan, but I'm too tired to think and my stomach is growling even though I don't feel hungry. I haven't eaten anything since last night, so it makes sense my stomach is begging for food but it's not getting any so I try to ignore it.

I take a seat on the sidewalk and search my purse for a mint or some gum. Then I search my wallet for money as if some might have magically appeared between the time I paid the taxi driver and now. There's not even a quarter in there, but in the zippered side pocket I find a business card. It's the card Arlin gave me.

I decide to call him. I'm not sure how he could help me, but I'm desperate and tired and out of any other ideas.

His phone rings twice and then I hear a recording of a woman's voice. *This number requires a passcode. Please enter it now.*

I forgot Arlin said I had to enter a code. He told me the code. What was the code? I can't remember.

Please enter the passcode now or you will be disconnected, the recorded voice says.

"Yeah, I know!" I yell at her. "Just give me a minute!"

Arlin said something right after he told me the code. What did he say? My birthday! He said he was sorry he missed all my birthdays. I quickly put in 1008 and the phone starts ringing again. It rings and rings and I'm sure he's not going to answer but then I hear a voice.

"Jade? Is that you?"

How did he know it was me? The code. Man, I'm slow today.

"Yes, it's me."

"I'm glad you called."

"Are you busy? Because I could call you back later."

Why did I just say that? I can't call him back later. I'm stranded here with nothing but gated mansions around me and a cell phone with an almost drained battery. Wake up, Jade! And get your freaking head on straight.

"Is something wrong?" He asks it like he already knows the answer, which I find very strange.

"Yes, something's wrong. I need help."

"Of course. Tell me what you need."

I hear the concern in his voice and it makes me want to trust him. Soon the words are spilling from my mouth before my brain can filter them.

"I was home on spring break and when I got back this morning, I found Garret in his dorm room. He was really drunk and saying all these things that didn't make sense, like how he was sorry and how he didn't know, and he kept telling me I had to go away. I called his dad and he came and got him, but he told me I had to go back to Iowa and that he was taking my scholarship away. So I took a taxi to Garret's house but the guards won't let me past the gate and now I'm stuck here. I'm out of money and I can't get back." I stop to take a breath.

"Just calm down. Where are you right now?"

"I'm down the street from his house."

"I'll send someone to pick you up. I'd get you myself, but I'm in Manhattan and with traffic it will take forever to get there."

"But I came here to talk to Garret. I can't leave before I find out what's going on."

"You need to go, Jade. I told you I would help you and I will. We'll get you enrolled in a different college. I'll take care of your expenses."

"Wait. Do you know what's going on here? Because you're acting like you do."

"Just stay where you are. I'll send someone to get you."

"I'm not leaving here until I know what's going on. So if you don't tell me I guess I'll freeze to death sleeping out here tonight."

"Jade. You need to get out of there."

"What I need is answers. And I'm not leaving until I get them."

He lets out a long sigh. "I told you when we met that there were plans for Garret. Those plans have now been approved and will soon be finalized."

"What plans? The ones from your secret organization?"

He doesn't answer.

"So what are the plans?"

"I can't tell you."

"I swear if you don't tell me, I'll tell everyone about this organization you're part of and then I'll tell them the truth about Royce. I'll go to the press. I'll tell them everything."

Now I'm blackmailing my own grandfather? I've never blackmailed anyone before, but I'm desperate and I need to know the truth.

"If you do that, Jade, you won't like the consequences."

"Which are what? The people in your organization will come after me? Hurt me?"

"Not you. But Frank and Ryan. The people you care about."

171

Shit! Who are these people? I take a deep breath as I try to think of a way to get Arlin to tell me the truth. I decide to guess at what might be going on and see how he reacts.

"This group is trying to make Garret's dad pay for killing your son. And you said Mr. Kensington didn't want Garret involved in anything this group does."

"Jade, don't start down this path."

"This group does something with politics. They hand-pick candidates. In the last presidential election, they rigged the voting machines in Ohio and Florida."

I can't believe I've resorted to repeating Carson's crazy conspiracy theories, but I have to say something, and shit, maybe he's right. He was right about *some* of the stuff he said. Maybe he's right about this, too.

"Why would you say something like that?" Arlin's words are rushed, his tone harsh. "That's not true."

"It *is* true. Some reporter proved it. And right before he was going to tell people about it, your group killed him."

"Stop talking such nonsense. This is not helping—"

"Let me finish." With my limited sleep, I can't figure out how I'm making sense of this, but my brain is somehow putting the pieces together. It may be totally wrong, but it's at least a theory. "You said this group had spent years preparing your son to be president. Now that he's dead, they have to find someone else. But they don't have time because it takes years, right? They'll have to settle for someone they didn't want, like Kent Gleason. He was at Garret's house a few weeks ago and Garret's dad told Kent he'd be president, like it was a done deal. Because it *is* a done deal, isn't it? They'll make it happen."

"Enough of this. You're confused and you've obviously been reading conspiracy theories spread by some nutcase on the Internet with a blog and an active imagination."

I ignore him and continue. "This plan they have for Garret has something to do with politics. Something big. Something important."

As I say it, it hits me.

The reason they want Garret.

The plan.

"They want him to be president." I say it slowly as I get up off the ground. "They're preparing him to be president. That's it isn't it? You said it takes years to prepare someone. You have to be at least 35 to run, so they have at least 15 years to get Garret ready."

Arlin is silent and his silence speaks volumes. It's true. That's the plan.

The silence continues as I think this through. Back when Arlin told me there was a plan for Garret, he said this plan would be Pearce's punishment for killing Royce. Arlin said it was something Pearce would never approve of. Pearce wouldn't approve of it because this group will take over Garret's life. They'll control him. He'll never be free to do what he wants. And he'll be the freaking president! No way. That can't be right. I start to come to my senses and realize my conclusion is too insane to be true.

But Arlin is awfully quiet.

"Go ahead," I say. "Tell me I'm crazy."

He finally speaks. "You're not crazy."

"They really want Garret to be the president of the United States someday? Just to punish his dad?" I realize I'm pacing the sidewalk and stop. "There's no way they would make a decision like that just to punish someone. I mean, how do they even know Garret would be good at that? They don't even know him. Shouldn't they hold interviews or make him take a test or something?"

"They've done their research. He meets the criteria. In fact he's the perfect candidate."

"Okay, back up a minute." I start pacing again. "So you're saying this organization is so powerful they can actually pick who they want to be president? And they can do it years in advance? And somehow make it happen? Why? Just so they can control things?"

"That's enough. You need to stop—"

I interrupt. "But how do they do it? They have to rig the system somehow, right? Are people in the government in on this? How long has this been going—"

"Stop it! Right now!" Arlin almost yells it. "You can't ask questions like that. Ever! Not even to me."

I'm so sick of this don't-ask-questions rule. I'm sure Arlin will yell at me again but I have to ask him about Garret.

"Why Garret? Why would they pick him? He doesn't even like politics."

"I can't say anymore. You just need to get away from this whole situation."

"But why would Garret go along with this? Did they threaten to hurt his dad? Or Lilly?"

"I'm getting a car over there and you're going home." His tone implies I have no choice, which I refuse to accept.

"I'm not going anywhere. I need to talk to Garret."

"He won't talk to you. He can't."

"What do you mean he can't?"

"Think about it, Jade. Think about what you just said. About why he's going along with this."

"Yeah, they threatened him. But you didn't answer me when I—" My sleepy brain finally gets it. "Me. They threatened to hurt me."

Arlin's quiet.

"Or they threatened to . . . kill me?"

"You need to leave. You understand why, so we're done talking about this."

"No! I'm not letting them take over Garret's life like this. There has to be something we can do. You're part of this group. Do something!"

"There's nothing I can do. They've already approved the initial plan."

"Who's they? How many people are in on this?"

He doesn't answer.

"You said you'd help me, so help me. I need to talk to Garret one last time. I need to at least say goodbye. Just help me get past the gate. Please. I'm begging you."

"If I do, then you'll say goodbye and agree to never see him again?"

"Yes." It's a lie, of course, but after what Arlin's son put me through, I feel a lie or two is justified. We wouldn't even be in this situation if Royce had just left me alone.

"I can't guarantee this will work, but here's what you need to do. When you get off the phone with me, walk back down to the entrance gate of the Kensington estate. When you get there I want you to text Mr. Kensington. I'm going to tell you what the text should say and I'm not going to repeat it. Are you ready?"

"Yes."

"G40K4." He says it slowly. "For the letters use all capitals."

"Okay. Anything else?"

"No. That's all you need. That will get his attention. If he lets you in, say your goodbyes to Garret and get out of there. I'll have a car waiting out front to take you back."

"Thank you. Thank you for helping me." I pause. "And um, I'd be okay with us meeting again sometime. Maybe you could bring your wife."

"She would like that very much. We both would. Goodbye, Jade."

We hang up and I walk as fast as I can back toward the house. The scene hasn't changed. The same girls are still sitting there waiting for some kind of activity. I stand a foot away from the gate as directed and text Mr. Kensington. Then I wait.

Not more than a minute later I see Brad coming up to the gate. When he gets there, the gate opens and he walks out to the sidewalk where I'm standing. "Mr. Kensington has asked to see you."

The girls across the street notice the open gate and come running over to it. The other security guards hold them back as I walk past the gate with Brad and enter the property.

It's a long walk to the house and Brad and I don't say anything to each other. I can tell he feels bad for turning me away earlier, but I don't hold it against him. He was only doing his job.

When I get to the door, Mr. Kensington answers. "Jade, come inside, please."

"Where's Garret?" I step into the foyer.

"He's in his room."

I turn to go upstairs but Pearce takes hold of my arm. "Let him sleep. He needs to get the alcohol out of his system. Let's talk in my office."

"Hello, Jade." Katherine walks by the foyer, smiling smugly like she won. Like she got what she wanted. To get rid of Jade forever.

Well, she can wipe that smug smile off her face because I'm not even close to letting her win.

I follow Pearce into his office. He sits behind his desk in his black leather office chair, leaning back and crossing his arms.

I sit across from him in the chair that I have sat in so many times before. Every time there's a crisis, I end up back in this same chair.

"So I take it you got my message?" I ask.

"I'm guessing you spoke with your grandfather."

"Nobody here would tell me anything. You wouldn't let me inside. I had to do something."

"I'm not saying what you did was wrong. Arlin is your family. I can't stop you from talking to him. But it's not his place to discuss matters dealing with the Kensington family. So what exactly did he tell you?"

"He didn't tell me anything. I figured it out myself and when I told him, he didn't deny it."

"I see. So why are you here, Jade?"

"I want to find a solution. Garret doesn't want to be part of this. The plan. The organization. He doesn't want to be involved in any of it. I know he doesn't. And I know you don't want that for him either. So let's figure out a way to fix this."

"It's not that simple. I've been part of this for 30 years, Jade, and believe me, there's no way out."

"How do you know that? We haven't even tried."

He sighs and looks down at his desk. "Years ago I tried to get out. I learned about the organization when I was 18. I told my father I wanted nothing to do with it, but I was young and my father insisted, so I went along and did what they said. I followed their rules. I went to the college they told me to go to. I took over the family business. I even married the girl they told me to marry. When the marriage ended, I'd decided I'd had enough. I didn't want them controlling my life. Shortly after my divorce I met a girl I actually loved and I married her. She grew up on a farm in Indiana. We met while she was out here attending graduate school."

"Garret's mother?"

He nods. "I knew I wasn't even supposed to date her, let alone marry her, but I did it anyway. I disobeyed the rules. And if you disobey the rules you get punished and you never know when it will happen. You're left waiting, wondering, just wanting it to be over. For years I never knew what my punishment was for marrying Garret's mother. Whenever something bad happened, I wondered if that was my punishment, but they don't tell you so you're left wondering. In the back of my mind, I had an idea of what the punishment was, but I wouldn't let myself believe it. Until I received this at the meeting Garret and I attended yesterday."

He slides an envelope across his desk. I pick it up and take out a sheet of paper. This is what it says.

Grievance against: Member 1479K.

Order: to remove obstacle created by Member 1479K

Obstacle: 35-year-old female, mother of member 1525K.

Previous attempts to rectify this matter: several attempts, including private meetings and warning letters; all met with resistance and a refusal to cooperate

Remedy: flight from DC To Hartford

There's a red stamp at the bottom of the page.

Obstacle Removed Successfully. Grievance closed.

CHAPTER SIXTEEN

I slowly slide the paper and the envelope back across the table. "They killed her. The plane crash wasn't an accident."

He puts the paper back in the envelope. "This was a warning for Garret. He tried to fight them. He tried to walk out of the meeting. And then they gave him what I just showed you."

It's starting to make sense now. Garret telling me to leave. Telling me it's over. Pearce sending me home. Arlin telling me to get away from Garret. They all know that this organization, whatever it is, would kill me if I stood in the way of their plans for Garret. And by threatening to kill me, they'll get Garret to do whatever they tell him to do.

"I never wanted my son to be part of this," Pearce says. "I wanted him to have what I couldn't. A normal life. One in which he could make his own decisions. I don't want him repeating the life I've had. After Garret's mother died, I didn't have the energy to fight them anymore. So I did what they said. I followed orders. I married the woman they told me to marry. I did things I didn't want to do. Things that were wrong and—" He clears his throat. "Anyway, it's too late for me."

I want to ask him what things this group made him do, but I know he won't tell me so I ask about Katherine instead. "So they made you marry Katherine?"

He nods. "Her father is a member. They prefer us to marry women whose fathers are members. If that doesn't work out, they find you a woman who is used to a life of wealth and privilege. Those women tend to marry for money and are less likely to care or notice what their husbands are doing on the side. Typically they never know about the organization or by the time they do, they're so immersed in the lifestyle they'll keep the secret to make sure the money doesn't go away."

"Did Garret's mother know?"

"No. Back then I held out hope that I could someday get out of it, so I never told her."

"But Katherine knows about it?"

"Yes, because her father is a member. Our marriage was arranged, and for years I tried to make it work. And after we had Lilly, Katherine and I grew closer, but it didn't last. Our marriage has always been a struggle and they refuse to let me divorce her. This will be Garret's life now. His wife will be chosen for him and he won't like the choice."

"Why didn't you ever tell Garret about this? He knew about the organization so why didn't you tell him he had to a member?"

"Because I was hoping he wouldn't have to be."

"I don't understand."

"Our younger members, myself included, don't like the rule that says you're born into this group. They'd rather hand select members based on certain criteria. Find people who actually want to be part of this rather than having to force people into it and coerce them into keeping quiet. They've been watching Garret since he was a young boy and they've seen how difficult he is to control. He's always been independent and rebellious. They knew he'd be a lot to handle and nobody has time to manage him."

"So get them to change the rule. Get Garret out of this."

"I tried. I've spent years trying to get him out. And just recently I thought I'd convinced everyone to let him go. In fact, right before I held that fundraiser for Royce, there was an initial vote to let Garret, and some of the other young men, out of this obligation. The vote passed and although the senior members could override it, they didn't. I assumed that meant Garret was free. That's why I allowed him to keep seeing you. I know how much he loves you and I wanted him to have that. To have love in his life. Real love, like the kind I had with his mother."

I can't believe Pearce is telling me all this. It's like as soon as he showed me that envelope about Garret's mom, his guard came down and he's letting everything spill out. But I know at any minute he could revert back to his old self, so I try to keep him talking.

"This group wouldn't make this plan for Garret's life just to punish you, right? It's too big."

"The punishment is just a side benefit. This plan would've happened anyway. The senior members have been interested in Garret for some time now, but they purposely hid it from me because they knew I'd be against it."

"Why were they so interested in Garret?"

He sighs like he's not sure he wants to tell me, but then he starts talking again. "As you know, this reality show Garret's been unwillingly involved in since his senior year in high school has given him a great deal of press. I ignored it because I thought it was too trivial to get into a legal battle over." Pearce looks down, shaking his head back and forth. "But I should've taken it seriously. I should've taken action like Garret wanted me to and stopped it right away."

"Why? What does the reality show have to do with this?"

"Yesterday Garret and I learned that the organization has been monitoring the public's response to him ever since he was featured on that show. They have records of all Internet searches for him and all comments made about him online. They compiled the data and found that people consider Garret to be trustworthy, attractive, intelligent, confident, and decisive—all criteria we look for in a possible presidential candidate. His appeal is not just with young girls, but includes other key demographics. At the meeting, they had charts and graphs showing how well Garret resonates with people. They can use this information and build on it to eventually create a consensus among the voting public that he's presidential material."

"I thought you rigged the voting. What difference does it make if people like him or think he's presidential material?"

"We don't rig the voting. We prepare candidates. Another organization handles it from there. I know nothing about them and I'm not just saying that. I really don't."

Another organization? What the hell? How deep does this thing go?

"I overheard you talking to Kent Gleason that day he was here at the house. You made it sound like he'd be president. Some guy brought in a video and—"

"You shouldn't eavesdrop, Jade. You'll find out things you don't really want to know."

"Do you rig photos? Videos? How did you cover up what happened to Royce Sinclair?"

His eyes narrow and I know I shouldn't have asked—or more like accused—him of that, but it's too late now.

"There *is* some media manipulation that occurs, but we are certainly not the only organization that feeds lies to the press. Almost every company in the world does that. Even governments do it. Sometimes you need to change public perception and the media can be very effective for that. People tend to believe what they see on TV or read in the newspaper."

I wasn't prepared for him to admit to manipulating the media and I'm not sure how to respond. So I turn the topic back to Garret. "Was Garret their only option for this plan? Or were there others?"

"Garret was one of four young men being considered. He was put on a list about a year ago. Again, I didn't know this. I had some suspicions when they forced me to make him intern in Washington last summer. But he showed no interest in politics the entire time he was there, so I figured they wouldn't consider him to be groomed for even a Senate position. But apparently he rose to the top of the list after that reality show aired last year."

"But Garret said he didn't get much press the first time it aired."

"Yes, he wasn't as well known as he is now, but the people who *did* know about him had very positive things to say. And when the public develops strong feelings about a person, it makes our job much easier. When grooming a candidate you need a good starting base and Garret has that. He's perfect actually. I never even considered it before, I guess because I didn't want to. But I see why they selected him. And making him do this fulfills my punishment for what I did to Royce. They know it kills me to see this happen to Garret. His life is over. It's theirs now, not his."

"Why is Garret going along with this? Because of me?"

Pearce doesn't answer.

"Then I'll go into hiding. I'll move out of the country."

"If Garret thinks there's even a possibility they would harm you, he'll do what they say. And now that he knows what happened to his mother, he won't call their bluff."

Pearce's cell phone rings. He looks to see who it is, then answers it. "Hello, Arlin. Yes, she's still here. You shouldn't have told her this. You know better than that. If they found out—" He stops and listens. "Yes, I suppose." His eyes dart up at me. "Garret is sleeping now. I'll have someone take her back when she's ready to go."

He hangs up. "Arlin has a car waiting out front for you, but I assumed you'd want some time to say goodbye to Garret."

"This isn't goodbye. I'm not letting them win."

"There's nothing we can do. If there was, I'd be doing it. Now I have some work to get done, so perhaps you could wait in the living room until Garret wakes up."

"Can I see Lilly?"

"It's best if you don't. She's grown very attached to you and seeing you one last time will only confuse her. We'll come up with a story to tell her later."

I get up to leave.

"Oh, and Jade, I don't think I need to tell you this, but just so we're clear, this conversation never happened. You know nothing about any of this, including what Arlin told you. Do you understand?"

He says it in that threatening tone he uses whenever he tells me to keep his secrets. It always freaks me out.

I nod. "Yes, I understand."

He turns on his computer, ignoring me.

I don't get Garret's dad at all. Sometimes he acts caring and then two seconds later he turns cold and emotionless. It's like turning a switch.

I walk out of his office and go sit in the sunroom. My cell phone has a bunch of messages from Harper, so I check one of her voicemails while I wait.

"Hey, Jade. Sean and I are at the airport. Our plane's delayed because of Kyle Andermeyer, that actor from those kid movies. Sean what's the name of those movies? Sean's in the ticket line. He can't hear me. Anyway the guy was a total jerk. He got on the plane drunk and was cursing and grabbing the stewardess' ass and then he brought out some suspicious liquid and we all ended up having to get off the plane. The liquid turned out to be an energy drink, but now we have to wait for a new plane. Someone got the whole thing on video and posted it online. His career's over. There's no way parents will take their kids to his movies after they see that video. Anyway, just wanted to give you an update. Hope you and Garret are enjoying your reunion." She giggles before hanging up.

Harper always leaves *really* long voicemail messages. That was a short one. I check my text messages. There's a whole string of them from Harper, mainly about how the video of Kyle has gone viral on the Internet and how people are trashing him online. She sent me a link to the video and told me to watch it but my battery is running low so I turn off the phone.

I look for something to read. There aren't even any magazines. I glance around at the house with its all-white decor. Carson's house was so much better. It felt like a real home, not this stark white, hospital-look Katherine has created.

It's making me feel sick so I decide to go wait in the game room. As I'm walking over there, I stop when I get to the stairs.

Why am I waiting down here? I should be upstairs with Garret. I don't care if he's asleep. I don't even care if he reeks of alcohol. I just want to be with him.

I make my way up the stairs and down to his room. His door isn't locked so I go inside. He's sprawled out on his bed, his head face-down in a pillow. I gently smooth his messy hair with my hand. He jerks up at my touch, then flips on his back, still asleep.

Now that I know what's going on, seeing him again makes my eyes tear up and my heart hurt. I literally feel pain in my chest as I think about us not being together anymore. This isn't fair. There has to be a way to stop this.

I kiss his cheek and lie next to him.

"Jade?" He whispers it, his eyes still closed. I assume he's saying my name in his sleep, but then I feel his arm lift up and land on my leg.

"Garret? Are you awake?" I ask softly.

He slowly opens his eyes. When he sees me there he bolts up, his body ramming against the headboard. "Jade, what are you doing here?"

"I came to see you." I try to hold his hand but he yanks it away.

"No! You can't be here. They'll—"

"They're not going to kill me right this second. They have a good 20 years to get you ready. My being here right now isn't screwing with their plan."

"What did you say?"

"I know everything, Garret. I put the pieces together and figured out part of what was going on and your dad filled in the rest."

"What do you mean when you say you know everything?"

"I know about the plan they have for you. I know about the organization. I know about your dad's marriage to Katherine."

"What about their marriage?"

186

"That it was arranged. He never wanted to marry her and now he can't get divorced. Didn't your dad tell you that?"

Garret shakes his head no. He's not as drunk anymore, but he doesn't look good. His eyes are red and puffy and he's rubbing his head like he has a headache.

"Do you know about my mom?" he asks quietly.

"Yes. And I'm so sorry, Garret." I reach over and hug him. At first he's tense, but then he relaxes and hugs me back like it's the last hug we'll ever have.

"They killed her. They killed my mom. She'd be alive right now if they hadn't—" He stops and it sounds like he's softly crying behind my shoulder. I've never seen him cry and even if it's a hungover, still-partially-drunk cry, it breaks my heart and fills me with overwhelming sadness. And because it's *his* sadness I feel, it hurts ten times more than if it were my own.

I used to be able to push away sadness and all the other painful emotions and bury them deep inside, but now I feel all of them. And I'm finally okay with that, because feeling them is part of living and I never would've realized that if it weren't for the man who's now holding on to me so tight I can barely breathe.

I want him to keep holding on but he doesn't. Instead, he takes hold of my arms and pushes me back so we're face to face. "I'll never let them hurt you. I'll do whatever they say. I'll do anything . . . anything at all to make sure they leave you alone."

"We're not letting them do this, Garret."

"You can't stop them. At this meeting they had all these charts and graphs and all these projections. Every part of my life will be planned out. And you're not in it, Jade. You're not allowed to be. You have to leave. If they did that to my mom, they'll do it to you, too."

187

I shake my head. "No, I'm not leaving."

He holds my face in his hands, forcing me to look at him. "You have to."

I shove his hands away. "I'm not leaving so stop telling me to!" I swallow hard past the lump in my throat and take a deep breath, determined not to cry. "You're one of the few people in the world I can stand being around. And even when you piss me off, I still want to be with you." I don't know why I'm joking at a time like this, but it makes Garret's eyes soften just a tiny bit so I continue. "It's true. You know how much I don't like people. And I liked you from the first day we met."

He takes my hand, holding it gently in his. "No, you didn't. You said I annoyed you at first."

"You annoyed me because you made me feel something. And I hate feeling shit. You know that." I get serious again. "Garret, I know for a fact I'll never find someone like you again. And I don't want to. You're it. You're all I want. And I'm not letting you go."

He holds my hand tighter. "Jade, you know I want that more than anything but—"

"Then we're fighting this! We're not just giving up."

"You can't fight these people."

"Yes, we can! We just need to think. Go take a shower and wash all that alcohol off you and then we'll talk."

He lifts my hand up and kisses it because he knows I don't want his alcohol-smelling mouth on my face. "I had this whole welcome home thing planned for you. I was going to fill your room with flowers, but then the meeting happened and well…"

"Go shower, Garret." The lump in my throat keeps getting bigger as tears well up in my eyes. I need a minute to get myself together but he keeps talking.

"I ordered you more of those Belgian chocolates. They're in my room at school if you want them." His gorgeous blue eyes are so full of hurt and sadness I almost can't look at them.

Dammit, he's going to make me cry.

"I was going to take you out for a really nice dinner tonight. And I had this box made for you. It's filled with stuff for California like sunglasses and flip flops and . . . maybe it was stupid, but I wanted to do it because you were so excited about living there, which made me excited and . . . anyway, it'll be delivered on Monday, but I guess you won't be here so—"

"Stop it! I'm not leaving on Monday! Just take your damn shower."

He goes in the bathroom and I slide off the bed and onto the floor, hugging my knees and letting my tears finally fall. When I hear the shower shut off, I stand up, wipe off my face, and plaster on my best fake smile as he walks back in the room.

"Do you feel better?"

"No." He goes to his dresser and pulls out some clothes.

"I've obviously never had a hangover, but I hear it can take a while to feel better."

"It's not the hangover. Physically, I don't feel that bad. Before I met you I drank way more than that." He faces the window as he puts his clothes on. I wait until he's dressed, then go over and hug him. But instead of turning to face me, he just stands there with his arms at his sides.

Something happened when he was in the shower. His body is stiff and refuses to soften when I touch him. He must've built up a keep-away-from-Jade wall because now he's cold and distant.

He breaks free from my hug and goes and sits on the chair by his desk.

I sit across from him on the bed. "Don't you want to sit here with me?"

He won't even look at me now. "You're making this harder, Jade. Why did you even come here?"

I get up, placing myself directly in front of him. "What the hell kind of question is that? I love you. I want to be with you. After everything we've been through, did you really think I'd listen to your dad and just leave? Not even ask for an explanation? Not even try to talk to you?"

His eyes are fixed on the floor and his arms are crossed. The emotion he expressed just minutes ago is completely gone. He's shut down. Given up.

"What happened while you were in the shower? Did you just decide you hate me now and you want me gone?"

I stand there, watching him, waiting for him to respond. But he won't answer me and he still won't look at me.

"I never should've trusted you, Garret. You lied to me when we first met and now I find out you've been lying to me this whole time." I walk to the end of the bed and sit down with my back to him. "I guess it's true. You can't change people. You'll always be a liar."

He storms over, landing in front of me and pushing on my shoulder to get me to look at him. "What the hell are you talking about? I haven't been lying to you! I didn't know about any of this until yesterday!"

I jump up and get in his face. "I'm not talking about the plan. Or the organization. You lied to me about *us*! You said I could have this forever. You said if we ever broke up it would be because *I* did it, not you. You said that nobody could ever break us apart unless we let them. And like an idiot, I believed you! I believed everything you said! But it was all just lies!"

"Those weren't lies!" He yells it, then lowers his voice. "I meant all of that. But everything is different now. When I said those things I didn't know this would happen. So it's not fair for you to say that I lied. Because I didn't."

"You lied, Garret! None of what's happened should matter if you really meant those things. You should still want to be with me. But instead you're breaking up with me!"

He raises his voice again. "Are you fucking kidding me? You think I *want* you to leave? I'm fucking dying inside right now! I can't even look at you! It's killing me to have you here in my room, this close to me, knowing I'll never see you again!"

His eyes are wide awake now and he's breathing fast. He's finally coming out of the comatose fog he was in. I knew he felt that way about me, and about us, but I needed him to say it. I needed to get some type of emotional response out of him so he'd stop acting like this was over. Like he'd shut down and given up.

"You WILL see me again!" I yell back at him, tears rolling down my cheeks. "I'm right here! And I'm not going anywhere, so stop trying to send me away! Stop telling me to leave!"

"I don't have a choice! Don't you get that? They fucking own me, Jade!"

"No! They can't have you! I won't let them!"

The room gets quiet, but I hear his breathing, fast and heavy. I wipe the tears off my face and try to get control of myself. I can't break down. I need to think. There has to be a way out of this. They can't take him away from me. I need him. And he needs me. And what we have is so real and so rare that I refuse to let it be taken from me without a fight.

I look up and see Garret studying me, like he's not sure what I want from him.

"Garret, if you really—"

He doesn't let me finish. He draws me into him and puts his lips just inches from mine, hesitating because he knows if we start this, it'll be that much harder for him to force me to leave. I gently kiss him and feel him giving in. He pulls me closer and kisses me back. It soon becomes a deep, intense kiss that for a moment takes my mind off all the events of this horrible day. I focus on the familiar feel of his soft lips and his warm breath and his strong arms around my waist.

I can't imagine ever having anyone else kiss me. Or hold me. Or be with me. I only want this. Him. Forever.

The thought wakes me into action, and as much as I want the kiss to continue, I pull away. "Garret, we have to talk. We don't have much time and we need to come up with a plan. Our own plan, not their plan."

"There's no plan we can come up with that will fix this. If we try to keep this going in secret, they'll find out. If I don't follow orders, you know what will happen."

"Yes, so you need to think differently. You can't just tell them no. You need a different approach."

"Like what?"

I take a moment to think, forcing my tired brain to work. "Like what if you weren't so popular with people anymore? Would this group still want you to be president?"

"They're going to make sure I'm popular. That's part of the plan. They build on the popularity I already have. So if people online say I seem trustworthy because of the way I smile, then they'll make sure I'm smiling in every photo, at every event. Yesterday they said people think I'm loyal because the fake me hasn't cheated on Ava. Older people said I seem responsible because I'm not seen at clubs and because I have short hair and don't have tattoos. This group plans to use stuff like that to make me even more appealing to voters."

I pace the floor hoping it will help me think better, but it doesn't. My cell phone dings and I pull it out of my pocket. "I swear I turned this thing off." As I go to shut it down, I notice more texts from Harper.

Text 1: Kyle Andermeyer just got booted from the airport.
Text 2: Still waiting for our flight. We're sooo bored.
Text 3: My dad called. Said Kyle just lost a movie role worth $4M!
Text 4: Finally getting on the plane!

"What are you reading?" Garret asks.

"Just some texts from Harper. Some actor delayed their flight because he was being an ass. She said he just lost a—"

"Lost a what?"

An idea hits me and I feel a rush of energy as I think of the possibilities.

"That's it," I say.

"What's it?"

"I think I have an idea."

CHAPTER SEVENTEEN

I hold up my phone. "These texts from Harper about this actor. That could be you, Garret."

"You want me to be an actor?"

"No. Well, kind of, but not like you're thinking."

"I don't know what you mean."

"Just go with me here. You know Kyle Andermeyer, the guy who stars in all those kid movies? Anyway, he was being a total ass on the plane and they couldn't take off. Everyone was delayed at the airport for hours. Harper said one of the passengers got video of the guy and posted it online just minutes after it happened. Within the hour Harper said the story was all over the Internet. Social media. Celebrity websites. Fan blogs. And now Kyle just lost a huge movie role. All because the public turned against him."

"Yeah? So?"

"The public turned against him, Garret. He lost a big acting job because the studio thinks people won't go to the movie if he's in it. Do you see what I'm saying?"

"No, but I'm kind of slow right now."

"If we could generate the same type of bad publicity for you so that people turn against you, don't trust you, maybe even hate you, then there's no way you could even be considered for this plan."

"Huh." He pauses to consider it. "But by the time I run for office people will have forgotten about what I did when I was 19."

"Not if you do something people won't forget. We're not talking about losing an acting job here. We're talking about the presidency. People expect more from a president than an actor. A few bad things may be all it takes for people to decide that you're not presidential material. The point is that the organization won't want to take a chance on you if the public doesn't like you or can't forgive you. You'll lose the starting base they think they have to build from."

"I don't know, Jade. They seemed determined to make this work."

"It's not up to them. The public will decide your fate. If they hate you, there's no way they'd vote for you, even 20 years from now. And if you ended up running and winning the election with little public support, it would draw attention. Reporters would be all over that. So even if that group messed with the voting machines to make sure you got elected, they wouldn't get away with it. Too many people would be looking into how you won."

"And how am I going to get people to hate me? Or lose interest?"

"We don't want them to lose interest. At least not at first. We want them to talk about how much they don't like you. Post it on their blogs. Tell their friends. We want people to instantly have a bad image of you when they hear your name."

"So I just do some bad stuff and make sure it gets photographed? That doesn't seem like it would work."

"No. You take all that research you learned about yesterday, the stuff that people like about you, and you do the opposite. So if people think you're faithful to Ava, we'll make up stories about you cheating on her. If people think you're responsible, we'll post stories about you crashing your dad's expensive cars. You could grow your hair longer and get tattoos. Have you ever seen a president with a tattoo?"

"No, but—"

"So go cover your body in tattoos. Whatever it takes." My mind is working so fast it's giving me a headache. "Or get fake tattoos. You don't actually have to do this stuff. We'll just make it look like you did. We could make fake videos of you acting out at clubs, destroying hotel rooms, smoking weed. We could make fake photos and post them online."

"And people are going to believe this?"

"Are you kidding? A fake Garret has been on TV for two weeks now and people are convinced it's you. I even overheard these girls in my chem class talking about you and Ava like you're actually dating, even though they see you and me together all the time. They just believe whatever they read in a gossip magazine or on a website instead of what's right in front of them. Think about it, Garret. For the past few months, you've done nothing but go to school and hang out with me, and yet during that time people have become obsessed with you. You have millions of fans even though you haven't even done anything. Your popularity is all engineered. Fake stories, fake photos. We can do the same thing only make the stories and photos negative instead of positive."

"That would take a lot of resources. We'd need other people to help."

"Your dad has a lot of resources. And he already feeds fake stories to the media. That's how he covered up what happened to Sinclair."

"Yeah, but he had a lot of help. Other members in the organization used their power and money to make that happen. He'll be working on his own to do this."

"I'm sure there are plenty of people who owe him favors."

"Not enough for what you're describing."

"We also have Arlin. He said he'd help me any way he could. He knows I want to be with you and he feels like he owes me because of Royce. So now we have two very powerful, very rich men who can help us with this. And we have Harper who has friends in film school who could help us make some realistic videos."

I'm out of breath from talking so much. I stop for a moment and notice Garret staring at me. I assume he thinks I'm insane but then he smiles.

"God, I love you."

I go over to him. "You don't think I'm crazy?"

He shakes his head no, still smiling as he wraps his arms around my waist. "You're not crazy. You're a freaking genius."

"Are you serious? So you think it might work? You're willing to try it?"

"I'm willing to try anything if it means I can be with you. I want my life back. I want OUR life back."

"I do, too, and I have no idea if this will change their decision, but we have to try something. We can't just give up."

He rests his forehead against mine. "I don't know why you stay with me after everything I've put you through. I don't deserve you."

"I know," I say, smiling. "And once this is over you're going to owe me big time."

"Just name it. Anything you want is yours."

"I just want a promise. A promise that you won't give up on us again. That's it. And I don't want it now. You've already screwed this up and saying it now would be meaningless."

He kisses me. "I totally screwed up. I did everything wrong. But when I found out what they could do to you, I panicked. I'm still panicked. If they find out we're together—I don't know if I can do this, Jade. I can't put you at risk."

"We're doing this. And you're not backing out. When does this plan they have for you go into effect?"

"It hasn't been finalized yet and it can't move forward until all the members have officially approved the final plan."

"When will they approve it?"

"In a couple months. Now that the plan has been presented, the members are given time to review it and make comments up until the final vote. Once they vote to approve the plan, I'll have to start going to their meetings and by late summer they'll have me attending public events to get my face out there more. And I have to change my major to prelaw and transfer to Yale and get more involved in politics and—"

"Wait. So this isn't final? We have time to change their minds?"

"Technically yes, but it's not going to be easy. Almost everyone wants me to be the candidate. At the meeting Friday, the ballot had three other guys and me. I don't know who the other guys were. I'm not allowed to know. Anyway, almost everyone voted for me. The final vote is just a formality. It's in the bylaws for the organization and they have to follow the bylaws."

"If this plan for you isn't final yet and it's not happening for months, then why am I being sent away on Monday? What's the rush? Did they tell you to get rid of me?"

"No, not specifically. But you're not part of the plan, and when talk of my future fake wife came up and I protested, they gave me the envelope about my mom."

"So they never actually came out and told you to break up with me?"

"My dad said they never come right out and say stuff. They prefer more discreet tactics that make their message clear. The memo about my mom's death made it very clear what could happen to you."

"But they wouldn't do anything to me anytime soon, right? I mean, it would look awfully suspicious if the girl you've been dating for months showed up dead. Even if they tried to cover it up, Frank would have his journalist friends all over that story trying to expose the truth. Then the public would always question whether you were a killer or not. That could destroy any chance of a future political career."

"That's true. I didn't think about that."

"So they can't kill me. At least not anytime soon."

"You're really making my head hurt with all this. I think the hangover's kicking in."

"Let's get some coffee in you. And I could use some food."

When we open the door, Pearce is standing there. "I was just coming to get you, Jade. Are you ready to leave?"

"She's not leaving," Garret says.

"Well, hurry up and say your goodbyes then."

"She's not leaving as in she's not going back to Iowa. She's staying in school and finishing the semester."

"Garret, you know the rules," Pearce says. "We've already decided what's going to happen here."

"No, *they* decided. But like Jade just pointed out, they're not going to do anything to her today or tomorrow or next week.

And if they *did* do something to her, Frank would have every reporter in the country looking at me as a possible suspect."

It's like a light bulb went off in Pearce's head. His eyes glaze over and he looks off to the side. "I hadn't considered that."

"I hadn't either." Garret puts his arm around me. "But my girlfriend is smarter than both of us and she's figured out a plan that might get me out of this."

Pearce still has that glazed-over look. "Once an idea like that was planted in the minds of the public, even if it wasn't true, it would destroy your chances. A good percentage of the public would never vote for you. They'd hold protests telling people they can't vote for a suspected killer."

"Yeah, but I don't want people to think I'm a killer. I just want them to dislike me enough that they'd never consider me for any political office."

Pearce wakes up from his daze. "Say that again."

"Let's go downstairs." Garret walks past him. "Jade needs to eat and I need some coffee. We'll meet you in your office."

His dad remains standing there while Garret and I go down to the kitchen.

"I think you just really confused your dad," I say as I take a seat on one of the tall stools along the kitchen island.

"We'll explain it to him later. So what can I get you?"

"Anything. But make it something quick because I'm starving."

He opens one of the big stainless steel refrigerators. "We have some ham and cheese. I can make you a sandwich."

"That works."

He hands me a bottle of soda, then pulls out the sandwich ingredients and grabs some bread from the counter.

"I can make it, Garret. You don't have to do it."

"You're not doing anything. After the way I acted, I owe you. I'll be making all your sandwiches from here on out." He puts the bread down and comes over to where I'm sitting.

"What are you doing?"

He doesn't answer, but just picks me up and sets me down on the floor. He wraps his arms around me and holds me against his body. The tightness in my chest begins to unravel and I finally feel like I can breathe. I rest my head on his chest and just listen to the beating of his heart. It calms me even more so I close my eyes and just listen.

"I missed you so damn much," Garret says softly. I feel him gently kiss the top of my head, then feel the warmth of his breath as he remains there, his head hung just above mine.

"I missed you, too."

"I don't mean just this past week. I mean when I thought you were gone. I missed you like I've never missed anyone. I missed the future I was going to have with you. I missed the feeling of having you in my arms like this. I missed hearing your voice and seeing your face and sleeping next to you. I missed all of it because I was sure it was gone. I kept trying to tell myself that it was for the best. That I had to do it to protect you, but it ripped me apart inside, Jade. I couldn't fucking handle it, so I drank. And I know that's not the way to handle shit, but I just wanted the hurt to go away." He pulls back, and when I look at him I can still see the pain in his eyes. "I knew I had to let you go, but I didn't know how. I could barely go a week without you, so how the hell could I go a lifetime without you?"

A few stray tears run down my face. He puts his hand on my cheek and wipes them away. "I'm sorry, Jade, for how I acted earlier. Pushing you away like that. Telling you to leave. But I swear I was only doing it to protect you. I thought if I made you hate me, it'd be easier for you to go."

I glance down. "I'd never hate you. It's not possible."

"I shouldn't have given up so easily. I should've tried to find a solution. But at that meeting, I felt like there was no way out of this. All these rich, powerful men were sitting around a table with an entire outline of my future. And then when they threatened to hurt you, I couldn't think straight. I couldn't—"

"Garret, stop." I lift my head and our eyes meet. "Don't talk about it. We're going to fix this. We're getting you out of this."

He smiles, then takes my face in his hands and kisses me. And it's like I can feel every ounce of love he has for me in that kiss. I can't even describe it, but I know I'll never feel a kiss like that with anyone but him.

He rests his forehead on mine. "I love you."

"I love you, too." I pull away before I start crying again. "Now go make the sandwich so I can eat and we can get to work on this plan."

"Okay." He hesitates. "But I just need one more." He kisses me again.

"You better stop kissing me because you're making me want to do things we don't have time to do right now."

"We'll make time." His lips brush mine as he says it.

I back away. "The sandwich, Garret." I point to the plate across from us.

He keeps his eyes on me. "Jade, if this plan of yours doesn't work, I don't know what will happen with us. There's a possibility that—"

I put my hand over his mouth. "We'll talk about that when we need to, but we're not talking about it now. Should I just make my own sandwich?"

He laughs. "I'm making it. Just hold on." He returns to his spot across from me. "So how was the drive back?"

"It sucked because my idiot boyfriend wouldn't answer the phone, so I assumed he was dead which ruined the trip."

His eyes lift slightly as he cuts my sandwich in half. "Sorry about that." He slides the ham and cheese sandwich over to me and reaches in a cupboard for some potato chips. "Besides that, anything else happen? Did Carson behave? Did he get back with his ex-girlfriend?"

"No. He said he wanted to date someone he could see everyday."

"Like you," Garret mumbles as he makes a pot of coffee.

"No, not me." I take a bite of my sandwich. It's really good. I always think food tastes better when someone else makes it. Or it could be because I haven't eaten anything since last night. "For most of the trip Carson didn't talk about you, but then in the last hour or so, he started telling me all these conspiracy theories."

I've never told Garret about Carson's obsession with the Kensington family, but I think it's time to fess up.

"So Carson's one of those freaks who believes that shit on the Internet?"

"Yes, and ever since he met you, he's been digging up all this stuff about your family. And your company. He thinks your dad's doing stuff that's illegal and covering it up. That's why Carson doesn't like you and why he's so protective over me."

"Was that the first time he mentioned anything?"

"No, he's been saying these things since I first met him. I didn't tell you because you already hate the guy enough. I keep telling him he's crazy so he'll stop talking about it, but he keeps bringing it up. In the car yesterday, he said he thinks your dad's part of some secret group and he claims there's proof this group rigs elections and does other bad things."

"Carson got all this off the Internet?"

"That's what he made it sound like, but I think his uncle sends him stuff, too. His uncle's a reporter in Chicago and he's the one who got Carson interested in this conspiracy stuff. Anyway, Carson said some reporter ended up dead right before he was about to break the story about election fraud. Carson's convinced that someone from your dad's secret organization killed the reporter and covered it up. He didn't say your dad did it, but he implied that your dad does stuff like that—has people killed if they know too much. And that soon you'll be doing it, too."

"What did you say when he told you all this?" Garret brings my empty plate to the sink, then takes a plastic container from the counter, opens the lid, and slides it over to me.

"I told him he shouldn't believe what he reads on the Internet." The container has homemade cookies inside. I take two chocolate ones and slide the container back.

"Did he believe you?"

"No. But he'll never believe me. He's convinced this stuff is going on." I take a bite of the cookie. So good. Charles makes great cookies.

"That's a problem, Jade. If he's that obsessed with me or my family, he could find out what we're up to with this plan of yours and ruin the whole thing." Garret goes to put the lid on the container and I reach over and grab one more cookie.

"I'll deal with him. Maybe we'll have to make up a conspiracy to post online to keep him occupied. Get him off track."

"Who knew you were so devious? This is a whole new side of you I've never seen." He smiles as he holds the lid over the cookie container. "You good now?"

"Hmm, maybe one more." I grab another cookie.

The coffee machine beeps and Garret pours himself a cup.

"I could use some of that," I say. He gives his full cup to me and pours another one. "So I guess our summer in California is off."

He comes over and stands in front of me. "It's not off. Even if I can't go, you're still going. I already paid for the place. Harper and Sean will be there, so it's not like you'll be alone."

"I can't go there with all this going on. Or if it doesn't work, then—"

"Jade, whatever happens with this, you can't stop living your life."

"There's no way I can go live in California without—"

He presses his lips to mine, then pulls away just slightly. "No matter what happens, you're going to live on the beach this summer. You've been looking forward to this ever since we first talked about it and you're not going to miss out because of me."

Just the thought of being there without him makes my eyes watery, but I don't want to cry so I try to lighten the mood. "You've seen Harper and Sean together. They can't keep their hands off each other. I can't watch that all summer."

He tucks my hair behind my ear. "Then bring some books and read on the beach. Or take a nap under an umbrella and listen to the waves."

I force out a half-smile, refusing to cry. "Maybe you'll still be able to go."

"I don't think so. Our plan may take a while to have an effect which means the final vote will probably get delayed into the summer. Come on. Let's go talk to my dad."

He helps me down off the tall stool. "How's your knee? With so much going on I forgot to ask."

"It's better. I'm ready to go running again."

He puts his arm around me and leads me out of the kitchen. "You're not going running. We have enough problems to deal with. We don't need you tearing your knee open again."

As we get near Pearce's office we hear him talking to someone, so we stop just outside his door. Pearce sees us waiting. "Come on in. We were just discussing some things."

We walk in and Arlin is sitting there. He gets up when he sees me. "Jade honey, it's good to see you." He hugs me, which is still strange, but I let him. I'm not okay with him calling me 'honey' either, but he's old and that's probably what old people do.

"What are you doing here?" I ask him.

"I came to check on you and give you a ride back to school, but Pearce said we needed to discuss some things first. He said something about an idea you had."

I explain the idea to them. They both listen, not asking any questions.

When I'm done, Pearce looks over at Arlin. "I think it's worth a try. What do you think?"

"It'll make a lot of people angry."

"But their plan for Garret doesn't even start until the fall."

"Yes, but time and effort is being put forth now in anticipation of that."

"All the more reason to get this started immediately."

"We have to change the minds of more than half of the members. That's never happened before."

"I know the realities of this, Arlin." Pearce looks across his desk at Garret and for the first time ever I see real emotion in Garret's dad. He usually acts so strong and stoic. Even when Garret was shot, he kept his emotions hidden. But now he looks panicked, fearful, and furious that his son's future is being taken away.

"We're doing this," Pearce announces, his eyes still on Garret. "If you don't want to be involved, Arlin, I understand."

I look at Arlin, hoping he was serious when he told me he'd do anything to help me.

"If that's your decision, then tell me what you need and I'll take care of it," Arlin says. "In fact, it's probably best if I manage the operations side of this instead of you. If you get caught, Pearce, well . . . you know what will happen."

"What?" Garret asks. "What will happen?"

Pearce ignores the question. "Arlin, let's talk specifics later."

I glance at Garret who seems just as surprised as me that his dad actually wants to do this. I was prepared for him to list all the reasons why it wouldn't work. But now I'm thinking that maybe it will.

CHAPTER EIGHTEEN

Everyone's quiet for a moment and then Arlin says, "If they let your son go, Pearce, they'll have to find a different way to punish you for what you did to Royce."

Pearce nods. "Yes. I'm aware of that."

"Like what?" Garret asks his dad. "What do you think they'll do to you?"

"It doesn't matter. That's not a concern right now."

"There will be other consequences as well." Arlin turns to Garret. "You're destroying your reputation by doing this. You won't be able to take over Kensington Chemical. The board would never allow it."

"Garret hadn't planned to do that anyway." When Pearce says it he doesn't even seem mad about it. I'm starting to see that Pearce really does want his son to be happy. A few months ago I never would've believed that.

Arlin continues lecturing Garret. "Finding any type of job will be difficult with these indiscretions in your past. You may even find it hard to get into an MBA program."

"I know." Garret acts like he's already considered that, but I hadn't even thought about it.

"And you realize that you can't see Jade while this is going on," Pearce says. "They might be watching you and being with her would put her in danger. You two will need to pretend to break up and then have limited contact until this is over."

"So I can't talk to him?" I ask.

"You can talk to him like you would talk to any other student, but you have to avoid doing anything that would indicate you're still together. You need to treat Garret like an ex-boyfriend. One who's seeing other girls and doing things you don't approve of. This is an acting job. For all of us. I plan to do my part as well."

"Are you saying I can stay at Moorhurst? You're not taking my scholarship away?"

"Arlin and I discussed this before you came in and we agreed that sending you home in the middle of the semester would draw suspicion from your classmates, your professors, as well as Frank and Ryan. We think it's best if you stay at Moorhurst, but pretend that you and Garret are no longer together. And don't worry about your scholarship. Your tuition, room and board have already been paid through the end of the year. But after this semester, Arlin has asked if he could fund the rest of your education. That's something the two of you can discuss later."

I glance at Arlin, then back at Pearce.

"But I thought the organization wanted me to leave. Isn't that why you were sending me home on Monday?"

"As long as you stay away from Garret, they won't care that you're still at Moorhurst. So you need to make it clear to everyone that you're not dating him and are not even friends with him."

"Can I tell anyone that we're not really broken up? Like my friend, Harper?"

"No. This needs to be kept a secret."

"But Harper will never believe it. And she'll never believe Garret would do the things he'll be doing. She'll ask me tons of questions. Plus, I was thinking we could get some of her film school friends in LA to help us make some fake videos."

"We have to be very careful about who we let in on this," Pearce says. "We don't want Harper interfering so she might need to be told, but we'll have to devise a story. She can't know the truth. And we don't need film school students. I already know people in film production who owe me some favors. In fact, Harper's father owes me one."

Pearce knows Harper's dad? I guess I do remember Garret saying Harper's parents had been to his house for some fundraisers. But why would her dad owe Pearce a favor? And why is Pearce willing to let Harper's dad know what we're doing but not Harper? It's another one of those things I probably don't want to know, so I don't ask. Even if I did, Pearce would never tell me.

We spend the rest of the afternoon brainstorming all the possible ways to make Garret lose public appeal. Pearce comes up with some really good ideas. He's clearly destroyed people in the past, which is a little disturbing but useful in the current situation. Arlin has some good ideas, too. Garret and I provide all the online and social media ideas since the two old guys aren't as familiar with how that works, although Pearce is pretty up to date on most of it.

When we're done, I feel a lot more confident. I'm not at all happy about the fake break-up between Garret and me, but I'm willing to do anything to make this work.

"How long do you think this will take?" I ask Pearce.

"The public will begin making their judgments about Garret after the first or second incident. We'll continue to feed the media negative articles, photos, and videos and hopefully, a couple months from now, most people will never want to see or hear another thing about him."

"And that's when the organization will make their decision," Arlin says. "Hopefully, they'll decide Garret's not worth the trouble to fix all the problems he's caused and they'll let him go."

There's some noise in the hallway and I look out thinking it's Katherine, but it's the maid. "Is Katherine going to know about this?"

"No, I don't want her involved," Pearce says. "She left about an hour ago for her parents' house in New York. She took Lilly with her, so if you'd like to stay here tonight, Jade, you can."

I almost jump for joy at his invite. Of course I want to stay. If Garret and I have to fake a break-up, this could be our last chance to be together for weeks, or months. Or forever if this plan doesn't work, but I'm not ready to consider that yet.

Garret puts his hand around mine and gives me a sideways glance. We both know I'll be expected to sleep in the guest room, but that won't stop me from sneaking down to Garret's room in the middle of the night.

"I'd love to stay. Thank you, Mr. Kensington."

"You can call me Pearce," he says. "And I should be thanking *you*. You might've just given my son a real life again."

"She's a very smart girl," Arlin says, smiling at me. "But what else would you expect? She is a Sinclair after all." He gets serious again. "Pearce, we need to discuss what to tell your father. He can't know about this. He'd never allow it."

Pearce nods. "Yes, I'll keep him out of it. I'll just go back to my role as the father who can't control his son. No offense, Garret, but your behavior in the past wasn't exactly something to be proud of."

"Yeah, I know, Dad."

"But your past will actually help us now because the people who know you will just assume you've gone back to your old ways. We can use your break-up with Jade as the catalyst. Your grandfather won't suspect a thing, although he will think poorly of you and I know his opinion of you matters."

"It's okay. I won't be bad forever."

Pearce stands up. "Well, it's getting late. Should we have some dinner? I thought it would just be me tonight, so I didn't have Charles make anything. But now that it's the four of us, I'll see what he can put together. Jade, do you have any requests?"

"Um, no. Whatever everyone else wants is fine." I'm surprised he's asking me that. Does he think I'm a picky eater?

Garret leans over and whispers. "You get to decide because you saved my ass with this plan of yours."

Pearce is still waiting for an answer.

"I could really go for a cheeseburger if it's not too much trouble."

"Burgers, huh?" Pearce smiles at me. "I think Charles can handle that. Katherine doesn't allow hamburgers, so this will be a real shock when I tell him."

"Katherine says burgers are poor people food," Garret explains as his dad walks out of the room. "So they're banned in the house."

"She banned pancakes, too. You and your dad need to take control of the menu."

"Poor people food? That's nonsense," Arlin says to Garret. "I'm worth more than your father and I enjoy a good burger on a regular basis."

I turn to Arlin. "That reminds me, I've been meaning to ask you, do you have an office in that pharmacy next to The Burger Hut?"

Garret starts laughing.

Arlin nods. "Yes, it's in the back. You were there. That's where I took you that day you passed out on campus."

"That's what I thought. But Garret and I went there later and the pharmacist acted like we were crazy."

"The employees don't know it's there. They think it's a maintenance closet. Royce made that room into an office last summer. I never understood why he wanted an office in some small town in Connecticut, but now I think he used it when he was here spying on you."

As he talks about Royce, I realize how strange it is that I'm sitting here with his father, right across the hall from where Royce tried to kill me. Arlin's son was shot dead in this very house just feet from where we're all sitting. And now Arlin is going to help Pearce, the man who killed his son, save Garret. It's all too weird.

"I'll be right back." Garret gets up from his chair. "I want to see Charles' reaction when my dad asks him to make burgers."

It's just Arlin and me left in the office which is awkward because I still don't know how I feel about him.

"So, Jade, I talked with my wife and told her you're willing to meet with her. She was very happy to hear that." Arlin looks down and smooths his tie. "She's, uh, well, she's cried nearly every day since she learned the truth about Royce. I haven't been able to console her. Grace is usually a very energetic, optimistic person, but after Royce passed, she just hasn't been herself. Then today, when I called and told her you were willing to meet her, she sounded like my wife again." He looks up. "Anyway, I appreciate you doing this. I know it might make you uncomfortable and I told her she may only get one meeting with you but—"

I put my hand on his. "Let's just see how it goes, okay? I was thinking we could meet for lunch. We could schedule it for next week sometime. Do you live around here?"

"Not here in Connecticut, but we have an apartment in Manhattan which is where I've been staying all week while I take care of some business. Grace and I actually have several homes but currently we're living at our home in Florida."

"Oh. Then we can just have lunch the next time you're both in town."

"We have a private plane. We just need to pick a time and Grace and I will fly up for the day."

Garret pops his head in the room. "Charles has the burgers started. He put some appetizers out if you want to come to the kitchen."

A half hour later, the four of us are eating burgers on fancy china plates in the formal dining room. If only Katherine could see this. I'd love to take a photo right now and send it to her.

Pearce has two cheeseburgers because he says it might be the last time he gets to eat a burger in his house. It's hard to believe how much control Katherine has over him. He doesn't like her but he's stuck married to her and for some reason he does what she says, at least when it comes to what they eat.

After dinner, Arlin and I make plans for lunch on Thursday and then he heads back to the city.

It's only 9, but I haven't slept for two days and Garret hasn't slept much either, so we decide to go to bed early. Besides, we both know I'll be sneaking in his room in a few hours and we could use a nap before then.

When we get upstairs, his dad is coming down the hall. I head to the guest room I've stayed in before and Garret goes to his room, which is at the very end of the hall.

Pearce stops me at the door to my room. "What are you doing?"

"I'm going to bed. I know it's early, but I'm really tired."

"You're not staying with Garret?"

I stare at Pearce like I heard him wrong. I glance down the hall and see Garret standing outside his door looking back at his dad.

"What?" Pearce smiles. "You think I don't know what goes on in the middle of the night?" I blush what I'm sure is a shade of bright red. "Just go down there, Jade."

"But I wasn't going to—"

"You haven't seen each other in a week and the next few months you'll have to spend apart." He motions to the end of the hall. "Go stay with Garret. I'm sure you two will just watch some TV and go to bed, right?" He's trying not to laugh.

"Come on, Jade," Garret calls out. "Let's watch TV."

My face is now burning hot. It's not like Pearce doesn't know his son and I are having sex, but the fact that he acknowledged it right in front of us is so embarrassing.

"Goodnight, you two." Pearce turns and goes downstairs. I hurry to Garret's room, shut the door, and collapse on the bed.

"I can't believe your dad just said that!"

"You're bright red." Garret's laughing at me. "It's not a big deal, Jade. We're adults."

"Yeah, but parents are supposed to ban it under their own roof. You have to be married before they let you sleep in the same room. It's in the parent handbook."

"These are special circumstances. Like he said, we can't be together until this is over."

I groan. "I feel like I've been given a conjugal visit or something. Your dad was basically telling us to do it! He probably thinks we're doing it right now!" I flip on my stomach and bury my face in the pillow.

"You're getting too worked up about this." Garret continues to laugh at me. I feel the mattress sink in as he lies beside me. "Jade, are you falling asleep?" He rubs my back.

"Yes," I mumble, my voice muffled by the pillow.

"Do you want one of my t-shirts to sleep in?"

I lift my head up. "Crap! I don't have pajamas. Now your dad will think I'm sleeping naked in here. That's just great!" I fall back into the pillow.

"I'm sure he's not thinking about that." Garret moves my hair aside so he can see my face. "Can I at least have a kiss goodnight?"

I flip over on my back and see him propped up on his forearm, gazing down at me, his aqua blue eyes no longer red and groggy but gorgeous and inviting. His hand rests on my stomach as he leans down and kisses me.

I close my eyes and focus on the feel of his hand on my lower abs, the warmth of his breath on my face, the mix of sensations flooding my core each time his lips brush mine. It brings my body to life and I forget all about being tired. I pull him closer until I can feel the weight of his body over mine.

"I thought you were going to sleep," he says between kisses.

"Sleep can wait."

I lift his shirt up and he takes it off. I gaze at his ripped abs as he strips off my clothes. He lies over me again as we kiss. His warm, smooth skin feels so good I could lie like this for hours. But maybe later. Right now my body is aching for him. His mouth moves to my breast, licking, teasing, and setting my entire body on fire. I undo his jeans. He gets up and quickly takes them off along with his boxer briefs. The sight of him naked gets my insides all tingly, yearning to be with him. I yank him back on top of me.

"You in a hurry?" He gives me a sexy smile.

"Yes."

He shifts to the side and slips his hand between my legs. "But I'm just getting started." He whispers it by my ear and a shiver runs through me.

"I know but . . ." I always find it hard to talk when he does these things to me.

"Tell me what you want, Jade."

I pull his hand away. "You. Right now."

He flashes that smile again as he gets back on top of me. With one thrust he's inside me and his lips crash into mine. I wrap my legs around him and he reaches his hand under my hip and draws us even closer as he says my name in a low, sexy groan. We begin to move together in a perfect rhythm until we both can't take the mounting tension a second longer. We finish at nearly the same time, our bodies wet with sweat.

Garret rests his head on my shoulder and I feel him softly kissing it. "I'm so damn in love with you, Jade."

"I love you, too."

After a few minutes, I gently push on him to move. "I could really use a shower. Can you get up?"

He lifts his head and grins. "I could if you wait a couple more minutes."

I brush his hair off his forehead and smile at him. "I asked if you could get up, not get *it* up."

"I thought you were inviting me in the shower with you." He doesn't move, but instead leaves kisses along my collarbone.

"If you want to you can, but I'm only planning on showering."

"Yeah, okay." He says it like it's a challenge.

We get up and go into the walk-in shower. I don't know if it's from months of dating a swimmer or that first kiss we had in the pool or what, but I find water to be like some type of potent aphrodisiac. Garret knows this, which is why he invited himself to shower with me.

As soon as I feel the slickness of his skin, see the beads of water forming along his broad shoulders, and slide my tongue past his wet lips, I lose all control. Before I know it, my legs are locked around him, my arms go around his neck, and we're doing it against the shower wall. With the water and the steam, it's even hotter than doing it in the bed. I hold onto him as we hit the peak of pure intoxicating pleasure, me first and him following seconds later.

Garret turns off the shower and sets me down. I rest my body on his as he reaches out to get the towels. He wraps one around me but I won't move. I'm too comfy, leaned against him, savoring the feel of his warm skin and the steam that still surrounds us.

He laughs. "Jade, are you falling asleep on me while standing up?"

"I think so."

"Let's get you to bed." He dries me off, then dries himself off and helps me out of the shower. I wake up enough to walk to the bed while he grabs one of his super soft t-shirts from his drawer.

"I don't have any clean underwear," I say as he puts the shirt on me.

"You don't need it. This is plenty long on you." He kisses me. "And it'll make things easier when we do this again in a few hours."

I kiss him back. "That's true."

Even though I've reached a level of exhaustion I've never felt before, I'll sacrifice another night of sleep to be with him because I have no idea when we'll be together again.

"Garret, what are we going to do?"

"About what?" He's at his dresser pulling out his pajama pants. He doesn't bother with boxers or a shirt.

"About this? Kissing? Sex? I can't go months without any physical contact."

He slides under the covers next to me and nuzzles my neck. "Maybe my dad could arrange some conjugal visits."

I playfully hit him. "I'm serious."

"So am I. If Katherine and Lilly aren't here, we could take separate cars and meet here. We'll have the car service take us. Nobody will see us with the dark windows."

"You think your dad would go for that?"

"Why wouldn't he? He did just now."

"But you have all these people working here. They could tell someone."

"Yeah, that's true. I guess it won't work, but let's not worry about it right now."

I yawn. "I really wish I could stay awake, but I think I'm falling asleep."

"It's okay, Jade," he says softly. "Just go to sleep." He kisses my head and hugs me closer, the back of my body fitting perfectly into the front of his.

I'm going to miss this. I'm going to miss it a lot.

CHAPTER NINETEEN

Around 3 in the morning, I wake up from a really hot dream starring Garret and me in the pool and I can't help myself. I'm ready for more. I kiss him until he slowly wakes up.

"What time is it?" he whispers, turning to me.

"Time for this." I slip my hand down his pajama pants.

The blue lights strung around his bedroom window are on, giving off enough of a glow that I can see him smiling, his eyes still closed. He stretches his arms out. "You're waking me up for sex? I swear you're the perfect woman, Jade. Did I mention how much I love you?"

"Yeah, you did. Now show me."

And he does.

Afterward, we fall sleep again and don't wake up until noon.

"I'm surprised your dad didn't get us up," I say.

"He knows better than to do that. He doesn't want to walk in on us doing something."

I sit up straight. "Didn't you lock the door last night?"

"I don't remember," he says, yawning.

I get up to check. "Garret, it's unlocked! Someone could've walked right in. Your dad. The maid."

"The mailman. The gardener. The delivery guy."

"This is so not funny. You have no shame, you know that? You walk around naked. You leave doors unlocked."

"I'm at my house, Jade. I'm not worried about people walking in my room seeing me naked or having sex."

"Well, I am." I lock the door.

"You feel better now?"

"Yes."

"Then why don't you come back to bed?"

He's sitting up, his arms casually resting over his bent knees, which are covered with the white sheet. The combo of his strong arms, chiseled chest, and muscular shoulders is so damn appealing. Add in the tousled dark hair, those beautiful blue eyes, and that perfect smile and he's like a male model. I could take a photo of him right now and put it on a calendar and it would easily sell millions of copies.

There's no way I'm turning down his invitation, especially now that the door's locked.

After another round of sex, we finally get out of bed, dress, and go downstairs to the kitchen.

Pearce is there and I feel like I'm doing the walk of shame, stuck in the same clothes as last night. But it's all I have and I'm not borrowing something of Katherine's.

"Hey, Dad," Garret says.

Pearce looks at both of us and I feel my cheeks heating up again. Garret, of course, isn't the least bit embarrassed.

"Did you eat yet?" Garret asks him.

Pearce smiles. "Yes, Garret. I've already had breakfast and lunch. It's 1 in the afternoon."

"Yeah, okay. Well, I'm gonna have breakfast." Garret walks over to the fridge. "What do you want, Jade?"

Why is he asking me questions? I'm trying to fade into the wall here or dissolve into the floor. Anything to not be noticed.

"You two eat and then come to my office," Pearce says. "I have some updates to share." He refills the cup of coffee he's holding and walks out.

Garret comes over to me. "You didn't answer me. You want breakfast or lunch?"

"Whatever. Breakfast is fine." I cover my face with my hands.

"Are you seriously still embarrassed?" He pulls my hands away and kisses me.

"Did you see how your dad looked at me? And that comment he made about it being the afternoon? He thinks I'm some nymphomaniac!"

Garret laughs and kisses me again. "You *are* a nymphomaniac. It's another thing I love about you. Now let's figure out breakfast."

He goes back to the refrigerator and starts pulling stuff out; eggs, cheese, green peppers. "I'm making an omelet. You want one? I make really good omelets."

"I'll just have cereal."

"That's not enough. You need to replenish your body after that sex marathon we had last night."

"Garret! Someone could hear you." I look around to make sure nobody's there.

He rolls his eyes and shakes his head. "I'm still waiting for an answer here."

"Okay, I'll have an omelet."

He whips up two omelets and some toast and we sit and eat breakfast at the kitchen island.

"You're a good cook," I tell him.

"Thanks," he says, biting into his toast.

His cooking reminds me of our plan to live together and a wave of disappointment goes through me. "I just thought of something."

"Let me guess. Now that your stomach's full you want to go have sex again."

I punch him. "No! That's not at all what I was thinking."

He shrugs. "Yeah, whatever, my little nympho girlfriend." He tenses up, preparing to be punched again but I leave him alone.

"What I was *really* thinking is that now we can't get an apartment together next fall."

"Why not?"

"Because people would think it's weird if bad-boy Garret went from having a different girl every night to living with just one."

"I'm hoping by then people will have lost interest in me." He gets up and takes the juice carafe from the fridge. "You want some more?"

"Sure." I hold my glass out. It's fresh-squeezed juice, not the canned stuff I had as a kid that wasn't even juice but more like orange-colored sugar water.

"Besides, I'm not planning on going back to Moorhurst next year." He puts the juice back in the fridge and comes back around to his seat.

"You're not? When did you decide this?"

"Yesterday. When we were in my dad's office."

"Why you didn't you tell me?"

"I'm telling you now." He shoves his plate aside and turns to me. "I think we both should leave Moorhurst and get a fresh start somewhere else. Too many people at school know our history. And if we show up there in the fall, they'll start gossiping and spreading stories about us and I'll end up on the front page of a celebrity magazine again. I can't have that, Jade. When this is over, I can't reappear in the press. I need to hide out somewhere quiet and let people forget about me."

"Where do you plan to go?"

"I don't know yet. But I'm not going anywhere unless you're going with me. So what do you think? Would you be okay leaving Moorhurst?"

"I'd miss Harper, but yeah, I could leave. It's a good school but you're right about the people. They gossip too much and I've never really felt like I fit in there. But we'd still go to college, right?"

He picks up our plates and takes them to the sink. "Well, yeah. But we need to find a small private college where people have no interest in me and are more focused on academics than celebrity gossip and reality shows."

"And we'd still get an apartment together?"

"Yes." He comes back over and lifts me up and into his arms. "We'll definitely get an apartment together."

"And you'll do all the cooking?"

His eyebrows raise. "I'm pretty sure I never agreed to that."

I tilt my head. "But you're so good at it."

"I'm good at a lot of things, but that doesn't mean I want to do them all the time." He pauses when he sees me smiling. "Okay maybe some things I want to do all the time, but not cooking."

"I'll do the laundry if you do the cooking."

"Hmm. Okay, but I think you got the better deal."

I got a *way* better deal. Laundry is easy. The machine does all the work. I'll just have to fold and put clothes away which is so much easier than cooking something.

Garret and I go down to his dad's office but Pearce is on the phone. We wait for him to finish his call then go sit down.

"So here's what's going to happen." Pearce goes into a detailed plan of what will transpire this week. I'll tell people at Moorhurst that I broke up with Garret over spring break. Then the story will be that Garret was so upset over the break-up, he took his dad's plane to Bermuda and rented a house on the beach. While in Bermuda, Garret got drunk, hooked up with some girls, and trashed the house he rented.

Pearce shows us some fake photos he already had made up. They look so real I almost punch Garret, like he really cheated on me.

When the rest of the world sees these photos, they won't be thinking he cheated on me because they don't know me. Instead they'll think he was cheating on Ava which is what will get people talking and spread the story across the Internet.

Pearce gets out his laptop and plays footage of a fake interview from the fake homeowner in Bermuda who rented his house to Garret. The homeowner describes how Garret destroyed his house last week and left condoms, marijuana joints, and broken liquor bottles on the beach behind his property.

"I did a lot of bad shit in just a few days," Garret says. "You sure people will believe that?"

"The public doesn't know you so yes, they'll believe it," Pearce says. "You already have the image of a privileged trust fund kid, which the public usually finds unappealing. But for the reasons we learned about on Friday, people are able to look past that with you. They think you're different. What we're doing here is showing them you're not. You're just a selfish, spoiled, rich kid who does what he wants and doesn't care who or what he destroys in the process."

"Yeah, but people who know me will think it doesn't make sense."

"That's where Jade comes in. The people closest to you know your past, so when Jade breaks up with you, it makes sense that you'd go back to this type of behavior. It's not like people forgot what you used to be like."

"I was never that bad," Garret assures me.

His dad's expression seems to disagree with that statement.

"What happens after this story gets out?" Garret asks his dad.

"It's already out. People are already talking about it online. Now we just keep it going. You'll need to hide out every weekend so people at Moorhurst buy into the stories about all the wild weekends you'll be having. I got you a small house in the woods not far from here. It's very secluded. You'll go there every Friday night and stay there until Sunday night or Monday morning. You'll need to stay there the whole time. You can't be seen in public."

"Can Jade meet me there?"

"No. Absolutely not. It's too risky. And Jade, you need to hang out with your girlfriends. Do whatever girls do after a break-up. And I agree that Harper may not buy the break-up story, so I came up with something to tell her."

He goes over the details and tells me to give the same story to Frank and Ryan, who would also be suspicious of the break-up.

"So that's it for now," Pearce says. "Oh, and Jade, you can take your car back to school. If anyone asks how you got it, just tell them I bought it for you as a congratulatory gift for doing so well in your classes. In the past I've given my scholarship recipients gifts for excelling in their first year. Nothing this big, but given you were dating my son, people shouldn't question it too much."

"Okay." I say it calmly, but inside I'm jumping up and down. I finally get to drive the car! I finally *have* a car! It still doesn't seem real. "But what if Garret's fans see me when I drive out?"

"They're not out there. As soon as we posted the story about Garret being in Bermuda, the fans and photographers went away." Pearce stands up. "It's time for you two to say goodbye." His eyes dart from Garret to me and back to Garret. "A short goodbye, son, meaning stay downstairs. Jade needs to leave now. She needs to be seen on campus as people start arriving back from break. You'll show up there later tonight."

Good thing Pearce isn't looking at me because I'm sure I'm blushing. Did he really think Garret and I would go upstairs and have sex again? Like we haven't done it enough already? Okay, he's probably right, but still.

We go out into the foyer, closing the door to Pearce's office. Garret gets his phone out and sends a text. "Brad's bringing your car around. It'll just be a minute. You sure you're okay to drive? It's been a week since I checked for any concussion symptoms."

"I'm good. I haven't had any symptoms."

He gets up close and gazes into my eyes. "Who am I?"

"Not the questions again." I laugh, then get serious, playing along. "You're the jerk who trashed some guy's house in Bermuda and did it with two girls you just met."

"Nope. Sorry. You're too confused to drive." He gets his phone out again. "I'll text Brad and tell him to leave the car in the garage."

"Wait! Let me try again."

Garret slides his phone in his pocket and circles his arms around my waist. "When's my birthday?"

"August 22."

He kisses me and keeps his lips on mine as he asks another question. "My favorite color?"

"Green."

It earns me another kiss, this one longer.

"Sports I played in high school?"

I squeeze my eyes shut. "Swimming, football, basketball, baseball, soccer, and lacrosse."

"Correct." He gives me one last lingering kiss. When he starts to break away I hold on, not ready for it to end. Because what if this really is the end? We have to be apart from now until that group makes their decision, and what if their decision doesn't change?

"Jade." Garret pulls back. "We'll be here all day if we don't stop."

"I know. But what if this is it?"

"Don't start thinking that way. You need to stay positive. And we'll still see each other. We live in the same dorm. Eat in the same dining hall."

"But I can't talk to you or touch you or—"

"Yeah, it's gonna suck, but we can do this."

I nod, then look up at him. "One more kiss?"

We come together for one final kiss and I feel us both struggling to end it. Eventually he does. "Now get out there and drive your new car."

He turns me around and opens the door and there it is all shiny and new. "I'm so excited I can finally drive it!" I step outside.

"You forgot your coat. Wait here. I'll go get it."

When he returns I'm in the car, buckled in and ready to go. I roll the window down and he hands me my coat. "So I guess a final goodbye hug is out."

"Oh, just a second." I undo my seatbelt and get back out to hug him.

"I love you." He squeezes me tight, then lets me go.

"I love you, too."

Garret holds the car door open. "Okay, now you can go."

I get back in and drive away. The parade of girls is gone, just like Mr. Kensington said, along with the photographers.

Back at Moorhurst, I go to my room and find my suitcase still sitting unpacked next to my closet. As I'm putting my stuff away, I call Harper.

She answers on the second ring. "Jade, come down to my room."

"I didn't know you were here. I thought you were still at Sean's."

I wait for her to respond but she already hung up the phone, so I walk down to her room. Her door is open and as soon as I walk in she grabs me for a hug.

"Hey, neighbor!" She lets me go and I shut the door. "I still can't believe we're going to be living next to each other all summer. My parents can't wait to meet you guys. They have the greatest summer parties. Full of A-list stars. We're totally going to at least a couple of them."

"You look great, Harper. You always do, but today you're almost glowing."

"Because I'm in love." She spins around with her arms out which makes me laugh, but also makes me sad because it reminds me how much I love Garret and how I can't be with him.

"Sean is so great." She stops spinning. "You know how taking a trip with someone can be super stressful? You're tired. You get on each other's nerves. You start fighting. We didn't do any of that. Even at the airport when that asshole delayed our flight, Sean was so cool about it. He kept me calm the whole time and made up these silly games every time I complained about being bored. God, I love him." She gazes dreamily at a spot on the wall behind me.

"Um, Harper." I get in her line of vision to wake her out of her trance.

"Oh. Sorry. So where's Garret? I thought the three of us could go out to eat. Sean can't come with us because he had to go to the restaurant to prep for tomorrow."

"Yeah, about that. Garret's still at his parents' house."

"Why? I figured you two would've been shacked up in his room since the second you got back."

"I need to talk to you about something. And you can't tell anyone about this. Even Sean."

She hesitates because she doesn't like keeping secrets from Sean. "Okay, I won't tell anyone."

"Garret and I broke up."

CHAPTER TWENTY

"What?" Harper grabs my shoulders, almost knocking me over. "When did this happen?"

"It's not real. It's just an act so I can stay out of this media frenzy he's got going on right now."

She pulls me over to sit on her bed. "But that's been going on for months. Why are you doing this now?"

"Because it's gotten really bad. The photographers are getting really aggressive. I've already been hurt once by those guys and if they found out I was dating Garret they'd start following me around."

It's the fake story Garret's dad gave me, and from her expression and nodding, Harper seems to be buying it.

"Garret's dad should just sue the show. That would stop all of this."

"It's not just the show. Garret's got tons of fans now and fans buy magazines, so even when the show ends the photographers will still be following him around wanting to get his picture."

"How long does this fake break-up have to last?"

"Long enough for the fans to stop caring about Garret so the photographers will leave him alone. It could be months."

"So you guys can't spend the summer in California?"

"I'm still going, but Garret probably won't be able to."

"Jade, this totally sucks. How are you going to go all those months without being together? Can you meet somewhere private so you could at least hang out a little?"

"Probably not. We can't risk people seeing us together. I'm not even supposed to call him. And just so you know, Garret's going to be doing some strange things during our fake break-up."

"Like what?"

I describe how Pearce hired people to purposely make Garret look bad so people won't like him. And how in the next few months she may see photos of him or read stuff online that will make him seem like a jerk but that none of it is real.

"That'll just make people even more interested in him," she says.

"If he were a real celebrity it might. But once the reality show ends, he'll go back to being a regular guy and start losing some of his fans. We're hoping the fans he has left will get tired of him being a jerk and will eventually lose interest in him."

Harper's right. The plan could make Garret even more popular. But being popular because you trash hotel rooms or crash cars won't make you a popular presidential candidate someday. And that's all we care about. Of course I can't tell Harper that.

"Doing that will ruin his reputation," Harper says. "It could mess up the rest of his life. Or at least the next few years."

"He's willing to risk it. He doesn't want to keep living this way. You should see how many texts and phone messages he gets. He changes his number and his fans still find him. And he can't leave his house without photographers following him around."

"Yeah, my sister has the same problem. The paparazzi are already taking photos of her and her movie hasn't even come out yet. But they haven't been aggressive like they've been with Garret. They keep their distance and shoot from across the street, so it hasn't been that bad."

"Remember that you can't tell anyone about this, including Sean. Just tell him that I broke up with Garret and that Garret didn't take it well and that's why he started partying and drinking again."

Harper's eyes narrow. "Okay, but I wouldn't do this for anyone else. I've never lied to Sean and I hate doing it now."

"I know, but I really need you to keep this a secret. Even Garret's stepmom doesn't know the truth."

"This is so weird. But I understand why Garret's doing it."

"I just hope we won't have to do this for very long. The fake break-up just started and I already miss him."

"I'm sorry." She pouts her lips, then scoots off the bed and races over to her suitcase. "I have some gifts that might cheer you up."

"Harper, you didn't have to get me anything."

"I didn't." She sorts through the clothes in her suitcase taking certain items out and forming a pile off to the side. "These are some more freebies my sister got."

I go over and sit next to her on the floor. "Did you bring me more t-shirts?"

"A few t-shirts, a few more skirts, a couple casual dresses, some bikinis." She holds up a neon green bikini that Garret would love and I can't even model it for him. There's also a red one, a hot pink one, and a white one.

"I know this skirt looks kind of frumpy, but I have one just like it and it's totally cute on." She hands me a white, cotton skirt with an elastic waist. "And I really love this dress. I wish it was in my size, but it'll look great on you."

I take the dress and hold it up. It's a short, navy blue, sleeveless knit dress. It's more sporty than fancy, so definitely my kind of dress.

When she's done making me a pile of new clothes she insists I try them all on which is good because it's something to do. It's better than sitting in my room wondering what Garret is doing and wishing I could be with him.

"You should wear that to dinner," Harper says.

I have on a dark denim mini skirt with a light blue sweater. The sweater is super soft and comfortable. Harper knows exactly what I'd buy if I had money to buy new clothes. She could be a personal shopper.

"I don't have the right shoes for this," I tell her, checking myself out in the mirror.

"Shoes! I almost forgot." She opens another suitcase and pulls out several pairs of shoes; a few pairs of sandals, and some shoes that are almost like sneakers but nicer. "I knew you'd say you didn't have shoes, so here. Now you don't have any excuses. Put these on and let's go." She hands me the sneaker-like shoes.

"Where are we going for dinner?" As I ask I remember my empty wallet that was drained by the taxi ride to Garret's house. "I can't go. Sorry, I'm out of money. I had to take a taxi earlier and—"

"It's my treat. Don't worry about it. You know my family's loaded and you never let me pay for anything." She's at the mirror, applying lip gloss and smacking her lips together.

"Because you shouldn't pay. I should pay for myself."

"I thought you agreed never to mention the money thing again." Now she's adjusting her ponytail which always takes forever. She has to get it just right. Not too high, but not too low.

"That was only with Garret."

"Well, I'm making it a rule with me, too. No more complaining if I offer to pay for stuff. I'm not saying I'll pay all the time, but tonight I want to take my friend out for dinner. And don't say it has to be fast food because I don't feel like having that tonight." Her ponytail is finally where she wants it. She turns away from the mirror and grabs her purse, linking her arm with mine and dragging me out of her room.

"Where are you taking me?"

"I haven't decided yet. Maybe a sushi place."

"Ugh," I mumble.

She laughs as we go outside. "I was kidding. I know you hate sushi."

It's 7 now and everyone appears to be back from break. The parking lot is packed with cars.

Harper gets her keys out. "There weren't many spots left, so I had to park down by Lisker Hall."

When we get to her SUV a car pulls into the space next to hers just as I'm going around to the passenger side. The bright headlights blind me and I shield my eyes while I wait for the driver to turn the car off. I look up and see that it's a black BMW. Garret's car. Seriously? What are the odds? I sigh as I watch him get out of the car.

People are all around us on the sidewalk and in the parking lot, so it's time to start playing my role of the ex-girlfriend, but it's freaking hard when he's right there and I just want to run up and kiss him.

I'm not sure what to do. Ignore him? Say hi? We should've discussed this before I left his house. Harper's waiting inside her SUV and even though it's dark out I'm sure she sees it's Garret who pulled in next to her. I walk to the side of the SUV. Garret's standing there, pretending to look at his phone.

"New outfit?" he asks, his eyes still on the phone.

"Yeah. It's from Harper." I smell his cologne and out of habit I step closer to him. He shouldn't be allowed to smell that good when we're not dating.

"I like it." He's trying not to look, but I catch him staring at my bare legs, then up to my fitted sweater and it totally turns me on.

"Kensington!" a guy yells out. He's standing on the sidewalk in front of Garret's car. "I gotta hear about Bermuda. Two girls at the same time? Was that shit true?"

Obviously the fake stories about Garret are already spreading.

"I should go." I put my hand on the door handle but don't open it.

"Hey, Shane," Garret says to the guy. "I'll tell you about it upstairs."

Garret's hand brushes the back of my skirt as he walks away.

I quickly get in the car before I lose all control.

"What did you say to him?" Harper whispers as if the people outside could somehow hear us talking in the car.

"Nothing." I put my seatbelt on.

"You said *something*. The way he was looking at you I thought you two were going to jump in his car and do it."

"He just hadn't seen me wear this before so he asked if it was new."

She starts the car and backs out. "I don't know how this fake break-up is going to work. It's obvious you two can't get enough of each other. Maybe I need to give you some acting tips. I took lessons growing up. It's basically a requirement for a kid in LA."

"Yeah, I think you might have to. This is harder than I thought."

Our brief encounter in the parking lot just proved it. Being forbidden from Garret made me hyperaware of everything about him. The pitch of his voice. His scent. His proximity to me. He barely touched me and my body got all hot and tingly.

"Jade." Harper says my name in a way that sounds like she's already said it several times.

"Did you say something?"

"I was thinking of going to Fresh, that organic restaurant. But it's like 20 miles away. Are you in a hurry to get back?"

"No. That sounds good." The farther away I am from Garret right now the better.

By the time we drive there, eat, and drive back it's 9 o'clock. I thank Harper for dinner, then go to my room and watch my new TV. It's still strange to have a TV in my room but I'm really glad Garret got it for me. It'll hopefully take my mind off him.

Or maybe not.

As I'm flipping through the channels, I see a photo of Garret on Hollywood Today, a celebrity news show.

"Garret Kensington, on-again, off-again boyfriend of Ava Hamilton, star of The Prep School Girls' Reunion, had quite a spring break," the perky blond show host says. "Rumor has it he traveled to Bermuda on his father's jet and hooked up with numerous women, despite recently getting back together with Ava. Fans of the reality show are saying Ava deserves better, but for now it seems that she and Garret are still together."

They cut away to Ava walking through a parking lot wearing big sunglasses, tight dark jeans, and a low-cut black sweater.

"Garret's always been a bad boy," she says, tossing her hair around as she walks. "I can't change him. It's one of the reasons I fell in love with him. I've always been attracted to bad boys."

"So you're still dating him?" someone off camera asks. The camera shakes a little as the cameraman tries to keep up with her.

"Yes." She gets into a black SUV and drives off.

They cut back to the show host. "Sources say Kensington nearly destroyed the house he rented in Bermuda and trashed the beach behind the property."

They cut to the fake footage I watched earlier in Pearce's office. An old man with a deep tan and white hair says, "That kid broke everything in my house and left the place uninhabitable. I won't be able to rent it out again for months. And then he doesn't even apologize. His parents should be ashamed."

The host appears again. "We contacted Kensington's PR rep but haven't received a response. Stay tuned for more updates."

I flip the channel and find an old movie to watch just as my phone rings.

"Jade, are you okay?" It's Frank. I totally forgot to tell him the story I told Harper.

"Yeah, why?"

"Chloe just called Ryan and said that Garret was in Bermuda destroying some guy's house." Frank doesn't mention the girls.

Ryan picks up the other phone. "That asshole's cheating on you! I swear, I'm going to kill him!"

"Both of you need to calm down and let me explain."

I tell them the made-up story I told Harper.

"We didn't realize the fans and the photographers had become so aggressive," Frank says. "I know it'll be tough for you to be away from Garret, but I think it's for the best, honey."

Once I'm convinced Frank and Ryan bought the story, I say goodbye and watch the rest of the movie. But my mind wanders to the situation I'm now stuck in. It's hard to fathom that just a few days ago everything was going great, and today I'm part of a conspiracy to make Garret one of the most hated men in America. Not to mention the fact that I'm one of the few people who know that our presidents are chosen by a small group of rich, powerful people and not the public. It's a secret I wish I didn't know and one I can never tell anyone. Doing so would definitely get me killed. Not that anyone would believe me.

Monday morning I check my phone and find three messages from Carson. I'm sure he heard the Garret news by now and can't wait to ask me about it. Or more accurately, he can't wait to gloat. This is like a Christmas present for him. Garret misbehaving? I'm surprised Carson didn't text me *'I told u so'* a thousand times.

I arrive at physics class with not a minute to spare hoping to avoid any pre-class conversation with Carson. But then the professor is late. Of course.

"I'm sorry about Garret," Carson says when he sees me. He doesn't sound the least bit sorry.

"It's no big deal." I pull my laptop from my bag and set it up on the table.

"No big deal? Did you hear what he did?"

"Yes. But he can do whatever he wants. We're not together anymore." I don't look at him as I get my laptop fired up. "I broke up with him last week. That's why Garret is acting this way. He didn't want us to break up."

Carson is quiet and when I glance over at him, he's staring at me like he doesn't believe me.

"Listen, Carson. I didn't tell you about this during our road trip because I didn't want another one of your lectures about

Garret and how I never should've dated him. So on the drive back here, I just pretended to be calling and texting Garret but I really wasn't."

"You could've told me. I wouldn't have lectured you. I swear. Do you want to go somewhere after class and talk about it?"

"No, I'm okay. I had a lot of time over the break to think about things and although part of me still loves Garret, it just wasn't working. I don't fit in his world. He knows that. He just doesn't accept it."

"Are you still talking to him?"

"I haven't since we broke up, but I'm not going to ignore him. If I see him on campus I'll still say hi and be friendly. It's not like I hate him."

"Even after what he did last week?"

"I knew he was like that when I met him. You've heard the stories about him from high school. He likes to drink and party and be with lots of different girls. He gave that up when he was with me, but now that I'm gone it makes sense that he would do that stuff again. I can't worry about what he does."

"Sorry I'm late everyone." The professor appears, hurrying to the front of the room. "Bring out today's notes and let's get started."

After class Carson walks back to the dorms with me. "You want to have dinner with me tonight?"

He's asking me out already? Wow. I thought he'd at least wait a couple weeks.

"I'm not ready to start dating again."

"Dating? I thought we'd just eat at my dining hall. I wasn't asking you out. I just didn't want you sitting alone at dinner. That's all."

"Oh." I stop in front of my building. "Well, I usually eat dinner with Harper."

"Then maybe some other night. See ya, Jade." He turns and walks off to his dorm.

Despite what he said, his invitation seemed like a date. An innocent meal in the dining hall would lead to a meal at a restaurant and then a movie and soon we'd be dating, at least in Carson's eyes.

I hadn't considered all the ramifications of not dating Garret. I'm single again, which means guys might ask me out.

This fake break-up is getting even more complicated.

CHAPTER TWENTY-ONE

The next few days I try to occupy every minute so my mind doesn't drift to Garret. I haven't seen him on campus or in the dining hall. He's changed the route he takes to class and his eating schedule to avoid running into me. And thank goodness he did because I'm so Garret-deprived right now I'd probably jump him in the cafeteria if I saw him there. I'm so worried about that actually happening—well, not about jumping him, but more like kissing him with maybe a little groping—that I've actually been practicing how I'll react when I finally do run into him.

On Thursday I go to morning classes, then drive to a restaurant in town to meet Arlin and Grace for lunch. I'm really nervous. Although Arlin is nice, I have no idea what his wife is like. If she's like Royce's wife, the only other Mrs. Sinclair I've met, I'm in trouble. I didn't like that woman at all. When she met me, she immediately asked for my last name so she could assess how much money I was worth. And when she didn't recognize the name as being anything of value, she looked at me like I was just that—of no value, completely worthless. If she only knew I was her husband's daughter.

I'm meeting Arlin and Grace at a small cafe that's in an old house. Not a run-down old house, but a historic house that's been turned into a restaurant. I've been there one time with Garret. The food is good but it's expensive. The chef makes up the menu each day and there are only four or five items to choose from. The last time I was here it was filled with people around Arlin's age and today is the same.

I tell the hostess I'm meeting Arlin Sinclair and her face suddenly perks up and a huge smile appears. "Yes, right this way." She leads me to their table.

"Mr. Sinclair, Mrs. Sinclair. Your guest has arrived." She quickly walks away, almost like she's nervous. I'm guessing she knows that Grace and Arlin are billionaires and it has her on edge. She probably wishes she was the waitress getting a tip from these people. I wonder who she thinks *I* am. She must assume I'm important if I'm eating lunch with these two. That would explain the overly enthusiastic greeting she gave me at the hostess stand.

Arlin stands up along with his wife. She's very small, not more than 5'2, with delicate features. Her straight, chestnut-brown hair hits just below her chin, styled in a clean-cut bob just like she had in the photo Arlin showed me. She has on a plum-colored, short-sleeved dress with a patterned scarf draped across the neckline.

"Jade, good to see you again," Arlin says. "This is my wife, Grace."

She extends her hand and smiles. "Hello, Jade. I'm so happy to finally meet you."

I can already tell she's not like the other Mrs. Sinclair. I can hear the sincerity in her voice and see it in her eyes. She really *is* happy to meet me.

Arlin motions for us to sit down. We're at a small round table that barely fits four people. One of the chairs has been removed, so I center myself in the space that's left so that Arlin and Grace are across from me.

The table is silent. This is awkward. For all of us.

"Should we go ahead and order?" Arlin asks, breaking the silence.

We all look down at the small paper menu that lists today's entrees. Everything here is gourmet, so even if it sounds normal it will have some special sauce or strange ingredient that turns it into something you're not expecting. The waitress arrives and I order a sandwich, Arlin orders the salmon, and Grace gets a salad.

Then we sit there again in silence. Grace keeps staring at me. She's probably noticing the similarity of our eye color. Our eyes are the exact same shade of green. My mom didn't have green eyes and neither did Royce, so it must only show up when two recessive genes come together.

"So Jade, how is school?" Grace asks. She's still smiling and it's a very real smile, unlike the fake one I got from the other Mrs. Sinclair.

"School is great. I like all my classes. My professors are really good."

"And what are you studying?" She unfolds her napkin and places it on her lap, so I do the same.

"Just general studies for now."

"What classes are you taking this semester?"

"Chemistry, microbiology, physics, sociology, and European history."

"That sounds like quite a workload."

"It's not too bad."

The waitress brings a basket of rolls and I take one, then realize they're probably meant to go with Arlin's salmon and

Grace's salad, not my sandwich. Oh well, they don't seem to care.

"You're taking a lot of science courses. Are you planning on pursuing a career in science?"

Grace asks this just as I'm taking a bite of the roll. I finish chewing then say, "Yes, I'm thinking of going to med school."

Arlin and Grace smile even wider, looking at each other then back at me.

"Jade, that's wonderful," Arlin says.

"Yes. You're clearly a very bright young woman," Grace says. "I barely passed chemistry when I was in college."

I ask her where she went to college, which keeps the conversation going for a good 10 minutes. Then Arlin tells me about *his* college days just as our meals arrive.

Now that we're all talking I'm feeling more relaxed. As we eat I tell them about Frank and Ryan and growing up in Des Moines. I don't mention my mom and they don't mention Royce. Those are off-limit topics, at least for now while we're getting to know each other.

When the waitress clears our plates, Arlin insists we get dessert. I was planning to leave so I could look over my notes for a quiz I have later. But I can tell Grace wants me to stay longer, so I order the chocolate torte. During dessert I ask Grace what she does when she's in Florida and she tells me all about her flower gardens. She says she's a Master Gardener, whatever that is.

"If you'd ever like to come visit we'd love to have you," Grace says, sipping her cappuccino.

"Yes, anytime, Jade," Arlin says. "You can take our private plane."

"I'll think about it. I'm pretty busy with school right now so I don't know." Although they both seem really nice, I'm not sure if I'm ready to go to their house for a visit. "I should really be getting back to campus. I have chem lab at 1."

Grace quickly sets her cup down and pats her lips with her napkin. "Yes, of course. We didn't mean to keep you."

"It's okay." I get up and put my jacket on. Arlin and Grace push their chairs out and come around the table to stand in front of me. "Thank you for lunch." I smile awkwardly, not sure how to end this.

Arlin puts his hand out. "Maybe we could do this again sometime."

"Sure." I shake his hand and look over at Grace. "Next time you're up here just let me know."

"Would next week be too soon?" she asks cautiously.

She wants to fly up here again just for lunch? I guess she likes me.

"Um, no, that's not too soon."

Her eyes light up and she hugs me, which I was not at all prepared for. I loosely hug her back and she backs away, realizing it might too early for that.

"Let's say a week from today," Arlin says in a take-charge tone. "Same time. Same place. Unless you'd like to go somewhere else."

"No, this place is fine. I'll see you next week."

As I start to leave, I hear Arlin behind me. "Jade." He comes over with his wallet in his hand and takes out a $100 bill. "I almost forgot to give you this."

I feel like he's paying me for showing up for lunch and it makes me tense up. "No, I don't need it."

Actually, I *do* need it because I have no money, not even a quarter, and I don't want to have to ask Ryan for money.

Arlin senses my hesitation and steps closer, lowering his voice. "It's from Pearce. To reimburse you for the cab ride last week."

"Oh. Yeah, okay. Thanks." I take the bill and put it in my purse.

"Goodbye, Jade," Arlin says, smiling. "We'll see you soon."

As I walk to the car, I have to remind myself that those two people were my grandparents. My real grandparents. It doesn't even seem possible. The journey to get to this place was completely insane. Their son destroyed my mom. Destroyed my childhood. Tried to kill me. And I just had lunch with his parents. Very weird.

Back on campus I race up to the second floor to tell Garret about the lunch, but then turn and go back down to my room, realizing I'm not supposed to be up there. I hate not being able to go up to his room. I desperately want to talk to him and I can't and it's driving me crazy.

I check my phone just in case he slipped up and accidentally called or texted me. But he didn't.

My phone rings as I'm checking it. "Hi, Harper."

"Hey, I was calling to see if you want to come over to Sean's place with me this weekend. We'll just get some movies and hang out at his apartment."

"That's okay. I know you guys want to be alone."

"Jade, I just spent an entire week with the guy. I want to hang out with you. So what do you say? Sean will do all the cooking."

"Okay, that sounds fun."

"Great! I have to run to class, so we'll talk later."

That takes care of one weekend. Now what do I do with the rest of them? I can't spend every weekend with Sean and Harper.

Around 6, Harper and I have dinner like we normally do. The dining hall is packed but there's no sign of Garret. How is it possible I never see him here? Does he not eat anymore?

"Stop looking for him," Harper says as she sees my eyes darting around the room. She just finished another one of her monstrous green salads and is eating a cup of yogurt for dessert. I, on the other hand, had a bowl of sugary, rainbow-colored cereal for dinner and am now enjoying a bowl of chocolate pudding. Not the most nutritious meal, I know, but I heard people crave carbs after a break-up, so I'm actually making the break-up seem more real.

"I wasn't looking for him," I say, but it's a total lie.

She stands up. "I'm going to get some fruit. I'll be right back."

While she's gone I finish my pudding, then push my tray aside.

"Hey, Jade." I hear a guy's voice behind me. As I turn to look back, he takes the seat next to me. "How's it going?"

It's a guy from my history class. What's his name? I can't remember. I'm so bad with names. There are only 20 people in the class. I should know his name.

"Hi. Did you want this table?" I glance around noticing the lack of open tables.

"No, I'm sitting over there." He points to a table a couple over from mine. It's full of guys, some of whom live on Garret's floor. "I just came over to see if you were doing anything tomorrow night?"

It takes my mind a moment to process what he said. *Doing anything tomorrow night.* What's tomorrow night? Friday? What am I missing here? Do we have something due for history? Wait! Friday night is date night. Is he asking me out?

I'm taking far too long to answer and he's giving me a strange look. "Jade? Did you hear me? It's kind of loud in here."

"Um, yeah. Something about tomorrow night?" I'm trying to buy time to find a way to turn him down. I'm supposed to be single now, so technically I could date him, but of course I wouldn't because I'm secretly still dating Garret.

The guy smiles at me. He's very cute, whatever his name is—wavy black hair, olive skin, dark brown eyes. He's thin but has decent arm muscles. On the first day of class when we had to introduce ourselves, I remember him saying his parents are from Greece and that he spends every summer there.

"I wanted to try this new Thai restaurant," he says, angling his body toward me. "I was wondering if you'd like to go with me. Do you like Thai food?"

"I do, but I'm busy tomorrow night."

"How about Saturday?"

"Some friends invited me to spend the weekend with them, so I won't be around."

"Okay, so maybe next weekend?"

Obviously I need to be more direct. I used to be really good at turning guys down, but after dating Garret for so long I'm out of practice. I scan the crowd for Harper but can't find her. Instead I spot Garret walking toward the table where what's-his-name was sitting before he came over here to ask me out. Garret stops when he sees me with what's-his-name, whose close proximity to me clearly indicates he's interested. Garret sets his tray on the table and slowly sits down, keeping his eyes on us.

"I really can't." I pause, wishing I could think of this guy's name. "I'm kind of taking a break from dating right now."

"Yeah, okay. I understand." He stands up.

"Hey, Nic." Harper appears, carrying a small bowl of blueberries.

Nic! I knew it was a one-syllable name. Nic. I've now stamped it in my brain, not that I'll need it again. This is probably the last time the guy will ever talk to me.

"Hi, Harper. I've gotta go. I'll see you guys later." Nic leaves and goes back to his seat, which is right next to where Garret is now sitting. Nic seems nervous seeing Garret there. He quickly grabs his tray and takes it to the conveyor belt.

"What was that about?" Harper asks.

"Nic just asked me out." My eyes are glued on Garret who is now the center of attention at his table. He's apparently become quite popular with the other guys after his wild weekend in Bermuda.

"He asked you out?" Harper drops the blueberries she was spooning into her yogurt and they go rolling down the table. "What did you say to him?"

"I told him I was busy this weekend."

My eyes are still on Garret, who looks so damn good it's not even fair. His dark hair is sexy messy, he's got stubble on his face to fit his bad-boy image, and he's wearing one of the fitted black t-shirts that I love on him. It clings to his shoulders and fits snug on his chest. I just want to run my hands under it and feel his skin, his muscles, his—"

"Jade." Harper kicks my foot under the table. "Stop staring," she scolds, glancing back at Garret.

"What? I can't look at my ex?"

"Not that way. You look like you want to rip his clothes off."

"Because I do."

She kicks me again. "Come on. You need to get out of here."

As I get up from the table I see Garret lift his eyes slightly, watching me. It sends a rush of fiery heat through my core. I swear this no-contact thing makes me want him even more than when we were together, which doesn't seem possible.

Harper practically has to pull me back to her room. "You need to get it together, Jade." She plops down on her bed, leaning against the wall. I do the same.

"I haven't seen Garret since Sunday. I couldn't help but look at him. And I'm sure nobody even noticed."

"You were gawking, not looking." She lets out a deep sigh.

"What? What are you thinking, Harper?"

"I think you should go out with Nic."

CHAPTER TWENTY-TWO

"What? No way! I'm not going out with Nic."

"You want this to look real, right? In the real world, you'd start dating again."

"That's not gonna happen, Harper. First of all, I don't want to date anyone, even if it's fake dating. Second, Garret would be pissed. And third, it wouldn't be fair to use Nic like that."

She considers it. "Yeah. I guess. But I wasn't saying you had to date him for weeks or months. Just one date. It would show people that you're moving on."

"Nic's a nice guy. I don't want to lead him on like that."

"Well, you have to do something so people believe this break-up is real."

"I'll mope around my room. Pretend I'm depressed."

"You're the one who dumped Garret. So you're the one who's supposed to be moving on. Dating again. Garret's supposed to be the depressed one. And instead he was in Bermuda last week with other girls."

"Fine. I'll think about it."

She reaches over to the table by her bed and picks up the TV remote. "Are you watching the last episode?"

I check the clock and see that it's time for the final episode of The Prep School Girls' Reunion show. "Might as well."

She turns the TV on and clicks through to the right channel. The show is just starting with the cheesy music and quick shots of the stars flashing on the screen. The first scene shows one of the girls fighting with her ex-boyfriend and then getting back together with him. How convenient. A happy ending for the last show. It's so staged.

Scenes with two other girls follow after that. The final scene is with Ava and fake Garret and I start to get nervous. If they waited till the very end, there must be something big planned.

The scene is at Ava's apartment, in her bedroom of course. The fake Garret has his shirtless back to the camera and they're sitting on her bed. She's facing him so the camera can catch her over-the-top, ridiculous expressions.

They flirt with each other, then kiss a little until the actor pushes her away.

"I have to tell you something," fake Garret says.

Ava sits back, wide-eyed and tilting her head. "What is it?"

"I got drunk last night and slept with another girl."

Cue Ava acting shocked and hurt. She covers her face and pretends to cry. She's such a horrible actress.

"Babe, I'm sorry," fake Garret says. "But you know I'm messed up. I always have been."

What's with the "babe" thing? Garret would never say that.

Ava lowers her hands from her face and looks at him. Her makeup isn't even running, which it would be if she was really crying as hard as she made it sound.

She pouts her shiny red lips. "You're messed up because of your mom, aren't you?"

Did she really just bring up Garret's mom? No way the show would stoop that low. Would they?

"When my mom died, I died with her. I've been this person I don't even know." Fake Garret starts fake crying and Ava gasps, then leans over to embrace him.

"It's okay," she says, not sounding at all sincere.

"No, it's not. It's not me. Getting drunk. Cheating on you. It's all wrong. I'm so sorry, babe."

"I forgive you," Ava says. "And I'll help you get through this. I'm here for you. I love you."

The cheesy music begins and they fade out. Then words go across the screen telling people to go online for future updates on Ava and Garret.

Harper turns the TV off and waits for me to respond.

"That was so bad." I get up to leave. "Thank God that was the last episode. I'm going to bed."

"Don't you want to talk about it?"

"No. I don't even want to think about it anymore."

I go to my room and despite what I said, all I can do is think about the show. The producer's took something extremely personal in Garret's life and used it to get ratings. And I hate them for that. And I hate Ava even more. She grew up with Garret. She knows what he's been through and yet she somehow thinks it's okay to talk about his mom's death on a stupid reality show? How could she be that cold and heartless?

I consider going upstairs to Garret's room. I need to see him and talk to him and give him a hug, but instead I have to sit down here and hope that he didn't see the show, and if he did, that he's okay.

Being apart from Garret all this time is starting to affect me more than I thought it would. I can't stop thinking about him. I love him so much and he's my best friend, and not being able to see him or talk to him is pure torture. Every little thing reminds me of him. And now, when I think he might be hurting and I can't be with him, my heart actually aches. When I used to hear the word heartache I never understood it. But now I totally get it.

The next day, I keep an eye out for Garret, hoping I'll see him so we can maybe sneak away somewhere private and I can talk to him just for a minute. But the day goes by and I don't see him anywhere.

After classes, Harper and I head to Sean's house. It's Friday night and we drive separately since she'll be spending the night over there.

Sean thinks Garret and I really broke up, so he's being even nicer than normal. He makes tacos for dinner, which is one of my favorite meals. Then he insists that I pick out the movie we watch.

Harper gazes at him all night as if his kindness toward me has made her fall even more in love. It's kind of annoying. I know I shouldn't say that. I like that she's happy. But now that I don't have Garret, seeing her with Sean is almost painful.

On Saturday the three of us go to an afternoon movie. Harper and Sean snuggle and hold hands and I sit there, feeling like a third wheel. After that we go back to Sean's apartment and he makes his famous homemade pizza and for dessert he makes brownie sundaes. If Harper marries this guy, she better work out a lot or she'll gain 100 pounds.

Later we play a board game where you have to find clues and solve a crime. It's based on one of those TV crime shows. Sean says he got it for Christmas and this is the first time he's played it. It's not very fun so we quit halfway through the game and watch TV.

"Sean, Jade doesn't like basketball," Harper says when he stops on a game. "Let's watch something else."

He switches the channel and Garret's picture is in the corner of the screen. Sean quickly flips to another channel.

"No. Go back," I tell him. "I want to see that."

He looks at Harper who nods in agreement, then flips back to the other channel.

"—was in Vegas last night and caused $10,000 in damages to his hotel suite. Sources say they found traces of cocaine in the room but can't prove who it belonged to. When hotel staff discovered the mess, Kensington was already gone. Friends say he was headed to Lake Tahoe on the Kensington jet for a round of golf. Garret's father, Pearce Kensington, released a statement to the press apologizing for his son's recent behavior and promising he'll pay for the damages. In other celebrity news…"

"You can change the channel now," I say to Sean as I get up from the couch. "I should leave. It's getting late." I grab my purse and head for the door.

"You don't have to leave." Sean sounds like he feels even more sorry for me than before.

"Yeah, Jade," Harper says, playing along. "Let's watch a movie."

"No, I just need to go. Thanks for dinner, Sean."

"Sure. What time are you coming over tomorrow?"

"I can't come over. I have to do homework. See you guys later."

Harper invited me to come over on Sunday, too, but I know she wants to be alone with Sean. Today was fun, but hanging out with the two of them is starting to get uncomfortable. We need Garret there to balance things out.

Back in my room, I go through my mail and notice an envelope from Grace and Arlin. I open it and inside is a card with a letter saying how much they enjoyed our lunch. There are also some photos of Grace's flower garden. On the back of the photos she wrote the names of the flowers in her old-lady, cursive handwriting. I pin the photos up on the cork board above my desk. They're so pretty they almost look like postcards.

I've never had a grandma, but after meeting Grace just one time she already seems like the type of grandma I imagined in my head growing up. I'm really glad I agreed to meet her. I really like Arlin, too. And I've decided that I want to spend more time with them.

I've given this a lot of thought because after our lunch the other day, I felt a little guilty for meeting with them, like I shouldn't agree to see them again knowing what their son did to my mom. But that's my head talking, not my heart. If I go with my heart, it tells me to give Grace and Arlin a chance.

Arlin said he didn't raise his son to be that way and I believe him. From our brief encounters, I can tell that Arlin's a nice man. It's just that there's this part of me that wants to punish his son, and since Royce isn't around I feel the need to punish his father.

I wish I could talk to Garret about this, but I think I already know what he'd say. He'd tell me to let it go. To not punish Arlin for his son's actions. To forgive.

I've never been very good with the whole forgiveness thing but I'm getting better at it thanks to Garret. He's really good at forgiving people, like his dad and even Katherine. He says you shouldn't waste energy being angry about stuff from the past. He used to tell me that whenever I'd get mad about my mom and how she treated me. He'd tell me I need to forgive her because it's the only way I can move on. And he's right. I've slowly started to forgive her the past few months and it makes my heart feel more open and more free to let people in.

When I think about that, I realize what a huge influence Garret's had on me. Sometimes I forget that, but now that we're not together I'm more aware of how much I've changed since he came into my life. And being reminded of that makes me miss him even more.

The weeks that follow go by excruciatingly slow. I sometimes see Garret from afar but that's it. His car is gone every Friday around 3 and doesn't show up again until Monday morning.

Celebrity news shows and talk shows report on whatever bad things he did over the weekend and it's starting to affect people's opinion of him. There are comments online about him being an alcoholic and a drug addict and needing to go to rehab. People are calling him inconsiderate, spoiled, out-of-control, immature, and other negative things.

Fake Garret's wild weekends have included property damage, car crashes, binge drinking, lots of girls, and evidence of possible drug use. None of this stuff is actually happening but it really does seem real. I don't know how Arlin and Pearce are pulling this off. Does nobody check these stories to see if they're true?

Arlin and Pearce obviously have enough connections and enough people who owe them favors to make these things happen but it still baffles me. After seeing this, I'll never believe another news story again.

As for Ava, she fake-dumped Garret a week after the last reality show aired, saying she couldn't take his constant cheating. She went on talk shows and used social media to tell everyone it was over. Now she's dating a male model from Brazil and her teen fans have moved their attention from Garret to this new guy.

My life seems boring in comparison. I've been meeting Arlin and Grace every Thursday for lunch for the past three weeks. Now that it's spring and the weather is warmer, they've moved back to their home in the Hamptons. They usually wait until May to go there, but they moved up earlier this year so they could spend time with me before school's out.

I went to their house last weekend for the first time. It's a huge mansion, but it isn't at all like the Kensington mansion. It's decorated more like Carson's house with warm colors and comfortable furniture. It's right on the ocean and has a big wraparound porch in the back. Arlin even grilled steaks for dinner when I was there. I didn't think billionaires cooked, but Arlin does. Grace said they have a chef but that he only works there in the summer months.

I really like hanging out with Arlin and Grace. We still avoid the topic of Royce and what happened, and maybe we always will. There isn't a reason to bring it up and doing so might risk the relationship we're developing.

Arlin is my only source of updates on Garret. He says the organization hasn't even addressed the public's shifting attitude and that the plan for Garret's future has not been discussed in over a month.

I'm trying to stay positive, but Arlin's updates have me worried. I thought by now this group would at least be holding meetings about Garret, discussing his bad behavior and reassessing their decision. But they're not, and that makes me think that maybe this was all for nothing. Maybe this group is determined to go forward with their plan and there's nothing we can do about it. I'm just not ready to accept that.

CHAPTER TWENTY-THREE

It's now the first week of April and the weather is really warming up. It also stays light outside for longer, so I've started running after dinner. I keep the runs short because my knee isn't fully healed. And I run on the trail because the ground is much softer than the track.

Tonight the trail is a little wet from the rain we had earlier in the week and mud is splattering up on my ankles. People don't like using the trail when it's muddy so I have it all to myself. Plus it's Friday night and everyone is getting ready to go out.

When I'm about a quarter mile down the trail I hear my name.

"Jade. Over here."

I look to my right and Garret is standing there under a large oak tree.

"Garret!" I run over and he hugs me so tight he lifts my feet off the ground. "What are you doing here?"

"I had to see you." He sets me down but keeps me close. "I can't do this anymore."

"What do you mean? We have to stick with the plan."

"Yes, we're still doing the plan, but I can't go another day without seeing you. Or talking to you." He pulls me off the trail behind a tree and draws me closer. "And I definitely can't go another day without kissing you." He gently presses his soft lips to mine and my legs get weak. No joke. Like he actually has to hold me up a little as I sink into him while we kiss.

When he stops I take a breath and stand up again. "Wow. I've really missed that."

"Yeah. I know. " He kisses me again.

We hear a rustling noise and break apart, but it's just a squirrel running through the leaves.

I wrap my arms around him again and hug him really tight. "I'm so happy you showed up here. I needed this so bad. I've missed you so much."

"I'm sorry I couldn't arrange something earlier. I kept trying, but you haven't been around."

"I've been spending a lot of time with Harper. And Arlin and his wife."

"Oh, yeah? What have you been doing with Arlin?"

"Having lunch. And I went to their house in the Hamptons last weekend. I have so much to tell you."

"Then let's talk. But we need to get off the trail in case someone comes by."

"We don't have anywhere to go."

"We do if you're up for a hike." He takes my hand and leads me down a steep hill into the woods.

"How did you know I'd be on the trail tonight?" I carefully step over a fallen tree branch so I don't trip again and get another concussion.

"I noticed you were going out there every night after dinner." He glances back at me and smiles. "I keep an eye on you, Jade."

We walk for a few more minutes, then come to a stop next to a small stream. There's a clearing in the woods where Garret has laid out a sleeping bag, unzipped so it forms a big rectangle. There's a picnic basket on top holding it down.

"I've been searching for the right spot for a week. What do you think?"

"It's great. Very secluded."

"Exactly. It's just what we need." He takes my face in his hands and kisses me. I don't know why, but I feel like I'm kissing him for the first time—butterflies in the stomach and everything. He parts my lips with his tongue and takes the kiss deeper. He tastes like mint and his skin has the scent of his signature cologne. Even when I close my eyes, I know it's him. I know his taste, his smell, his touch. And I've missed all of it. I've missed everything about him.

We kneel down on the blanket, our lips still joined. I lie on my back and he lies over me. Some birds rustle the leaves just above us and I break from the kiss. "Are we really doing this? Outside?"

He sits back on his knees. "Not if you don't want to. I guess I did say we were just coming to talk so—"

"Are you kidding me? We'll talk later."

He smiles and takes off his shirt, exposing the ripped muscles and smooth skin I've been longing to feel against me again. I quickly take my clothes off not even letting him do it. Sensing my urgency, he strips the rest of the way, then pulls a thin blanket from the basket.

"In case you get cold or want to cover up."

I sit back on my elbows, smiling at him. "So you just assumed I'd go for this?"

He kisses my neck and coaxes me back down. "I knew you'd go for it, my little nymphomaniac."

It's so mean, but it makes me laugh. "That's the last time you get to call me that."

We kiss and touch like we can't get enough of each other, breathing heavy and starting to sweat in the cool night air.

"I'm trying to go slow for you, Jade, but it's been too long and I don't—"

"I don't need slow. I'm more than ready."

He instantly joins us together and I hear him groan my name as he goes deeper. My core is fired up with sensation, ready to burst. He's still trying not to hurry as he slowly rocks his hips, his breathing ragged, his head resting on mine. I push my hips into his and guide him to a quicker pace. He seems relieved at my signal and moves faster and deeper until we both finally get relief from the desire that's been building inside us for weeks.

Garret moves off me and holds me in his arms, pulling the blanket over us. "Okay, now we can talk," he says, kissing my forehead. "By the way, I love you. I should've said that when I first saw you. I'm out of practice. I haven't been able to say that for weeks."

"Yeah, and I've missed it. I love you, too." I snuggle closer to him and wrap my arm across his chest. "When is this going to end? Have you heard anything?"

"My dad said the organization has been monitoring what's going on, but they haven't addressed it any of the meetings. He's just heard stuff from other members. So far, it sounds like nothing's changed. They still want me to go through with this and that's why they've been trying to interfere."

"By doing what?"

"They've been planting fake articles saying the rumors about me are false. That I'm a good guy, but just struggling with some issues. They got the reality show to reshoot the last episode so the actor playing me could blame my mom's death for why the fake me is doing all these things."

"So the producers of the show are working for the organization? Are they members?"

"No, I think they were just offered a shitload of money to reshoot the scene. They probably didn't even ask why."

"I saw that episode and I wanted to talk to you so bad after that. I almost went up to your room, but I knew I shouldn't."

"I'm over it. I'm just trying to forget about the show. Oh, and now that Ava dumped me I'm getting a new fake girlfriend to cheat on. Some 20-year-old blond actress. She's done some modeling but hasn't had any real acting jobs yet."

"Great. Competition from a hot blond. Just what I need."

"You have nothing to worry about." He flips me on my back and hovers over me. "I don't even like blonds. I only like girls with long brown hair, jade green eyes, around 5'5 with larger-than-average breasts."

"I was just your type until that last part."

"I disagree." He cups my breast with his hand. "See? A perfect handful, and I have large hands."

"And how do you know that's larger than average?"

He smiles. "I've done some research over the years."

I laugh. "Yeah, I'm sure you have. I hope you're done with that research."

"You know I am." He leans down and kisses me. "You're all I think about, especially now that I can't be with you. And speaking of competition, what's with all the guys asking you out?"

"One guy. That's it. Nic's in my history class. He just asked me to dinner."

"What did you tell him?"

"I told him I wasn't ready to start dating again. He hasn't bothered me since."

"And why do you keep wearing skirts? Are you trying to torture me?"

"Harper gave me a bunch of new ones from her sister along with a few more bikinis. You'll get to see them in California this summer."

He's quiet as he rubs his hand up and down my arm.

"You're not going, are you?"

"Probably not. This is going slower than we thought it would. My dad was sure they would've given up on me by now and picked someone else. But they haven't, so we need to keep this thing going."

"I've been reading the comments online about you and they're pretty bad."

"That's the thing. A lot of people either don't like me anymore or have lost interest, so I don't know why the organization isn't giving up on me. Hardly anyone would vote for me now or in twenty years. People think I'm a drug addict. Even if fake Garret went to rehab, nobody wants a former drug addict for a president."

"If you can't go to California I don't think I should go either."

"We've already discussed this. You're going. A driver will take your car out there. You can just fly out and take a cab from the airport. Did you want to stop in Des Moines on the way out there and see Frank and Ryan?"

"Yeah, but I don't have money for all those plane tickets. And you can't buy them for me. If someone found out, it would look suspicious."

"You should have Arlin pay for it."

"I can't do that. I don't want him and Grace thinking I'm only being nice to them for their money."

"Well, I might've mentioned to him that you need some plane tickets. And he might've already offered to get them for you."

I sit up. "Garret, why did you do that?"

"He called and asked me if you needed anything because he said he knows you'll never ask. So I just said you might need a plane ticket to Des Moines and another one for California. He really wants to do this for you, Jade."

"Yeah, because he thinks buying me stuff will make up for what his son did."

"That's not what he's doing. And he's afraid to offer to pay for anything because he knows you'll assume that's why he's doing it. But it's not true, Jade. I told you before. He loves doing stuff for his grandkids and now he's got you. A whole new kid to spoil. So don't read so much into it. Just let him be a grandfather." Garret gets up and gathers our clothes from the ground. "I almost forgot the picnic part of this secret meeting. But we should probably put something on first."

After we're dressed, he opens the picnic basket and pulls out a bottle.

"Sparkling water. I was in a hurry and it's all we had. But it's cherry flavored." He takes out two champagne flutes and hands them to me.

"Are these crystal glasses?" I ask, noticing how heavy they are.

"Yeah. I just grabbed some from the cabinet at home." He fills our glasses, then holds his up for a toast. "To people continuing to hate me so this will end and we won't have to have our dates in the woods." We clink glasses.

He reaches in the basket again. "And here are the Belgian chocolates I was supposed to give you after spring break."

I take a chocolate and pop it in my mouth. "This is definitely the best chocolate ever."

"You can take the rest of them back to your room." He sets his glass down. "So what are you doing for Easter? Do you have a place to go on Sunday?"

"Sean is making brunch, so I'm going over there with Harper. He's having a whole bunch of people over."

"Before you go over there, I need you to go on the trail."

"You want me to go running on Easter?"

"No. Just show up on the trail around 9. I'll have a surprise waiting for you."

"What kind of surprise would you have on the trail?"

"Just go there and find out. I promised you I'd make each holiday special with all the traditions you didn't get growing up. I'm guessing you didn't celebrate Easter either?"

"No." I take another chocolate. "But you don't need to keep doing this holiday thing."

"Why not?" He nudges my leg. "I know you love it."

"I never said I loved holidays. You're just assuming I do because *you* like them."

"Maybe you didn't like them before, but you do now that you have *me* around." His cocky smile appears. I've missed it.

I smile back. "Okay, there might be some truth in that."

"It's getting dark. You should probably head back. The coyotes and raccoons will be out soon, if they're not already."

I jump up on his lap, spilling my sparkling water. "Are you serious? Did you see one?"

He's laughing at me. "No, I just wanted you on my lap." He takes my glass and sets it aside, then reaches his hand behind my head and draws me in for a kiss.

When he lets me go, I hold on. "No, it's too soon. I'm not ready."

"We'll do this again. I just don't know when yet. But next time I'll tell Harper so you'll know when to meet me out here." He hands me the box of chocolates.

"Okay, but it better not be weeks." I reluctantly get up.

"It won't." He stands up and takes my hand. "Come on. I'll walk you back to the trail. I parked up on the road in the opposite direction."

"You left your BMW on the side of the road? But you're supposed to be out partying tonight. Everyone around here knows your car. They'll know you were here."

"I drove Charles' old pickup truck. He only drives it when he goes fishing. He let me borrow it."

"What did you tell him for an excuse for why you needed a pickup?"

"I didn't tell him anything. I just asked if I could use it. I think he knows that I was trying to sneak off and see you."

"Then he knows what we're doing? Garret, what if he tells someone?"

"He'd never do that. He wants us to be together. He always tells me what a great girl you are and how I should never let you go." Garret smiles and lifts my hand up to kiss it. "All stuff I already know."

The walk up the hill is way too short. I want to go back down and walk up it again, but it's getting darker and I don't want raccoons attacking Garret on his way back to the truck.

"Goodbye, Jade." He kisses me, then gives me a hug.

"Don't say goodbye. I hate goodbye. Say 'see ya later.' That's all I'll accept."

"Okay. See ya later."

We kiss once more before he disappears into the trees.

CHAPTER TWENTY-FOUR

I return to my dorm practically giddy. Giddy means really happy, right? I think so, but I could be wrong. I've heard it used in old movies to describe girls twirling around in their dresses like they're so happy they can't help but twirl. I'm not the twirling type, but right now I'm so happy I think I could actually twirl. But instead I walk down the hall with my box of chocolates wearing what I'm sure is a big, goofy grin on my face.

Harper sees me as I walk by. "What's wrong with you?"

"Nothing's wrong. Why?"

She follows me to my room. "You haven't smiled like that since—" She stops and lowers her voice to a whisper. "Did you and you-know-who just you-know-what?"

I open my door and drag her in my room. "Yes!"

"But how? Where?"

"In the woods. Like really far into the woods."

She makes a face. "Didn't you get eaten by bugs? And what did you do it on? The ground?"

"He had a sleeping bag. And I didn't notice any bugs."

"Huh. Well, whatever works. So can you two start dating again?"

"No, we still have to wait. And it sounds like he can't come to California this summer."

"But it's still weeks away. Things could change by then, right? Or maybe he could just come for part of the summer."

"Yeah, maybe. Hey, I wanted to ask you a favor."

"Sure, what is it?"

"I need you to help me communicate with Garret. Like next time he wants me to meet him in the woods, he'll tell you beforehand and you'll tell me."

"Okay. That's easy enough. Anything else?"

"Nope. That's it."

"You should've thought of this weeks ago. You two could've been secretly meeting this whole time." She checks the clock on my desk. "I gotta go. Sean will be here any minute. We're going to a party. Do you want to come with us?"

"Harper, you know I never go to parties."

She shrugs. "I had to ask. Someday you might say yes."

When she's gone I change into my pajamas and grab my laptop. I search Garret's name on the Internet and see what comes up. Lots of shirtless photos of him. Below that are some recent articles. One is about him crashing one of his dad's expensive cars. Another one mentions his spending habits, claiming he spent a half million dollars on a watch. People seem really upset about that one. There are lots of negative comments. The next few articles are from some online celebrity magazines. I check the comments section and only a few people have anything good to say about him.

The anti-Garret plan seems to be working, which makes me feel hopeful again. I know the organization hasn't changed their mind, but I have to keep thinking that this will all work out. I don't even want to consider the alternative.

It's strange for me to think that way because I've always assumed bad things will happen, not good. But the past few months have taught me that bad things sometimes turn into good things. Like having Royce come into my life was really, really bad, but meeting his parents was good. Plus, Royce is the reason I'm at Moorhurst and if I hadn't gone to Moorhurst I wouldn't have met Garret. So I have proof that good things can come from bad. And right now, that's the only thing keeping me going.

On Easter Sunday at 9 a.m., I go outside to find whatever Garret left on the trail. It's a warm, sunny spring day and I'm already dressed for brunch at Sean's apartment. I wore one of the dresses Harper gave me. It's a light green, short-sleeve chiffon dress that's fitted on top and flows out at the waist. This is the first time I've worn it. The green reminded me of the color of dyed Easter eggs so it seemed like a good dress for today.

Where the trail begins there's a big basket and a little basket sitting on the ground. The big basket is overflowing with Easter candy; jelly beans, chocolate bunnies, marshmallow chicks, and chocolate eggs. The small basket has a note in it that says, *The Easter bunny hid 10 plastic eggs for you to find. All are no more than 20 feet down the trail. Good luck!*

I pick up the basket and start hunting for the eggs. I feel like a little kid. But I've never done this before and nobody is watching, so I might as well let my kid side out and have fun. If I'd known I was going on an egg hunt I probably wouldn't have worn a dress and heels. At least the ground is dry instead of muddy.

The first five eggs are easy to find behind some trees, right off the trail. The next three are more hidden, just barely peeking out from under some fallen leaves. I have to really search for egg nine, but I eventually find it up in a tree branch. After searching up and down the trail, I can't find the last egg and am ready to give up when I hear a noise.

"You're getting warmer."

I whip my head around to see Garret standing there in a dark gray suit, white shirt, and blue tie. I'm so excited to see him my heart gets all fluttery in my chest.

I run up to him. "What are you doing?"

"Helping you find your eggs." He leans down and plants a kiss on my lips.

He looks really hot in that suit. He smells good, too. It makes me want to forget the brunch and sneak off into the woods with him.

"How long have you been here?" I ask, setting my basket down.

"Long enough to watch you hunt for eggs. You're pretty good for a first timer."

"I couldn't find the last one."

He smiles. "Keep looking."

"I already looked everywhere and I couldn't find it. Can you give me a hint?"

"Do that thing I taught you when we first met."

I give him a hug and find the last egg in his hand behind his back.

He circles his arms around my waist. "Open it."

"The egg? Why? Is there something in it?"

"Well, yeah. There's stuff in all of them."

"Oh, I thought they were just plastic eggs."

He laughs. "So that explains why you didn't open any of them. I couldn't figure that out. Well, open this one and you can open the other ones later."

I twist open the pink plastic egg. Inside is a necklace; a silver chain with a silver starfish hanging from it.

"I thought you could wear it this summer."

"Thank you. I love it." I hug him again. "And thanks for the Easter basket."

"You've never gotten one before, have you?"

"No," I say, looking back at the candy-filled basket.

"Then it's a good thing I've got connections with the Easter Bunny."

I laugh. "I didn't know you two were friends."

"We're not. He just owed me a favor." Garret kisses me. "Happy Easter, Jade. You look really beautiful in that dress. You'll have to wear it for me someday."

"I will." I look around to make sure nobody is around. "Hey, did you drive here?"

"Yeah. The fake Garret is behaving this weekend and going to his grandparents' house for brunch. So it's okay if people see me around campus or in town. But I do need to get going."

"Thanks again for Easter. It was great."

"We'll have a better one next year." He give me a kiss, then moves his lips to my ear and lowers his voice. "Plan for another picnic in the woods this week." His breath on my neck gives me chills and I want to kiss him again, but he walks off toward the parking lot.

Garret's surprise visit puts me in a good mood for the rest of the day. After Sean's Easter brunch, I return to campus and go for a run. When I get back to my room I open up the remaining plastic eggs. They're filled with fun stuff that didn't cost much, like a candy ring, a candy bracelet, some new headbands to use for running, my favorite lip balm.

I love the necklace he gave me earlier but I also love getting these inexpensive gifts, especially when they show how much he knows about me. Just the fact that he remembers my favorite headbands and lip balm is so sweet. And a while back I told him how when I was little I always wanted candy jewelry, and he remembered and got it for me.

I want to thank him and give him a huge hug for doing all this. But that will have to wait until I can see him again, which hopefully will be soon.

The dining halls are closed all day, so I raid my Easter basket for dinner, putting myself into a sugar coma before falling asleep.

Tuesday at breakfast, and then again on Thursday, Harper gives me a heads-up to meet Garret at our secret spot. There are a lot of bugs now so it's not the greatest place to hang out, but we get to see each other so I don't care. Even seeing him just a couple times a week is so much better than not at all.

Saturday morning, I go out to the Hamptons again to visit Arlin and Grace. This time, they're taking me out on their sailboat. I've never been boating and I'm a little worried I might get sick, so I stopped at the drugstore near campus and bought some wristbands that are supposed to keep you from getting seasick.

When I arrive at their house, Grace is dressed in navy pants and a white and navy shirt. It's the first time I've seen her wear pants. Arlin is in a white polo shirt and khaki trousers, a much more casual look than his usual suit and tie.

"Are you ready to sail, Jade?" Arlin's smiling from ear to ear. I've never seen him so excited. He's like a little kid.

"Arlin loves his boat," Grace says quietly to me. "He can't wait to take you out on the water. He's been wanting to for weeks."

I turn back to Arlin, holding up my wrists. "I got these so I don't get seasick."

He waves his hand in the air like he doesn't want to see them. "Nonsense. You're a Sinclair. We were meant to be on the water. We don't get seasick. Take those silly things off."

Grace leans over to whisper. "Just put them in my purse for now. If you feel sick you can wear them later."

"Do you need help with anything?" I ask her. "I can load stuff on the boat or whatever else you need."

"We don't need anything. Everything's ready to go. Come on, honey." She leads me out back. I no longer mind that she and Arlin call me honey. They are my grandparents, after all.

The boat is huge. I've only seen sailboats on TV or in photos. I've never seen one up close. I wonder what these things cost. I went to a boat show with Frank and Ryan a couple years ago, but all they had were pontoon boats and speedboats. They were really expensive but not nearly as nice as this sailboat, so I know this thing cost a fortune.

Arlin helps Grace get in and I step in behind her. Then he messes with some ropes and we take off into the ocean. Crap! I'm sailing in the ocean! I could die! This suddenly seems really dangerous.

"How long has Arlin been sailing?" I ask Grace as we sit there watching him.

"Don't worry, honey. He's been sailing since he was a young boy."

I feel a little better knowing that, but then we hit a wave and the boat sways and I'm sure we're going to die. I instinctively hold on to Grace who laughs.

"These waves are nothing. Arlin and I have sailed in heavy storms and he's always gotten us back safe and sound." Another wave hits the boat. "See? That wasn't so bad, was it?"

"I guess not." I release my hold on her. "I've just never been on the water before."

"Well, we're hoping we can do this again before you leave for the summer." She turns to me. "Speaking of summer, Arlin and I heard that you need some plane tickets and we'd like to offer to pay for them."

"I don't know. We're just getting to know each other and I'm not sure if I should be accepting gifts like that."

"Jade, you're our granddaughter. Let us do this for you." She puts her hand on mine.

"But—" I stop, remembering what Garret said about Arlin doing this because he wants to, not because he feels guilty for what Royce did. "All right."

"Good. Then it's settled. Arlin will set you up with a credit card. Use it to get the plane tickets and whatever else you need. We'll take care of the bills. They'll go directly to us."

"But I just need the plane tickets."

"We want you to have fun this summer, so use the card for whatever you need."

"I really don't need—"

She interrupts. "You need gas for your car, right? And groceries? Suntan lotion? Sunglasses?" She smiles. "They have great shopping in California. You might see something you like."

The old Jade is coming back telling me there must be a catch. There's always a catch.

Grace notices my hesitation and it's almost like she read my mind. "All I ask in return is that you call us. Once a week would be nice, just so we know you're okay."

"Of course I will. I'll call you even more than that. I'm going to miss you guys."

"Jade, get over here," Arlin yells from behind a giant wheel. "I want to show you how to sail."

"I'll see you in a couple hours," Grace kids, patting my knee.

I make my way up to where Arlin is standing.

"Grab hold of the wheel and I'll show how to steer." He's so happy out here on the sailboat. He can't stop smiling. "I've taught every one of my grandkids how to sail. Usually we start a lot younger, but you can catch up."

After he explains how to steer the boat, he takes me over to the ropes and shows me different ways to tie knots.

As he's talking, a wave hits and I panic again. "Hey, um, shouldn't you be steering the boat?"

"It has a self-steering mechanism." Arlin must see the worried look on my face because he says, "It's perfectly safe. I use it all the time."

He goes back to talking about the ropes and then tells me how the sails work.

"There's a lot to learn," I tell him after our hour-long lesson. We're standing at the wheel again and he's letting me steer.

"I can already tell you're a natural." He puts his arm around my shoulder. "Should we take a break and I'll show you more later?"

"Yeah, okay."

He glances back at Grace who's reading a garden magazine near the back of the boat. "Can we talk for a minute?"

"Sure."

We take a seat on the small bench that's next to the wheel.

"Did Grace tell you that we'd like to help you out with some expenses?"

"Yes, she mentioned it."

"Are you okay with that? Garret said you might not be given the circumstances."

"Um, yeah, I guess I am."

"We're not trying to get you to forgive our son for what he did. And we're not doing this out of guilt. We want to help you because you're part of our family. I know we've only known you for a few months, but Grace and I love you like we do all our grandchildren."

I don't know what to say. I know they both like me, but I wasn't expecting him to say that they *loved* me.

Arlin continues. "I know I've mentioned this before, but we'd like to pay for the remainder of your college. And med school if you decide to go."

"That's very generous but—"

"You think about it and let us know later." He glances back at Grace again. "Have you decided if you want to meet the rest of the family?"

Arlin asked me this a few weeks ago at lunch when Grace was in the restroom. I'd given it some thought and had no doubts about my answer.

"I don't want to meet them," I say. "I shouldn't say it that way. I'd like to meet them, but then they'll know about Royce and I think it's better if they remember him as the man they knew and not the man who—well, you know."

"Yes. I understand. I thought you'd say that. And I have to admit I agree. It's probably best if they don't know."

"Are you two ready for some lunch?" Grace calls out.

"Yes, we're ready," Arlin yells back to her as he returns to the wheel.

"I'll go help her." I see Grace going down some stairs in the middle of the boat and I follow her. "Can I help with lunch?"

She turns around. "Jade, I thought you were still up on deck. Come on down. I'll show you around."

I meet her at the bottom of the stairs and she leads me down a narrow hallway and points to a small room. "We have a bedroom here and one on the other side. The bathroom is back there." She points behind me, then walks back to the area near the stairs, which has a small kitchen and a table. "And this is where we eat."

"This is a great boat. I've never been on a sailboat. Or any boat."

"Thank you for going along with Arlin's little lesson up there. He just loves teaching the grandkids how to sail. None of them are very interested, but he teaches them anyway."

"*I'm* interested. I was hoping to learn more, not that I'll ever own a sailboat, but I like learning about them. And I love it out here on the water. I don't even feel seasick."

"If you tell my husband you like sailing, he'll have you out here every weekend."

"That wouldn't be so bad." I smile at her.

She smiles back, her eyes wide and hopeful. I think she gets that I've finally accepted them as my grandparents and that I really do want a relationship with them.

Grace and I take out the salads and sandwiches she brought and arrange them on the small table in the kitchen. Then she calls Arlin to come down and the three of us have lunch. Afterward, Grace reads a book while Arlin teaches me more about sailing.

We get back to the house late afternoon. They invite me to stay for dinner, but it's a 2 to 3 hour drive back to Moorhurst depending on traffic around New York City and I don't want to drive in the dark. I don't know the area that well. This is the first time I've driven out to their house. When I came here last Saturday, Arlin and Grace drove me. But I insisted on driving myself this week. Arlin wanted to send his private plane to pick me up, but there's no way I'm getting on one of those small planes knowing what happened to Garret's mom.

Before I leave, I say goodbye to Grace in the kitchen. Then I go outside and meet Arlin by his car. He's putting a bag of golf clubs into the trunk.

"I'll see you next week, Arlin."

"Looking forward to it." He shuts the trunk. "Have a safe trip back. Call when you get there so we know you made it."

I turn to leave, then stop and turn back around and give Arlin a hug. "Thanks for teaching me how to sail."

I pull away, but he keeps me there a moment longer. "Anytime, honey. We love having you here."

I've already agreed to come back next weekend and the one after that, but next time I'll spend the night and drive back on Sunday. Hanging out with the grandparents in the Hamptons is a lot more fun than sitting alone in my room all weekend. Plus, it keeps my mind off Garret.

CHAPTER TWENTY-FIVE

The rest of April goes by really fast. I've been buried me in homework and I still have two big papers to finish before the semester ends.

Every weekend I've been going to the Hamptons to hang out with Arlin and Grace. I take my books and study on the deck overlooking the ocean, which is the absolute best place to study. The sound of the waves. The cool breeze. The warm sun. It's way better than studying in my room. Grace sits out there with me and reads a book. She loves to read.

We always spend the afternoons on the sailboat. I'm learning a lot about sailing. Arlin's face lights up whenever I ask him to teach me something new. Grace says I'm the only grandkid who's ever shown that much interest in learning how to sail. But I like learning about it. And I like spending time with Arlin. He tells me these old people jokes that aren't that funny but still make me laugh because of the way he says them. And then he laughs at his own jokes, which makes them even funnier.

During the week, Garret and I have been meeting in our secret location almost every night after dinner. A couple weeks ago, Garret set up a tent because the bugs were getting so bad. It's a big tent and he outfitted it with sleeping bags and pillows and got some lanterns so we could stay out there really late. I keep worrying we'll get caught but Garret assures me that nobody goes down that far into the woods.

It's hard to believe that it's now the first week of May and finals are next week. This past weekend I left for the Hamptons on Friday instead of Saturday morning and didn't get back until late Sunday, which means I haven't seen Garret for days.

Monday night I hurry through dinner because I'm dying to see him. We're meeting earlier than usual so we can both get back to our rooms and study.

When I get to the tent, Garret's already there waiting. I crawl inside, zipping it up to keep the bugs out. He grabs my waist from behind and pulls me down on the sleeping bag with him.

"Nice of you to stop by," he says, kissing the side of my neck.

"I haven't seen you for three whole days. I needed my Garret fix."

"I needed my Jade fix three days ago." His kisses move to my mouth as he slides his hand under my white cotton skirt. "I love it when you wear these."

Lately I've been wearing skirts when I come here, which always leads to sex right away and then we hang out and talk. The same thing happens tonight. After the sex part I get right to the talking.

"Did you get any updates over the weekend?" I ask Garret as he's pulling his shirt on.

"I got an update, but I don't know if it's good or bad. The organization is having a big meeting two weeks from today. My dad said they didn't send an agenda so he doesn't know what it's about."

"When I was with Arlin yesterday he mentioned the meeting, too. He said he heard it's about you."

"Shit! Really? My dad thought it was still too soon for them to vote. He thought it'd be late June or July."

"Garret, this is good. They'll finally make a decision."

"Yeah, and their decision could be to keep moving forward with the plan."

"Why would they still want you to be president? Nobody would vote for you. Even 20 years from now people will remember you as being some spoiled trust fund kid who got drunk, did drugs, and trashed his dad's expensive cars. Hardly anyone is talking about you online anymore, and the few people who are have nothing good to say about you."

"I know, but there's still a possibility they'll make me do this."

"No. I'm not even considering it." I secure my arm around him and lay my head on his chest.

He kisses the top my head. "What happened to you? Just a few months ago, you never thought anything would work out. You were always planning for the worst. And now you won't even think about it."

I push myself off him and sit up. "Because it can't happen. You promised me I could have you forever. And at the time I wasn't sure I wanted you for that long, but now I do. I want that damn forever."

He smiles and runs his hand along my arm. "I want it, too, Jade."

"So if they decide to go ahead with the plan, then we'll run off together. We'll go into hiding. We won't let them get to us."

"They have too many resources. They'd find us."

"That doesn't mean we can't try." I gaze down at the blanket, trying to keep it together. I refuse to cry about this, because if I do it'll seem more real.

"I can't risk putting you in danger." He pushes my chin up. "You know I won't do that. If this goes forward, then we just can't—"

"See each other anymore. Yeah. I know." I say it without an ounce of emotion because I'm not ready to accept that as a possibility. "Talk about something else."

He sits up across from me. "Jade, we need to discuss this. If this happens we only have two weeks—"

I put my finger to his lips. "I can't, Garret. Please. Not now. Just talk about something else."

He takes my hand from his mouth, keeping hold of it as he sets it between us on the sleeping bag. "How was your weekend?"

"Great. I went sailing again. I'm getting pretty good at it. Arlin's taught me a lot. I'm really going to miss him this summer. And Grace, too."

"You should ask them to come out and see you in California."

"Yeah, I think I will. I don't want to go all summer without seeing them." As I think about Arlin, my mind wanders to a topic that's been bugging me ever since I met him. "Garret, do you um . . . do you think Arlin's done things? Like bad things?"

"What are you talking about?"

"It sounds like the organization makes their members do things that are wrong and illegal. Maybe even have people killed, like that reporter who found out about the election fraud in Ohio and Florida."

"You don't know if that story was true. You can't listen to Carson." Garret's phone vibrates and he checks it. "It's my dad. I'll call him later."

"So do you think Arlin has done anything like that?"

"Jade, they've all done things. My dad. Arlin. And if I'm part of this group, they'll make me to do things, too."

"No. You can't. And why would Arlin? He's such a nice man."

"Because they threaten to do whatever they know will hurt you the most. And if you don't do what they say, they make good on their threats."

"You really think Arlin has hurt people? Or maybe had someone killed?"

He sighs. "I don't know so I'm not going to assume anything."

"But with your dad, you've seen stuff and heard stuff that makes you think it's possible?"

He nods. "But Jade, I don't know anything about Arlin when it comes to that and neither do you."

"I know. I just can't imagine him hurting anyone."

Garret's phone vibrates again and he checks it. "It's my dad again." He scrolls through his phone. "He left me four text messages, too. I should call him back. He doesn't know we've been meeting like this, so don't let him hear you." He calls, and his dad answers right away. "Dad, what's with all the messages?"

Garret listens and keeps listening for almost a minute, his expression growing darker by the second.

It has to be about the organization. They must've called Garret's dad and told him they're continuing with the plan. But it's not time yet. It's too soon! My heart goes into overdrive, beating so fast I feel like I can't breathe.

"Okay." Garret looks at me. "No, I'll tell her." He hangs up and sets his phone down.

"It's the plan, isn't it? They're making you do this? But why? Did he say why?" I'm gripping Garret's shirt tightly in my hands and don't even realize it until he pries my fingers open and I release the fabric. He keeps hold of my hands.

"Jade, that wasn't about me. Or the plan. It was about something else. Something happened." He lightly rubs the top of my hand with his thumb which he knows always calms me down.

"What is it? What happened?"

"It's Arlin. He had a heart attack. They took him to the hospital but he . . ." Garret has that sad look on his face that I hardly ever see, but when I do I really don't like it. "He didn't make it. I'm sorry, Jade."

"No! I just saw him yesterday! He was fine. He wasn't sick." Tears quickly fill my eyes and run down my cheeks. "He took me sailing and he was healthy. Your dad is wrong! Call him back and tell him he's wrong!"

Garret pulls me onto his lap and wraps his arms around me, pressing my head down on his shoulder. "I'm so sorry, Jade."

The tears keep flowing and my rational side can't figure out why. I just met this man a few months ago. I shouldn't be this sad. But I am.

"I wasn't done getting to know him. I needed more time."

"I know." Garret keeps me held against him. He kisses my head and rubs my back and we stay that way for several minutes.

My tears finally let up a little and I reposition myself in Garret's lap to face him.

"When did it happen?"

"A few hours ago. My dad said the funeral will probably be this weekend."

"And I can't go. I can't go to my own grandpa's funeral."

"Why can't you go?" He takes the tear-stained strands of hair off my cheek and tucks them behind my ear.

"Because his family can't know about me."

"It'll be a huge funeral. You won't even have to talk to the family."

"But Sadie knows me and so does her mom. They think I'm your ex-girlfriend and it would be weird if they saw me. It wouldn't make sense." I move off Garret's lap and sit across from him. "I don't want to go to the funeral anyway. I want to remember Arlin on a sailboat, not in a casket." Saying it makes me cry again.

"What can I do, Jade?" Garret asks, cupping my cheek.

I push his hand away and wipe the tears off my face. "You can promise me you won't leave. I'm sick of people leaving me! Promise me you won't let that group take you away from me."

"You know I can't promise you that," he says softly.

He reaches for me but I shove him away. I get up and stand on the other side of the tent. "Then just leave! Just go away! Let's just end this now. We both know you're not getting out of this."

He jumps up and gets right in front of me. "We have no idea what's going to happen."

"Yes, we do. If these powerful people want you to be president someday they'll find a way to make it happen. It's over, Garret."

"It's *not* over. Don't even say shit like that. You're just upset because of Arlin."

"I can't do this anymore. I can't meet you down here and act like we're still together when I know this is ending in two weeks."

"It's not ending in two weeks!" He screams it and for the first time I can see that he's scared. I see the panic in his eyes and I hear it in his voice. He's scared that this really *is* ending. That two weeks from now his life will be over. We'll never see each other again and he'll be forced to be with someone he doesn't even like. Be forced to marry her and have children with her. Be forced into doing things that are bad and wrong and illegal. And years from now he'll be the president and they'll still control him. Who knows what they'll make him do.

I hadn't even been thinking about how awful his life will be. I've been so focused on us and what effect this plan would have on me. But it's so much worse for him. And he's only going along with it because of me. Because he's afraid of what they might do to me if he says no.

"Sorry," he says quietly. He hugs me and I feel his heart pumping hard and fast against my chest. "I didn't mean to yell at you."

I pull away. "You're freaking out, aren't you? And I haven't been here for you. I should've been helping you, supporting you, doing whatever you need me to do. You should've said something. You should've told me I was being a shitty girlfriend. I haven't even been a good friend."

He looks at me, confused. "What are you talking about?"

"Your life is over if this happens. You'll have no choices ever again. You'll have no freedom. They'll make you do things. Really bad things. This is way worse for you than it is for me and I haven't even been thinking about that. I'm sorry, Garret."

"You don't need to be sorry. I'm prepared for all that. I can handle it. Am I freaked out that my life will be controlled by other people? Yes. But I'm more freaked out by the idea that I can never see you again. That's what scares me, Jade. Because I don't think I can do it. I'm afraid I'll try to find you and then they'll find out and hurt you to punish me."

"So what are we going to do? I'm out of ideas. Our plan didn't work. If it did, they would've let you go by now. They wouldn't have waited this long."

He puts his hands on my shoulders and looks me in the eye. "You don't know that, so stop thinking that way."

"I DO know it. And so do you. You just won't admit it." He doesn't respond which basically tells me he's thinking the same thing. That our plan didn't work. "I don't know what else to try. I don't know how to fix this."

"We're not even sure if this meeting they're having is about me. We're just guessing based on rumors. It could be about something totally different."

"But if it *is* about you, then we have no time left. I leave a week from Friday to go home and that might be the last time I see you."

"Then let's spend as much time together as possible over the next two weeks. We both have to study for finals, so we'll study down here. We could even sleep down here. I'll get some more blankets and sleeping bags. We'll just camp out until you have to leave. We'll spend our days in the dorm and our nights here. What do you think?"

His eyes are bright and eager as he waits for my answer. I love him so much for trying to make the best of this horrible situation.

"I think it's crazy," I tell him. "But I can do crazy."

"Then go get your books and I'll go get some stuff at the store. We'll meet back here in an hour." He unzips the tent and helps me out.

"What if wild animals eat us?" I call back as I make my way through the woods.

"Raccoons don't eat people, Jade," he yells from inside the tent. "But I'd keep an eye on your potato chips."

I find myself laughing as I imagine a raccoon with his paws in my potato chip bag. Damn, that idiot can make me laugh even when I'm really sad. And I need that in my life. I need *him*. But I'm not sure how much longer I'll have him.

When we meet up again, Garret has more sleeping bags, pillows, and blankets, a flashlight, and four really bright lanterns. He also bought chips, soda, and candy—basic study food.

I set my backpack down and get my books out. "I've never been camping before. Have you?"

"Not really. When my mom was alive and we lived in the other house, my dad let me set up a tent in the back yard but that wasn't really camping."

My phone rings and I check to see who's calling. "Garret, it's Grace. What do I say to her?"

"Just say what you feel."

"I can't. I feel terrible."

It continues to ring. "Just answer it, Jade."

"Hello."

"Jade. It's Grace." She sounds really tired and very serious. "I have some bad news. Your grandfather passed away earlier today. He had a sudden heart attack."

"Yeah, Garret told me. I'm so sorry, Grace. Can I do anything?"

"No, honey. I just wanted to let you know. The funeral is Saturday if you'd like to attend."

"I don't think I can."

"I understand." And the way she says it makes me feel like she does. "Maybe we could have lunch once more before you leave for the summer."

"Yes. Definitely."

"I'll call you next week and we'll figure out a time." She says goodbye and I set the phone down.

I look up at Garret. "Well, that really sucked. I had no idea what to say to her."

"Nobody ever knows what to say when something like this happens."

I rest my head on Garret's lap and he runs his fingers gently through my hair. The tent is quiet except for the sound of an owl off in the distance. I close my eyes and imagine Arlin sailing somewhere up in the clouds. He looks happy and peaceful. It's odd, but I never pictured my mom like that after her death. So I do it now. I see her meeting Arlin, introducing herself as my mom, and Arlin taking her sailing. It makes me feel a little bit better.

"Are you okay?" I open my eyes and see Garret gazing down at me.

"Yeah. I'm okay."

We spend the rest of the night studying, then I fall asleep in Garret's arms, which I haven't done since I stayed at his house after spring break.

In the middle of the night I wake up and hear Garret talking in his sleep. He keeps saying my name and then he says, "No, don't take her." He says it several times, then gets quiet again but tightens his hold on me.

I don't have to be an expert in analyzing dreams to know that he's worried his future has already been decided and there's no way out of this. He's losing hope. And so am I.

CHAPTER TWENTY-SIX

Why is it that when you're desperate for time to slow down, it suddenly speeds up? The past week has gone by faster than any week in my entire life. Garret and I spent every night together in the tent and even snuck down there during the day. But it still wasn't enough time with him.

Now it's Monday and my last week at Moorhurst College—not just for the semester, but forever. I won't be coming back here again. Garret and I already decided that when we thought this would all work out and we'd be together. Now I'm assuming we won't be together after this week, which means that in the fall Garret will go to Yale as dictated by the plan because apparently presidents go to Ivy League colleges and Moorhurst isn't good enough.

I'll be going to college somewhere else. I can't come back here. There are too many memories. Plus Yale isn't that far from Moorhurst and Garret and I need distance between us or we both know we'd try to sneak out and see each other.

I've already sent out applications to other schools. I haven't heard back yet so I don't know where I'll end up. And I'm not sure how I'll afford it. Arlin always said he wanted to pay for my college, but now that he's gone I don't know what will happen.

I'm not going to ask Grace about it, especially so soon after Arlin's death.

Garret and his family attended Arlin's funeral last Saturday. Garret said there were so many people at the church that some people had to stand. I probably could've gone and hid in the back but I'm glad I didn't. I prefer that image I have of Arlin sailing in the clouds.

Today is the start of final exams and the physics final is my first one. As I walk to class I remember how I felt when I arrived here last September. I was so afraid I wouldn't do well in my classes. I never would've guessed that the classes would be the easiest part of college.

I get to class right as the professor begins handing out the final. The answers come easily to me and I'm the first one to finish it. My brain has been really fired up this past week. I guess it was trying to occupy itself with school so it wouldn't have to think about all the other stuff going on.

Carson turns in his final just seconds after I do and follows me out the door to the outside. "I haven't seen you around all week. Where have you been?"

"Just hiding out studying. The dorms are too noisy. I had to get out of there."

I'm not in the mood to talk to him but he keeps following me as I walk back to the dorm.

"Is something wrong?" He's got his conspiracy tone going. I hope he's not getting ready to tell me a new story about Garret's family. He hasn't said a word about them since Garret and I broke up, which just confirms that he was only telling me that stuff so I'd stop dating Garret. A few weeks ago Carson asked me out. He wanted to take me to dinner and a movie. As usual, he claimed it wasn't a date but just two friends hanging out. I said no, of course, and after that, he gave up asking me out.

Knowing Carson, he's probably still trying to find out what's going on with Garret's family and their company but I can't worry about it anymore.

"Nothing's wrong, Carson. I'm just tired from all the studying."

"When are you done with finals?"

"Wednesday. Thursday I'm packing and Friday I'm flying home."

"Are you leaving your stuff in storage?"

"I don't have much stuff. Mainly clothes."

"What about your car?"

Carson asks way too many questions. He's a nice guy but his constant prying gets on my nerves.

"A friend of mine is going to drive it out later," I say, hoping he won't ask for the friend's name. The truth is that I'm packing the car with all my stuff and a guy will come get the car a week from today and drive it to California. Before he died, Arlin hired the driver for me. It's the guy he uses for his own cars. Apparently rich people do this all the time. They prefer to fly long distances and have their car delivered.

"Maybe we could meet up this summer," Carson says. "I'll be in Des Moines in July to visit my grandma."

"I won't be there. I'm spending the summer in California."

"Without Garret? I thought you weren't going since you guys broke up."

"I'm still going. Harper and her boyfriend are renting the place next to mine."

"Then I guess after Friday I won't see you until September."

"Yeah. Probably not."

We say goodbye and he goes to his dorm and I go in mine. Carson will be the first person to investigate why I'm not here next fall. Truthfully, he'll be the only one who cares. Nobody else will even notice. Except Harper. I haven't decided what to tell her yet. But I have all summer with her, so it's not like I have to tell her this week.

I haven't told Frank and Ryan my plans either, and I'm not going to until I know for sure where I'm going in the fall. If I told them now, they'd ask too many questions and I don't have the energy to come up with a story they'll believe. I'll tell them later when all this is over.

The week continues with more finals during the day and more campouts at night with Garret. We only sleep a couple hours each night. There's no time for sleep. As much as I don't want to believe it, this could be our last week together and just the thought of that makes me want to savor each moment we have left.

Part of our nights are spent being together physically, but most of our time is spent lying in each other's arms talking. Telling each other things that bring us even closer. Things we wouldn't tell others. Things we probably wouldn't have told each other for a very long time, but now time is running out and we have to fit it all in during these last few days. I want to know everything about Garret, even though I may never see him again after this week.

He tells me more about his mom and all the stuff he went through after she died. He tells me a story about when he was 14 and got drunk for the first time. He came stumbling home and his dad pretended to not even notice and that's when he assumed his dad didn't care about him anymore. That single incident started the years of drinking he now regrets.

Tonight we're on the topic of my mom. I don't know why but for some reason I tell him a story about when I was 8 and had the flu and threw up on the carpet because I couldn't get to the bathroom fast enough. I was so sick I could barely move, but my mom made me scrub the carpet until it was clean. I hated her for it. Part of me still does. Maybe that's why I told Garret that story. Maybe by telling him I can move on and not be so angry about it.

"Okay, your turn," I say. "Tell me something else. Anything."

We've been taking turns telling each other stuff. I wait for him to talk, but he doesn't. Instead he looks at me like he wants to say something but isn't sure if he should.

"Go ahead," I tell him.

"Jade. . . did you love your mom?"

I stare back at him, surprised that he would even think to ask me something like that, especially after I just told him that story about her.

Deep down I know the answer to that question, but I've never admitted it to myself because it's wrong and crazy and makes absolutely no sense. And I'm not sure why Garret even cares. What difference does it make?

"Jade?" He's still waiting for me to respond, sitting across from me holding both my hands.

I notice that I'm shaking a little as I nod. "Yes. I loved her." I pick my arm up and use my sleeve to quickly wipe away a tear. "Why are you even asking me that?"

"Because I think you needed to hear yourself say it."

I don't respond because now I'm pissed I said it at all.

He reaches for the hand that's now in my lap. "It's okay, you know. You can love her even after everything she did to you."

"No, it's not okay!" I rip my hands from his and scoot back a little, hugging my knees to my chest while a few more tears manage to escape my eyes. "She doesn't deserve it. She deserves nothing but hate from me."

He comes over and wraps me tightly in his arms so I can't pull away despite my all-out effort to do so.

I'm so angry. Not at Garret, but at myself for saying I loved her. I give up fighting him and just let my body relax into his.

"I shouldn't have loved her. It's wrong." I keep my head down against his chest. "But I did. And I don't know why."

"Because she was your mom," Garret says softly.

It's true. It seems like the reason should be more complex than that but it's not. She was my mom and as horrible as she was to me, I'm her child and children love their moms. And I loved her because even as a child, I knew she was struggling with some kind of deep, devastating pain that never went away and I wished more than anything that I could help her somehow. Now I know the cause of her pain and the reason she acted that way, but it's still hard for me to say that I loved her.

"Jade. Can I ask you something else?"

"Yeah."

He hesitates, then asks, "Are you afraid to have kids someday because you think you'll treat them like your mom treated you?"

It's another question I didn't expect and one I've never even asked myself. I feel Garret's arm muscles tense up as he prepares for me to try to yank away from him again.

But I keep still and take a moment to think about his question. It doesn't take long for me to realize that he's right. I'm scared to death I would abuse my child the way my mom abused me. Not that I would hit a child, but that I might say the same awful things my mom said to me. The words that used to haunt me until Garret came along and stopped them.

I don't look at him when I answer. "Yes."

And that's all we say about it.

But he's given me something to think about. How did Garret know this about me when I didn't even realize it myself? Because he gets me. That's why. He gets everything about me

297

and I'll never meet anyone ever again who understands me like he does. He knows who I was last year and who I am now, and he was at my side for that journey and is the reason I went on it in the first place. That's how I know that this thing we have between us can never be replicated with someone else. This is it. And soon it's going to end.

On Thursday Garret finds out that the organization's meeting next Monday is definitely about his future. He's not allowed to attend the meeting, but his dad will be there. Garret's going home on Friday at noon and once he's there he isn't allowed to leave the house until after the decision has been made. It's a mandate from the organization.

At the meeting they'll take a vote and Garret's fate will be decided. If the plan is approved by a majority of the members, his every action from that point forward will be decided for him.

Friday morning Garret and I get up early like we've been doing so we can sneak back in the dorm.

"I guess this is it." I fold up one of the blankets and start on another. I sound cheery for some reason. I guess I'm trying to deny this is really happening. "You need help packing up all this stuff?"

"No. I'll do it later." Garret doesn't sound cheery at all and his serious tone knocks me back to the cold hard reality I don't want to exist. He takes the blanket from me and throws it on the ground. "Jade, don't act like this is over."

"I'm not. I just wanted to help clean up." The cheerful tone returns as I fight against that damn reality.

I go to roll up the sleeping bags but he grabs me around my waist and draws me into him. "This will all work out, Jade. I promise."

"That's just mean!" I shove on his chest but he won't let me go. "You know that's not true! Why would you even say something like that?"

"Because it's what I believe, so I'm saying it."

He's holding me so tight that it's no use fighting him but I still try. I don't know why. It's not like I want him to let me go. But that fucking reality is now staring me in the face, ripping at my heart, and being this close to him, being in his arms . . . it's killing me. I can't do it a second longer.

"Let me go."

"Don't be this way. This isn't the end."

My gaze remains on the ground. I can't look at him. "Yeah, whatever. I'll make sure to vote for you in 20 years."

"Hey." He pulls back a little and nudges my chin up. "Stop it. You're trying to shut your feelings off just like the old Jade would. You're trying to push me away and I won't let you do it. This is the last—"

"Last time we'll see each other? Yeah, exactly. So much for the promise you just made."

All of a sudden, a rush of emotion shocks my system, flooding every cell and I can't stop it. I don't where it came from and why it's happening now when I'm trying so hard to be strong. Tears well up in my eyes and my throat burns as I struggle to keep the tears from falling.

"I was going to say it's the last time I'll see you until I get to California." Garret smiles at me and for a second I believe that he really *will* see me in California, but then I come to my senses.

"You're not going to California. They'll probably make you spend another summer in DC learning how to be a politician. Going to fundraisers and—"

"Jade, stop." He hugs me even closer, pressing my cheek against his chest and kissing the top of my head. "We'll see each other again." Even though his voice is strong, I feel him trembling a little as he holds me. "You're not getting rid of me."

"Maybe I'm ready to get rid of you." I close my eyes and breathe in the scent of him one last time. "Being with you is exhausting." It comes out sounding funny for some strange reason. I don't even know why I said it. It sounds like something stupid I would've said before all this happened.

He gently pushes me back to face him. "What are you talking about? Being with me is awesome and you know it." He gives me the cocky smile that only he could get away with and it somehow lightens the mood. And for just a moment I let myself go back to the way things used to be between us, before we started counting the minutes to the end, because I miss those times so bad and I'd do anything to get them back.

Garret keeps talking. "I make you laugh. I buy you the world's best chocolate. I have sex with you whenever you ask. I keep my body in shape for your visual pleasure. I—"

"Are you done complimenting yourself? Because I could give you a whole list of things that need work." I really can't think of anything he needs to work on. I love him exactly the way he is, but I try to find something to prove my point. "Like you could really use a haircut. The bad-boy Garret look isn't working for you."

"See? There's no way you could go the rest of your life without giving me one of your insults."

He lets me go and I get the feeling he wants to end this now, while we're still in this make-believe happy place. While the mood is light and not so sad.

But I'm not ready for it to end.

I'm not ready to say goodbye.

I can't do this. I can't.

Garret takes both my hands in his. "So I'll see you later, okay?" He uses an upbeat tone, but his face is serious and struggling to form even the slightest smile.

My heart is running fast, skipping beats, like it's in total distress.

I need more time. This can't be the end.

But it is. And I need to say goodbye.

I swallow hard past the giant lump in my throat, begging my eyes not to cry. "Yeah. I'll see you later."

I turn to leave, but Garret keeps hold of one of my hands. "Hey."

I turn back around.

"Before you go. One more thing." His beautiful blue eyes are wet now, ready to drop tears at any second. It just confirms that he, too, believes this is the end, no matter what he says.

"Yeah?" I bite my bottom lip hard to keep from crying.

"I love you, Jade Taylor." He smiles even though a tear is running down his face. "I always will."

I somehow manage to smile back, tears now pouring from my eyes. "I love you, too, Garret Kensington. I'll love you forever."

With those final words, I tear my hand from his and run out of the tent, through the woods and up the hill to the trail, not looking back.

When I get to my room, I cry like I've never cried before, hoping it will help relieve all the hurt, loss, and sadness I'm feeling. But it doesn't. It's going to take a long time to feel better. A really long time. Even so, I tell myself that I'm not going to cry about this after today. I knew this was coming and crying about it doesn't make it any easier.

I have to accept that this chapter of my life is closing. And I'll be okay. I'll move on, just like I did after my mom's suicide.

I'm strong and I can get past this.

CHAPTER TWENTY-SEVEN

At noon I leave to meet Grace for lunch. I don't feel like going out, but I told her I'd be there. As I'm driving to the restaurant I realize that I'm actually glad I'm going to see her. We're both experiencing loss and sadness and maybe just by being together we can make each other feel a little bit better.

We meet at the cafe in the old historic house, the one we went to when I first met her. It's weird not having Arlin there. And really sad. Grace gives me a hug when I see her.

"I'm so sorry," I say softly as we hug.

She rubs my back. "It's okay, honey. I'll see him again someday."

When we pull away and take our seats, I see her taking deep breaths to keep her emotions in check. She looks thinner, like she hasn't eaten since it happened.

We talk a little about the funeral, but then she quickly changes the subject to her flower garden, telling me what she's planting next week and about the new flower seeds she ordered. She talks about it all through lunch and I just listen because I know that talking about geraniums and petunias is the only way she can get through the pain she's feeling. We all have our own way of dealing with these things and this is hers.

When we're done eating, she gets her purse out and I assume that means she's getting ready to leave.

"Thank you for lunch." I get my car keys out.

"No, honey, we're not leaving yet. I just had to get something from my purse. Your flight leaves later tonight, right?"

"Yes. At 6." I put my keys away.

"Then we have time." She runs her hand up and down an envelope that's now lying on the table.

"Did you get a letter?" I ask her.

"No. This is something for you."

"Oh." I look at it, confused. "Do you want me to open it?"

She shakes her head. "Not yet."

She's struggling and I don't know why. I put my hand on hers. "What is it Grace? Is something wrong?"

"I just have a hard time talking about him." I notice that her lips are quivering and her eyes are watery.

I scoot my chair closer to her. "I know. I miss him, too."

She smiles and wipes the corners of her eyes with her napkin. "He was so happy taking you sailing. I can't tell you how much that meant to him." She laughs a little. "After you'd leave he'd say how quickly you learned what he taught you. He'd repeat all the questions you asked him. His whole face lit up when he talked about you. Even before I met you, he told me all about you. How you were valedictorian of your high school. How well you were doing at Moorhurst. He was so proud."

Now she's making *me* tear up. Dammit!

She takes a deep breath and smiles like she's determined to stop crying about Arlin's death. I know because it's the same determination I'm trying to force upon myself with the loss of Garret.

"Jade, honey," she continues. "You already know Arlin and I wanted to pay for your college. So this will take care of that."

She taps the envelope but still doesn't give it to me. "But we wanted to do more for you."

The waiter comes to refill her coffee and she waits for him to leave before continuing.

"Arlin was a very successful man and he wanted to share that success with his family. So before he passed, he put some money into a trust for you. We did it now because if we waited until both Arlin and I were gone, it would cause confusion among the rest of the family. They wouldn't understand why we gave you this."

She hands me the envelope. I open it and pull out a sheet of paper. There's some legal jargon on it and a seal at the bottom. And then I see my name. And next to it is a number. A very large number with a dollar sign in front of it.

I can't speak. I don't even think I'm breathing. I'm too shocked. I stare at it thinking I must be reading it wrong but the number doesn't change.

It's 50 million dollars. Fifty. Million. Dollars.

I force myself to breathe again.

"It's yours, Jade, to use as you see fit. Arlin and I wanted you to have whatever type of future you want. This will help you do that."

"No. It's way too much. I don't need this much."

She smiles. "It's a lot, but it's not too much. Remember, honey, we're billionaires. It takes a lot of millions to make a billion."

I guess that's true, but still. Fifty million? I get my wallet out and give her the credit card she gave me back in March. "Then I don't need this anymore."

She gives it back. "Take it. Use it until you get out of school and then you can get your own. That's the deal we have with all the grandchildren."

"But I have—"

"Jade. Use the credit card until you graduate. Arlin was very insistent on that and so am I. You can use the money from the trust later on."

I look at the paper again and the amount and my mind immediately thinks of Frank and Ryan. "Are there any restrictions on how I can use this? Because I was just wondering if it's okay if I give a little to Frank. With his illness, he hasn't been able to work, so he could really use some money. He wouldn't waste it. I swear. He'd just use it for groceries and maybe to fix up his house. And his son really needs a new car and some help paying for med school."

She nods. "It's your money. You can give Frank as much as you want."

Knowing I can help Frank makes me even more excited about the money. He could get a new house. Move to a better neighborhood. Pay off Ryan's loans. This will change their lives.

I reach over and give her a hug. "Thank you for this. I don't even know what to say." I pull back and look at her. "Other than that I need you to know that I never, *ever* expected you and Arlin to give me money. I only wanted to get to know my grandparents."

She pats my hand. "Yes, I know, honey."

"So when will I see you again?"

"Whenever you want to see me. I do enjoy California." She smiles. "In fact we have a small cottage in Santa Barbara. I plan to spend a few weeks out there this summer."

I'd love to know what she considers to be a small cottage.

"Then I'm coming to see you. Or you can come stay with me. I have a whole condo and it's just going to be me there."

"Jade." She clasps her hands around mine and waits for our eyes to meet. "This issue with Garret will get resolved. I'll take care of it myself if I have to. If those idiot men would just let women into their little club they wouldn't make such stupid decisions."

Grace is usually soft spoken, but she said those words forcefully like she was both fed up and pissed off. I didn't realize she knew about everything going on with Garret. It's not something we talk about. Plus, Garret said the members usually don't tell their wives what goes on within the organization.

"I'm not feeling good about it. There's a meeting on Monday."

"Yes. I know about the meeting. My son, William, is a member. He'll be there."

"Does he know what's going to happen?"

"No. But you shouldn't give up yet, Jade."

"I'm not. I'm—"

"Yes. You have." She squeezes my hand. "I could see you struggling all through lunch because you think this is over. But you're giving up too soon. You need to have hope. Sometimes things just work out."

I nod like I believe her even though I don't at all.

"You should know that before Arlin passed, he fought hard to keep Garret out of this. And I don't just mean with the negative press that was created. I mean that he let his feelings be known to every member of the organization. And that's not something you do. It's against the rules."

"Then why did he do it?"

She takes a sip of her coffee. "When Royce was picked years ago, Arlin asked them to pick someone else, but he didn't do anything else to get it stopped."

"But Royce wanted to be president, didn't he?"

"Yes, but it wasn't right for him. He always had an obsessive personality. He'd set his mind on something and wouldn't let anything or anyone stop him from getting it. The organization took advantage of that. When we learned about their plan for Royce, Arlin and I knew it would destroy him. And it did. Arlin always regretted that he didn't do more to stop what they did to our son. I think helping Garret was his way of trying to fix the past. That and the fact that he wanted you to be happy."

I wonder what exactly Arlin did. What if his attempts to help Garret caused him to get in trouble? What if the organization did something to Arlin? What if the heart attack wasn't natural but was caused by something they did? Wait—what am I saying? I sound like Carson, coming up with his crazy conspiracy theories. I quickly shake them from my mind and notice Grace getting up from the table.

"You should get back to school and finish packing. I have some issues to take care of at the lawyer's office and then I'm heading home to work in my garden."

We walk out together to the parking lot.

"You should try gardening, Jade. It's very relaxing. Whenever I'm feeling stressed I find that I have to do something physical like take a walk or work in the garden."

"Me, too. Except I go running."

"Running's hard on the knees." She winks. "Try gardening."

I smile. "Okay. I'll see you later."

"No goodbye?"

"I don't like goodbyes."

"Then I'll see you later, Jade."

We have one last hug before leaving.

Back at Moorhurst it's total chaos as people pack up cars and moving trucks with all their stuff. I get out of my car, still trying to comprehend the fact that I am now a millionaire. A multimillionaire.

I'm not ready to go back to my room, so I sit on a bench under a big maple tree. Everywhere I look I see things that remind me of Garret. There are so many memories here. This is where we met, where we became best friends, and where we fell in love.

I get up and walk to the edge of campus over to the trail that leads into the woods. A few people are running on it today and I wait for them to pass me. Then I sneak down and go deep into the woods to the tent so I can see it one last time.

But it's gone. Everything's gone. Like it was never there.

I collapse down on my knees and the tears start pouring again. I know I said I wouldn't cry, but I can't stop myself. I feel like I've lost everything. And I'm afraid that soon I'll turn back into the old Jade who didn't trust people and didn't believe in happy endings. *Good things never last, Jade.* That's what my mom used to say and I used to believe her. But now I've changed and I don't want to go back to the person I used to be, but part of me thinks that I will.

My phone rings and I see that it's Frank calling. I sit up and take a deep breath before answering. "Hi, Frank."

"Hey, I just wanted to wish you a safe trip." He sounds really happy. "Ryan and I will both be at the airport tonight to pick you up. We can't wait to see you."

"Yeah. It'll be good to be home." I do my best to match his happy tone but it doesn't come out that way.

"Are you okay, Jade?"

"I'm fine. Just tired."

"Well, we'll let you sleep in tomorrow. See you soon."

When he hangs up I check the phone for any messages. There's one from Harper. She's driving to California with Sean. They left yesterday and her message says they're somewhere in Pennsylvania.

The alarm on my phone beeps reminding me I need to head to the airport soon. I make my way up the hill and back to my dorm room. The suitcase Garret bought me last year is packed and ready to go, sitting next to the door. I packed all my other stuff in the car. My room is as empty as when I arrived here last fall.

I sit on the bare mattress on my bed and look around. It doesn't seem like that long ago that I walked in this room for the first time, feeling really sick because I was scared to death to be so far away from home. And then I met Garret on that very first night. I couldn't take my eyes off him. He was the hottest guy I'd ever seen. And he was nice to me from the second we met. I pretended to be annoyed with him, but deep down I liked him right away. I liked talking to him and hanging out with him. I liked that he kept forcing me to do things with him. He made me feel welcome, and after just one day with him I forgot all about missing home. And even after I told him we couldn't date, he stuck around. He was my friend from my first day here and ended up being the best friend I'll ever have.

Garret's at his house now, so I go up to his floor. Guys fill the hallway, carrying boxes and furniture. Music is blaring and guys are yelling stuff to each other. I squeeze past some guys carrying a couch and make my way down to Garret's room. The door is open and the room is completely empty, just like mine. I go inside and shut the door. It still smells like him and I feel the tears forming again and realize that coming up here probably wasn't the best idea. But I had to see this room one last time. This is where Garret first said that he loved me. And where I first said it to him. It's where he hugged me, again and again, until I finally learned how to do it right. It's where he talked to me and listened to me and helped me get the voices out of my head.

There are so many memories between these four walls. And on this campus. In this town. But it's time to let them go.

It's not at all what I want. I don't want to forget. I want to remember everything. Everything Garret and I shared since the moment we met last September. All the movie nights in his room. All the trips to Al's Pancake House. Racing each other on the track and in the pool. Every hug. Every kiss. All of it. But I can't. I have to find a way to shove those memories in the back of my mind where they'll never be found. And then force myself to never go looking for them. It's the only way I'll ever move on without him.

My phone dings reminding me it's time to leave. I go back downstairs and wheel my suitcase into the hall, then look at my empty room once more before shutting the door for good.

When I go outside, a taxi is there waiting to take me to the airport. The driver takes my suitcase and puts it in the trunk.

As the taxi drives away, I say goodbye to Moorhurst. Not 'see you later,' but goodbye. Because I know for sure that I'll never come back here again.

CHAPTER TWENTY-EIGHT

Back in Des Moines, I wait until Sunday night to tell Frank about the money. Ryan is out with Chloe, which is good because I didn't want him around when I talked to Frank. Ryan can't know the money came from me. For one, he knows nothing about my relation to the Sinclairs and two, he'd feel weird taking money from his little sister.

"Frank, I need to tell you something." I'm kind of nervous to tell him this. I'm worried he'll get mad at me for accepting the money or take offense that I'm offering him some of it.

"What is it, Jade?" He turns the TV down.

We're sitting in the living room, him in his recliner and me on the couch.

"Well, as you know, I spent a lot of time with Grace and Arlin the past few months and I really got to know them."

"Yes, and I'm glad you did that. It was good for you. I'm just so sorry about Arlin."

"He treated me like a granddaughter since the day we met. And Grace did, too. Well, she still does. She has a house in California so she's coming out to see me this summer."

"That's good, honey." Frank takes a drink of water from the glass by his chair.

"So anyway, they wanted to help me pay for college. I guess I already told you that. But what you don't know is that they set up a trust fund for me."

Frank's eyebrows raise. "To cover your college expenses?"

"Yes, but the money can be used for other things, too. And I, uh . . . I wanted to give some of it to you."

"No. Absolutely not. You need that money for school, and if you go to medical school, well, that's very expensive. I still don't know how I'm going to pay for Ryan's tuition."

"That's why I'm giving this to you. You can pay off Ryan's loans. And he won't even need loans for med school. You can just pay for it. You'll have plenty of money. And you can get him a car that works. One that has air conditioning and doesn't break down every week. And you can pay off your medical bills."

"No, that's too much money. Ryan and I will figure something out. We always do."

"Just let me do this for you. Please. I never would've gone to college if you hadn't taken me in after my mom died. I would've ended up in state custody. Stuck in foster homes. I might not have even graduated from high school."

"That's not true, Jade. You're a very determined, very bright young woman. You would've graduated no matter what."

"Whatever. The point is that you kept me on the right path. And you've always taken care of me and treated me like a daughter. Please, Frank. I want to do this for you."

He sighs. "How much money are you talking about here, because I'm not taking—"

"I have 50 million dollars," I blurt out. "So you can have as much as you need."

His jaw drops and he's speechless, just like I was when I found out.

"I know. It's a lot of money."

He clears his throat. "Yes. I thought you were going to say they gave you a million. But 50 million. Wow. You're set for life, Jade."

"And I want you and Ryan to be, too."

"I appreciate the offer, but I can't accept it. It would be wrong to take your money."

"It's not wrong. And don't think of it as my money. Think of it as the money Royce owed us for what he did to my mom and me. And to you, since you had to support me after my mom died. You bought me clothes and food and let me stay here. I at least owe you money for that."

"Don't be ridiculous, Jade. You don't owe me anything. You were a child. I was taking care of you just like I took care of Ryan. The money never even crossed my mind."

"Will you please just take some of this? If you don't, I'll mail you a check and if you don't cash it I'll keep mailing them until you do."

He thinks for a moment. "Okay. I'll use some to pay for Ryan's tuition."

I scoot to the end of the couch closer to Frank's chair. "And get Ryan a car that works. A car he really wants. Not a cheap car or a used car."

He smiles and pats my hand. "Fine. I'll get him a car."

"You can't tell him this money is from me. Make something up. Say a long lost uncle died and left you five million dollars."

"Jade, I am not taking five million dollars from you."

"Yes, you are. That's nothing. I'll still have 45 million left."

"You know I'll never spend that much money."

"Then when you die, which I'm not letting you do until you're at least 110, you can leave whatever's left to Ryan. Or give him part of it now. It's yours. Divide it however you want."

I cross my arms across my chest and glare at him. "You're taking that money, Frank. I won't take no for an answer."

He shakes his head. "You're very stubborn. You always have been."

I keep glaring at him.

"How about one million? That's more than enough."

"Nope. You're getting five."

We argue about it some more, but he finally takes it.

Now that I've settled that issue, on to the next; the meeting to decide Garret's fate. I already know what the outcome will be and now I just want it over with so I can attempt to move on.

Monday comes and goes and I don't hear a word about what happened. I didn't expect that I would. The meeting was at night and Garret's dad said that afterward, a vote would be taken and the outcome would be discussed by a smaller group of higher level members. That wouldn't happen until Tuesday. After that, Garret and his dad would be called in for a private meeting in which they would be told the final decision before it was announced to the entire organization.

If they decide to go ahead with their plan, Garret will have to spend the rest of the week learning what will happen next. They'll start training him on the basics of being a politician, like what he can and can't say in public, how he should dress, who he'll be dating. He won't be allowed to call anyone. Even if he could, the members think Garret broke up with me months ago, so he couldn't call me anyway, which is why we said our goodbyes in the woods.

All day Tuesday I wait to hear the decision. The plan was for Pearce to call and tell me but he never said when he'd call. And he said if he was unable to call, he'd send me an email or a text. But I haven't received anything.

Even though I'm completely on edge I try to act normal in front of Frank and Ryan, who know nothing about what's going on. While I'm a nervous wreck, Frank is more relaxed than I've ever seen him. He's always had to worry about money and now he doesn't have to.

I love that I'm able to do this for him. He can rest and take care of his health and not worry about finding freelance work. And Ryan can quit his job and focus on school. Frank isn't going to tell Ryan about the money until he has it in his own account, which he will once I figure out how to access the money in my trust fund.

Around 11 I go to bed realizing that I'm not going to hear from Garret's dad today. There must be some delay. Either that or his dad doesn't want to have to tell me the bad news. But I wish he'd just call and get it over with.

I can't sleep. I toss and turn, then check the clock and repeat the process every couple minutes.

Then at 12:14, my phone rings. I don't recognize the number but I answer it anyway.

"Hello?"

"Jade, it's me."

My heart stops when I hear his voice. Why is he calling me? His dad was supposed to call me, not him. What does this mean? He doesn't sound happy or excited. He doesn't really sound like anything other than tired.

"Garret?" I shove the covers off me and stand up. "Is it really you?"

"Yeah, it's me."

"So they're allowing you to call me? Why? Did they give you one last phone call to say goodbye?"

He's quiet and I get a sick feeling in my stomach as I sink back down on the bed. I'm not prepared for this goodbye. I can't do this again. I thought our goodbye in the woods was the last one, and now he's calling me to say one last final goodbye? Why is he doing this to me? I don't even know what to say to him. I finally hear his voice again.

"I'm not saying goodbye. And this isn't our last phone call."

"What are you talking about? What does that mean?"

"They let me go."

"Don't joke about this, Garret. I swear I'll—I don't know what I'll do to you, but something really bad for playing this sick joke on me."

"I'm serious. The plan wasn't approved. They didn't have enough votes for it to pass." Now he sounds happy. Why the hell didn't he sound that way when I answered the phone? I was having a freaking panic attack here!

"Wait. So it's over?"

"It's over."

"But how? What did—"

"How was the flight to Des Moines?"

His sudden topic change is a sign that he can't talk about what happened over the phone. Someone might be listening. I don't know who or why, but in Garret's crazy world there's always a possibility someone's listening.

But I'm having a really hard time acting calm and normal when I just want to jump up and down and tell him how happy I am. How relieved I am. How I want to see him again as soon as possible. I take a moment to calm down and try to contain my excitement.

"The flight was okay."

"Good." He gets quiet.

This is very odd. I'm not sure what I'm allowed to say. And I don't understand this. If someone from the organization is listening to the call, then why is Garret calling me at all? Are they allowing us to date now? That doesn't make sense. Even if he's not their presidential pick, he's still a member of the organization. He was born into it. He has no choice. Or did his dad manage to get him out of it?

I need Garret to give me a clue, anything that will at least hint about what's going on.

"So are you going to California?" I ask.

"In a week or so. I have to take care of some things first."

From his tone I get the feeling I'm not supposed to ask what those things are, so I don't. But the fact that he's going to California seems like a good sign.

"And, um, you'll be staying there a while? In California?"

"Yeah." His tone lightens and he sounds even happier. "I'll be there all summer."

Another good sign.

"And then you're going back to Moorhurst?"

"No. I've decided to go to a different college next year. I don't know where yet. But my options are open. I can choose wherever I want to go."

He puts a slight emphasis on the words 'options' and 'choose' which I'm taking to mean that he's somehow not part of that group anymore. Or if he is, they eased up on the rules and are letting him make his own choices, something his dad was never allowed to do.

"Okay, well, when you figure out your plans, just let me know."

"I will. Hey, I can't really talk now and things will be a little crazy the next couple days, so I probably won't call you until Friday."

"All right." I go along with it, but find it strange that he can't talk to me for the next two days. "Did you get a new phone? I didn't recognize the number."

"I'm calling from the home phone. I kind of trashed my cell." He pauses. "I had to say goodbye to someone I didn't want to say goodbye to and I um, got really pissed and threw my phone in a creek in the woods."

I almost laugh. It's not really funny, but the image of him throwing it in there is a little funny.

"Tell Frank and Ryan I said hi. I'll talk to you soon."

"Yeah. Bye."

He hangs up without an I love you or I miss you or anything like that. He obviously wanted to make it sound like we're just friends and not dating. So what does that mean? I'm so confused.

Maybe I'm getting all worked up about nothing. Maybe Garret was just being extra cautious, just in case someone was listening in.

I'm not going to worry about it. Besides, Garret sounded happy. And he wouldn't sound that way unless he knew he could be with me. Unless he knew we could have a future together. It takes a moment for that to sink in. Garret thinks we can be together? So this whole thing is over? We can be together without people trying to break us apart?

Then what I am doing in bed? I get up and jump around like a lunatic. I know I'm acting crazy but I'm too excited to go to sleep.

Who would've ever thought that Jade Taylor would be jumping around her room in the middle of the night because of a guy? Anyone who knew the old Jade would never believe it. But in the past year, I've learned that love can make you do crazy, silly, stupid, ridiculous things. And the fact that one person can make you feel this way and do those things is amazing to me. Now I just need to get that one person back and never let him go.

CHAPTER TWENTY-NINE

The next two days go by and as Garret said, I don't hear from him. On Friday morning, I pack up for California. Frank and Ryan take me out for breakfast and then we head to the airport. Ryan parks at the drop-off area and gets out to give me a hug.

"I'll definitely make it out there to see you this summer," he says. "I just don't know when yet. This car will never make it. I'll have to fly, which means I need to get some extra shifts at work to pay for it. But I'll be there."

"You better be," I say, hugging him tight. I smile knowing that as soon as Ryan finds out about the money he'll be able to quit his job and not worry so much.

Frank gives me a hug next. "Have a good trip, honey."

I whisper near his ear. "I'll get you the money as soon as possible. I don't know how all that works, but I'll figure it out. Get Ryan a car before anything else. And then get yourself something."

He pulls away, smiling. "You have fun this summer. Be sure to call us."

"I will. See you later."

The plane ride to California is a few hours so I use the time to sleep. Since getting the news about Garret I've been too excited to sleep, but I sleep really well on planes for some reason. When we land, the guy next to me has to wake me up.

Harper is picking me up at the airport so I get my suitcase, then wait for her outside the terminal.

This is my first time in California. Harper told me the weather here is almost always perfect. Today it's sunny and dry and feels like it's about 75 degrees. Perfect, just like she said.

I hear my phone ringing while I'm waiting and I have to dig through my carry-on bag to get it out.

"Hello?"

"Hey, it's me."

"Garret?" I instantly smile just hearing his voice again.

He laughs. "Yeah. It's Garret. Why were you asking like you weren't sure? I thought we were on the 'it's me' level."

I start laughing. "We are. We totally are. I just wasn't expecting it to be you. I've been dying to talk to you. I can't believe you made me wait—"

"Where are you right now?"

"I'm at the airport. Harper's picking me up. She should be here any minute."

"Yeah. About that. Harper called and said she isn't coming."

"What? Why not?"

"Because I told her not to."

"Why would you—" I stop when I notice a white BMW convertible parked two cars down from where I'm standing.

"So you want a ride or what?" I turn around and Garret is right there in front of me, looking all California-like in his white polo shirt, navy shorts, sunglasses, and a golden-brown tan.

My heart explodes with happiness. If I were a cartoon, little pink and red hearts would be floating around my head right now. I don't think I've ever been more excited to see someone. In fact I know I haven't.

I go to hug him but he hugs me first, lifting me off the ground.

"Garret, how did you do this?"

"I'll tell you later." He sets me down and gives me a long, not-so-innocent kiss that is probably causing the people around us to stare. Who cares? They have no idea what we've been through.

"You need to move your car, sir."

We stop kissing and notice a police officer pointing back at the car.

"Yeah, we were just leaving," Garret says.

The guy shakes his head, annoyed. Garret just laughs and grabs my hand, pulling me toward the car. He opens the door for me, then goes back for my luggage and puts it in the truck. When he gets in he asks, "Do you want to drive? It's your car."

"You go ahead. I have all summer to drive it."

He takes off away from the airport.

"I can't believe you're really here! That you're actually sitting here next to me." I move my hand up and down Garret's arm to make sure he's real and this isn't a dream.

"So it was a good surprise?" He brings my hand to his lips and kisses it.

"Are you kidding? It was the best surprise ever. You'll never top that one."

His cocky smile appears. "Oh, I think I can."

I have no idea what that means, but I don't bother asking.

"Is this really over? Their plan for you?"

"It's over. And they already picked someone else."

"Do you know who? I mean, not that you'd know the guy but—"

"I know him. And so do you." He glances at me like I should know who he's talking about, but I give him a blank stare. "Evan Cauldwell."

"Evan." I repeat it as I try to think of how I know that name. "Evan as in Sadie's boyfriend? That guy from Yale?"

"Yeah, the one who was so rude to us that night of the fundraiser. I got a bad feeling from that guy as soon as we met him. I don't know why they didn't pick him originally. He's a way better choice than me. I'm sure he'll do whatever they ask without even thinking about it."

"Is Sadie still dating him?"

"Yeah, and get this. Apparently she aspires to be first lady someday. One of the members told my dad that she actually volunteered to marry whichever guy they picked. I guess before he died, Royce told Sadie how the system works and she was all set to make herself part of it."

"Is that why she wanted to get back together with you? Did she know about their plans for you before *you* even knew?"

"I can't say for sure, but that's what I'm guessing. After I talked to her that day you were in the car with me, she broke it off with Evan. And she just got back together with him after she found out he was taking my place."

"Huh. My half sister's going to be first lady someday."

"That's what it sounds like." He opens a compartment in the dash of the car and pulls out some sunglasses. "Here. I got these for you."

"Thanks!" I try them on and check out how they look in the visor mirror. "So why were you acting so weird on the phone the other night? Was someone listening in?"

"Probably not, but I didn't want to take any chances. My dad always says to never trust the home phone. That's why we hardly ever use it. But I didn't have my cell phone and I had to talk to you."

"Well, now that we can talk, tell me what happened at the meeting."

"I don't want to talk about it right now. We're here in California. It's a beautiful day. Let's just enjoy it."

"Okay." I'm a little worried he doesn't want to talk about it. Is he not telling me something? Is this group making him do something else now? He seems really happy so I decide to let it go. "Have you been to our place yet?"

"Yeah. I got here yesterday and scoped out the area. It's a great condo. You're going to love it."

"You got here yesterday? Why didn't you call me?"

"Because that would've ruined the surprise." He reaches across the seat for my hand. "You still don't understand the concept behind surprises, do you?"

I roll my eyes at him, smiling. "So the car was already here?"

"It got here Wednesday. I unloaded all your stuff but didn't put it away. I figured you'd want to decide where to put everything."

"Are we going there now?"

"I thought we'd stop at the beach first. You're in California. You have to check out the beach."

He turns onto a small road lined with strip malls that turns into a smaller road that eventually comes to a dead end. There's a metal railing and just past it is a beach and beyond that, the ocean. I can see it from the car.

Garret parks next to the metal railing and comes around to let me out.

"I don't think you're supposed to park here," I tell him.

"Don't worry about it. We're good." He clicks the car remote, locking the doors.

"I have to go see it." I run off toward the beach. Garret runs after me and scoops me up into his arms.

"Not yet," he says and plants a kiss on my lips.

I love being in his arms again. And hearing his voice again. And feeling his lips again. I love everything about him.

"I can't go to the beach?"

"I'm taking you to the beach. But I'm taking you to a different part of the beach. Over there." He points to a giant black rock formation jutting out from the sand that has stairs so you can climb to the top. It's so big it's like a small hill.

"Why there?"

"It's a lookout point. It has a great view of the ocean." He sets me down. "Come on. I'll show you."

We run along the sand and climb to the top of the rock. There's nobody up there, but near the edge of it there's a blanket with a picnic basket on top.

"That looks just like the blanket we used in the woods."

"Because it is." He grabs my hand and leads me to it.

"But how did you. . . When did you . . ."

"What do you think of the view?" He puts his arm around my waist as we face the ocean.

"It's incredible." I scan the beach, which is a never-ending stretch of sand with small houses on one side and the roaring ocean on the other. "Is this a private beach?"

"Yeah. It's just for the people who live here."

"Then we should get out of here. We'll get in trouble."

"We won't get in trouble. We live here, Jade." He points behind me to some two-story condos. "We live in that white one and Sean and Harper are in the blue one next to it."

I turn to get a better look. "Seriously? This is our beach? We're really going to live here?"

"Yes. This is where we live now." He turns me back toward him and takes my sunglasses off and sets them on the blanket. I notice his are off, too. "But before I take you to our place, I have to do something."

"Okay, what?" I kiss him quick, but I want to kiss him a lot more so I hope he hurries up with all this talking.

"I'm kind of old-fashioned. You know that, right?"

"Old fashioned how? What do you mean?"

"Like I'm into traditions and stuff like that."

"Yeah, I guess you are."

"So I was thinking that if I'm going to live with a girl, she should be more than just a girlfriend. Living together is kind of a big step."

"What are you getting at here?"

He smiles at my impatience, but now I feel bad for rushing him. I can tell by his tone that whatever he's trying to say is important. I'm just really anxious to get to the kissing part.

"I'm sorry. Go ahead." I give him my full attention, gazing at his gorgeous blue eyes.

He takes my hand. "When I made that list for you last Christmas with all the things I love about you, I was serious when I said I could fill a whole stack of notebooks." He pauses, but his eyes remain on mine. "And I find it amazing that even now, you continue to add to that list. I keep finding more things to love about you. I don't even know how that's possible but it's true."

I glance down at the blanket. I never know what to say when he says these nice things to me.

Garret nudges my chin up and our eyes meet. "I love you more than anything in this world, Jade. And when I promised you forever, I meant it."

He lets go of my hand and reaches into his pocket and takes out a small blue box. As in Tiffany blue.

My heart starts beating really fast, but then I relax, thinking it's probably a pair of earrings like last time. Or a necklace. Or maybe a bracelet.

Then again, it could be something else.

Garret gets down on one knee and my heart beats even faster. It's definitely not earrings.

He holds the box out in front of me and slowly opens it. "Jade, will you marry me?"

CHAPTER THIRTY

The box holds a very large and very sparkly diamond ring.

I look at Garret, studying his face to make sure he's not joking. *Say something, Jade!* I'm yelling at myself in my head because no words are coming out and Garret is starting to look concerned.

"Yes! I'll marry you!" I hug him and he bursts up and hugs me even tighter back.

"What the hell took you so long? I didn't think you were ever going to answer."

"Sorry. I just had to make sure you weren't kidding."

He laughs. "The ring didn't make that clear?"

"I guess not. Can I see it?"

"You can do more than see it. You can wear it." He takes it out of the box and slips it on my finger. It fits perfectly. And it's so beautiful.

"Is this the ring I saw in New York?"

"It is. Do you still like it?'

"I love it." As I see it on my finger, I'm flooded with emotions. All good ones. Happiness. Love. Excitement.

"Jade, you're crying." Garret sweeps his thumb along my cheek.

"No, I'm not." I feel my face and he's right. I *am* crying. "What the hell? I make fun of people who cry when they're happy."

He leans over to whisper. "I won't tell anyone."

I wipe away the rest of the tears and kiss him. "I love you, Garret. I love you so much." I must be smiling a lot because my cheeks are starting to ache. I gaze down at the ring again, watching as it sparkles in the sun. "I can't believe you proposed! I did not expect this. At all."

"I told you I could top my surprise appearance at the airport."

"When did you get the ring?"

"Right after you picked it out."

"I didn't pick it out. I just said I liked it."

"You *really* liked it. I could tell."

I hold it up again. "Okay, I admit it. I really liked it. And now that I see it again, I love it. It's perfect. I can't believe my perfect ring just happened to be sitting in the window of the jewelry store that night."

"Yeah. Crazy, huh?" He's trying not to laugh.

"What is it, Garret? What are you not telling me?"

"I have a confession to make. I picked those three rings out beforehand and had the sales lady place them in the window. Then I had our driver drop us off in front of the store so I could quiz you on which one you liked." He points to my ring. "That was my favorite one, too."

"How did you get the jewelry store to do that for you?"

He smiles. "Let's just say I know the right people."

I smile back, then glance at the ring again. "So you bought this ring months ago even though I kept telling you I didn't want to get married?"

"That didn't mean I couldn't propose. And I needed the ring in case you said yes."

"You really wanted to marry me, didn't you?"

"Jade, I told you that like a million times."

"I didn't believe you."

He rolls his eyes. "Yeah, because guys just say that to girls all the time."

"Maybe they do. How would I know?"

"Believe me. They don't."

"So what's in the basket?" I ask him.

He opens it and takes out two bottles. "Real champagne and fake champagne. I wasn't sure what you'd want."

"This is definitely worthy of real champagne."

I reach in the basket and take out the glasses as he opens the champagne.

After he pours it, he takes his glass and holds it up. "To forever."

Forever. I smile even more as we clink our glasses because the thought of having Garret by my side forever fills my heart with a happiness I can't even put into words.

"I have one more thing to tell you." He takes my glass and his and sets them aside. "Let's sit down."

We both take a seat on the blanket, facing each other.

"This sounds bad. Can it wait until later? Because I'm really happy right now."

"It's not bad." He reaches over and holds my hand, which now has a sparkly diamond ring on it. "Well, I guess some people might think it's bad, but it doesn't have to be."

"You're making me nervous. Just say it."

"Before I do, tell me again that you'll marry me."

"Why?"

"Just do it."

"You're being really strange, but yes, I'll marry you."

"And not like in 50 years, right? Like sooner than that?"

"When do you want to do this?"

"I don't know. Next year. Two years. Three years. Whenever you're ready."

"I'd marry you this summer if you wanted me to."

"Are you serious? Because I would totally do that."

"Then let's not wait. We can get married on the beach. I don't need a fancy wedding. I just want this. Us."

"I do, too, but we're only 19."

"We both turn 20 in a few months. And I don't care about our age. I love you and that's not going to change, so why wait?"

"I agree. But you know that some people aren't going to be happy about this. Like Frank. He may be okay with us getting engaged, but he'll want us to wait until we're older to get married."

"He'll have to get over it. I'm done letting other people make decisions for us. They've been trying to do it since we met, but they're not going to do it anymore. We're together now and I'm not letting anyone come between us."

Garret's smiling at me. "You did it again, Jade."

"Did what?"

"You added to my list again. You gave me another reason why I love you. I'm going to have to stock up on notebooks."

"I don't get it. What's the reason?"

"You'll find out when I give you the updated list."

"When's that going to be?"

"I don't know. Maybe our 10-year anniversary."

"I have to wait that long to find out?"

"Yeah. Why? You aren't planning to stick around for that long?"

I lean over and kiss him. "I'm not going anywhere. I told you. You're stuck with me."

"Yeah, that's right." Once again, he pretends this is a bad thing. "So how long am I stuck with you for?"

I kiddingly shove his shoulder, laughing. "I thought you wanted me to stick around."

He kisses me, then stays close to my lips and says, "You didn't answer my question."

"Forever. You're stuck with me forever." I smile as I say it.

"Good answer. Just had to make sure we're in agreement on that." He kisses me again, then slowly pulls away, smiling. "So back to this wedding of ours. You really want to get married on the beach?"

"It's exactly what I want." I peer out at the ocean. "Look at this. It's beautiful. It's the perfect place to get married. Plus it's a lot cheaper than a traditional wedding. And yes, I know you'd pay for a big, fancy wedding but that's just not me."

"Jade, I should probably tell you my news now."

"Yeah. Go ahead.

"Well, since this plan for me isn't happening now, the organization had to find a different way to punish my dad for what he did to Royce."

"Yeah." I feel my heart racing and not in a good way. "So what is it?"

He hesitates, then says, "The punishment is that he has to disown me from the family."

"What does that mean? You can't see them anymore?"

"I can still see them. It's more of a financial disownment. I can't have access to their money." He gets a really serious look on his face. "I'm broke, Jade. My trust fund was taken away. My credit cards. Bank accounts. All of it."

I try really hard to be serious like he is right now, but I can't. I just start laughing and I can't stop. I can't even sit up anymore. I have to lie down on the blanket.

"What the hell, Jade? This isn't funny. Did you hear me? I'm broke. Well, they let me keep my college money, but it can only be used for tuition. Nothing else. And I can keep the car. So at least we'll have two cars. And the condo is already paid for through the end of August, so it could be worse."

I'm still laughing. Garret lies next to me. "Are you drunk? From half a glass of champagne?"

"No. It's just funny."

"Your fiancé being broke is funny?"

"Hey, I like that. My fiancé. That's a strange word, isn't it?"

"Yeah, I guess." Garret tilts his head. "You sure you're not drunk?"

I turn on my side so we're face to face. "Garret, I don't care if you're broke. I never cared that you had money. You know that."

"But we're getting married now and my money was supposed to be your money and now it's gone. I didn't want you to ever have to worry about money again. And I'm going to do all I can to make sure you don't. I'll get a job, or two jobs, or three. Whatever it takes."

"And what kind of job are you planning to get?" I ask, scooting closer to him. "You've never even had a job, have you?"

"I've had internships, but they didn't pay. I don't know what I'll do. I guess I could work construction or something."

"Somehow I can't see you working construction. Have you ever built anything?"

"No, but I can learn." He considers it, then says, "Fine, then I'll go be a waiter somewhere. It doesn't matter. I'll find something that'll pay the bills."

He's so determined and it's so damn sweet that it makes me want to hug him and kiss him and never stop, but first I need to tell him my news. "Garret, you don't need to worry about money."

"Why not?" He looks so confused.

I smile at him. "Because I have 50 million dollars. Well, 45 million. I gave five to Frank."

Now Garret's laughing. "Yeah, I wish."

"I'm not joking. I have 45 million dollars. Arlin set up a trust fund for me before he died."

"Wait. Are you serious?"

"Totally serious. Grace and I had lunch last Friday and she told me about it. I told her it was too much, but then she went on about how many millions it takes to make a billion. Basically she insisted it wasn't too much and told me it's mine to use however I want. Oh, and she's making me keep that credit card she gave me and told me I'm supposed to use it until I get out of college. I tried to give it back but I guess all the grandkids get one and she wants it to be fair."

Garret is listening to my every word but his expression hasn't changed so I don't know what he's thinking. I think he's speechless. It seems to be a common reaction to the mention of 50 million dollars.

"So anyway, I guess I'm the rich one now." I kiss him to wake him from his daze. "If you want anything, just let me know and I'll buy it for you. And don't complain about me buying you stuff or I'll make you strip for me." I nudge him. "Garret? Are you alive over there?"

A smile slowly forms across his face as he pulls me on top of him. "I think I'll be stripping a lot. It's payback time. You know I'll be giving you a hard time. You buy me a pack a gum I'll be saying, 'Jade, no, it's too much.'"

"Hey, I never said that for a pack of gum."

"I'm pretty sure you did."

"Whatever. Go ahead and say it. I'm still buying you stuff."

"So I'm broke and you're rich. I get why you were laughing now."

My smile fades as I remember why he's broke. "Garret, how do you feel about being disowned by your family? I wasn't laughing about *that*, by the way. It's not funny."

"It's not as bad as it sounds. It's really more about making sure I don't have access to my dad's money, which includes cutting me out of the inheritance. Being part of that organization has rewards. Financial rewards. And with my bad behavior, I was kicked out and banned from ever being a member. Therefore I can't benefit from the financial rewards my father and grandfather have received. The members consider this a punishment for my dad because they assume my dad wants to be able to share his money with me and all the benefits that come with having that kind of money. But secretly, he'd rather have me free from the organization. And I would, too. I'd take my freedom over the money any day."

"So you never have to be part of that group? You're out for good?"

"I'm out for good. In fact I think they were kind of glad to get rid of me."

I hug him. "Garret, you should've started with that."

"Instead of the proposal?"

"Yes. Well, no. Whatever. It doesn't matter. You're finally free from them! We need to celebrate. You want some more champagne?" I sit up and reach for our glasses.

"Actually we have dinner waiting. We should probably get down there."

"Down where?"

"To our place. Sean made us dinner. By the way, I told him what was going on last semester and how I wasn't really acting that way. I gave him the same story we gave Harper and Frank. So Sean's no longer mad at me. Anyway, Harper's setting everything up on the deck so we can eat outside. She says it's our engagement dinner."

"What if I'd said no?"

"When you were checking out your ring, I texted her with your answer so she'd know whether to do this or not. But I had a feeling you might say yes." Cue the cocky smile. "Let's go eat."

We walk down the beach to a two-story condo with windows all along the back. Harper is on the deck, barefoot and wearing a short white sundress, her bright blond hair held back with a glittery silver headband. She runs down on the beach and hugs me, kicking up sand everywhere.

"Congratulations! I'm so happy for you guys!"

She hugs Garret, too. "Sean has everything ready. He's just keeping it warm in the oven."

Sean comes out from the other condo wearing a light blue, button-up shirt and white shorts, already tan from being here a few days. "Congratulations, Jade." He gives me a hug, then goes up to Garret and shakes his hand. "Bet you feel better now that she said yes."

"Sean," Harper scolds.

"What? Like she didn't know he was nervous as hell? Every guy is."

"You were nervous?" I ask Garret, laughing a little. "You, Mr. Cocky Smile? Mr. I-Knew-You'd-Say-Yes?"

He shrugs. "Maybe a little. But not as much as Sean's making it sound like." He pretends to be annoyed with Sean, but he's not. I can tell they're back to being friends.

"Ready to eat?" Sean asks.

Harper moves closer to me so the guys won't hear. "Garret invited Sean and me to eat with you two, but if you want to have a romantic dinner without us, we totally understand."

"Don't be crazy. You guys are having dinner with us. This is our first night here together and we have a lot to celebrate."

She hugs me quick. "Okay, then I'll pour the drinks. Go inside and check out your place."

I grab Garret's hand and pull him toward the door. "Come on. Give me a tour."

He picks me up and carries me through the door.

"You're not supposed to do that until we're married."

"I'm practicing." He carries me past the living room and goes straight up the stairs.

"I missed the whole downstairs. Where are you taking me?"

"To our bedroom." He goes down a short hallway into the bedroom and sets me down on a king-size bed that's covered in white cotton linens. The room has warm wood floors and light-colored furniture. There's a tall dresser along one wall and a nightstand on each side of the bed. Windows line the back wall. The windows are open and the cool ocean breeze is blowing in. You can hear the waves crashing on the shore.

"What do you think?" he asks.

I stretch out on the bed. "I think this can't possibly be real. It's too great."

"It's real." Garret lies beside me and kisses me and I know that if we don't stop we'll never make it to dinner.

"Garret, we should go outside. Harper and Sean are waiting."

"Yeah, I know," he says, continuing to kiss me, "but let's make this a short dinner."

"We're not racing through dinner." I push him back a little and smile. "But after that, I'm all yours. In fact I don't think we'll be leaving this room tomorrow. Maybe not the next day either."

"And there's my little nympho girlfriend," he says, tickling my side.

"Hey." I push him back again. "It's *fiancé*. Get it right."

He laughs. "Sorry. You're right. My nympho *fiancé*."

We go back downstairs. The living room has a big, U-shaped couch that faces the windows looking out to the ocean. A flat-screen TV sits on a stand in the corner. The room is open to the kitchen which has a long center island with barstools and a small table off to the side. I notice a vase of red roses on the table.

"You got me roses?"

Garret comes up behind me. "I wanted to fill the whole place with them but I'm a little short on cash."

I turn to face him. "A dozen is plenty. Thank you." I loop my arms around his neck and kiss him. "I love you, Garret Kensington."

"I love you, Jade Taylor. Soon to be Jade Kensington. Unless you're keeping your name."

"Jade Kensington," I say, hearing how that sounds. "Wow. I'm going to be a Kensington. And a wife. And someday a mo—" I stop, not sure how that thought even got in my head. A mom? Me? Must be the champagne talking.

Garret ignores my slip up, but now he's smiling even more. "So I guess you're going with the name change. That's good. Makes it easier on the mailman. Multiple names at one address could be confusing."

"Yeah, that's true. Let's go eat." I grab his hand and drag him to the deck where Harper and Sean are waiting.

"We wondered if you two were ever coming out of there." Harper laughs and picks up her glass. "Let's toast." The rest of us lift our glasses. "To my best friend and the guy who was lucky enough to get her."

"I second that," Garret says and we all clink glasses.

Then the four of us sit at our ocean-view table, eating the delicious dinner Sean prepared. We reminisce about the past year, reliving all the memories that led us to be together at this table on this beautiful night, on this picture-perfect spot of the California coast.

We remain there talking and laughing and watching the sun set. Sean and Harper move their chairs to face the orange and pink sky. Garret and I do the same. He puts his arm around me and I lean in and whisper, "We're going to have a really great summer."

He tips my chin up and gives me a soft, sweet kiss. "Not just the summer, Jade. We're going to have a really great life."

Made in the USA
San Bernardino, CA
08 October 2017